Leif G.W. Persson is Scandinavia's most renowned criminologist and a leading psychological profiler. He has also served as an advisor to the Swedish Ministry of Justice. Since 1991, he has held the position of Professor at the National Swedish Police Board and is regularly consulted as the country's foremost expert on crime.

He is the author of ten bestselling crime novels, three of which feature the irrepressible Evert Bäckström. He is also the recipient of many prestigious awards, including The Piraten Award, The Glass Key for Best Scandinavian Crime Novel, The Swedish Academy of Crime Writers' Award (three times), The Finnish Whodunnit Society's Annual Award for Excellence in Foreign Crime Writing, The Petrona Award for Best Scandinavian Crime Novel, and The Danish Academy of Crime Writers' Palle Rosenkrantz Prize.

Praise from around the world for Leif G.W. Persson
and his novels:

'From a country known for terrific crime novelists, Sweden's great crime writer Leif G.W. Persson brilliantly takes the reader into a world of fascinating mystery and secrets' Joseph Wambaugh

'Persson shines a light on Swedes and their society, and in that broader sense may be the most interesting of the novelists in the current Swedish crime boom' Barry Forshaw, *Crimetime*, UK

'Persson outperforms most of his competitors in the Swedish crime genre by miles . . . hardboiled, clever, suspenseful' *Svenska Dagbladet*, Sweden

'Leif G.W. Persson's books are both brilliant and unique – stylish crime requiems marked by pitch-black humour and an unparalleled satirical sting' Hakan Nesser

'[Persson] remains unthreatened as the King of Swedish crime writing. Period' *Kvällsposten*, Sweden

International acclaim for *The Dying Detective*:

'Persson is more authentic than Stieg Larsson . . . With this amazing novel, Persson proves himself to be a significant voice, classic yet original, on the overly-exhausted Scandinavian crime fiction scene. A blend of tradition and innovation.'
La Repubblica, Italy

'Persson combines the humour of Håkan Nesser and his hero Van Veeteren with the energy of detective Kurt Wallander, created by the famous Henning Mankell.'
Trouw, Netherlands

'Persson's novels contain everything you expect from good crime literature: an irresistible plot, subtle storytelling and interesting characters.'
★ ★ ★ ★
Crimezone, Netherlands

'Read the book for its teeming sarcasm, its humour and its portrait of a dying detective and his tender, almost beautiful, relationships to friends and family – and perhaps to get a sharpened view of morals and revenge, also within the police force. Gifted entertainment set in a macho world.'
★ ★ ★ ★ ★
Fyns Amts Avis, Denmark

'A meticulous masterpiece.'
Sydsvenskan, Sweden

'The novel has all the qualities that readers have come to expect from this author: intelligent entertainment, suspense, coarse humour and small portions of self-irony.'
Svenska Dagbladet, Sweden

The Dying Detective

Leif G.W. Persson

Translated from the Swedish by Neil Smith

BLACK SWAN

TRANSWORLD PUBLISHERS
61–63 Uxbridge Road, London W5 5SA
www.penguin.co.uk

Transworld is part of the Penguin Random House group of companies
whose addresses can be found at global.penguinrandomhouse.com

Penguin
Random House
UK

Originally published in Sweden as *Den döende detektiven* in 2010
by Albert Bonniers Förlag

First published in Great Britain in 2016 by Doubleday
an imprint of Transworld Publishers
Black Swan edition published 2017

A CIP catalogue record for this book
is available from the British Library.

ISBN 9780552778374

Typeset in 11/14pt ITC Giovanni by Thomson Digital Pvt Ltd, Noida, Delhi.
Printed and bound by Clays Ltd, Bungay, Suffolk.

Penguin Random House is committed to a sustainable
future for our business, our readers and our planet. This book
is made from Forest Stewardship Council® certified paper.

The Dying Detective

I
Eye for eye . . .
Book of Exodus, 21:24

1

Monday evening, 5 July 2010

Karlbergsvägen 66 in Stockholm is the location of Günter's, the best hotdog kiosk in Sweden. It's surrounded by sturdy stone buildings many storeys high, all constructed at the start of the last century. Solid brickwork, carefully laid, brick upon brick, with lime-mortar rendering, bow windows and old-fashioned leaded glass. There are generous lawns in front of the properties and – at this time of year – leafy trees lining the street. When you enter the buildings there is usually red marble in both the lobbies and stairwells, friezes on the ceilings, ornate plasterwork, even dado panelling in places. The skirting boards and doors are made of oak. It is an area that gives a bourgeois, affluent impression.

Günter's is also located within the old city boundaries of the most beautiful capital in the world. Just a few hundred metres south of Karlberg Palace and Karolinska University Hospital, and close to two of the major roads leading away from the north of the city centre.

The former head of the National Criminal Police, Lars Martin Johansson, really ought to have been at his summerhouse up in Roslagen today, but that morning he had been obliged to come into the city for a meeting with his bank, to conclude a deal about a patch of forest that he and his eldest brother had an interest in.

Once that had been arranged, various other matters and errands of a miscellaneous and private nature which, for practical reasons, he might as well sort out then and there, had, as usual, cropped up. The list of things to do had rapidly become very long, and by the time he was ready to return to his wife and the summer tranquillity on Rådmansö it was almost eight o'clock in the evening and Johansson was as hungry as a wolf.

Just a few hundred metres before he would be passing the old tollgate at Roslagstull on his drive north, his hunger got the better of him. There was no way he was going to spend an hour driving when his stomach was already screaming at him. So he took a quick detour to the best hotdog kiosk in Sweden for a well-spiced Yugoslavian bratwurst with salt-pickled Åland gherkins, sauerkraut and Dijon mustard. Or maybe a Zigeuner sausage with its taste of freshly ground pepper, paprika and onion? Or should he stay true to his Norrland roots and partake of a lightly smoked elk sausage with Günter's home-made mash of salad potatoes?

Absorbed in these pleasant considerations, he parked just a few metres from the kiosk, immediately behind one of Stockholm Police's minibuses, and, like them, halfway on to the pavement, before getting out. Given that he had been retired for three years, this was not entirely legal, but it was eminently practical, and some of the habits he had developed during his almost fifty years in the force were deeply ingrained.

It was a warm and sunny day in early July, and the evening was as warm as the day had been – far from ideal weather for a hotdog, which presumably went some way

12

to explaining why the queue ahead of him consisted of just four younger colleagues from the Stockholm rapid-response unit. Former colleagues, to be more precise, but they still recognized him. Nods, smiles, their commanding officer raising his right hand to his cropped head even though he had tucked his cap under his belt.

'How's it going, boys?' Johansson asked, having made his mind up what to choose as soon as he detected the heavenly smells drifting towards him. The elk sausage could wait until the autumn. Smokiness, well-balanced flavours and Norrlandic stoicism were all very well, but an evening such as this required something stronger. But not too strong, nothing from the southern Balkans. Paprika, onion, pepper and lightly salted, coarse-ground pork would do very nicely indeed. In fact, considering the weather and his mood, he couldn't think of anything better.

'Nice and calm, so we thought we'd take the opportunity to refuel before the storm breaks,' the officer replied. 'You're welcome to go first, boss, if you like. We're not in a hurry.'

'I'm a pensioner,' Johansson said, for some reason. 'And you've got to work. Who's got the energy to harass ne'er-do-wells on an empty stomach?'

'We're still making up our minds.' The officer smiled and nodded. 'So, please, go ahead.'

'Well, in that case,' Johansson said, and turned to the man behind the counter, 'a Zigeuner with sauerkraut and French mustard. And something to drink. A bottle of water, with bubbles. The usual, you know.'

He nodded encouragingly to the latest in the succession of Günter's associates. This one was a youngster called Rudy, an Austrian like Günter himself, and even though Günter had been dead for almost a decade, new staff were almost always recruited from his former homeland. Günter's best friend, Sebastian, who had already taken over before Günter died; Udo, who had worked there for many years; and Katja, who was only there occasionally. There was another one, whose name he had forgotten, and finally there was Rudy. Johansson knew them all, and they had known him over the course of several hundred hotdogs, and while Rudy was putting together his order Johansson turned to make some agreeable small talk with his younger colleagues.

'This year it will be forty-six years since I started as a beat officer in Stockholm,' Johansson said. Or is it forty-seven? he thought. Sod it – who cares?

'Back when you still carried sabres?' A broad grin from the youngest-looking one.

'Watch yourself, kid,' Johansson said. Nice lad, he thought.

'And then you moved to surveillance,' the younger officer's boss said, evidently well schooled in Johansson's history.

'Ah, you know about that? Fifteen years,' he added.

'Together with Jarnebring,' another of them said.

'That's right. You remember the big beasts, then.'

'Used to work there. Jarnis – Bosse – was my commanding officer. Best boss I've ever had,' he added, for some reason.

'Would you like it in French bread, or would you like it on a tray, sir?' Rudy interrupted, holding up the freshly cooked sausage.

'The usual,' Johansson said. 'Take a baguette, pull the innards out, then stuff it with sausage, sauerkraut and mustard'. That can't be too hard to remember, can it? he thought.

'Where were we?' he asked, nodding to the colleague who had worked under his best friend.

'Jarnebring, Bo Jarnebring.'

'That's right,' Johansson said, with unnecessary emphasis, given that he was the one who had forgotten what they were talking about. 'Jarnebring, yes. He's a pensioner as well now, retired at sixty-five, last year. Doing well, by the way. We meet up regularly and fabricate old memories to tell each other.'

'Send him my best, sir. I'm Patrik Åkesson, P-2. There were two Patriks in the group and I was second to arrive, so Jarnis called me that to avoid unnecessary confusion when we were out on jobs.'

'Sounds like Jarnebring,' Johansson said. He nodded, pocketed his change and took the sausage and water he had ordered. Then he nodded again, mostly because he didn't have anything else to say.

'Take care of yourselves, lads,' he added. 'As I understand it, it's not like it was back in my day.'

They all nodded back, suddenly serious, and their commanding officer once again signalled his respect by raising his hand to his close-cropped head.

In my day you'd have been fired for saluting without your cap on, Johansson thought as he managed, not without some difficulty, to squeeze into the driver's seat, put his drink into the cup-holder between the seats and move the sausage from his left hand to his right.

At that moment someone must have driven an ice-pick into the back of his neck. No rumbling forewarning of an ordinary headache, but a sharp, searing pain that

15

tore through the back of his head. The sounds from the street blurred and became hard to hear, and then disappeared altogether. Darkness spread across his eyes, first the right one, then the left, as if someone had pulled a blind that had been hung up askew. His arm went numb and his fingers felt stiff and unresponsive. The sausage fell between the seats.

Then nothing but darkness and silence.

2

Monday evening, 5 July, to Wednesday afternoon, 7 July

Lars Martin Johansson is unconscious. Just after midnight, and as soon as his condition has been stabilized, he is moved from intensive care to neurosurgery. Close at hand, in case complications should arise and an operation be required.

Hypnos is the god of sleep in Greek mythology, the twin brother of Thanatos, the demon of death, both the sons of Nyx, goddess of the night, but none of them, not even Nyx, is Johansson's divinity, because Johansson is unconscious. He reacts to light in a purely physiological sense, whenever any of the white coats who come and go at his bedside get it into their heads to hold his eyelid up and shine a light into his eye, but because he is unconscious he is unlikely to be bothered by this.

Hypnos is not his god, because he isn't asleep, and there certainly aren't any dreams to exacerbate, or perhaps alleviate, his torment. Dreams require the presence of people and events, and in the absence of those one might perhaps manage with irrational creatures or inert objects such as a green casting net, even one that is the wrong colour, or perhaps a sledge one used to ride

17

on as a child, but above all dreams require a degree of consciousness upon which to act, and Johansson does not have this.

Nor is he governed by Thanatos. Because Johansson is alive, he is breathing and his heart is beating under its own power. Never mind the fact that he needs medication to stabilize its rhythm, lower his blood pressure and thin his blood. Medication to ease his pain, sedate and calm him; all the needles, wires, tubes and pipes that had been attached in or on his body. But he is alive, and now he is in the care of Nyx, he is in night and darkness, so it doesn't really matter that he isn't aware of this. It's probably just as well, in fact, because Nyx isn't a particularly pleasant woman, even in a mythological sense. Among other things, she is also the goddess of vengeance, but what decent person could possibly hold a grudge against Lars Martin Johansson?

Perhaps Hypnos is actually the one closest to him, after all. In ancient depictions he is usually shown as a young man with poppy seedheads in his hand, and, if nothing else, this shows that even extremely ancient Greeks knew things that it had taken medical science and the international narcotics trade another couple of millennia to work out. And if only Johansson had been aware of what was dripping into his veins, he would surely have nodded in appreciation. No matter. Johansson is unconscious. He isn't dead, he isn't asleep, and he certainly isn't dreaming, there's zero chance of him nodding his head, and all this business of light and dark makes no difference whatsoever.

3

Wednesday afternoon, 7 July

It starts as a rumbling ache in the back of his head and a faint perception of light, quite when and why is unclear, but suddenly he has woken up. He realizes he is lying in a bed, and that he must have been lying on his right arm, because it feels numb. His fingers feel clumsy and he can't clench his fist properly. Beside his bed sits a short-haired woman in a white coat. A stethoscope is sticking out of her breast pocket, to remove any lingering doubts as to her role.

What the hell is going on? Johansson thinks.

'What's going on?' he says to the woman in the white coat.

'My name is Ulrika Stenholm,' the woman says, looking at him with her head tilted. 'I'm acting senior consultant here at Karolinska Hospital, and you're on my ward. I thought I might start by asking you if you can remember your name.'

She smiles and nods amiably, straightening her head as if to soften her question.

'My name?' Johansson asks. What the hell is going on? he thinks again.

'Your name. Can you remember?'

'Johansson,' Johansson replies. 'My name is Johansson.'

'What else?' Another nod, another friendly smile, another tilt of the head, to the other side this time. But she's not backing down.

'Johansson. Lars Martin Johansson,' Johansson replies. 'If you want my ID number, my driving licence is in my wallet. I usually keep that in my left trouser pocket. What happened?'

An even broader smile now from the woman beside his bed.

'You're in the neurology department of Karolinska Hospital,' she replies. 'On Monday you suffered a blood clot in your brain and were brought here.' Her head changes position again, short, blonde hair, a long, thin neck without any trace of wrinkles.

'What day is it?' Johansson asks. She can't be a day over forty, he thinks, for some reason.

'It's Wednesday today. It's five o'clock in the afternoon and you ended up here with me almost two days ago.'

'Where's Pia?' Johansson asks. 'That's my wife.' He suddenly remembers sitting in his car and feels a severe anxiety that he can't explain.

'Pia's on her way. She's fine. I spoke to her a quarter of an hour ago and told her that you were waking up, so she'll be here soon.' Dr Stenholm goes so far as to nod this time, twice. As if to underline what she's just said.

'So she's fine? I can remember driving my car,' he adds. The anxiety that he can't explain is relenting now.

'You were alone in the car. Your wife was out in the country, and we called her as soon as you arrived in A&E. She's been with you pretty much the whole time since then. And, like I said, she's fine.'

'Tell me,' Johansson said. 'What's happening? Or what happened, I mean?'

'Well, if you think you're up to it.' Another nod, serious, and a questioning expression.

'Tell me. I feel great. Never felt better. Like a pig in shit,' he adds, just to be on the safe side. What the hell is really going on? he thinks once more, because suddenly he feels unfathomably elated.

'I must have slept on my arm,' he adds, even though he already has a suspicion of why he can't lift it off the bed.

'We'll get to that,' she replies, 'a bit later. There's no need for you to worry. If we work together, you and me, I'm sure we'll be able to sort your arm out.'

4

Monday evening, 5 July, to Wednesday afternoon, 7 July

It was the driver of the police minibus who discovered Johansson. When he got out of the vehicle to stretch his legs he saw Johansson's head leaning motionless on the steering wheel, and when he opened the driver's door to see what had happened the unconscious Johansson would have fallen out and hit his head on the road if his colleague hadn't caught him with his arm.

Things moved fast after that. They were told over the radio that the ambulance would be another five minutes, which in practice usually meant double that, but because the commanding officer of the rapid-response team had no intention of letting one of the force's very own legends die as a result of that, still less in his own arms, they lifted Johansson into the van, laid him on the floor, switched on the engine, siren and blue lights and set off at top speed for Karolinska Hospital. It wasn't, perhaps, an altogether orthodox means of transportation, but they were dealing with a colleague who was in dire straits, in which case all the rules and regulations in the world could get stuffed.

It was barely a kilometre as the crow flies to the A&E department of the Karolinska, and they stuck as close to that path as they could, and pulled up two minutes later in front of the main entrance. Considering the life he had led, and which was now threatening to leave him, Johansson made both a grand and a fitting entrance. Lying unconscious on a trolley, surrounded by rapid-response-unit officers and medical personnel, straight into the intensive-care unit, past all the bog-standard patients sitting or lying there waiting, with their chest pains, broken arms, sprained knees, ear aches, allergies and common colds.

From then on everything went according to routine and, four hours later, once the immediate danger had been fended off and the diagnosis was more or less settled, he had been transferred to the neurosurgery ward.

'I spoke to the doctor who was on duty on Monday evening,' his female doctor said. 'He'd talked to one of your colleagues, who brought you in. You caused quite a stir, by all accounts.' She nodded. Smiled slightly, but without tilting her head.

'A stir?'

'Evidently someone recognized you and got it into their head that you'd been shot in the stomach.'

'Shot? In the stomach?'

'You had sauerkraut and mustard on your shirt. Loads of it. And there were all those police officers, of course. Someone thought your guts were falling out.' She looked even happier now.

'Sweet Jesus,' Johansson said. Where do people get it all from? he thought.

'Apparently, you collapsed at that hotdog kiosk up on Karlbergsvägen. Before you had a chance to stuff yourself with all the unhealthy food you'd bought. Sauerkraut, fried white bread, a fat, greasy sausage and God knows what else.'

What's she going on about? Johansson thought. Must be Günter's. He had stopped at Günter's, the best hot-dog kiosk in Sweden. He had talked to some younger colleagues. His memory was coming back. He could remember that much.

'I had a workmate who died while he was standing in the queue for that kiosk. He had a heart attack. He more or less lived on that sort of food, despite the fact that he was a doctor.' Head tilted, serious now.

'Sauerkraut,' Johansson said. 'What's wrong with sauerkraut?' Sauerkraut must be pretty fucking healthy, he thought.

'I was thinking more of the sausage.'

'Listen,' Johansson said, feeling inexplicably furious now that his head had started to ache really badly. 'If it hadn't been for that sausage you're going on about, I'd be dead now.'

She contented herself with a nod and adjusted the angle of her head. Didn't say anything.

'If I hadn't stopped to get a hotdog, I'd have been sitting in my car on the way out to the country, and then things would have gone seriously wrong.' At worst, for far more people than just me, he thought.

'We can talk about this later,' she replied, then leaned forward and patted him on the arm, the arm which wasn't asleep but had simply stopped working.

'Have you got a mirror?' Johansson asked.

She must have heard the question before. She nodded, put her hand in her coat pocket and pulled out a small mirror and put it in his outstretched left hand.

You look fucking awful, Lars Martin, Johansson thought. His whole face seemed to have slumped, his mouth was tilted off balance and he had a number of small bruises under his eyes, like dots, bluish-black, no bigger than pinheads.

'Strangulation marks,' Johansson said.

'Petechiae,' his doctor agreed with a nod. 'You stopped breathing for a minute or so, but then one of your colleagues got you going again; it seems he was an ambulance driver before he joined the police. A trained paramedic. I have to say that I agree with you,' she went on. 'All things considered, in spite of everything, it was lucky that it happened where it did.'

'I look fucking awful,' Johansson said. But I'm alive, he thought. Unlike everyone else he had seen with similar marks under their eyes.

'I daresay your wife must be here by now,' she replied. 'I thought I'd leave you alone to talk in peace. I'll come back and see how you're doing before bedtime.'

'Do you know what?'

She shook her head.

'You look like a squirrel,' Johansson said. Why am I saying that? he thought.

'A squirrel?'

'We can talk about it later,' Johansson said.

5

Wednesday afternoon, 7 July

Pia, his wife, walked straight up to his bed. She was smiling at him, but the smile didn't match the expression in her eyes, and when she went to sit down on the chair beside the bed she managed to knock it over. She pushed it out of the way with her foot, leaned over and wrapped her arms round him. She held him tight, pressing his head to her chest, rocking him like he was a small child.

'Lars, Lars,' she whispered. 'What have you got yourself into this time?'

'It's nothing to worry about,' Johansson said. 'Some crap happened up in my head, that's all.'

At that moment something tightened in his throat and he started to cry. Even though he never cried. Not since he was a little boy. Except for his mother's funeral a few years ago, and his father's a couple of years before that, but then, of course, everyone had been crying. Even Johansson's eldest brother had rubbed his eyes and hid his face behind his hand. But, otherwise, Johansson never cried. Not until now, and without really understanding why. You're alive, aren't you? he thought. What the fuck are you blubbing for?

Then he took some deep breaths. He stroked his wife's back with his good hand. Wrapped his arm round her and hugged her chest.

'Can you get me a handkerchief?' Johansson asked. What the hell is going on? he thought.

After that he was himself again. He blew his nose loudly several times, fended off his wife's attempts to dry his tears and wiped his face with the back of his hand instead. He attempted a smile with his crooked, drooping mouth. The ache in his head was suddenly gone.

'Pia, lovely Pia, little Pia,' Johansson said. 'It's okay now. I feel like a pig in shit, on top of the world. I'll soon be walking about with a skip in my step.'

Then she smiled at him again. With both her mouth and her eyes this time, leaning forward on the chair she was now sitting on.

'Do you know what?' Johansson said. 'If I budge up a bit, you could hop up and lie here next to me.'

Pia shook her head. She squeezed his healthy hand, stroking the one that wasn't asleep but just felt like it was.

Then she left him and, because his need to be alone was stronger than ever, he had made her promise to go home to their flat in town and talk to everyone who would be worrying unnecessarily. And then get a good night's sleep and not come back until the following afternoon.

'Once all the white coats have finished messing about with me,' Johansson explained. 'Then we'll be able to talk in peace and quiet.'

'I promise,' Pia said. Then she leaned over and took hold of his neck, even though it was usually him who took hold of hers, and kissed him. Then she nodded and walked out.

You're alive, Lars Martin Johansson thought, and even though his headache had come back again he felt happy, suddenly, without knowing why, and in spite of the pain.

After that he fell asleep. The ache in his head had eased, and someone touched his arm, a woman who couldn't have been a day over thirty. She nodded towards the tray of food she had left beside his bed. A woman who was smiling at him with dark eyes and a generous mouth.

'I can help you, if you like,' she said.

'It's not a problem,' Johansson said. 'I'll manage. Just give me a spoon.'

Half an hour later she came back. During that time Johansson had tasted the boiled fish (two spoonfuls), the white sauce (half a spoonful), the creamed rhubarb (three spoonfuls) and drunk a whole glass of water.

While she was standing there again he pretended to be asleep, evidently successfully, seeing as he was already thinking about Günter's, the best hotdog kiosk in Sweden, smelling the heavenly aromas that always greeted him several metres before he reached the counter.

Then another young woman dressed in white emptied his bedpan, and he promised himself that next time he would make his way to the toilet. Like any normal person, even if he had to balance on his good arm to get there.

After that his very own squirrel paid him a visit.

'A direct question,' Johansson said. 'How old are you?' Mostly to divert any more nagging about his dietary habits and generally useless state.

'I'm forty-four,' she replied. 'Why do you ask?'

'Ulrika Stenholm,' Johansson said. 'I swear to you, not a soul would believe you were a day over forty. We can take up that squirrel business another day.'

And with that he fell asleep again.

An anxious sleep, to start with, and his head had begun to ache again, but then Hypnos must have stuck his oar in – he had a vague memory of someone moving about by his bed and fiddling with one of the many tubes that led from the drip-stand above his head – because the ache in his head had disappeared and he started to dream.

Enjoyable dreams. Dreams that healed more than just an ordinary headache. Dreams about all the squirrels he had shot when he was a young lad living at home with Mother Elna and Father Evert, home on the farm in northern Ångermanland. How it had all started with Great-uncle Gustaf sitting on their kitchen sofa complaining about his rheumatism and saying that the only thing that would help was an old-fashioned waistcoat made of squirrel skin, with the fur facing inwards.

'I can get you one if you like, Uncle,' Lars Martin Johansson had said, sitting on a stool by the woodpile, just a third the size of all the others in the room.

'That's very kind of you, Lars,' his great-uncle had replied. 'You can borrow my rimfire rifle, then you won't have to mess about with that air rifle your father gave you last Christmas.'

'Why not?' his dad, Evert, had said. 'The lad's got an unChristian talent for shooting, so that would be fine. Give him your rifle and he'll get you a waistcoat.'

That was how the business of the squirrels had started, because of his great-uncle's offer and his father's consent, in reality as well as in the dream, and it would be only sixty years before he met Ulrika Stenholm, qualified doctor and neurosurgeon, and she reawakened his childhood memories. Forty-four years old, even though she didn't look a day over forty.

6

The night between Wednesday, 7 July, and Thursday, 8 July

Johansson dreams of all the squirrels he has shot. About the waistcoat made of the skins of squirrels which he, in little more than a year, shot for his great-uncle Gustaf. Admittedly, he had to cheat slightly in using both summer and winter pelts, but his mother, Elna, who had to act as furrier, said that didn't matter. As long as you put the winter pelts at the back where the pain was, there wouldn't be a problem.

During that first year he had shot just over fifty squirrels, because, like all the other men in the family, his great-uncle was generously proportioned across both back and chest. The shooting had taken less than a minute in total.

Tiny, jet-black eyes, heads that jerked and twisted as they darted between the pines and scampered up and down the trunks. Sometimes they would stop halfway, no matter whether they had their heads facing up or down, and would turn their necks to look at everything and everyone, and even at him. Curious, alert, wary eyes, tiny and black as peppercorns, and even though he already had them in his sights and was just about to fire, they always used to sit quite still, with their heads tilted. Then he would squeeze the trigger. He would barely hear the whip-like shot of the rifle, and it was goodbye to another squirrel.

On numerous occasions his prey would snag on a branch on the way down. When he was still a little boy he would poke them down with another branch cut from a birch or aspen tree. When he got older and had arms that were almost as thick as those of his eldest brother, Evert, he would climb the trunks and grab them. No problem, even when the pines were frozen and slippery in winter, covered with patches of snow and ice: he would manage with a length of rope tied round his waist and a hunting knife clutched in his right fist to help him get a better grip.

Then, one day, he stopped shooting them. Their little heads darting about the whole time, the black eyes that could even be staring right at him when he fired. They never seemed to grasp the fact that they were staring at death. They were just as curious about that as everything else. Only a few minutes in total to squeeze the trigger and shoot hundreds of them. Hundreds of hours in between those shots in which he just sat and watched them.

Much later in life, in a different life, he met Ulrika Stenholm. A neurologist at Karolinska Hospital, with short, fair hair, a wrinkle-free neck and no trace of either a brown pelt or a bushy tail. Not remotely like a squirrel, if it weren't for the way she turned and angled her head when she looked at him.

That, more or less, was when he woke up. He tried to lift his arm from the bed, without succeeding. It was still asleep, but he was wide awake. He was also thirsty, but when he reached for the glass of water he tipped it over, and when he made to call for the night nurse, he dropped the little gadget with the button on he needed to press.

'What the hell is going on?' he yelled. Straight out, just like that, and then the night nurse came in and gave him a glass of water, patted his right arm even though it was already asleep, adjusted one of the drips, and then he drifted off to sleep again. Without dreams, this time.

7

Thursday, 8 July, to Tuesday, 13 July

On Thursday he went to the toilet. Admittedly, with the help of a male nursing assistant and a stick with a rubber stopper at the end. But he had shaken his head at the offer of a wheelchair or a walker, and he peed all on his own. In spite of the drip-stand, his dangling right arm, his unsteady right leg and the ache in his head. He was filled by a strong sense of happiness, so strong that he couldn't help sniffling. But no tears welled up.

'Stop whining,' he muttered to himself. 'You're getting better, for God's sake.'

Anything else would have been rather odd, because these days he was a challenge for the latest developments in medical science. Over the next few days Johansson's bed was pushed around all manner of different departments, Johansson was lifted off and on, given new needles, wires, tubes and pipes, surrendered more blood samples, was X-rayed once more, strapped to a bare trolley and rolled back and forth in a large tube that made a whirring noise. He was examined from every angle. Torches were shone in his eyes, people squeezed him, bent, poked and twisted his arms and legs, hit his knees with a little metal hammer and then ran the hammer across the soles of his feet, and pricked him with tiny needles. In every imaginable place, and pretty much without interruption.

Then he encountered the physiotherapist who showed him the most basic, introductory exercises. She assured him that 'soon the pair of us' – careful to stress 'the pair of us' – would see to it that he regained both feeling, mobility and strength in his right arm. As far as his face was concerned, it was already regaining its former appearance. More or less of its own accord, as if by magic. The physiotherapist also gave him some brochures to read and a little red rubber ball for him to squeeze in his right hand. And if he didn't have any questions just then, it wasn't the end of the world, because they would be seeing each other again the following day.

Ulrika Stenholm had gone off on holiday. Just for a few days, so there was no reason for him to worry about that either. While she was away her colleagues looked after him. A younger male junior doctor, originally from Pakistan, and a middle-aged blonde with fake breasts who had come to Sweden from Poland twenty years before and had spent pretty much her whole life working as a brain surgeon. Neither of them bore the slightest resemblance to a squirrel.

His wife, Pia, visited him every day. If it had been up to her, she would have moved into his room, but Johansson had vetoed that. Once a day was fine, and if anything were to happen which necessitated other arrangements, she would find out about it in plenty of time. He was also careful to avoid questions about his health. Johansson felt better with each passing day. Soon he would be back to his usual self, and that was all there was to it.

Anyway, how was she? He made her promise to look after herself. And would she mind bringing him his mobile phone, his laptop, and the book he had been reading when it happened? He had forgotten the title, but it was on his bedside table out at the cottage. Pia did as he asked. The book, of which he had read half, to judge by the bookmark, remained untouched. He discovered that he didn't have a clue what it was about, and he couldn't summon up the energy to start again. Not now; maybe later, when he was back on form again.

His children were due to arrive that weekend, first his daughter and son-in-law, then his son and daughter-in-law. It was decided that the grandchildren would stay at home without him even having to request this. But they sent him messages and presents instead.

The eldest, who was now seventeen and would be graduating from high school the following spring, wrote him a long letter in which she encouraged 'the best grandfather in the world' to stop getting so stressed, to take things easy and relax, 'chill out' and 'chillax a bit more'. To underline this point, she wrote that she was sending him a book on meditation and a pirated CD entitled *Soothing Favourites*.

Her little sister had sent him a picture she had drawn, showing Johansson lying in bed surrounded by white coats with a big bandage around his head. But he looked happy, and was even waving, and beneath it she had written: 'get wel soon granddad'.

Her cousin, two years younger, sang to him on his mobile in his delicate boy's voice, and sent him 'half' his weekly sweets – foam bananas and jelly babies, sticky from childish fingers – but only after some hesitation, apparently. His twin brothers, two years younger than him, had set aside their differences for once and drawn him some stick figures and something which was probably supposed to be the sun.

A much-loved husband, father and grandfather, but more than anything he would have liked to be left alone, so they didn't have to see him looking so weak and he didn't have to see the concern in their eyes.

Pia had diverted all visits from other friends and acquaintances. Jarnebring kept calling, pretty much the whole time, and Johansson's eldest brother called every morning and every evening, and also wanted to discuss business with him. Then there were all the other relatives, friends, acquaintances and former colleagues, who wanted at the very least to be given ongoing-status updates.

'It can't be easy for you, love,' Johansson said, patting his wife's hand. 'But it will soon be over. I'm thinking of asking them to discharge me on Monday, as soon as the weekend is over.'

'Let's talk about that later,' Pia said with a weak smile.

Because he'd had that response before, he knew it wouldn't be happening on Monday.

Despite the fact that he kept improving. The number of tubes, pipes, wires and needles had halved. The headaches were coming less frequently. He took almost all his medication in the form of differently coloured pills, carefully counted and lined up in tiny plastic cups, and he swallowed them all himself and rinsed them down with water. On Monday he was given his very own little box by one of the nurses: it was important that he learned to organize his medication and, the sooner he could get into the routine, the better.

Johansson showed it to his wife that same evening. A small box made of red plastic with seven transparent little lids. A total of twenty-eight tiny compartments for morning, midday, evening and night, for all the days of the week. Well-filled tiny compartments, a total of about ten pills each day.

'Medals and a decent pension are all very well, but getting your very own health-service pillbox feels pretty special,' Johansson declared with the crooked smile that now came naturally.

'Yes,' Pia said. 'That's when you know you've really made it.' Then she smiled, with both her mouth and her eyes, and she seemed as happy as the first time she ever smiled at him. I'm so grateful to have you back, she thought.

8

Wednesday morning, 14 July

On Wednesday morning he met Ulrika Stenholm, who this time brought with her a notebook full of writing.

'You've got the verdict with you, then,' Johansson said, nodding towards the notebook.

'If you feel up to it?'

'I'm listening,' Johansson said, and as he spoke it happened again: a sudden, strong and inexplicable feeling. Elation, this time.

Dr Stenholm was both organized and pedagogical. Johansson had suffered a stroke in the left side of his brain which had led to 'partial paralysis of the right side of his body', which had, among other things, 'reduced mobility' in his right arm and also caused a reduction in feeling, movement and strength in his right leg. Because he had stopped breathing for a minute or so, his lungs had evidently also been affected, but she couldn't find any signs of lasting damage there.

'Brief interruptions in breathing aren't uncommon and can be caused by a lot of different things,' Ulrika Stenholm explained.

'What I can't understand is why it happened to me,' Johansson said. 'I've never had any problems with my head. I hardly ever have to take headache pills even.' And my prostate's absolutely fine, he thought, but that was none of her business, so he kept that to himself.

'That isn't actually the problem, either,' Dr Stenholm said. 'The problem's your heart.'

'My heart,' Johansson said. What the hell's the woman saying? he thought. He sometimes got a bit out of breath when he over-exerted himself, felt a bit of tightness in his chest, maybe his pulse raced on the odd occasion, and he could get a bit dizzy if he stood up too quickly, but that was hardly the end of the world, was it? Things usually sorted themselves out after a few deep breaths and a short nap.

'I'm afraid your heart isn't in great shape.' She moved her head and nodded twice to underline what she'd just said.

'So that stroke was just some sort of bastard bonus, then?' Johansson said.

'Yes, that would be one way of describing it.' She was smiling now. 'Let me explain,' she continued.

Not a bad list, Johansson thought when she had finished. Atrial fibrillation, arrhythmia, enlarged heart, enlarged aorta, a heart that beat far too fast and far too unevenly, and something else he had already forgotten, and all because he ate too much, and the wrong kind of food at that, did too little exercise, was seriously overweight, suffered from too much stress, had high blood pressure and atrocious levels of cholesterol.

'Your atrial fibrillation is the worst of the bad guys in this particular drama. That's what lets blood cells cluster together and form clots,' she explained, and her expression left no room for doubt that there were plenty more bad guys romping about in his chest.

'So what are you thinking of doing about it, then?' Johansson said. He wasn't planning on just giving up. Not after all the tax he had paid into the health service over the course of a long, industrious life, and not considering all the hypochondriacs who had effectively stolen from him on that front with the help of their gullible doctors.

'Medication,' she said. 'The sort that will lower your blood pressure, thin your blood, lower your cholesterol. You're already on those drugs. The thing that's going to make the biggest difference long term, though, is entirely down to you.'

'Lose weight, eat less, stop getting stressed, start exercising,' Johansson said. So there's no need for you to sit there nagging, he thought. And no more Günter's.

'There, see?' Dr Stenholm said with a smile. 'You already know what to do. You need to start looking after yourself. There's no more to it than that.'

'Am I allowed to have a Christmas tree?' Johansson asked. He hadn't felt this cheerful for ages. Quite incomprehensible, he thought.

'I'm serious,' Ulrika Stenholm said, not looking even remotely amused. 'If you don't change your way of life, and I mean radically, then you'll die. If you stop taking your pills, or even skip them occasionally, then I'm afraid that could happen very soon.'

'But the clot in my brain was just a little bonus. Because my heart suddenly had a flutter and started fucking with me.'

'That was a warning,' she replied. 'And you got off lightly. I've got patients who have received considerably more serious warnings than you. You must have had these problems with your heart for a number of years.

Hasn't your doctor ever said anything?' She looked at him curiously.

'I have regular medical checks. Annually, and he usually listens to my heart and all that,' he explained. 'But no, he's usually happy with me. He's never said anything.'

'He's never said anything?'

'No,' Johansson said. 'Just that I should take things a bit easier. But no drugs or anything.'

'Sounds like a strange doctor, if you ask me.'

'Not at all,' Johansson said. 'He's an old hunting buddy of mine. We go elk-hunting together back where I grew up. He was born in the next village, his dad was a vet in Kramfors. He studied medicine in Umeå. He usually gives me the once-over when we meet up to go hunting in September.'

'You'll have to excuse me if I'm labouring the point, but he's never said anything about your heart?'

'Nooo,' Johansson said, now getting seriously fed up of this endless nagging. 'The last time I saw him he praised my good health. Said he was jealous of me, and that I must be a happy man.'

'Praised you? What for?'

Okay, Johansson thought, deciding to put an end to this utterly pointless conversation.

'For my dick and prostate,' Johansson said. 'His exact words? He said that if he had my dick and my prostate, he'd be a happy man. And he's a urologist, so he must know what he's talking about. I daresay he's seen several kilometres' worth of dicks in his time.' That told her. Mind you, she was asking for it, he thought.

Dr Stenholm contented herself with shaking her blonde head regretfully. She seemed cross.

'Do you have any questions of your own?' he added with an innocent expression.

'If there's anything I'm wondering about? What would that be?' Still cross.

'That business with the squirrel,' Johansson said. 'If you feel up to listening.' His own sudden flare-up of temper seemed to have died down.

He went on to tell her about all the squirrels he had shot when he was a lad. And the way they moved their heads. And the hundreds of hours he had spent watching them. But he added that, otherwise, and certainly for a layperson who lacked his special insights in the subject, she wasn't at all like a squirrel.

'I daresay it's just a tic I've picked up.' Ulrika Stenholm nodded, as if to emphasize what she'd said.

A bit happier now. She even smiled, but without tilting her head.

'On a completely different subject,' she said. 'Not about you. Well, about your job. Your old job,' she clarified. 'I thought I'd take the opportunity while we're talking one to one. I've got a question.'

Johansson nodded.

'If you're sure you feel up to it? It's quite a long story.'

'I'm listening,' Johansson said. And that was how it all started. For Lars Martin Johansson, anyway. For everyone else involved, it had started long before then.

9

Wednesday morning, 14 July

A long story. The outline was long. The questions that popped up afterwards were many. What she was wondering about was simple enough. Did he remember the murder of Yasmine Ermegan? She had been just nine years old when she was raped and strangled.

First the outline, which unfortunately was far too long and messy for Johansson's liking.

Ulrika Stenholm had a sister who was three years older than her, Anna. She was a prosecutor, and Lars Martin Johansson was the great idol of her professional life. She had related countless stories about Johansson to her younger sister, Ulrika.

'She worked for you for a couple of years, back when you were head of the Security Police. She used to say you could see around corners. I mean, without having to lean forward and look.'

'I daresay that's the point,' Johansson said. Who did she take him for? And I don't remember her sister, he thought. As for 'head' – he had been operational head. Not some deskbound paper-shuffler.

'Our father was a vicar, Åke Stenholm. He had a parish in Bromma,' she went on. 'This is really about him. He died last winter, just before Christmas. He was old – eighty-five years old – when he died of cancer. He was already retired by then, of course. He retired in 1989, when he was sixty-five.'

Okay, Johansson thought, with rapidly growing irritation. What's this got to do with me? he wondered.

'I'm making a mess of this,' Ulrika Stenholm said, shaking her head nervously. 'I'll try to get to the point. A couple of days before he died, my dad told me that there was something that had been tormenting him for many years. One of his parishioners had apparently told him, when she was making her confession, that she knew who had murdered a little girl. The girl's name was Yasmine Ermegan. She was nine years old when it happened, and she lived in the parish of Bromma. But she, the woman making the confession, made him promise not to say anything, and because it was part of a religious confession there wasn't a problem with that. As I'm sure you know, priests have an absolute oath of confidentiality. Unconditional and with no exceptions, unlike mine and my colleagues'. But it tormented him badly, because the perpetrator was never found.'

What a uniquely messy story, Johansson thought. It wasn't made any better by the fact that his head had started to ache again.

'So, what I'm wondering, and this was what I wanted to—'

'Give me a pen and paper,' Johansson interrupted, snapping the thumb and forefinger of his left hand commandingly. Whatever the hell do I want them for? he

44

thought quickly. 'Wait,' Johansson said. 'It's better if you write. Make notes. Start a new page. What did you say the victim's name was? The girl, the nine-year-old. The one who lived in your dad's parish.'

'Yasmine Ermegan.'

'Write that down,' Johansson said. 'Like this: victim, colon. Yasmine Ermegan, nine years old, lived in the parish of Bromma.'

Ulrika Stenholm nodded and wrote. She stopped writing, looked up and nodded again.

'When is this supposed to have happened?' It can hardly have been very recent, he thought.

'It was in June 1985, there was something about it in the papers just a few weeks ago. A big article to mark the fact that it was twenty-five years since it happened.'

'Hang on,' Johansson said. 'When in June? When in June 1985?' he added, to be on the safe side. I've talked to plenty of confused informants over the years, Johansson thought. Things weren't made any easier by his damn headache, and the fact that he himself was both a pensioner and a patient and was expected to take things very, very gently. And why in the name of holy fuck had he suddenly started swearing like a navvy in his thoughts or when he was alone, and why was he so angry with pretty much everyone except Pia?

'She went missing on the evening of 14 June 1985, the Friday before Midsummer. And she was found murdered a week later, she'd been raped and strangled, on Midsummer's Eve. The murderer had buried her in the forest outside Sigtuna. He'd wrapped her up in those awful black bin-liners.'

'Hang on,' Johansson said. 'What day is it today?' His head was completely blank all of a sudden.

'Wednesday,' Ulrika Stenholm said. 'It's Wednesday today.'

'Wrong,' Johansson said. 'The date, I mean. What date is it?' What the fuck's going on inside my head? he thought.

'It's 14 July today. Wednesday, 14 July 2010.'

'And how long does that make it?' Johansson said. 'Since they found her, I mean.'

'Twenty-five years and three weeks, more or less. Twenty-five years and twenty-three days, if I've counted right.'

'In which case it's passed the statute of limitations,' Johansson said, and shrugged his shoulders: even the right one worked now. 'That means people like me can't do a thing about it now. Whoever did it can act as suspiciously as he likes, and people like me can't so much as talk to him about it.'

'But that rule has been abolished – the statute of limitations, I mean. It went through Parliament back in the spring, didn't it? These days there's no statute of limitation for murder. The murder of Olof Palme, for instance. That'll never be prescribed.'

'Listen,' Johansson said. She's pretty damn persistent, he thought. 'The statute of limitation for murder, and a number of other crimes with a lifetime sentence, was abolished as of 1 July this year. Parliament voted it through in the spring, but the law was changed only from 1 July. Murders that had already passed the statute of limitations before 1 July are therefore not covered by the change in the law. They're dead and buried for good. You can talk to your prosecutor sister if you don't believe me.' She seems a bit simple as well, he thought.

'Okay, but what about Palme, then?'

46

'Because Palme was murdered in February 1986, that crime wasn't already prescribed by 1 July this year, meaning that it's covered by the new legislation. And will never be prescribed. But this Yasmine you're talking about was murdered in June 1985, so her case was already prescribed when the law was changed. You see the difference,' Johansson said.

'But that's awful,' Ulrika Stenholm said. 'Suppose they found the murderer. Suppose one of your colleagues found the man who killed Yasmine. Suppose you found him today. You'd be forced to just let him go. You wouldn't be able to do a thing.'

'We couldn't do diddly-squat,' Johansson said, nodding as he lay in bed. 'Diddly-squat,' he repeated, just to be on the safe side, seeing as law didn't seem to be her strong subject.

'But that's just awful,' Ulrika Stenholm repeated. 'In spite of all the DNA and other stuff you've got these days.'

'Yes, it's bloody ridiculous,' Johansson said, suddenly in an inexplicably good mood again.

'Yes, it is ridiculous,' Ulrika Stenholm agreed.

'Yes, and do you know what makes it even worse?' Johansson asked.

'No.' She shook her short, blonde hair.

'That I didn't get that blood clot in my brain six months ago. That was very remiss of me. Then we'd have had plenty of time to solve this problem between us. Before it got prescribed, I mean. Or you could have talked to one of my colleagues in good time. Or your dad, the good priest, could have done. Or the man who murdered Yasmine could have had the decency to wait a few weeks before he killed the poor girl.'

'I'm sorry,' Ulrika Stenholm said, and looked like she meant it. 'I really shouldn't be bothering you . . .'

'Never mind that now,' Johansson said. 'This informant, the woman who spoke to your dad, the one who knew who killed Yasmine . . .'

'Yes?'

'What's her name? The informant, I mean.'

'I don't know, he never said. He wasn't allowed to say. Dad had his oath of confidentiality, after all.'

'For God's sake,' Johansson said. What the hell is she saying? he thought. 'When did she tell your dad this, then?' he went on. 'The informant, I mean.'

'As I understand it, it was a year or so after Yasmine was murdered. It can't have been after the summer of 1989, because that's when Dad retired. Reading between the lines of what he said, I understood that she was an elderly lady who was a member of his congregation. And that she told him because she was seriously ill – that was why she was making confession.'

'But you don't know her name? This woman? No idea at all?'

'No, no idea.'

'How do you know she was telling the truth, then? Maybe she was just a bit crazy. Or wanted to make herself more interesting. That sort of thing isn't unusual, you know.'

'Well, my dad believed her. He was a wise, thoughtful man. And he'd heard a few things over the years, so he wasn't easily fooled.'

'So did your dad tell you that she told him who did it, then?'

'No, he didn't say. Not to me, anyway.'

'It wasn't her husband or her son, a relative, a neighbour, workmate? Someone she knew? No clues of that sort?'

'No. But I'm fairly sure she told my dad. Who'd done it, I mean.'

'So how did she know? That this individual had actually done it?'

'Don't know. I just know that Dad believed her, and it caused him a lot of anguish.'

'Okay, okay,' Johansson said. 'Tell me what happened when your dad told you.' Let's take this from the start, he thought. Or what was your start, anyway.

The former vicar of the parish of Bromma, Åke Stenholm, had died of cancer at the age of eighty-five early in December the previous year. In his final days his daughter was with him more or less the whole time. His wife, Ulrika's mother, had been dead ten years, and her father's relationship with Ulrika's older sister was poor. They hadn't been speaking to each other over the previous few years. His daughter Ulrika was the only person he was really close to. As well as being his beloved daughter.

He had spent most of the last few days of his life asleep. Heavily medicated to ease his pain. But two days before he died he had been fully conscious for several hours, and that was when he had told her.

'He started by telling me he hadn't taken his pills for that precise reason. That he wanted to be right in the head – that was how he put it, right in the head – so he would be able to talk to me.'

'I see,' Johansson said. 'Was that all?'

'Yes,' Ulrika Stenholm conceded. 'I can understand that you don't think it's much to go on. Even if the case wasn't prescribed, I mean.'

'Nonsense,' Johansson said. 'There's one thing you need to know, Ulrika: if you're going to investigate a murder, you take things as you find them. There's no point moaning about how hard it is and how little you know, rubbish like that. No proper police officer would waste time on that. Make the most of what you've got, that's the point.'

'Yes, but it's not—'

'Don't start arguing,' Johansson interrupted. 'Let's sum up what we've got instead. And make a note of this.'

Ulrika Stenholm nodded and sat ready with the pen and notepad.

'In December last year, just before he dies, your father tells you what an elderly female parishioner once told him. Some twenty years earlier, just a couple of years after Yasmine's murder, under the seal of the confessional, and when she herself is about to die. Is that correct?' 'Under the seal of the confessional' – not bad, Johansson thought.

'Yes,' Ulrika Stenholm agreed.

'Nothing else that you can recall?'

'No,' Ulrika Stenholm said.

'Okay,' Johansson said. 'Well, we really are going to have to make the most of this. Just so you're clear.'

'I realize that. But there was one thing that struck me, the very first morning I saw you. The day after you were admitted.'

'I'm listening,' Johansson said.

'This story didn't only torment my dad, it's been troubling me as well. Especially recently, what with

50

everything that's been in the paper. And then all of a sudden you show up here . . .'

'And?'

'My father had a very strong faith.'

'That sounds practical. Considering that he was a priest, I mean,' Johansson said.

'And I suppose I'm a bit like that, like he was, but not as much as Dad, I have to admit. Do you know what Dad would have said?'

'No,' Johansson said. How the fuck would I know that? he thought.

'He always said it, when strange things happened. Odd coincidences and so on, things you couldn't explain. Good and bad alike.'

'I'm still listening,' Johansson said.

'Dad used to say that the Lord moves in mysterious ways.'

'You'll have to forgive me, but that sounds like blasphemy to me.' All of a sudden it had happened again. He was elated, instantly. His headache had completely gone.

'How do you mean?'

'The idea that the Lord would have sent you a former police officer, unconscious with a blood clot in his tiny little head, to help you get to grips with a twenty-five-year-old murder. Which just happens to be prescribed already because it was, sadly, a couple of weeks too old to be covered by the new law.' When you thought about it, that was pretty much the only piquant aspect of the whole story, Johansson thought.

Ulrika Stenholm, doctor and neurologist, forty-four years old, even if she didn't look a day over forty, hadn't moved her head at all.

51

'The Lord moves in mysterious ways,' she repeated.

'My problem is that I can no longer see around corners,' Johansson said. 'I can barely work out where I am, if I'm honest. Some things I don't remember at all. The other day it took me an hour to remember what my daughter-in-law's name is. I get cross, sad and happy in a flash, all muddled up, without knowing why. I say strange things, and I swear like a trooper. This murder you're talking about, little Yasmine – I don't remember it at all. To be honest, I haven't got the slightest memory of it, not a thing.'

'That's because of what you've been through,' Ulrika Stenholm said. 'It happens to everyone in your position, you know. And let me tell you . . .'

Johansson shook his head.

'Because we're dealing with you here, I'm pretty confident that it will pass.'

'My arm as well?' Johansson said. Best to make the most of this, he thought.

'Your arm as well,' Dr Stenholm said, and nodded.

Then she stood up, nodded again and patted his good arm.

'Look after yourself now,' she said. 'See you tomorrow.'

It was only when she had already left the room that he remembered. The first of all the obvious professional tricks that someone had erased from his head.

'Fuck!' Johansson yelled. 'Come back, woman!'

'Yes,' she said, standing by his bed again.

'Your dad,' Johansson said. 'He must have left loads of papers and notes when he died.' Old priests were quite phenomenal when it came to collecting stacks of paper.

'Boxloads.' Ulrika Stenholm said.

'See if you can find anything, then,' Johansson said.
Because I'm not going to look for you, he thought.

Then she left, and she was barely out of the door before he fell asleep. The man who had once been able to see around corners, Johansson thought, just before Hypnos grabbed hold of his good arm and led him gently into the darkness. Luring him with the green poppy seedhead he was holding in his slender white hand.

10

Wednesday afternoon, 14 July

In his prime, Lars Martin Johansson was known among his colleagues as 'the man who could see around corners', as well as a walking encyclopaedia when it came to violent crime. As soon as his associates came across an old case they couldn't place, they would start by asking Johansson. That usually saved a lot of time in front of a computer for the person in question, and Johansson was normally able to help, willingly, happy to be asked, and careful and thorough in his answers. He also had an uncanny ability to remember numbers and was often able to recall the case numbers of the investigation a colleague in need was looking for.

Now something had happened inside his head. He could live with the fact that he had forgotten the name of his only son's second wife. Besides, he had remembered after a while.

The fact that he was unable to remember the murder of Yasmine, apparently only nine years old when she was raped and strangled, was considerably more serious. That it had taken place twenty-five years ago only made matters worse. He was often able to remember murders from that time, from the prime of his career, better than those that had occurred later, and he was able to remember the most notable of them down to the smallest details.

Serious anxiety, almost angst, then – not because he had forgotten Yasmine's murder but because of what must have happened inside his head.

First he thought of calling for the nurse and asking for an extra tablet. One of those ones that made him feel detached, that increased the distance between him and whatever was bothering him and made him stop caring. As if it, whatever it was, were nothing to do with him any more.

But not this time.

'Pull yourself together,' Johansson said out loud to himself. Go on the internet and have a look, he thought. The simplest solution was that his little squirrel had got most of it muddled up and that was why he couldn't remember Yasmine's murder. He thought, took an instant decision, but then things started to go seriously wrong.

Problems, problems, problems. Getting the laptop from the bedside table, putting it in front of him on the bed, opening the lid, switching it on, all with his left hand, having a right hand that was only in the way. Then, once he had got that far, realizing he had forgotten his password. The same password he hadn't had any problem with that morning, before that nightmare of a doctor had come into his room and complicated his life. Now he could no longer use his own computer. As if he didn't have enough to deal with already.

Nevertheless, he made a number of attempts. He could feel sweat breaking out on his forehead, his head started to ache, his chest felt tight. It got worse each time he was denied access to his own computer. Fuck, fuck, fuck, Johansson thought, and it wasn't the change in his language that was bothering him now. Then he called Pia. She was in a meeting but answered straight away because it was him ringing, and made no effort to hide the anxiety in her voice.

'Lars, has something happened?' she asked.

'I've forgotten my password,' Johansson said.

'Your password?'

'The password for the bloody computer,' Johansson explained.

'God, you gave me a fright!' Pia said.

'My password,' Johansson repeated. For God's sake, woman, he thought, the first time he had ever thought anything like that about Pia. The first time since he met her more than twenty years ago.

'I've got it written down at home,' Pia said. 'You can have it when I see you this evening. I don't know it off the top of my head.'

'For God's sake, woman!' Johansson yelled. 'Is it really so fucking hard to remember a pissing computer password?' In an instant, he was unreasonably furious with the person he loved more than everyone and everything.

'Lars, you've never shouted at me before. This isn't you, Lars. We both know why, but please, don't shout at me.'

His throat tightened. That only took a second as well.

'Sorry,' Johansson said. 'I'm sorry, darling.'

Then he ended the call, but not quickly enough, because tears were already running down his cheeks.

He wiped his face on the sheet, and the fact that his laptop fell off the bed didn't bother him in the slightest. It might as well lie on the floor until someone came in and picked it up for him. Then he took three deep breaths, picked up his mobile and called his best friend. Easy enough, because he was on speed-dial, and Johansson was able to manage perfectly with just his left hand and thumb for once.

'Jarnebring,' Jarnebring said on the second ring.

'Hello, Bo,' Johansson said. 'It's me.'

'Christ! That's cheered me up! How are you? You sound pretty perky.'

'I was wondering if I could ask a favour,' Johansson said. 'You've got a key to my house. Could you call in and check the password for my laptop? There's a note of it in that secret place, you know . . .'

'No problem,' Jarnebring said. 'See you in an hour.'

'I'm fine, by the way,' Johansson said. 'Like a pig in shit.'

'Yes, you sound pretty alert. And you're not slurring or stammering.'

'Never felt better,' Johansson declared. A thought had just struck him, a very pleasant one, compared to everything else that struck him these days. And not too much of a stretch: a real bonus. Not like having a stroke because of your dodgy heart.

'There was one other thing. While you're in the flat, grab a bottle of vodka, then if you could stop off on the way, at Günter's, you know, and get me a large bratwurst with sauerkraut and mustard. Don't bother getting a drink to go with it, I've got that here.'

'You do sound kind of thirsty,' Jarnebring concurred. 'Weird food in those places, so I've heard.'

'Can you manage that?'

'Do bears shit in the woods?' Jarnebring said. 'Sausage, password, vodka, sauerkraut. See you in an hour!'

My best friend, Johansson thought. But he wasn't about to start crying. Instead he made himself comfortable in bed. He even managed to fold his hands on his stomach in a reasonably sensible way. No headache, no anger, no anxiety. Peace, Johansson thought. Finally, some sort of peace for a restless hunter like me.

That was how things progressed for Johansson. That was how it started up again for his best friend, Bo Jarnebring. After the first time, twenty-five years ago.

II
Eye for eye, tooth for tooth . . .
Book of Exodus, 21:24

11

Wednesday afternoon, 14 July

Jarnebring looked the same as usual. He stopped in the doorway to Johansson's room, assessed its security with his eyes, then occupied it in a purely physical sense. As if he were on a raid of a drug den. Only then did he come over to the bed and sit down beside Johansson. He smiled and shook his head.

'You look fucking awful, Lars,' Jarnebring said. 'Mind you, you look a lot more awake than I was expecting,' he added quickly when he realized what he had just said.

There's something that isn't right, Johansson thought. Something missing. Something that could hardly be inside the large brown bag that Jarnebring had put down next to the bed. And Jarnebring smelled of aftershave. Nothing but aftershave. Not like someone who had just been to Günter's.

'Where the hell's my sausage?' Johansson asked in an accusing voice.

'Look, Lars,' Jarnebring said, leaning forward and grabbing his shoulder with his large hand and squeezing him hard. 'You're my best friend. I'm fucking glad you're still alive, you know.'

'Same here,' Johansson said. 'So where the hell's my sausage?' And my vodka, he thought.

'Here.' Jarnebring emptied the contents of the brown bag on the bed. 'Apples, pears, oranges, bananas – I even got you some chocolate, that healthy stuff with nothing but cocoa.'

'No sausage.'

'No sausage, and no vodka either,' Jarnebring confirmed. 'If you want to kill yourself, you'll have to do it on your own. I'm not going to help you. But I have got the password for your computer, like you asked. And as soon as you sort yourself out and get out of here, I'm going to personally carry you down to my gym so we can knock you into shape.'

'Thanks a lot for all your help. With friends like you, who needs enemies?'

'Stop moaning,' Jarnebring said. 'You're not the only one having a rough time. Pia hasn't had a great time, you know. Nor me. On Monday evening last week, when you ended up here, some moron from *Aftonbladet* called and said you'd been shot in the stomach and were in intensive care. I was sitting out in the garden, relaxing with my wife, my sister and brother-in-law, drinking a nice chilled pilsner. Enjoying life as a pensioner, and then that idiot phones, claiming you've been shot and are on the way out. Wondered if I'd like to make a comment.'

'And did you?'

'I told him to go to hell. Then I called the Pit and asked if they knew anything. And there I got hold of another simpleton – a fellow officer, no less, whoever the fuck would recruit someone like him and put him in Central Control. Anyway, he says that all he knows is that the lads from the rapid-response unit said over the radio that they were taking you to A&E at the Karolinska because it was evidently too fucking urgent to wait for a proper ambulance. It's hardly surprising I was worried. So I got on the phone again, but the doctors refused to tell me anything and Pia's number was engaged the whole time, so obviously I got even more worried.'

'You haven't had an easy time of it,' Johansson said.

'No,' Jarnebring said. 'It wasn't easy, but just as I was about to get in the car, in spite of those three or four beers, to drive to the Karolinska and say goodbye to you, one of my old mates called and told me what was going on. He was one of the ones who drove you in. We're still in touch.'

'P-2,' Johansson said. 'Patrik Åkesson.' Suddenly, he could remember.

'There,' Jarnebring said. 'You haven't completely lost it. Anyway, like fuck had you been shot in the stomach. It was the same crap you've been trying for the past twenty years. Eating yourself to death. Fainting and making a right mess of yourself with sausage, mustard, sauce and other slop.'

'Well,' Johansson said, 'I don't know about fainting . . .'

'Don't interrupt me. All I was going to say is that I'm not going to budge when it comes to your sausage. But you can ask me for pretty much anything else. Obviously.'

'In that case, there is something I've been thinking about that you might be able to help with.'

'I'm listening,' Jarnebring said.

'Do you remember a twenty-five-year-old murder, summer of 1985?' Johansson said. 'A nine-year-old girl who was raped, strangled and buried outside Sigtuna – Yasmine Erdogan.'

Jarnebring looked at him in surprise.

'Why are you thinking about that?' he asked.

'Never mind that now,' Johansson said. 'We can do that bit later,' he added, to smooth things over. 'Do you remember the case?'

'Yes,' Jarnebring said with a nod.

'Tell me.'

'Yasmine Ermegan, that was her name. Not Erdogan. Ermegan. If we take the short version . . . she was from Iran. She and her parents arrived here when she was just a few years old. She went missing from her mum's flat out in Solna on a Friday evening, 14 June 1985. She was found a week later, on Midsummer's Eve, Friday 21 June. She'd been smothered, not strangled. Probably with a pillow, according to the pathologist, because he found traces of down and white cotton in her throat. Her body was wrapped in four plastic bags, sealed with ordinary packing tape. The perpetrator had dumped her in some reeds in an inlet of Lake Mälaren, a couple of kilometres north of Skokloster Castle. So she wasn't buried, just dumped. You could get a car to where she was found. The perpetrator only had to carry her a dozen or so metres, which most people could have managed, seeing as she didn't weigh more than thirty kilos.'

'How do you know all that?' Johansson asked. How could Jarnebring know all this while I can't remember a thing? he thought.

'It was my case,' Jarnebring replied. 'So it's not really all that strange. I know everything about little Yasmine's murder. There's only one thing I don't know.'

'What's that, then?' Johansson said, even though he already knew the answer.

'Who killed the poor kid. I'd like to have a few words with that bastard.'

64

12

Wednesday afternoon, 14 July

'So, tell me,' Jarnebring said, taking a large bite out of one of the apples he had just given Johansson. 'Why this interest in a twenty-five-year-old murder? Are you thinking of going back on the force or something?'

'No, definitely not. Someone who works here asked me, it was something she'd read about in the paper, and then I realized I didn't have a clue what she was talking about. It wasn't a pleasant feeling, because I'm so used to being able to remember things like that.'

'It's hardly that surprising,' Jarnebring said with a grin. 'You were on the National Police Board at the time. Buried under all those files, unable to see or hear anything.'

'Maybe,' Johansson said.

'Okay.' Jarnebring shrugged his broad shoulders. 'So, I'm not a doctor, but maybe it's got something to do with what happened to you. That must have occurred to you as well? Blood clots in your noggin can really fuck things up. I remember my old man. All of a sudden he couldn't remember anybody in his family. Spent the rest of his days either sitting there crying, or roaring with laughter at everyone and everything. He wasn't himself after that, if I can put it like that.'

'It's more patchy with me,' Johansson said. 'Some bits of my head are complete blanks,' he explained. 'But I still think I ought to have remembered this. There must have been loads in the press when it happened. I mean, I can still remember the murder of Helene Nilsson in Hörby in 1989 in detail, for instance.'

'No,' Jarnebring said, shaking his head firmly. 'It wasn't anything like Helene. There must have been a hundred times more about Helene in the papers than there was about Yasmine. The first week when Yasmine was missing, she didn't get a single mention. Nothing on television or radio either.'

'Why?' Johansson said. 'A nine-year-old girl going missing from her home on a Friday evening? There must have been a huge fuss.'

'Pretty much nothing happened,' Jarnebring said. 'The parents had separated a year or so earlier. Yasmine spent every other week with her dad and his new partner out in Äppelviken, and the other week with her mum in Solna. Her mum lived alone, incidentally. So that week she should have been with her mum, but they started arguing after just a few hours. The kid took her things and walked out. When the mother finally got in touch with our colleagues out in Solna a few hours later, even she believed that Yasmine had just gone back to her dad's. She'd called there, of course, but there was no answer. The duty officer in Solna sent a patrol car round to the father's house. The mother refused to go – she was terrified of her ex-husband – but the villa where he lived was empty and shut up. Which was a bit odd, seeing as his workmates, whom our colleagues had also spoken to, said he was going to be working that evening. He was a doctor. Involved in some weird experiment that involved him going back and forth between home and work to keep an eye on a load of laboratory animals while he slowly killed them. But that Friday evening he'd just disappeared. Persuaded a workmate to do his shift instead. But it was a week or so before we discovered that. This was where he worked, by the way.'

'Here? In Neurology?'

'No, here at the Karolinska. The Karolinska Institute. He was an associate professor in some research department.'

'Oh, I see,' Johansson said.

'Exactly,' Jarnebring said. 'So the general understanding was that when the kid showed up at her father's, he went mad, took the kid and vanished. They were in the middle of a messy divorce; things were getting really nasty. Mostly about custody of Yasmine, who was the only child, as well as everything else. Everyone thought that was what had happened, including us and Yasmine's mother.'

Classic, Johansson thought. A classic example of a case going wrong right at the start. Everything seemed right, everyone thought the right things. And then everything turned out to be completely wrong.

'But on Midsummer's Eve, when she was found, everything changed. That was when I was brought in. I was called in on the Saturday morning, together with the rest of my team, to help our colleagues out in Solna. Unfortunately, that went wrong as well, not because of me but because of the cretinous moron who was in charge of the investigation.'

'I thought you were in charge?' Johansson said. 'Didn't you say it was your case?'

'I was deputy. Another of our colleagues was officially head of the investigation.'

'Who was that, then?' Johansson asked.

'You don't want to know,' Jarnebring said with a broad smile.

'Yes, I do,' Johansson said.

'Evert Bäckström.' Jarnebring smiled even wider.

'Sweet Jesus!' Johansson said. Sweet Jesus! he thought.

13

Wednesday afternoon, 14 July

'Get me a glass of water,' Johansson said, nodding towards the carafe on his bedside table.

'Your face has gone bright red, Lars,' Jarnebring said. 'Maybe I should have done as you said, after all, and brought that bottle of vodka.'

Jarnebring poured a glass, then put it carefully in Johansson's outstretched hand. Johansson drank, deep gulps. He felt completely calm now. Completely calm, without any drugs.

'Too late now,' Johansson said, wiping a few errant drops from his top lip. 'The vodka, I mean.'

'Thanks,' he added as Jarnebring took the empty glass and put it back on the table.

'Maybe you could get a job as a traffic light, Lars,' Jarnebring said. 'They could put you next to a crossing, say something inappropriate, and you'd go red instantly.'

'How the hell,' Johansson said, with force, feeling and an acute need to lower the pressure building up inside him, 'can anyone come up with the idea, or even think the thought, of appointing Evert Bäckström head of the preliminary investigation in a case like that?'

'I think it was Ebbe's fault.' Jarnebring didn't seem entirely unpleased when he said it.

'Ebbe? Which Ebbe?'

'Ebbe Carlsson. That crazy little publisher who kept sticking his nose into police business. Everything from the West German Embassy siege, when he worked as head of information for the Minister of Justice, to the murder of Olof Palme twenty years later. When little Ebbe was a director at Bonniers Publishing House – whatever the hell they had to do with a murder investigation. Or rather that moron of a police chief we had back then, who appointed himself head of the investigation into the murder of our beloved prime minister, despite the fact that he had no idea about how to investigate a murder, and insisted on asking his best friend, Ebbe, to help him.'

'Explain.'

'Do you want the long or the short version?' Jarnebring asked.

'Give me the long one,' said Johansson, who was feeling brighter than he had in ages.

'You may remember that Ebbe was a poof,' Jarnebring began.

'What's that got to do with anything?'

'This time it is actually relevant,' Jarnebring said with a crooked smile.

'How?'

'Six months before Yasmine was murdered, the publisher had been at one of those clubs for like-minded souls, where he found a young man in a sailor's uniform, whom he invited home for all the things people get up to when they drag new friends home from bars. Regardless of whether or not they're gay, I mean,' Jarnebring added, for some reason.

'So what happened?' Johansson said.

'The young man in the Donald Duck costume robbed him. Beat him up badly and then disappeared, taking the publisher's wallet and various other valuables with him. Including some old dress that the publisher had bought at an auction. Supposed to have belonged to Rita Hayworth. That American actress, you know. Worth loads of money, apparently.'

'Go on,' Johansson said.

'The publisher filed a report with the police and had the great good fortune to end up with Bäckström looking after his case. Bäckström wrote it off, explained to the publisher that he had to expect that sort of thing if he didn't pull himself together and start behaving like a normal person.'

'Sigh,' Johansson said. Sigh and groan, he thought.

'Naturally, Ebbe was seriously fucked off. Mind you, who wouldn't be, given that he'd been beaten up and robbed? So he called his best friend and told him about little Bäckström and his performance. And the fact that Bäckström had called him an arse bandit, an anal acrobat, and other things of a similar nature.'

'And the chief of police went mad,' Johansson concluded.

'To put it mildly,' Jarnebring said. 'He's supposed to have lost it completely, and threatened to kill little Evert if he didn't behave better. So Bäckström got kicked out of Crime in Stockholm. As punishment, he was transferred to the crime unit out in Solna. He happened to be sitting there the evening Yasmine went missing, and because it was summer and everyone was on holiday and there was barely anyone else around, he ended up as head of the investigation a week later.'

'So what happened after that? With Yasmine, I mean,' Johansson asked. Stupid question, because he already knew the answer.

'Got shunted downstairs,' Jarnebring said. 'All the way down to the basement. But to be honest, that wasn't only Bäckström's fault.'

'Tell me.'

'Are you sure?' Jarnebring looked at the time. 'I mean, isn't Pia coming today?'

'In three hours. We've got plenty of time. Go on.'

Detective Inspector Evert Bäckström had the picture clear in his mind right from the outset. Yasmine had argued with her mum. She had gone home to her dad's, he had taken her with him and left the city, a straightforward way of putting an end to a difficult custody battle. Then, when Yasmine was found murdered a week later, he only had to make a minor adjustment. The father hadn't only abducted his daughter, he had also raped and murdered her. For the usual reasons that applied to people like him.

'Another wretched honour killing, the sort of thing Arabs and Muslims and others of that ilk got up to. Because, naturally, Evert understood that sort of thing better than anyone else.' Jarnebring nodded gloomily.

'But the rape? How could he believe that? The poor girl had been raped.' Johansson shook his head in disbelief.

'That wasn't a problem. According to Bäckström, men like Yasmine's dad fucked goats and sheep when they weren't shagging their own children. And, sorry to say, he got a degree of support for this from Yasmine's mother. Like I said, the parents had already filed for divorce when this happened, and by then the mother had reported the father for several instances of abuse. That investigation was dropped more or less at once but, if you ask me, I think he beat her pretty badly on more than one occasion,' Jarnebring said thoughtfully.

'Only a couple of months before this business with her daughter, the mother threw some more fuel on the fire by claiming that he had sexually assaulted their daughter. She was really going for it, basically. They both wanted custody of the daughter but, while they waited for the verdict, they had agreed to share Yasmine between them, one week at a time. By the way, she went to school in the centre of Stockholm. One of those fancy private schools. She started there when her parents were still together.'

'Was it true, then?' Johansson asked. 'Had he assaulted his daughter?'

'No,' Jarnebring said. 'I'm sure he hadn't. I'll get to that in a moment,' he went on. 'But I'm pretty certain he used to hit his wife, on the other hand. And, towards the end of the relationship, I reckon it happened pretty often.'

'What an incredibly depressing story.' Johansson sighed.

'It gets worse.'

'I'm listening.'

'When Yasmine was found, her father was still missing. He'd been gone a whole week by then. On the morning of the following day, on Saturday, the radio and television news reported that Yasmine's body had been found. Within a couple of hours he showed up at the police station out in Solna. Completely mad.'

'So what happened?'

'It was a disaster. A total fucking disaster. The first time Bäckström interviewed him it ended with the father trying to break little Evert's arms and legs. The father was a big man, kind of like me,' Jarnebring said. 'But Bäckström wasn't stupid, not like that, anyway. There were plenty of officers in the vicinity, so Yasmine's dad got a serious seeing-to before he was dragged off to the cells. The prosecutor immediately decided to remand him in custody. At that point he was in complete agreement with Bäckström. Most of our colleagues were, to be honest. Even I thought it was probably the father at that time. His story of what he'd been doing during the week he was missing sadly turned out not to be true.'

'What was he claiming, then?'

'That he'd been sitting in a cottage out in the archipelago, all on his own, thinking deep thoughts about life. He said he'd borrowed the cottage from a workmate, which, admittedly, was true, but apart from that it was all lies, and for the usual reason.'

'An affair. He was with another woman,' Johansson concluded.

'Of course he was,' Jarnebring confirmed. 'But it took several days before he managed to say that. The situation turned out to be rather complicated, if I can put it like that.'

'How do you mean, complicated?' Johansson asked.

'Well, like I said, he had a regular shag,' Jarnebring said. 'Another doctor, same age as him. This story's crawling with doctors, as you might have noticed. She was the one he lived with in that villa out in Äppelviken; it was her house. She'd been given it by her parents, and she and Yasmine's father had been seeing each other for a year before he left Yasmine's mother. She was away when all this happened. She'd gone to Spain for a fortnight's holiday – her parents lived there – and so her partner decided to make the most of the opportunity. He'd managed to pick up a younger model who worked in the same lab as him, borrowed the cottage in the archipelago from a colleague, and got on with it. Making the beast with two backs, morning, noon and night. The girl he'd picked up was only half his age, and she was also playing away from home. Had a fiancé doing national service.'

'Half his age, you say. So the father didn't kill his daughter?'

'Nope,' Jarnebring said. 'He didn't kill Yasmine. He certainly had an eye for the ladies and he was a bit handy with his fists, but he wasn't a paedophile. As little as you or me, Lars. He was thirty-four when his daughter was murdered – born 1951, if I remember rightly. The girl he dragged out to the archipelago may have been only nineteen, but she certainly wasn't a child. A young, attractive blonde. Neither you nor I would have said no if she'd asked.'

'When did you work this out?' Johansson asked. Speak for yourself, he thought.

'As soon as I met him. He was in custody, and was pretty much climbing the walls. After a few days I went up and talked to him. I realized it wasn't him almost immediately. He was basically mad with grief at what had happened to his daughter.'

'You're absolutely sure?'

'Completely the wrong type. Nothing about him felt right. At least I managed to talk some sense into him. To the extent that he said there'd been someone with him who could give him an alibi. A female acquaintance from work. But he didn't want to give me her name. So I took the gloves off. Told him the whole investigation was heading for the rocks if he didn't see sense. That we weren't going to make any progress until we could count him out. And if he was as innocent as he claimed, then he ought to give that some serious thought. And then I finally got the name out of him. I had a proper talk with her. And it turned out to be exactly the way he said. By this point we'd started to get hold of other information that backed up his alibi. People who'd talked to him on the phone, seen him and the girl out at that borrowed cottage. The usual sort of thing.'

'So what happened after that, then?'

'I had a chat with the prosecutor and Bäckström. The prosecutor was already having doubts by this point – he had the custody proceedings to worry about, and there wasn't a lot of hard evidence against the father. Bäckström was his usual self: anyone with a brain could see that the father did it – unless you were thick in the head, like me. And those witnesses who had just appeared were obviously lying to protect him.

'The day the father was due to be charged we got the results back from the National Forensics Lab. They'd managed to secure samples of sperm from Yasmine's body and clothes. The perpetrator's blood group didn't match her father's. There was no DNA technology back then, of course, but the blood group was more than enough.'

'So the prosecutor backed down and the father was released,' Johansson said.

'Exactly. I can tell you've been through this before. The only one who didn't back down was Bäckström. If it wasn't the father who'd raped the daughter, then it must have been one of his friends having a bit of fun with her. The result of this whole mess was that it took more than fourteen days from when she went missing for us to have any reasonable grasp of the nature of what we were dealing with. Not to mention the fact that the holiday season was in full swing and we couldn't get hold of anyone. We were about a third the strength we usually were. That we should have been, and needed to be to make any progress. And that's without even taking into account the little fat bastard who was in charge of it all.'

'Bäckström carried on being difficult?'

'Of course,' Jarnebring said. 'He told anyone who was prepared to listen that he now knew there were at least two perpetrators involved. The father and an as yet unknown friend of his. There were plenty of journalists who bought the story as well. But there were a few legally responsible editors who didn't, which is probably another reason why there wasn't much media coverage of Yasmine's murder. There was the fact that the family were immigrants. And those accusations the mother made against the father. Honour killing and violence against women and incest and immigrants and God knows what else. All of a sudden it was a bloody sensitive story.'

'I can imagine,' Johansson said. 'And all of it a load of crap that had nothing to do with the facts and just confused things.'

'You don't have to tell me that, but trying to explain that to Bäckström was a complete waste of time. He refused to listen.'

'What were you expecting?'

'It turned into a complete disaster, the whole case.' Johansson sighed deeply and shook his head.

'The investigation into little Yasmine's murder isn't a happy story. Not a happy story at all.'

Johansson made do with a nod. He sat in silence for so long that Jarnebring got worried and had to sneak a glance at him to make sure he hadn't fallen asleep. Or, even worse, had another stroke. But he hadn't. He looked like he was thinking. As if he were somewhere deep inside himself, thinking.

'Give me the really long version,' he suddenly said. 'I want to hear more about the start of the investigation. I want to know more about that little kid and her family. We've still got plenty of time.' He nodded towards the clock hanging above the door of his room.

'Are you sure you're up to it?' Jarnebring asked. I'm starting to recognize you again now, he thought. Even though you look a right mess and your face is all lopsided.

'Never felt better,' Johansson said. Even though I really feel like apple sauce that someone's just crapped out, he thought.

'Okay. But you'll have to give me some paper and a pen and five minutes to gather my thoughts.

'Have a word with the nurse. And I can have one of your bananas in the meantime?' At least they're the same shape as Günter's magnificent Polish bratwurst, he thought. But there the resemblance ends, sadly.

14

Wednesday afternoon, 14 July

'Are you asleep?' Jarnebring asked.

'No,' Johansson replied, shifting position on the bed. 'Just shut my eyes for a minute.'

'Okay,' Jarnebring said. 'Off we go, then. I think we'll start with the weather on the day she went missing.'

'I'm listening.'

'High summer in Sweden, not a cloud in the sky, barely any wind. Between twenty and thirty degrees. The weather stayed pretty much the same all week and, naturally, I was stuck at work, sweating my arse off. My usual luck.'

'At least little Yasmine was fortunate with the weather,' Johansson said. Because where his heart usually sat in his chest there was suddenly nothing but a black hole, but there was no chance of him bursting into tears because there was also, just as suddenly, a hatred so strong that it shut out love, sadness and common human decency.

Jarnebring looked at him, barely able to hide his surprise.

'How are you doing, Lars?' he said. 'Maybe we should wait with this, after all?'

'No,' Johansson said. 'I'm listening,' he repeated. 'Tell me what happened the day she disappeared. You said it was a Friday.'

'Friday, 14 June 1985,' Jarnebring confirmed.

'Friday, 14 June 1985,' Johansson repeated. A hot summer's day in Sweden. He tried to disregard the hatred he was feeling. Just remember that you can't see around corners any more, he thought.

15

Friday, 14 June 1985

Twenty-five years earlier, and the last time Josef Ermegan, thirty-four, spoke to his nine-year-old daughter Yasmine, he lied to her.

It was around six in the evening when he dropped her off outside the door of the house on Hannebergsgatan in Solna where her mother lived. He kissed her on the cheeks and forehead, made her promise not to argue with her mother, and himself promised to phone her as soon as he got time, but that it might be a few days because he had a lot to do at work. Then he drove out to the archipelago, to a house he had borrowed from a work colleague, with a young woman with whom he had just embarked upon an affair. A different woman from the one he had been sharing his home and bed with for the past couple of years, the woman Yasmine sometimes called 'Mummy' when she was tired and sleepy, or just forgot.

When he told Jarnebring about this a week or so later, he was sitting in custody in the police station in Solna suspected of having murdered his daughter. He was sobbing uncontrollably, like an abandoned child, and Jarnebring didn't know what to do. He patted him on the shoulder and said he believed him. Josef grabbed his hand, squeezing it hard between both of his, then pressed Jarnebring's hand to his face. Jarnebring felt 'seriously fucking awkward', even though he had seen most things and was used to all sorts of body language. He pulled his hand free, as gently as he could, then leaned across the table and took hold of Josef Ermegan's shoulders. He squeezed hard to get him to listen. Josef whimpered, pressed his knuckles into his eyes and dropped his head to the table between them. Jarnebring patted him on the back. Told him he needed to pull himself together so he could help Jarnebring find the man who had killed his daughter. Josef straightened up and removed his hands from his face.

'I promise,' Josef Ermegan said. 'I promise to toughen up, to summon up the worst in me. I swear I'll help you. I swear on my daughter's life.'

If only Yasmine had managed to keep her promise to her father, then what ended up happening would never have happened. Instead, she and her mother Maryam, thirty-two, started arguing before they even sat down to eat. Yasmine had taken a can of Coca-Cola from her rucksack, sat down at the table and started to read a comic she had brought with her. Her mum started nagging her, saying she wasn't allowed Coke, it wasn't good for her teeth, and that she, a dental nurse, knew better than Yasmine's dad. When she made to take the can from her daughter, Yasmine spilled the drink on her blouse and they started shouting at each other. Yasmine pulled on the little rucksack containing all her things, rushed into the bathroom and locked the door behind her.

Her mum decided to pretend it hadn't happened. Only when she had finished preparing the meal and the table was set did she knock on the bathroom door and say it was time to eat. Yasmine came out. She had swapped her white blouse for a pink T-shirt and pale blue jeans and went and sat at the table, where she started to eat in sullen silence. Her mother ignored that as well. Then the phone rang, and her mum went into the living room to answer. It was one of her colleagues at work. Maryam explained that she and her daughter were in the middle of eating and promised to call back later, but as she put the phone down she heard the front door close. Just before seven o'clock, on the evening of Friday, 14 June 1985. And if she had never started arguing with her daughter, what ended up happening would never have happened.

At first she rushed into the bathroom, although she was unable to say why when she was asked about it later. Yasmine's keys were on the floor in front of the basin, an ornate, plaited leather necklace that she usually wore round her neck with one key to her mum's flat, and one for the house where her dad lived. She had evidently taken it off when she changed her soaked white blouse for the pink T-shirt and forgotten to put it back on again when her mum told her food was ready.

Then Maryam ran out on to the balcony to call to her daughter. But the street was empty. Just a few adults walking past, staring up at her on the balcony in surprise as she called her daughter's name.

Then she put her shoes on and ran down the stairs, and just as she was about to run out into the road she bumped into a neighbour who lived in the same building, a police officer. He was considerably older than her but, to judge from the way he looked at her whenever they said hello to each other, he liked what he saw, maybe even had a bit of a crush on her and could imagine getting together with her. Even though he was Swedish and blond and a police officer and considerably older than her, a refugee from Iran who had only just been granted Swedish citizenship.

'You're in a rush!' Police Inspector Peter Sundman said, smiling broadly at the woman who had just run into his arms.

'Sorry, Peter,' Maryam apologized as soon as she saw who it was. 'It's Yasmine, my daughter, she's just run away from home.'

'Only just, surely?' Peter Sundman asked. 'I passed her a couple of minutes ago when she was on her way to the underground. She looked the way kids do when they've had a row with their mum. I waved to her, but I don't think she saw me. If you ask me, she's on her way back to her dad's to tell him how awful her mum's been and to get a bit of sympathy.'

He already knew about the situation between Maryam and her former husband. She had told him, and he had also heard about it at work. A beautiful young woman, seemed educated and smart, and if she fancied trying something new he was prepared to bide his time.

'She didn't take her keys,' Maryam said.

'If her dad's home, I'm sure he'll let her in.' Peter Sundman patted her arm sympathetically. 'If only to give him a reason to yell at you.'

'What if he's at work?'

'Then she'll call him there. If I had to guess, I'd say she'll phone you first because she's already regretting what she's done and wants to say sorry for being so silly. How about a cup of coffee?'

'In my flat,' Maryam said. 'So I'm there if she calls. When she calls, I mean.'

And if Yasmine hadn't forgotten to take her keys with her, it would never have happened.

Yasmine never phoned. After a couple of hours and numerous cups of coffee, Maryam and Peter started making phone calls. First, Peter called her ex-husband at home, because she refused to, then he tried calling him at work. Then Maryam called a few of Josef's work colleagues, and Yasmine's best friend. But they either got no answer or the person they spoke to had nothing to tell them. They didn't know where Josef was. If he wasn't at home, then he was probably at work. Maybe he was out getting something to eat, even though it was late. He was probably somewhere between home and the laboratory, a journey he had to make often because of the laboratory animals, which needed looking after the whole time.

If she hadn't started arguing with Yasmine, if her husband hadn't given her that can of Coca-Cola even though he knew she wasn't allowed it, if her daughter hadn't left her keys behind . . . If, if, if.

Over the course of the next few months Maryam and Josef would come up with hundreds of different explanations as to why what ended up happening shouldn't have happened. If only . . . They tormented themselves, and each other.

Just before midnight Peter Sundman called the officer at the Solna Police who had relieved him on the duty desk at Solna police station at half past six that evening. The duty officer put him through to the detective who was on call for the crime unit in Solna that evening and, when Peter Sundman heard who it was, he groaned silently to himself.

'Bäckström,' Bäckström said. 'What is it?'

16

Saturday, 15 June

Bäckström and Sundman had begun to squabble almost immediately. Bäckström had considerably more important things to do than take care of 'a little brat who's had a row with her mum and run off to her dad'. Surely even someone like Sundman could understand that? Sundman ended the call and rang the duty officer again. He got him to send a patrol car to the villa where the father lived. The car arrived just after midnight, but the house was locked and dark, no car in the drive, and the letterbox was empty. The officers drove around the neighbourhood, but the whole area was quiet and dark and seemed almost abandoned.

On the way back to the station in Solna the patrol car stopped off at the father's place of work out at the Karolinska. There were a few lights on in various windows, but when they rang the bell no one responded over the entry-phone. And they hadn't spotted anyone who looked remotely like Yasmine when they drove round the hospital grounds a few times just to be sure.

Before they finished their shift the following morning, they repeated the procedure, but in reverse. Same result as before. No one replied on the entry-phone at the father's workplace. The house where he lived was as before. Drive empty, letterbox empty, no morning paper, even though the man delivering them was on his way down the street. They stopped to talk to him, and he checked his list. The paper had been cancelled from Monday that week, for a fortnight. He had nothing else of note to contribute.

'Most people who live here have already gone off to their summer cottages,' he explained.

While his younger colleagues drove to and fro, the duty officer called the father's home and workplace. According to him, he tried at least three times during the night, at intervals of a couple of hours. No answer. What Bäckström had been doing was unclear. He didn't answer when the duty officer tried to call him at three in the morning. All of this was according to what the duty officer told Jarnebring when they discussed it just over a week later.

'Mostly to wind up the fat little bastard. When it comes to that man, Sundman and I are of the same opinion. If I had to choose, I'd pick haemorrhoids over him.'

On Saturday morning Peter Sundman talked to his boss, who talked to Bäckström's boss, who in turn saw to it that Bäckström at least filed a formal missing-person report for Yasmine Ermegan, nine years old. But, in principle, he shared Bäckström's opinion. 'Voluntary disappearance. No crime suspected.'

In a few days' time she and her father would doubtless show up in the best of health and then all hell would break loose again between him and the girl's mother. In the usual way, with the air thick with accusations and counterclaims. The way things always turned out when kids of that background and with that sort of parents ran away from home. Any proper police officer knew that.

But not this time.

17

Wednesday afternoon, 14 July 2010

'So, basically, not a damn thing happened during the whole of the first fucking week. Not until she was found on Midsummer's Eve, on the evening of 21 June,' Jarnebring said, glancing at his notes.

'I'm listening,' Johansson said.

'It was the usual,' Jarnebring went on. 'A dog-owner taking his mutt out for an evening piss. Wonder how many dead bodies have been found by them over the years?'

'You're right, there,' Johansson said. 'You can never go wrong with a dog. Dogs are good.'

Jarnebring glanced at him, slightly warily. Something's definitely happened to Lars Martin, he thought. Not that he could do much about that. No more than he was already doing, of course.

'Anyway,' Jarnebring said, 'he was renting a cottage out near Skokloster Castle, and when he was walking along the shore of the lake his dog suddenly races off, straight out into the reeds, and then starts barking like buggery. The poor girl was wrapped in some of those big plastic bags, but the dog was standing there tearing at them, so the owner saw what was inside. That put a rocket under him, naturally. He put the dog on the lead and rushed home to call 90000 – that was still the number in those days – and said he'd found a dead body wrapped in black plastic. It was a standard poodle, by the way,' Jarnebring said. 'The dog, I mean. Called Old Bosse, I seem to recall. Why the fuck would anyone call their dog Old Bosse?'

'Isn't your name Bo?' Johansson said.

'Yes,' Jarnebring said with a grin. 'Now I'm starting to recognize the old Lars. Nice to know you haven't lost it completely.'

'So she was lying there in the reeds?' Johansson said. 'She hadn't been buried?'

'No,' Jarnebring said. 'He'd dragged her out a few metres, to where the reeds were at their thickest, and then pushed or trod her down into the mud. There was loads of sludge down there. If the dog hadn't found her, she'd have been there for quite some time.'

'So where did the girl go?' Johansson asked. 'When she ran away from her mum's, I mean.'

'I'm getting to that – all in good time,' Jarnebring said, running his forefinger down his closely written notes.

18

Friday evening, 14 June 1985

Just before seven o'clock on Friday evening, Yasmine had run away from her mother's flat. When she got outside the front door she – in all likelihood – turned right and walked, or ran, the fifty metres from the building on Hannebergsgatan to the first junction with Skytteholmsvägen. There she turned right again and walked the hundred metres to the entrance to the underground. Twenty metres before she disappeared into the station she was spotted by the first witness, Police Inspector Peter Sundman.

They passed each other ten metres apart. He said hello to Yasmine, but she didn't appear to have seen him. She was marching determinedly towards the doors of the underground station, disappeared through the swing doors and out of his sight. Back straight, nose in the air, her jacket tied round her waist, holding her little rucksack in her hand, her whole body radiating anger and urgency.

She's had another row with her mother, Sundman thought, and for a moment he considered running after her and at least having a word with her. But he just shook his head instead, smiled to himself and, only a few minutes later, when he walked in through the front door, her agitated mother had run straight into his arms.

During the months and years that followed he had thought a lot about all this. If only I'd tried to talk to her, he usually thought, and the only consolation to be had in this context was that he was at least a far better witness than the ones who usually cropped up in similar circumstances, and that he had done all he could to help his colleagues try to find the perpetrator.

The police – that's to say, Bo Jarnebring and his five colleagues from the crime unit in Stockholm – found another four witnesses who had seen Yasmine. None of them was a particularly poor witness. At least three of them were considerably better than witnesses usually were. That was scant comfort, though, given what went on to happen.

The second witness was the guard sitting in the ticket office in Solna Centrum underground station. Like Yasmine, he was originally from Iran. He had seen her on numerous previous occasions when he had been in that particular booth. He had noticed the way she looked and had once asked her if she was from Iran, even asking in Farsi, but Yasmine hadn't replied, just shook her head and carried on towards the platform.

Jarnebring obviously looked into him thoroughly, and he even checked out his colleague, Sundman. The guard's alibi was even better than Sundman's. He had been in his booth until the station closed for the night, and there were plenty of people who could confirm that. There was also all the electronic evidence he left the whole time he was simply doing his job.

Yasmine took the underground from Solna Centrum to Fridhemsplan, then changed lines and travelled out to Alvik. There she got on the Nockeby tram line, where she encountered witnesses three and four.

Witness number three was the driver of the tram between Alvik and Nockeby. Just as he was about to close the doors and set off, Yasmine came running up. The driver was an immigrant from Turkey; he had arrived in Sweden in the sixties and had been driving the tram for almost ten years. He recognized Yasmine because she had been travelling to and from school on his tram for the past couple of years. Also inside the tram was witness number four, a female pensioner, seventy-five, who lived in the same district as Yasmine and recognized her.

The driver of the tram spoke to Yasmine, saying she was lucky to have got there just in time. Yasmine thanked him for waiting. The pensioner said hello to her – 'Hello, my little friend. I hope you're well?' – and Yasmine had smiled, curtsied politely and replied, 'Thank you, I'm very well.' Neither of the two witnesses noticed anything to suggest otherwise.

Yasmine travelled just one stop, as she usually did. Half a kilometre, taking about a minute. There she said goodbye to the old lady and got off, and walked the last of the way home, a distance of less than five hundred metres.

Halfway there, she was seen by the fifth and last witness. He lived in a villa on Äppelviksgatan, just a few hundred metres from the house on Majblommestigen where Yasmine lived with her father and his new partner. The witness was on his way out to his wife and children in the country, because it was 'the weekend, at last'. He saw her as he pulled out of his drive, when she was heading towards her home and had some hundred metres left to walk. He, too, recognized her: his youngest son went to the same school as Yasmine.

He drove off in the other direction. He was stressed, and a couple of hours late. His wife had already called and shouted at him. From then on, he kept checking the time. When he saw Yasmine it was 'quarter to eight, give or take'. Another reason for him looking at the time was that she was walking on her own and there had been a couple of break-ins in the area during the summer. Considering what went on to happen, not a day had passed since without him 'cursing' himself for not driving after her and 'at least making sure she got home okay'.

So, Yasmine left her mother's flat just before seven o'clock. She vanished into the underground at Solna Centrum a few minutes later. In all likelihood, she caught the train that left for Fridhemsplan at ten minutes past seven. There she caught another one to Alvik, at twenty-five minutes to eight. She got off at Alvik six minutes later and jumped on to the tram heading to Nockeby, which left on time at fifteen minutes to eight. She got off at the next stop a minute or so later and continued on foot for a few minutes. She was seen about a hundred metres from her home by the last person to have seen her alive: at 'quarter to eight, give or take'.

19

Wednesday afternoon, 14 July 2010

'We were basically able to track her from start to finish,' Jarnebring concluded, with some satisfaction. 'Apart from the last stretch along the road where she lived. Majblommestigen, that's what it's called. A little side street off Äppelviksgatan. The lads and I were actually pretty pleased with ourselves.'

'Hang on, hang on,' Johansson said. 'That last witness. What sort of clown was he?'

'Interesting character,' Jarnebring said with a smile. 'Good to see you getting back to your old self, Lars. That your thinking skills haven't vanished, I mean.'

'The last witness,' Johansson repeated. 'I'm still listening.'

The last witness was forty-two years old. Married fifteen years. He and his wife, who was a teacher, had three children, aged seventeen, fifteen and ten. He worked as a claims adjuster for an insurance company. He and his wife had bought the house where the family lived ten years earlier. No bad debts, no criminal record, not even a speeding ticket.

'And?' Johansson glared suspiciously at his best friend.

'His main hobby was swimming,' Jarnebring said. 'When he was younger he was one of the best in Sweden, and after he stopped competing he carried on as a youth coach and official. He held a number of posts in the national association, as well as the club he belonged to. He did quite a lot of work with sponsorship.'

'Youth coach. So what's a youth coach?'

'Quite. That's where it starts to get interesting. In this particular instance, it means training the young girls in the club, seven to ten years old. The same age as Yasmine, more or less.'

'Who'd have thought it?' Johansson said. 'Now where have I heard something like this before?'

'That's what I thought, too,' Jarnebring said. 'Especially once I'd spoken to his wife, who said that she didn't know what time it was when he eventually showed up at their summer cottage outside Trosa, and the normal driving time was one hour. She'd fallen asleep at nine o'clock that evening. According to her, she had a terrible headache, took two tablets, went to bed and fell asleep. Their kids had already gone off to spend the night with various friends. She didn't wake up before morning, by which time her husband was there. Lying next to her in bed. But, if you ask me, I reckon she'd consumed rather more than just a couple of headache pills.'

'Such as?'

'If we're to believe the neighbours, she drank pretty heavily. I'm inclined to agree with them. I actually met her, interviewed her again when the question marks started to pile up. The warning signs of alcoholism were pretty strong with that little lady, if I can put it like that.'

'So her husband didn't have an alibi,' Johansson said.

'Actually, no. That's precisely what he did have. He had a quite remarkable stroke of good luck, actually.'

'Go on.'

'At twenty past eight he was caught speeding on the motorway some ten kilometres south of Södertälje. About half an hour after he left home in Äppelviken.'

'I thought you said he didn't have any points on his licence?'

'He didn't. The officers who caught him – I talked to them as well – let him off with a caution.'

'What the hell did they do that for?'

'One of them used to be a swimmer, apparently.' Jarnebring chuckled. 'It took a while before that came out.'

'He could have put the kid in the boot,' Johansson said. 'Yasmine, I mean. Not very likely, perhaps, but, according to his wife, he could have been out all night.'

'We're dealing with a very rare man here. He had the most incredible luck, all the way through. When he turned up out in the country half an hour later, his closest neighbour had driven into a ditch. His summer cottage is roughly one hundred kilometres south of Stockholm, so the distance matches the time it took pretty well.'

'Who'd have thought it?' Johansson said. 'Drove into a ditch. In the middle of nowhere on an ordinary Friday night.'

'I know. And despite the fact that he was stone-cold sober, according to him.' Jarnebring grinned. 'We talked to him as well. To cut a long story short, first our witness helps his neighbour get his car out of the ditch. Then he drives home to see his wife. She's already asleep, alone in the house. So he returns to the neighbour, who is no longer in the ditch, and ends up sitting there drinking half the night away with half a dozen like-minded souls, all of them neighbours, before staggering home and falling asleep. So I bought his alibi. What would you have done?'

'Bought his alibi,' Johansson said. 'So what happened after that, then? With the investigation, I mean?'

'We did all the usual. Poked about in Yasmine and her family's backgrounds. Checked everyone in her vicinity. Other family members, friends, acquaintances, neighbours, schoolmates, friends and their elder siblings. We went door to door in the neighbourhood, checked everyone who lived there, plus the guy who delivered the papers, the postman, workmen and anyone else who just happened to be in the area. We checked to see if any taxis had been in the vicinity at the time she disappeared. Went through the usual sex-obsessed nutters. Looked into any other crimes that might be connected to Yasmine's case. Asked for tip-offs from the public. My lads and I, and a couple of female colleagues, too, for that matter, did all the things we were supposed to do. Everything by the book. And we pretty much came up with nothing. We never found a crime scene but, considering the state her body and clothes were in, most of the evidence seemed to suggest that it must have happened indoors. There were far too few of us. We were far too slow getting going. No crime scene, and whenever that's the case everything usually goes to hell. And no perpetrator either.'

'She was wearing her clothes?'

'No,' Jarnebring said, shaking his head. 'The body was naked, completely naked. No clothes, no jewellery, nothing. He'd dumped them in the same stretch of reeds, a

97

couple of hundred metres away from the body. One of our dog-handlers found them the next day, on Saturday, 22 June, when they were searching the area where she was found. Her clothes, shoes, rucksack, watch, the rings she'd been wearing – two, if I remember rightly – were all stuffed into a couple more of those bin-bags that her body was wrapped in. According to Forensics, they came from the same roll, one of those ones with ten bags, the sort you can buy at any garage or supermarket. He'd just tied the bags containing the clothes – ordinary granny knots, in case you're wondering.'

'From the same roll,' Johansson said. 'How do you know that?'

'It was one of our colleagues in Forensics who figured that out. Clever bloke, really smart. Yasmine's body and her clothes were wrapped in a total of six bags. The first five, and then the last one on the roll. The four in between were missing. He must have used them for something else when he was cleaning up after himself. We don't know what, seeing as we never found them.'

'Bloody sheets and the usual,' Johansson said. 'What about Bäckström, then? What was he doing?'

'Same as always. When he wasn't keeping out of the way, he mostly just sat and went on about Yasmine's father. He wouldn't let it go.'

'I can't help wondering how a man like Bäckström ever got to be a police officer.' Johansson's mind was suddenly wandering.

'His dad was in the force.' Jarnebring grinned. 'He's supposed to have been even worse than his son. His uncle was an officer as well. And his cousin – used to ride a motorbike, a complete cretin, so an obvious choice to be secretary general of the union. So perhaps it's not so strange. The force is crawling with them. The best thing about Bäckström is that at least he's had the good sense not to have had a load of kids who've gone on to join the force.'

'So the investigation was crawling along,' Johansson said.

'Everything went wrong, right from the start. By the time we were brought in it was already too late. Like I said. We didn't find out anything of any real use. Nothing we could pull on or even give a tentative little tug. We kept going through the autumn, until one of our many bosses decided to put the case on the backburner. That happened just after New Year, by the way. And then, of course, our prime minister was murdered a couple of months later, and that was the end of it. Everyone in Crime and Surveillance was switched to the Palme case.'

'I know,' Johansson said with a nod. Better than most, and better than you, my friend, he thought.

'Who'd have thought it?' Jarnebring grinned.

'Even so, there must have been a few question marks?'

'As I remember it, that's more or less all we had. The question mark I remember best was a car that was supposed to have been seen near the house where Yasmine lived on the evening in question. A red Golf, latest model. Good condition, definitely didn't belong to low-lifes. You know, the usual tip-off about a car that shows up in practically every murder investigation,' he said with a wry smile.

'Tell me.'

'We never got to the bottom of that either,' Jarnebring said.

'Tell me,' Johansson repeated. 'Tell me, anyway.'

20

Wednesday afternoon, 14 July

According to an elderly witness living in the area, there was a red Volkswagen Golf parked on Majblommestigen, where Yasmine lived. Just a few houses further down the road, right next to the junction with Äppelviksgatan.

Like so many similar witnesses before him, he had been out to walk his dog on the evening Yasmine disappeared and had observed the car 'some time between nine and ten o'clock in the evening'.

Everything had followed the usual routine after that. First, they checked to make sure that it didn't belong to anyone who lived on the road, on adjoining roads or in the immediate vicinity. It didn't, which instantly rendered it more interesting. Everyone who lived in the area or had some connection to it and who owned a Golf was written off, even though there were several of them, including two that had cars the right colour.

The next step was to get a list of all red Golfs in the Stockholm area from the vehicle registration database, whether they were owned privately or by companies, leasing firms or rental businesses. Even though they restricted the search to the latest model, they still ended up with hundreds of them.

While this was going on, their witness, like so many similar witnesses before him, had begun to have doubts. First, he wasn't sure about the day, then the model, because 'of course he wasn't an expert', and, finally, even the colour.

By that time Jarnebring and his colleagues already had an overflowing box full of files from the vehicle register just waiting for one of them to find the time to go through the mass of documents. Because of the other demands on their time, however, they ended up doing what so often happens. They started to check registered owners living in the area between Solna and Bromma who might possibly have come across Yasmine somewhere between her mum's and her dad's, as well as those with a criminal record for previous offences, particularly crimes that bore some resemblance to what had happened to Yasmine.

They didn't find anything of interest – the little that had initially looked promising was soon dismissed, and at that point the search was stopped, or at least put on hold.

'I regret not chucking that bastard car into the Palme investigation six months later,' Jarnebring said. 'Then no stone would have been left unturned.'

You shouldn't be too sure of that, Johansson thought, seeing as he knew better, but he didn't say anything because at that same moment he was struck by a thought. An obvious thought in circumstances such as these.

'We need to get out into the field,' he said. 'I need to see the house where she lived, check her route, put my ear to the ground, you know.'

'Out into the field,' Jarnebring repeated. Now he's gone all weird again, he thought.

'Exactly.'

'In a health-service nightshirt and hospital slippers,' Jarnebring said, nodding at Johansson as he lay there on the bed.

'Ah, yes. That doesn't work. Okay, when you come back tomorrow it would be a good idea to bring me some clothes. Doesn't have to be anything special. Just a pair of comfortable trousers, underpants and a shirt. And a pair of shoes. I need shoes.'

'You think?' Jarnebring said, trying to sound more positive than he felt.

'Thank Christ,' Johansson said, 'nothing seems to have happened in this case over the past twenty-five years.'

'Well,' Jarnebring said, 'a couple of things did happen, actually. In the spring of 1989, when Helene Nilsson was murdered down in Skåne, the investigation was dug up again. To see if there were any plausible connections between Helene's murder and that of Yasmine. There was nothing to suggest a link, and as soon as they got hold of Yasmine's killer's DNA it became obvious that we were dealing with two different people. So it was shut down again.'

'And nothing's happened since then?'

'The usual routine follow-ups and comparisons with new cases that have come in over the years. Last winter, six months before the case got prescribed, the idea was that the Cold Case Unit in Regional Crime in Stockholm would make one last attempt, but then someone shot that prosecutor out in Huddinge in the head and they got lumbered with something else to do instead.'

'Cold cases,' Johansson snorted. 'No one should waste their time on that shit. Murders are perishable goods.'

'Sounds like a wise attitude,' Jarnebring said. 'Very wise,' he added, for some reason.

'So what are you two sitting here plotting?' said Pia Johansson, who was suddenly standing in the doorway to Johansson's room.

21

Wednesday evening, 14 July

Jarnebring gave Pia a hug, even though she was already standing by the bed and stroking her husband's cheek. Then he cleared his throat and stuffed his notes in his pocket.

'Well, time to think about getting going,' he said.

'Yes, definitely. Look after yourself, Bo, and see you tomorrow. And don't forget what you promised.'

'What's he promised this time?' asked Pia, looking inquisitively at Jarnebring.

'Neither sausage nor vodka,' Jarnebring replied. 'I just promised to look in, that's all. He's starting to get back to his usual self again, so I've got good reason to keep an eye on him.'

Then he nodded, patted his best friend on the shoulder and walked towards the door. There he stopped briefly and nodded once more.

'Bo isn't quite himself,' Johansson said once the door was closed. 'I think this has hit him hard,' he explained. Why am I saying that? he wondered. She could see for herself that Jarnebring wasn't himself.

Pia sat beside him on the bed. She leaned forward as she gently stroked his cheeks and forehead with her fingers.

'So how are you, then?' she asked.

'Fine,' Johansson nodded. 'I'm tired, and a bit low, to be honest, but I feel better than I have for a long time.'

'I had a word with the nurse. She says you're not eating very well. You've got to eat. You realize that, surely?' She looked at him sternly.

'I do eat,' Johansson said. 'Soured milk and fruit and vegetables and fibre and loads of stuff like that. I've eaten two bananas and an apple. Bo brought a whole bagful.'

'No sausages,' Pia said.

'No.' Johansson shook his head. 'I don't feel like eating that sort of thing any more.'

'So, what were you and Bo talking about, then? I heard he's been here all afternoon.'

'Old memories,' Johansson answered. 'Old memories that I've forgotten. From work, mainly. Nothing that concerns us,' he added. Why did I say that? he thought.

'Are you sure you don't want anything to eat?'

'No, I'm fine.'

'Do you want to get some sleep?'

'Only if you want to sleep next to me,' Johansson said. 'If you budge over a bit and promise not to snore.'

'I promise.'

Then he budged over a bit and lay on his side. She lay down beside him. He put his good arm round her and hugged her carefully. Then he fell asleep. And slept, just slept; no dreams that night, even though he should probably have dreamed about Yasmine.

22

Thursday morning, 15 July

Life was becoming more structured and organized with each passing day. First, he hobbled to the toilet, managing with just the rubber-pointed stick, even though he couldn't actually hold it in the right hand. Never mind the fact that he was followed by an anxious nursing assistant.

Then he took his medication and ate his new, nutritious breakfast. He must have dozed off again, because when he looked up Ulrika Stenholm was sitting beside his bed. Smiling at him, her head tilted. But what else was he expecting?

'You're improving by the day,' she said.

'Have you found her?' Johansson asked.

'Found her?'

'That informant,' Johansson said. 'You promised to look through your father's papers.'

'I know,' she said. 'No, I haven't found her. But I have started looking. He left a huge amount to go through. There must be twenty boxes and bags of his old papers. All sorts of things: newspaper cuttings, notes, outlines of sermons, old diaries, letters: so many letters and postcards.'

'Is it in chronological order?' Johansson asked.

'I hadn't thought of that,' she said. 'But now you mention it, I suppose he collected it as time went on, so to speak. But there's not much of a system. It's all mixed up. But yes, there's probably some sort of chronological order. I suppose that did cross my mind yesterday, actually, when I was reading a load of letters he'd saved. They all seemed to be from the same year, the ones that were dated, anyway.'

'When did you say he retired?'

'In 1989, in the summer. I have a feeling it was the start of the summer. Why do you ask?'

'Try to find the papers covering the last two years when he was working. From the summer of '89 to the summer of '87,' Johansson said. 'Start with '89 and work backwards.'

'What about 1985, then? Yasmine was murdered in the summer of 1985, after all. You don't think I should start there?'

'Do as I say,' Johansson said. And she's supposed to be intelligent, he thought.

'Okay, now I'm getting curious. Why do you want me to work backwards?'

'It usually takes a while for people to squeeze out something like this,' Johansson said. You're definitely not a police officer, he thought.

Then he met his physiotherapist and set two new personal records. First, pressing his little red ball in his right hand, and then bending his right arm. He managed to lift it almost halfway as she stood alongside, pushing him on.

'Your shoulder, Lars. I know you can do it. Come on, touch your shoulder.'

'Tomorrow,' Johansson said. Tomorrow is another day, he thought.

He was certainly feeling more cheerful. Even though he hadn't managed to touch his shoulder, he felt so much brighter that he even dared to try the beef-and-beetroot patty he was served for lunch. But not the sauce, and not the potato. There had to be some limits.

And he managed it in good time as well, because the nursing assistant had only just taken his tray away when Jarnebring showed up in his room with three big folders under his arm. But no trousers, and no shirt. Not even a pair of shoes.

23

Thursday afternoon, 15 July
Jarnebring sat down beside the bed and put the folders on the sheets.

'What the hell is all that?' Johansson said, nodding towards the folders. Where the hell are my trousers? he thought.

'You remember Kjell Hermansson, Herman? You must remember him?' Jarnebring looked at him. 'That younger colleague who worked in Violent Crime when you and I were at Surveillance?'

'Stop nagging,' Johansson said. 'Yes, I remember Herman.' But what the fuck has he got to do with my trousers? he thought.

'Good lad. A smart policeman. He's been at Regional Crime for the past few years. He's head of the group working on cold cases.'

'Oh.' Still no mention of the clothes he'd been promised.

'When I realized how interested you were, I thought I'd have a word with Herman,' Jarnebring said. 'It turns out that he's got all the files relating to the investigation into Yasmine's murder. It's prescribed now, as you now. Only missed the new legislation by a couple of weeks. So I had a chat with him – he says hello, by the way – and asked him to dig out the sort of thing you usually like to look at.'

'What sort of thing?'

'The initial report, crime-scene analysis, all the forensic details, post-mortem report, all the witness statements from the mother and father and the people who saw her, a summary of the door-to-door inquiries – all the usual, you know.'

'Yes, I know.'

'So here it is,' Jarnebring said, opening the first folder. 'And I've removed all the staples to make it easier for you to look through them. And I've added blank paper after every couple of pages in case you want to make any notes. Makes it easier, what with your arm and everything. The first sheet's the list of contents, then the initial report, followed by everything else, exactly the way you like it.'

'That's very kind of you, Bo,' Johansson said. 'Extremely considerate,' he added, and realized he was on the verge of bursting into tears again.

Fortunately, he managed to grab a paper tissue so he could blow his nose loudly a few times until the worst of it had settled down.

'Are you okay, Lars?' Jarnebring asked, looking at him with concern.

'Fine. It's the drugs,' he lied. 'They fill you up with snot.'

'Are you sure?'

'Yes,' Johansson said. 'Anyway, what the hell happened to my clothes? Didn't you promise to bring them so you could take me out to get a look at the place where she lived? Get a feel for the route between her mum and

110

her dad? And I'd like to take a look at the site where she was found, too. Out at Skokloster.'

'I spoke to Pia,' Jarnebring answered. 'And the nurse here on your ward. Neither of them thought it was a good idea.'

'For fuck's sake, Bo. What's that got to do with anything? I'm an adult, aren't I? I haven't been sectioned. So it's high time you and Pia and everyone else started treating me like a full citizen.'

'Well, for the time being I'm going to treat you as an ordinary patient,' Jarnebring said. 'As long as you stop making a fuss, of course, because if not I'll treat you like an ordinary, awkward mental patient, and you wouldn't have been able to handle that even when your right arm was working properly.'

Johansson said nothing. He didn't really feel anything either. He certainly wasn't about to start crying.

'Where do you want to start?' Jarnebring asked.

'Tell me how she died.'

'You've got everything in the files,' Jarnebring said, holding up a different one. 'If you want to read it for yourself, I mean. That's all in this one. The post-mortem report, forensic examination, the results from the National Forensics Lab, analysis of the scene and her clothes – the whole lot.'

Johansson shook his head. He didn't feel like going through a load of paperwork. Anyway, as soon as he tried to read his headache began to come back.

'It's better if you tell me,' Johansson said. 'Start by telling me how she died. Who was it who did the original post mortem, by the way?'

'Sjöberg. The professor. The old legend, Sjöberg. He could do two post mortems at the same time while

111

simultaneously giving a lecture to people like you and me while he was dissecting them.'

'I thought he'd already retired by then?'

'He had,' Jarnebring said. 'But the forensic medical unit was in a state of total chaos that summer. You remember that pathologist, the one who was suspected of killing that prostitute? That was the previous summer—'

'Yes, I remember him,' Johansson interrupted. He was hardly any crazier than anyone else there, he thought.

'He was suspended from duty. A couple of his colleagues had already resigned, and Sjöberg's successor, that idiot from Yugoslavia, the one who was so short-sighted he used to say hello to the yucca plant down in reception when he arrived at work each morning—'

'I remember him,' Johansson said. 'What's he got to do with this?'

'Nothing.' Jarnebring shook his head to emphasize his words. 'He'd gone off abroad to do some research. That wasn't the biggest problem, though, if you ask me. Anyway. There was hardly anyone left there. So Sjöberg went back to make sure that there was at least some semblance of organization at his former workplace. And he was particularly diligent when it came to tracking down people who had raped and murdered young girls, as you doubtless remember.'

'Sjöberg,' Johansson said. 'Utterly relentless. When he got things right, you didn't need police, prosecutors or judges.' Couldn't be better, he thought. 'I'm listening,' he went on, and leaned back on his bed.

24

Wednesday, 26 June 1985

The post mortem on Yasmine Ermegan's body was conducted on Saturday 22 and Sunday 23 June 1985. The report was compiled and signed three days later, on Wednesday 26 June, by Dr Ragnar Sjöberg, professor emeritus and MD. His signature is perfectly legible, the handwriting neat, harmoniously rounded, gently backward-sloping. A fully rounded personality.

Jarnebring and his colleagues had received a preliminary report before that, on the evening of Saturday, 22 June. A few days later, the same day he sent the full report over by courier, Sjöberg rang Jarnebring and asked him and his colleagues from Surveillance to come over for a 'confidential and open discussion'. On the condition that they didn't bring Evert Bäckström with them.

'I can't even bear to look at that little idiot,' Sjöberg had explained. 'The only consolation when I do see him is that I'm convinced he's going to end his days in my old workplace, and probably in such a state that even I couldn't make any sense of it.'

With this pious hope fresh in his mind, Jarnebring and his colleagues enjoyed a long and very rewarding conversation with the old legend.

Yasmine Ermegan had weighed 'approximately 33 kilos' and had been 'approximately 133 centimetres tall' when she died. The reason why Sjöberg couldn't be more precise was that she had been dead for almost a week and her body had spent most of that time wrapped in black plastic and pressed into the mud in a patch of reeds a couple of kilometres north-west of Skokloster Castle in Uppland.

Yasmine had been smothered, probably with a pillow, seeing as Sjöberg had found a piece of down in her throat and a couple of threads of white fabric between her teeth.

'She bit into the pillow while he was smothering her, which explains the down and fabric,' Sjöberg said. 'I want to stress that,' he emphasized. 'The down didn't get there when she was lying among the reeds. That dog may have torn the plastic she was wrapped in, but that was at the bottom of her body. Besides, it was so far down her throat it could only have got there while she was still breathing.'

Before she was smothered, Yasmine had been raped, penetrated vaginally. The injuries to her genitals were those that always happened when a grown man assaulted a young girl in that way. Sexual secretions from the perpetrator had been gathered from her vagina but no actual sperm. There was, however, plenty of that on her stomach, chest and in her hair. And on her pink T-shirt.

'He pulled out before orgasm and ejaculated across her stomach, chest and head,' Sjöberg explained to Jarnebring and his colleagues.

Yasmine's body showed no traces of the expected defensive injuries, and Sjöberg and his colleagues at the National Forensics Laboratory had found the explanation for this in her blood and several of her internal organs in the form of a powerful and fast-acting sedative. More than three times the recommended dose, given her age and weight.

'The only consolation in this tragic story is that she must have been unconscious when he assaulted her,' Sjöberg concluded.

'But she bit the pillow when he smothered her?' Jarnebring queried. Best to ask, just to make sure, he thought.

'That sort of thing can happen out of reflex when you're being asphyxiated,' Sjöberg said. 'Unless, very regrettably, she was on the point of regaining consciousness. Because he had been busy with her for some time, or because she began to be aware of the pain in her crotch. Or both,' he said with a sigh.

'Apart from that, the little lass was in good health,' Sjöberg continued. 'No healed fractures, no sign of past inflammations. She seems to have been in perfect health.'

'Do you have any idea how it might have happened?' Jarnebring asked.

'Why do you think I asked you to come here?' Sjöberg said with a slight smile. 'I thought I'd let you have all the things you lot are always begging for and which every sensible practitioner of my profession never commits to paper.'

'In which case, we're extremely grateful,' Jarnebring said.

'Yes, well.' Sjöberg shrugged his shoulders. 'Anyway, I'm retired now, and who's got the stamina to argue with a pensioner? This is what I think happened . . .'

First the perpetrator tricked her into taking the sedative, which, seeing as it was fairly bitter, had probably been diluted in a very sweet, strong-tasting drink.

'According to the contents of her stomach, it could have been Coca-Cola,' Sjöberg said. 'Or juice – something like that. Something that would have hidden the taste of the drug, basically.'

Then she passed out, within ten minutes, at most. The perpetrator put her on a bed and undressed her, removing all her clothes, her wristwatch and rings.

'They usually do it in that order,' Sjöberg said. 'The pillow suggests a bed, and they usually take care to undress their victims completely. They usually stand and look at them before they get to work, exposing them, twisting and turning them a bit, looking at them from different angles. Small and defenceless, entirely exposed, at their mercy. They usually take their time with that.'

Then he raped her, subjecting her to full vaginal 'intercourse' and pulling out before orgasm. He ejaculated across her stomach, chest and head. Then he wiped his genitals with her pink T-shirt.

'At a guess, I'd say the perpetrator is fairly young,' Sjöberg said. 'A lot of semen, shot quite some distance. Not the sort of thing your average ugly old man can accomplish.'

'Did he assault her more than once?' asked one of Jarnebring's colleagues.

116

'I don't think so,' Sjöberg said. 'She bled heavily after the first assault. A lot of them have trouble with that. With real sadists, it's the opposite, of course, but I get the impression here that we're dealing with a more sensitive type of paedophile. Respectful, as one of them once described himself to me when I was conducting a physical examination of him.'

Finally, he smothered Yasmine with a pillow when he realized that there was no alternative but to kill her if he was to get away with what he had done.

'For the rape alone he'd serve at least seven or eight years,' Sjöberg continued. 'Better to take his chances. Then there are all the other things that they usually take into account. The social consequences, if I can put it like that. He doesn't seem to have been a madman. He didn't strangle her, didn't cut her throat, didn't smash her head in, even though any of those would have been much simpler. Not the slightest sign of sadistic violence either. He chose the most humane alternative and suffocated her with a pillow. And then, of course, he didn't have to look at her while he was doing it. Like I said, a sensitive paedophile, socially accepted by those around him, people who presumably don't have the slightest suspicion of his sexual proclivities. Someone who believes he doesn't have a choice. That what happened isn't really his fault. That it just turned out that way.'

'A cowardly little fucker, then,' Jarnebring said. I'll kill the bastard, he thought. A thought that was so strong that it had already taken root in his fists.

'Couldn't agree more,' Sjöberg said. 'If you happen to break his arms and legs when you arrest him, I promise to do everything in my power to show that the wounds were self-inflicted.'

What about the timing? What could he say about that? First the assault, and then the murder?

According to Sjöberg, everything he had described had occurred soon after she disappeared. She probably died that same evening, Friday, 14 June. Among other things, the contents of her stomach were a strong indication of that.

And the dumping of her body?

There was a good deal of uncertainty on that point. If Sjöberg were to hazard a guess, he would say that Yasmine's body was dumped the following night. Some time around midnight, perhaps, when it was dark enough not to be seen, light enough for him to see what he was doing and not trip over and fall. Seeing as he was so sensitive.

25

Thursday afternoon, 15 July 2010

'Sjöberg was a real rock,' Jarnebring declared. 'But he never got to stick his knife into our esteemed colleague Bäckström. The old boy died ten years or so back. He was over ninety, so I daresay he was still hoping. Tried to cling on but couldn't quite manage it.'

'The problem with men like Bäckström is that they never die,' Johansson said. 'But never mind him now. Tell me about Yasmine instead. Was she one of those happy, sociable, trusting little girls who might have gone off with someone she didn't know?'

'Not according to the parents. Both her mother and father had spoken to her about that on numerous occasions, about never going with anyone she didn't know. Avoiding any close contact with strangers, men and women alike. Even other children and teenagers if she didn't know who they were and whether they could be trusted. She's supposed to have been a sensible girl, mature for her age, well brought up, and she knew her own mind. A pretty little thing, too. I put some pictures of her in the file for you to take a look at. Dark, with big, brown eyes and long, black hair. Good at school, too. Popular with her friends, the sort plenty of boys that age would fancy. Very particular about how she dressed. A bit coquettish, as they say.'

'All according to her parents, of course.'

'I know what you mean. But also according to her teachers and everyone else we spoke to who knew her.'

'Under normal circumstances, that may well have been true,' Johansson said. 'But this was no ordinary evening. First, she runs away from her mum. When she gets home to her dad's, the house is locked up and he's gone, without telling her. And she's forgotten her keys, too. And she hasn't got a phone. I mean, there were no mobiles in those days. I think that opens up the possibility that she might have done plenty of things she wouldn't normally have done.'

'I agree with you,' Jarnebring said. 'Which didn't exactly make things any easier.'

'How did they end up here, anyway? The whole family, I mean,' Johansson said, even though his thoughts were focused on a time and a life that only arose much later. Maybe she just wanted to borrow a phone so she could call her mum, he thought. Knocked on the door of some trustworthy and helpful paedophile of the more sensitive variety. Who just wanted to look at her while she slept naked on his bed as he took care of himself. Until a rush of lust, which obviously wasn't his fault either, grabbed hold of him and left him with no choice.

'That political stuff isn't my strong point, but I could always—'

'Sorry, what did you just say? Something about politics?' Pull yourself together, he thought.

'Yasmine and her parents arrived as political refugees from Iran,' Jarnebring said. 'That was in the winter of 1979, when Yasmine had just turned three.'

120

'I see.'

'That political stuff' may not have been Jarnebring's strong point, but he had talked to Yasmine's parents and listened to what they had to say on the subject. He had compared what they had said with what was written in the files held by the immigration office on when they came to Sweden and – immediately upon arrival at Arlanda Airport on 20 January 1979 – they had applied for political asylum. Just for once, all parties concerned had been touchingly unanimous. The risk of them being subjected to 'political persecution' in the Ayatollah's Iran was deemed to be 'highly considerable and pervasive'. They themselves, along with their families, were members of the Christian minority, belonged to the old upper class and had supported the Shah. The father, or 'Jusef', as his name was spelled in his Iranian passport, his wife, Maryam, and their three-year-old daughter, Yasmine, had quickly been granted residence permits.

Both parents were highly educated, the father a doctor who had graduated from medical school in Tehran, the mother with a medical-technical degree from the same university. They also had an existing connection to what would become their new homeland. 'Josef' Ermegan – he changed the spelling of his name as soon as he was granted permanent residency – already had a number of relatives living in Sweden, among them an uncle who was a successful doctor and worked as a professor of medical chemistry at the Karolinska Institute.

'I have a feeling the father was given authorization to work as a doctor in Sweden after just a year or so,' Jarnebring said. 'He needed to do a couple of supplementary courses. Yasmine's mother trained to be a dental nurse and had also finished within a year or two of their arrival. The entire family became Swedish citizens in February 1985. Just a few months before their daughter was murdered. That was when they applied formally for a divorce. They had already separated a year or so earlier, but they kept that quiet. Presumably, didn't want to jeopardize their application for citizenship.'

Whatever their divorce had to do with that matter, Johansson thought, but instead of saying anything he contented himself with a nod.

'You remember those charges the mother filed against the father, about him assaulting her? I mentioned them yesterday.'

'Yes,' Johansson said.

'Those weren't filed either until they'd been granted citizenship.'

'Well, that was fairly practical. For the father, I mean. Why complicate things unnecessarily? He probably promised her the kid and a bit of extra maintenance if she kept her mouth shut.'

Off he goes again, Jarnebring thought. There's something not right.

'What happened afterwards, then?' Johansson asked. 'To the parents, I mean. Are they still alive?'

'I haven't heard anything to the contrary,' Jarnebring answered. 'But they've both left Sweden. The father moved to the USA in 1990. Alone – he didn't stay for long with the woman he was living with when his daughter was murdered. He's supposed to have done well for himself over there. As rich as Uncle Scrooge. Owns some big pharmaceutical company. He's been an American citizen for years. He changed his name again when he moved, to Joseph Simon, Joseph with a "ph", and Simon after his father. You know, like that singer in Simon and Garfunkel.'

'What about the mother?' Johansson asked.

'She lost it, apparently,' Jarnebring said. 'Moved back to Iran some time in the 1990s. Became a Mohammedan. With a veil and the whole shebang.'

'Converted to Islam, you mean.'

'Yes. Started going round in a burka, or whatever it's called.'

'Sounds practical.'

'No doubt,' Jarnebring agreed. 'If you're a woman living over there, it's probably essential.'

One who survived, Johansson thought. Who hardened himself, brought out the worst in himself and survived with the help of his hatred. And one who went under and was forced to give up the life she had lived before.

'I'm starting to feel a bit tired,' he said. 'Would you mind if I called time out and had a little nap?'

'Not in the slightest.'

'See you again tomorrow?'

'Oh, yes,' Jarnebring said. 'You can count on it: same time, same place.'

Then something strange happened. When Jarnebring leaned over the bed to give him a manly and comradely pat on the shoulder, Johansson held out his right hand. Without even thinking about it. He raised it from the covers where it had been lying the whole time and held it out.

Jarnebring took it. In a firm grip, but as gently as he would a child's hand.

'Squeeze, then, Lars,' Jarnebring said. 'Let me see some of the old energy I know you've still got in there.'

'It's coming,' Johansson said. It's coming, he thought. 'Listen, Jarnis,' he added when his best friend was on his way out through the door of his room. 'Don't forget my trousers.'

Then he fell asleep. On his back, with his hands folded over his stomach, the way he always did before he got that crap in his head which was actually just a bonus he got because of his dodgy heart.

When Pia came to see him that evening he was fast asleep.

She sat down on the chair beside his bed, and stayed there for a good couple of hours, just looking at him. He wasn't snoring, for once. He just lay there on his good left side, quietly, motionless.

She stroked his face and right arm softly. No movement, not the slightest change in his face. She felt a deep anxiety that she couldn't explain.

He's asleep, she thought. He's asleep, that's all, she repeated to herself. Just as long as nothing else happens.

Then she went home.

26

Friday, 16 July

Another day in Lars Martin Johansson's new life. A day he started by setting two new personal records. First, he more than doubled the amount of time he could squeeze the red rubber ball in his right hand. Then, and without the slightest hesitation, he raised his sleeping right arm and touched his right shoulder with his hand. His arm was also itching and aching the whole time, in the most encouraging way.

'I'm proud of you, Lars,' his physiotherapist said. 'You're making great strides.'

'Oh, I don't know,' Johansson said; deep down, he was a shy, modest person. 'Maybe not great strides, but at least it's going in the right direction.'

Things weren't quite so good with his doctor, Ulrika Stenholm. She looked tired, which is exactly what she was. She had been on call for the past couple of nights, and the most she had managed was four consecutive hours' sleep.

She hadn't had time to do much about her father's papers. But she had done a little, trying to pick out the bags and boxes containing documents from 1989, 1988 and 1987, as Johansson had instructed her. She had put them in a separate pile and was thinking of getting to grips with them seriously over the weekend.

'It's not the end of the world,' Johansson said. 'Those papers are hardly going to run away from us,' he added.

'Thanks,' Dr Stenholm said. 'It's nice to have someone show me a bit of patience.'

And you're not a lawyer either, are you? Johansson thought. Even though I've already explained the situation to you.

Then he ate lunch, the food pretty much the same as usual. He reinforced it with a banana and half a bag of morello cherries, as well as a chocolate biscuit which he ate in secret. Just as he was wiping the last crumbs from his lips, Jarnebring appeared. They had coffee in his room, a whole pot with a jug of warm milk alongside it, and then spent half the afternoon discussing their case.

'What do you think about this, then, Lars?' Jarnebring said. 'Yasmine's murder, I mean.'

'You start,' Johansson said. 'I'll listen. You were there, after all.'

'It all went wrong from the beginning,' Jarnebring started. 'When I think back to how it went wrong, I usually console myself by thinking that it might have been one of those cases that would have gone wrong anyway. I can tell you, this case has been eating me up from the inside.'

'How do you mean, "would have gone wrong anyway"?'

'Because it was too difficult,' Jarnebring said. 'When the girl was heading back to her mother's – because that was probably where she was going – she ran into one of those lunatics who get turned on by children. Someone she'd never met before, a complete stranger, and a totally coincidental encounter, but because she wasn't herself he managed to trick her into going with him. The sort of case we never manage to solve because it's simply too difficult,' he repeated.

'For God's sake, Bo,' Johansson said, and sighed. 'Now I'm starting to get seriously worried about you.'

I recognize you now, Jarnebring thought.

'So tell me what happened, then. I've always been a simple constable. I've never been able to see round corners. Tell me what happened.'

'I don't know,' Johansson said. Not yet, he thought. 'But there's one thing I do know,' he said.

'What's that?'

'That in nineteen out of twenty cases when we're dealing with crimes like this, the perpetrator is someone in the victim's immediate vicinity. Either in their social circle, or the perpetrator belongs to the same family, group of friends, all the usual, you know – or he's in the victim's vicinity geographically. They're neighbours, he lives in the same area, he sees the victim every day when she walks to and from school, because maybe he works in the cornershop across the street. Or he's in both – social *and* geographic proximity.'

'Hang on now, Lars,' Jarnebring said, putting his hand up to stop him, just in case. 'Take someone like that Anders Eklund, who killed little Engla, Engla Höglund, that young girl who lived up in Dalarna. Pure coincidence. He'd probably never seen her before in his life.'

'The twentieth case,' Johansson said. 'But you don't have to worry about him this time. Not when it comes to Yasmine.'

'How do you mean?'

'Eklund wasn't carrying sleeping pills or a pillow with a white pillowcase around with him,' Johansson said. 'He was a primitive simpleton, and the way he carried out his crime was perfectly logical, given the way things worked inside his tiny mind. It took the local cops less than twelve hours to find him. So you can definitely forget about men like him when it comes to Yasmine.'

'Ulf Olsson, then? The one who killed Helene Nilsson.'

'Classic nineteen of twenty,' Johansson said. 'Lived in the same place as her, had lived there all his life. His family knew her family; and his younger sister was best friends with Helene's older sister, wasn't she? The fact that it took sixteen years to find the bastard wasn't down to him. He can thank our colleagues down in Skåne for those years, for screwing up a perfectly simple case beyond all recognition. I'd have caught him within a month.'

I believe you, Jarnebring thought. Who knows, maybe even I could have managed that?

'The "girl killer", then, John Ingvar Löfgren? You know, the one in Stockholm back in the mid-sixties.'

'It was 1963,' Johansson said. 'Two little girls; I seem to recall the first victim was six years old, the other even younger – four, if I'm not mistaken. The dates of their murders were 12 August, out in Aspudden, and 2 September, in Vitabergs Park on Södermalm.'

Now I definitely recognize you, Jarnebring thought. 'But they were hardly victims he socialized with,' he said. No point giving in too easily, he thought.

'He tried,' Johansson said. 'Löfgren was thirty-two. He had the intellect of an eight-year-old and a grown man's body and desires. He spent his days drifting around parks looking for girls of the same mental age as him to play with. He forced himself upon them, or attempted to, then killed them and ran off. Compared with him, even Anders Eklund looks almost normally intelligent. Forget men like Eklund and Löfgren. Where Yasmine's concerned, you can even forget Ulf Olsson, although he was considerably more than normally intelligent, if we're talking about his IQ here.'

'I can forget him, too? Why?'

'Far too peculiar. A loner, a conspiracy theorist, always in conflict with pretty much everyone he runs into. Previous convictions for stupid crimes. Forget men like Olsson.'

'What's our bloke like, then?'

'Pleasant, helpful, sociable, good company, likes spending time with men and women his own age. None of them has any idea that all he really wants to do is have sex with little girls. The only thing you might be able to criticize him for is drinking a bit too much,' Johansson said with a smile. 'But he never gets annoying or out of hand.'

'You couldn't give me a name, could you?' Jarnebring said with a grin. Lars Martin is back in the saddle again, he thought.

'Give me a week or so. You mustn't forget that I've got a lot of crap going on inside my head. I've forgotten loads of things. I keep thinking of things I've forgotten. The worst part is that I can't remember what they are. Just that they're things I've forgotten.'

'Yes,' Jarnebring agreed. 'You've seemed perfectly normal recently. You've even shown a few human characteristics, actually.'

'There are three things I haven't forgotten,' Johansson said, not seeming to take any notice of what Jarnebring had said. 'When I forget *them*, I'm finished.'

'What are they, then?' Jarnebring asked.

'Make the best of what you've got, don't complicate things unnecessarily, and hate coincidence.'

'Lars Martin Johansson's three golden rules for investigating a murder. A week, you said. Then you'll give me a name?'

'Not that I can see why you want it,' Johansson said. 'You can't do anything about the case, not now.' None of us can, he thought.

'To satisfy my curiosity,' Jarnebring said. 'I might go round and see the bastard and have a serious talk with him. Man to man. And rip his arms and legs off.'

'Sounds like an excellent idea,' Johansson said. 'But you'll still have to give me a week or so. I'm not quite myself yet.'

27

Friday afternoon, 16 July

Johansson spent the rest of the afternoon looking through the files Jarnebring had given him. He sat for a long time with a photograph of Yasmine in his hand. It was an unremarkable portrait, probably a school photograph, half profile, with her smiling and flashing her eyes at the photographer. A child, he thought. A happy child, and just as pretty as Jarnebring had said. Then his chest started to hurt. He put the photograph back in the folder, and the pain eased.

He made do with merely leafing through the post-mortem report. What it said seemed to match what his best friend had already told him. Instead, he scrutinized the analysis of the place where she was found, as well as the other forensics reports. He carefully inspected all the photographs taken by the forensics team. He even wished he had the little loupe he had fixed to his key ring. They must have a magnifying glass in a place like this, Johansson thought, and rang for a nurse.

'How can I help?' A young woman in her thirties. Nice-looking, happy and positive. Someone like her was bound to have a magnifying glass.

'You wouldn't have a magnifying glass that I could borrow, would you?' Johansson asked.

'Of course,' she said. 'You can borrow the one we keep in the office.'

After he had raped and murdered Yasmine, her sensitive murderer had taken his time and gone to a lot of trouble wrapping her up in a neat parcel.

He pulled two bin-bags over her head, across her torso and down to her thighs. Then he pulled two more bags over her feet, legs and waist, the edge of the bags at roughly the level of her nipples. He did it in that order, because the bags at the bottom overlapped the ones at the top.

Then he sealed the parcel with tape. Ordinary brown packing tape, five centimetres wide. Pulled tight. First round her ankles, with her feet and legs pushed close together. Then her knees, and her thighs, just below her buttocks. Then round her waist and chest, with her arms by her sides. At each point he wound the tape round her body five or six times, even though once would probably have been enough. The result was a package that, in terms of its content and appearance, was strikingly like a mummy wrapped in bandages. Apart from the black plastic and tape, of course.

Despair, Johansson thought. Not just despair at what you'd done and the situation you found yourself in. This despair is older than that, he thought. You've learned to control it. Controlling your despair has become an essential part of your character.

He hadn't left any fingerprints while he was doing it. But there were marks made by fingers wearing rubber gloves. Fragments of pale pink rubber had been found on the underside of the tape.

Washing-up gloves, Johansson thought. Ordinary washing-up gloves. Probably well used, too, seeing as they had started to fray and leave traces behind. If you're in your own home, then these aren't your gloves, he thought. Because you'd have had a different colour. Besides, I don't think you're the sort who does the washing-up, still less wears gloves if you do. Women use washing-up gloves, so there's a woman somewhere in your life. Your partner? Or perhaps your mother or your sister? Or simply some other woman you know well enough to be able to spend time in her home without feeling any need to rush?

I wonder if you're still alive? Johansson thought. Or if your despair has killed you?

I think you're alive, he thought. Making the best of things. You're far too fond of yourself and, anyway, you don't feel any guilt. No despair that you can't control, at least. Besides, there are plenty more like Yasmine. You see them all the time. They occupy your consciousness practically the whole time.

Then Johansson put the files down to eat his dinner. He drank two glasses of water, ate about half his portion of wholemeal pasta and pesto, mostly out of duty, and so as not to worry the people responsible for his health and imminent recovery.

After that he fell asleep, and he woke to find Pia sitting in the chair by the side of his bed, running her forefinger across his cheeks and down his chin.

'How are you feeling?' she asked. 'You look a lot brighter. When I was here yesterday you were asleep the whole time. Sleeping like a baby; you weren't even snoring, not at all. I almost got worried.'

'I feel like a pig in shit,' Johansson said. 'So don't you go worrying about me now. Tell me what you've been up to instead.'

28

Saturday, 17 July, to Sunday, 18 July

The weekend, with all its visits. Just like the previous weekend, except that he had fended off the children. Just to make sure, he had even gone so far as to speak to both his son and his daughter on the phone.

'I'll soon be home,' Johansson said. 'It would be a lot nicer for everyone to come and see me and Pia at home and have a proper dinner. Spend time together like normal people.'

'Sounds like an excellent idea,' his son said.

'We'll do as you say,' his daughter said. 'Daddy's little girl always does what Daddy says,' she added, for some reason.

There was no getting away from his eldest brother, Evert, though. He came marching in before lunch. Big and heavy, unbowed, his back ramrod-straight, even though he was ten years older than Lars Martin, the youngest son of the Johansson family.

Cheerful and pleased with himself, as always, and 'what phenomenal luck' that they had been able to conclude the forestry deal before Lars Martin 'had his brainstorm'.

'We really were damn lucky,' Evert Johansson declared, grinning with his big, yellow, horse-trader's teeth. 'The price of timber and woodpulp is going through the roof. I've already got a load of people after me, wanting to do a deal on the patch we got hold of.'

'What have you been telling them, then?' Johansson asked. He was only half listening and could already feel his headache starting to rumble.

'Far too early to sell, far too early. So I've been telling them to go to hell,' Evert said, and chuckled happily.

'They don't get upset?' Johansson wondered.

'If they do, it's their problem, not yours and mine,' Evert grunted. 'To change the subject, I've found an industrial property outside Örebro, an old workshop and warehouse. Looks very promising. Very promising. What do you think?'

'Go on,' Johansson said, having made up his mind to stop listening altogether.

Then Jarnebring arrived, in the middle of one of his brother's long spiels, and he and Evert needed no more than a quick exchange of glances to understand that any attempt at a cock-measuring contest would be a waste of time. How often did you ever encounter an equal?

'Bo Jarnebring,' Evert Johansson said. 'Shake my hand, Bo. Thanks for taking care of my little brother. That used to be my job, but since he moved to Stockholm fifty years ago that's happened less and less, if I can put it like that.'

Then they shook hands on the matter, with hands of a size that hardly any other men went around with. They squeezed harder than usual, and resolved the issue by more or less simultaneously giving the other a fraternal slap on the right shoulder.

'If there's anything I can do for you, Bo,' Evert said, 'don't hesitate to get in touch. Let me give you my mobile number. And you can give me yours.'

After that, they mostly talked to each other. Not about crimes, not about forestry and property, but about cars, which was a common point of interest. Evert Johansson, who, along with all the forest, land and properties he owned, also happened to own a couple of large car-dealerships in Västernorrland. Bo Jarnebring, who had no money but was a devoted motorist, and naturally preferred the sort of cars he couldn't really afford.

'In that case, I've got just the right car for you, Bo,' Evert said. 'I'll get one of my salesmen to give you a call on Monday and we can do business. You'll never be offered a price like this again in your life, I can promise you that.'

Watch yourself, Jarnis, Johansson thought, but didn't say anything.

Then Pia showed up. She flashed a radiant smile at both Evert Johansson and Bo Jarnebring, gave them each a big hug and then told them both to go to hell.

Not that she put it quite like that, but that was what she meant, thought her husband, Lars Martin Johansson.

'It's a shame you have to leave,' Pia said. 'I suggest you go and sit down somewhere nice and have a proper boys' lunch, do a bit of arm-wrestling and take good care of each other. You, Evert, can pay for it, and I'll have a nice quiet chat with my husband in the meantime.'

'I know of a really good bar up on Regeringsgatan,' Jarnebring said, before they were even out of the door. 'Decent, traditional Swedish food, not too busy, reasonable prices. It's actually run by a couple of Yugoslavians,' he explained. 'Got to know them when I was at Surveillance here in Stockholm. But they've calmed down a lot now, and they're seriously good at cooking decent grub.'

'What are we waiting for?' Evert said. 'Good blokes need good food.'

'You're missing them already, I can tell,' Pia said as soon as the door closed.

'Not remotely,' Johansson said, and reached out both arms to her, to hold her the way he had always held her before he became someone different from the man he had been.

29

Monday, 19 July

A human being, no doubt, but primarily a patient, and therefore subject to fixed routines decided by people other than himself. First, he met the physiotherapist. The old record in squeezing the rubber ball still stood. His right arm was the same as before. No better, no worse. Maybe it tingled a little more. It itched, too. Prickling, pins and needles, even a bit of stinging now.

'You've reached a plateau,' his well-trained female tormentor explained. 'That's perfectly normal, nothing for you to worry about. Your recovery will happen in stages. Your arm will be exactly the same as before. But it will take time.'

Why don't I believe you? he thought. All of a sudden, he felt tired and depressed.

'Why don't I believe you?' he said.

'You mustn't think like that,' she said. 'That will only make it take longer. This will be sorted out, your arm will be exactly the same as before. That's what you've got to think.'

The medical version of 'make the best of things', he thought.

'In the police, we usually say that you have to make the best of things,' he said.

'Exactly,' she said. 'Exactly.'

Not so easy when it's you, though, he thought.

When he returned to his room, Jarnebring called. He was going to have to postpone their meeting. His daughter had a water leak in her kitchen and her clever old dad had to do a bit of plumbing.

'You can never get hold of a decent bloody plumber,' Jarnebring said, for some reason. 'But I'll see you as soon as I've finished.'

'You're a marvel when it comes to that sort of thing,' Johansson said. 'So it's hardly the end of the world. Anyway, I've got loads I need to be getting on with, so my suggestion is that we meet up tomorrow instead. If that's okay with you, of course.'

'Course it's okay,' Jarnebring said. 'What do you take me for? Take care of yourself now.'

Then his doctor, Ulrika Stenholm, showed up. She was feeling guilty about not managing to get through her dad's paperwork over the weekend, as she had promised. All manner of things had got in the way.

'I should have had children earlier. At my age and with my job, you really shouldn't have a five-year-old and a three-year-old.'

'It's not the end of the world,' Johansson said.

'It's not good, though, is it?' Ulrika Stenholm said. 'Tonight, I promise, I'm going to do something about it. I can drop the kids off with their father. Anyway, I've got some good news,' she added.

I'm going to get a new arm, Johansson thought. One of those ones with a hook on the end. But, naturally, he didn't say that.

Johansson was going to be allowed home. He would be leaving the hospital. Transferred to out-patient care and regular check-ups. Not tomorrow, though, but on Wednesday, because Dr Stenholm wanted to take a look at the results of the latest batch of tests before letting him go. And always assuming that nothing untoward happened in the meantime, of course.

'Which it won't,' Dr Stenholm said, smiling in a way that was both cheerful and professional. 'I think you've done really well. I've booked you in for a check-up with me in a week's time – next Monday. As for the rest, I thought I'd talk to Pia about that.'

Pia, Johansson thought. You're Pia and Ulrika to each other now. To him, she was still Dr Stenholm, Ulrika Stenholm, or 'my doctor', he thought.

'You're the doctor, so you know best. I want to go home,' he suddenly said.

'I can understand that very well.' Ulrika Stenholm smiled and nodded, and tilted her head.

After lunch, yet another meal that tasted like all the others, regardless of what was served, he made yet another attempt to pull himself together.

'Is it possible to get a cup of coffee in this place?' Johansson grunted at the nursing assistant who came to remove his tray.

'Would you like a magnifying glass on the side?' She smiled cheerily at him.

'Just coffee,' Johansson said. 'Black.'

Black, to help clear your head, he thought, and reached for one of the files. Pull yourself together. Make the best of things. This isn't all about you, after all.

Among all the papers in his folders he had found an expert's statement from the National Forensics Laboratory in Linköping, which in turn had prompted a further statement from a professor in animal biology at Stockholm University.

When Professor Sjöberg carefully pulled out the scrap of down that had caught in Yasmine's throat, and, with the same precision, removed the two white threads that had caught between her teeth, he had put each of them in a separate bag, filled in the usual forms and sent them with everything else to the forensics department of the Crime Division in Stockholm.

There, a forensics officer had looked at them. Two fragments of white cotton and a piece of bird-down approximately two centimetres long and one centi-metre across. He couldn't say much more than that, because he had neither the knowledge nor the necessary equipment. But, being a conscientious and thorough public servant, he had put them into two fresh bags, filled in even more forms and sent the lot off to the National Forensics Lab in Linköping. He had two ques-tions: what sort of thread was it, precisely? And was there anything else that could be said about the scrap of bird-down?

The relevant biologist at the lab had no difficulties with the first question. He had both the knowledge and all the equipment he needed. The two threads came from the plant *Linum usitatissimum*, or flax, to give it its common name.

The finest-quality flax and, more specifically, the sort of flax that was used to make fabrics. The finest-quality flax, and the idea of the pillowcase, which his colleague in the Crime Division in Stockholm had mentioned, seemed highly plausible under the circumstances. Or a sheet, a duvet cover or a handkerchief woven of the same fibres.

The notion that the threads might have come from – for instance – a tablecloth, a table runner, a towel or a linen napkin, was, on the other hand, highly improbable. Not only because of the circumstances but because such items were usually made of thread of a different structure and coarseness.

That left the little scrap of down, about which he, however, lacked the necessary knowledge. Because he was just as conscientious and thorough as his colleague in the forensics department, he had sent it on to one of his old lecturers at Stockholm University. The professor was a distinguished ornithologist, so it would present him with little difficulty.

His reply arrived by fax the same day he received the package containing the sample and the request from the National Forensics Laboratory. They were dealing with a member of the duck family, the professor explained. More precisely, a member of the subspecies of diving ducks, and, in this particular instance, down from the breast of a *Somateria mollissima*, an eider duck. Not a bad pillow, the biologist at the National Forensics Lab thought, as he forwarded the reply to the police in Solna. Stuffed with eiderdown and covered with a pillowcase woven of the finest linen.

What the fuck is this? thought the former head of National Crime, Lars Martin Johansson, when he had finished reading. How in the name of all that's holy did they manage to miss this? They must have been complete morons, he thought. And 'they' included, sorry to say, even his best friend, former Detective Superintendent Bo Jarnebring. After that, he wrote a whole page of notes. A new record with his left hand, Johansson thought, and then he fell asleep.

144

30

Tuesday, 20 July

Yet another day that started with the physiotherapist, as he had now reached the point where he chose to disregard the fact that it actually started with a walk to the toilet, having a shower and a shave and eating breakfast. His day started with the physiotherapist, and this penultimate day, if Dr Stenholm was true to her word and nothing unforeseen occurred, he was, regrettably, once again stuck on the same 'motor-function plateau' as the previous day.

'Make the best of things,' the physiotherapist said, and smiled.

'Make the best of things,' Johansson agreed.

Something's happened, Johansson thought as soon as Dr Stenholm sat down in the place where she always sat. Her cheeks even looked a little flushed.

'You've found something,' he stated.

'Yes, I have,' Dr Stenholm said. 'It was in a boxful of papers from 1989. I don't know how you could have known that.' She handed him a small plastic bag.

'Let's take a look, then.' Johansson reached out with his good hand. A hairgrip, he thought. A little hairgrip made of red plastic shaped like a Monchhichi doll's head.

'It's a Monchhichi.'

'I know,' Johansson said with a faint smile. 'I've got children and grandchildren. Was it in this bag?' he asked, holding up the little plastic bag.

'No,' Dr Stenholm shook her blonde head firmly. 'I put it in there. I thought—'

'I understand what you were thinking,' Johansson said, to pre-empt the usual explanations about finger-prints and DNA.

'The hairgrip was in this envelope,' Ulrika Stenholm said, passing him another small plastic bag containing a white envelope.

Egg-shell coloured, Johansson thought. Finest quality, with the owner's name printed on the inside of the flap. 'Margaretha Sagerlied', he read. Where have I heard that name before? he wondered, turning the envelope over. Where the stamp would usually be there was a brief note, written in ink with a fountain pen: 'USC/ÅS'.

'Under the seal of confession, forward slash, then your father's initials, Å. S., Åke Stenholm.'

'Yes,' Dr Stenholm said. 'Now I'm starting to think my sister wasn't exaggerating when she told me all those stories about you.'

'Well,' Johansson said, 'let's not get carried away. I don't suppose there's any way that this hairgrip could have belonged to you or your sister when you were lit-tle?' And that there was something else in the envelope to start with, he thought.

'No, neither of us ever had a hairgrip like that. Besides, we're both far too old. This sort of thing was popular

146

with young girls from the late seventies. Monchhichi dolls are still popular, as you're no doubt aware. Both my boys have got stuffed Monchhichi toys. Yasmine was nine years old when she was murdered in 1985; she might well have had a hairgrip like this.'

Johansson contented himself with a nod. There are no strands of hair on the grip, he thought as he inspected the bag it was in.

'This envelope,' he said, holding up the other bag. 'You didn't notice if there were any strands of hair inside it?' He couldn't just open it and take a look any more, of course.

'No,' Ulrika Stenholm said. 'I was very careful when I opened it. I mean, I'd seen what Dad had written on it, and his abbreviations – my older sister learned to crack his codes as soon as she could read. I am a doctor, after all, so I've picked up a bit over the years. There was nothing, just the hairgrip.'

A sensitive murderer, Johansson thought. Who had carefully removed her hairgrip so that his already sleeping victim could lie there with her long, black hair spread out across the pillow.

'This Margaretha Sagerlied,' Johansson said. 'What do you know about her?'

'Quite a bit,' Dr Stenholm said. 'I even met her a few times. I looked her up on the Net when I found the envelope. She's in *Who's Who*. You know, that book.'

'Tell me,' Johansson said. Always the Net, he thought.

Margaretha Sagerlied was born on 12 April 1914 and died on 6 May 1989, at the age of seventy-five. She was once an opera singer. Not one of the most famous, but well enough known to leave a trail in numerous newspaper articles, reviews and books about opera and other opera singers. And well enough known to appear in *Who's Who* in the 1950s.

'Like I said, I found her in an old edition of *Who's Who*,' Dr Stenholm said. 'My dad must have had a subscription, I've inherited at least twenty editions from him; they're all in my bookcase at home.'

'And what did it say, then?' Johansson asked.

'I was actually rather surprised,' Dr Stenholm answered. 'I mean, I knew she was famous, but I had no idea she was that well-known. There was almost as much written about her as about Birgit Nilsson. I'll get a copy for you.'

'Hmm,' Johansson said. He knew better from experience. 'The most likely explanation is that, once you're in that book, you get to write your own entry.'

'That would explain it, then,' Ulrika Stenholm said. 'She always was extremely pleased with herself. She came to dinner at my parents' several times when my sister and I were young. And she used to sing at christenings, weddings and funerals in the church out in Bromma, and she always had loads of stories to tell. How she'd met the king – the old king, that is – and about singing with Jussi Björling, and knowing Birgit Nilsson. And going to banquets at the palace and at the district governor's residence. And singing at the Nobel ceremony. Did I mention that she was very attractive? She was very particular about her appearance. But I never thought she was really that good as a singer.'

'You didn't?' Johansson said. 'Not like Birgit Nilsson.' Hardly sounds like the sort who'd stand bent over the sink wearing a pair of old pink rubber-gloves, he thought.

'No. I'm actually quite musical, you know. I used to play the piano and the organ in Dad's church. I still do, actually. I play the piano several hours each week. I find it's a good way of relaxing.'

'Husband and children, then?' Johansson asked. 'Any family?'

'No children.' Dr Stenholm shook her head. 'She married quite late. According to *Who's Who*, not until 1960, when she was close to fifty. Her husband was considerably older, born in 1895, died 1980. I have a vague memory of him as well. At some point, he came to dinner with my parents with his wife. According to *Who's Who*, his name was Johan Nilsson, and he was a company director. I have a feeling he was in the grocery business, and I remember Dad saying he was very wealthy.'

An eighty-five-year-old husband who died five years before Yasmine was murdered, no children, no grandchildren. Well, no known children or grandchildren. Some other younger male relative? Someone who was an admirer of the famous opera singer and for that reason was permitted to spend time in her company? Perhaps a member of her entourage, Johansson thought. Regardless of who might have been its members, it was a lovely word.

'Maybe I should ask my sister,' Ulrika Stenholm said. 'She's three years older than me, so she ought to remember more about those days.'

'No.' Johansson shook his head firmly. 'Don't do that. For the time being, I want this to stay between the two of us. I don't want you to talk to anyone about this.' The last thing I want is an inquisitive prosecutor around my neck, he thought.

149

'Okay,' Dr Stenholm said. 'I know what you mean.'

'Carry on with your father's old papers. See if you can find anything else.'

'I was thinking of carrying on anyway,' Ulrika Stenholm said. 'My ex has taken the kids off to the country, so I've got all the time in the world for the next few days.'

'To change the subject slightly,' Johansson said, 'you don't happen to know where she lived, this Sagerlied woman?'

'I suppose she probably lived in Dad's parish, in Bromma.'

'Bromma's a big place.'

'I know. I have a vague memory of her talking about moving into the city centre. To be nearer everything. To the opera and all the theatres, and Östermalmshallen and all her friends. Saying that the villa she lived in was far too big for her now that she was on her own. That must have been a year or so after she was widowed. But I wasn't very old at the time. I only remember fragments. But I do know that my dad was in charge of her funeral. I know that for certain, because he asked my sister and me if we wanted to go. So it ought to be possible to find out from his records of that. I can have a word with someone in the parish office out there.'

'It'll all become clear,' Johansson said. 'Is it okay if I keep hold of the hairgrip and the envelope?'

'Of course. I hope you don't think this is childish, but I can't help finding this all really exciting. Horrible, but exciting at the same time.'

'No,' Johansson said. 'I don't think you're being remotely childish. Did you go to the funeral, then? You and your sister?'

150

'No,' Ulrika Stenholm said. 'Neither of us had time, actually. He was a bit disappointed with us. Apparently, there weren't many people there. Hardly anyone, in fact.'

Not even a sensitive child-killer, Johansson thought.

As soon as she had gone, he called the Stockholm Police and asked to speak to Superintendent Kjell Hermansson, head of the cold-cases unit at Regional Crime, or, if he wasn't able to take the call, to his office.

'This is Lars Martin Johansson,' Johansson said. What on earth that has to do with anything! he thought. From the National Association of Retired Police Officers, he thought, and suddenly felt almost elated.

'I recognized your voice, boss,' the receptionist said. 'One moment, please.'

'Hermansson,' Hermansson said. Only fifteen seconds and three rings later.

'Johansson.'

'Johansson. How the devil are you? You sound very lively,' he added, for some reason.

'Living life to the full,' Johansson lied. 'I could do with a bit of help with something. I'd like to look at the log book for the Yasmine Ermegan case. You know, with all the people, vehicles, places and timings that cropped up in the investigation.'

'Now I'm getting curious,' Hermansson said.

'Don't be,' Johansson said. 'It's too early for that. Can you email it to me?'

'Nope,' Hermansson said. 'It isn't on the system. We had trouble with our computers a few years back and it all got deleted.'

This can't be true, Johansson thought.

'But I'm sure there's a back-up copy in our physical archive, so you can have that. I'll make a copy and have it sent over to you, if that suits you, boss?'

'Excellent,' Johansson said. 'When can I have it?'

'It's practically on its way. But on one condition.'

'What's that, then?'

'That I'm first to hear the bastard's name,' Hermansson said, sounding unexpectedly bitter. 'I was thinking of killing him, you see.'

'Naturally.'

'I'll send my son-in-law.'

Half an hour later, Detective Inspector Patrik Åkesson, P-2, walked into Johansson's room with a brown envelope in his hand. Plain clothes, unlike last time.

'Sorry, boss,' P-2 said. 'But I haven't brought you a sausage from Günter's. I spoke to Jarnis. He's had strict orders from Alpha One.'

'Alpha One?'

'Your wife, boss,' P-2 said with a broad grin. 'Just code we use at work. The alpha female of the family, code-name for the wife. Saves time and unnecessary chat.'

'Sounds like a good idea,' Johansson said. 'Thanks for last time, by the way. I didn't know you were married to Hermansson's daughter. Isn't she with Domestic Violence, down in the city?'

'Yes,' P-2 said, with an even broader smile. 'But, apart from that, she's completely normal. It's a small world, as they say.'

'Very small,' Johansson said. My family, he thought. If you ignored cuckoos like Evert Bäckström.

*

According to the log that was compiled in the summer of 1985 in connection with the investigation into the murder of Yasmine Ermegan, Margaretha Sagerlied was questioned during the door-to-door inquiries in the area on Tuesday, 2 July 1985. The officer who spoke to her was a female constable, Carina Tell, and the person responsible for deciding that she was of no interest to the case was the head of the preliminary investigation, Detective Inspector Evert Bäckström.

An elderly woman, seventy-one years old, a widow of five years, with no children or male contacts of interest to the case, away from home for the three days before Yasmine was reported missing. Returned home the day before she was questioned. The police had made the same checks on everyone who lived in the area. Margaretha Sagerlied had no criminal record, didn't own a car, had a passport but no driving licence.

The only reason she had been questioned at all was that she lived at Majblommestigen 2, at the bottom of the road, next to the junction with Äppelviksgatan. At roughly the same place where a witness had reported seeing a red Golf, latest model, on the evening that Yasmine disappeared.

The same Yasmine who lived at the top of the road, on the same side, at Majblommestigen 10. Together with her father and his new partner, who Yasmine sometimes called 'Mummy' when she was tired and sleepy, or just forgot.

Certainly a highly remarkable coincidence, thought the former head of the National Crime Unit, Lars Martin Johansson, who had learned to hate coincidences early in his career.

31

Tuesday, 20 July

Now, it was all really just a matter of time, Johansson thought, seeing as he had learned to make the best of things even before he started to hate coincidences. And assuming that he didn't have another stroke, of course, as he was now a different person to the man he had always been.

First, he thought he might have a little nap and rest on his newly acquired laurels. He had, after all, been told to take things very, very gently. But, of course, that didn't work. Too much going on in my head, he thought, after making a couple of attempts, and even going to the effort of rolling over in bed.

So instead he asked for some coffee and started to look through the files his best friend had given him, and because Jarnebring had arranged the papers in the exact order he knew Johansson would want them, he quickly found the inventory listing the clothes and other belongings Yasmine had had with her when she disappeared.

No hairgrip, Johansson thought when he had finished reading. He felt a sense of calm spread through his body when he saw that the inventory had been signed by his best friend, former Detective Superintendent Bo Jarnebring.

It shouldn't have been there, of course, not if she had lost it somewhere along the way. He tried to get rid of the image of her dark hair spread out across the white pillow.

Then he took out the portrait of Yasmine in which she was flashing her dark eyes and smiling at the photographer with her perfect white teeth. Even though she was only nine years old, while half of her classmates were walking about with braces on their teeth. Just as he was unable to see round corners, he was unable to see behind her eyes and mouth, see her thin neck and the way she wore her long, black hair. And it doesn't help much if I turn the photograph, he thought, feeling the same inexplicable delight as when he had felt like telling the police receptionist that he was calling from the National Association of Retired Police Officers.

Johansson put the photograph down on the bed covers. Drank a restorative sip of coffee, took three deep breaths and tried to buck his ideas up.

'Lars Martin Johansson, you're starting to go mad,' he said out loud to himself. So sort yourself out, he thought.

It worked. Suddenly, he felt calm and collected again. He picked up the picture and examined it once more.

Not that I'm a hairdresser, Johansson thought, but from this photograph it looks like her hair has been tied back, or pulled up, or whatever it's called. With a hairgrip, a hairband, maybe just an ordinary scrunchie, the sort his wife used to keep her unruly hair together when she was exercising at the gym or wanted to do pretty much anything at all.

155

Bo Jarnebring was a very thorough man. A legendary detective, for good reason, and compiling inventories was one of the disciplines he excelled at. Attached to the inventory was a list of the interviews he had conducted when he was trying to find out what Yasmine had been wearing, and what she had had with her, when she disappeared. Three interviews with her mother, two with her father, and ten in total, once you included the five witnesses who saw her on her way from her mother's flat to her father's home. There were another ten witnesses who thought they'd seen her but probably hadn't, largely because their descriptions of her and her clothes diverged widely from the information provided by the first seven witnesses.

Nothing about a small, red plastic hairgrip in the shape of a Monchhichi. Easiest to call Jarnebring, Johansson thought, but at that moment tiredness caught up with him, emptying his mind of all thought, all energy, all willpower. He was barely able to put the file down before he fell asleep, and when he woke up later he had trouble remembering what had happened after that.

He had declined dinner and dutifully nibbled at a sandwich instead, and crispbreads and cheese, he had drunk a couple of glasses of water and eaten a pear – or was it an apple? Presumably, he had gone to the toilet, rinsed his face, brushed his teeth. Talked to Pia about the practical arrangements that needed to be made regarding his return home to their large, two-storey apartment on Södermalm. Kitchen and study on the ground floor, their bedroom and bathroom upstairs, and a narrow staircase that he wouldn't be able to negotiate, not in either direction. Not in his current state.

'If you like, we can put a bed in your study – there's plenty of room. Or you could sleep in the guest room down there. Entirely up to you.'

'I can sleep on the sofa,' Johansson said, and promptly fell asleep again.

He slept the whole night through, dreaming about Yasmine. But no angst, no joy either, mostly contemplation – whatever that was doing in a dream – and perhaps grief. Grief which hadn't yet hit him, had barely even caught up with him.

The same Yasmine as in the photograph. But no smile. She's standing there looking at him. Serious, watchful, but not frightened.

'Hello, little thing,' Johansson says. 'There's no need to be frightened.'

She doesn't reply, but she does at least nod, and she isn't frightened.

'I've found your hairgrip,' he says, holding it out to her.

'Thanks,' she says, surprised, but now she's smiling. 'Thanks very much,' she says, and takes it from his outstretched hand.

32

Wednesday morning, 21 July

First the toilet, then the shower, then teeth-brushing. But he couldn't be bothered to shave. A bit of stubble is never wrong on a rough-hewn man, Johansson thought as he staggered into his room.

Lazy bastards, he thought once he was lying on his bed. It was the fourth time in a row that they had left him to fend entirely for himself on his potentially lethal walks. In spite of all the taxes he had showered on them throughout his life, without demanding anything in return.

Then breakfast. The healthy version, with yoghurt, muesli and fresh fruit. Three glasses of mineral water, but no coffee. He didn't feel like coffee this morning.

He didn't escape the physiotherapist, even though the bells of freedom were ringing loudly inside him. Regrettably, he was still stuck on the same plateau, despite the fact that he was trying really hard not to be viewed merely as his own very specific, if unforeseen, condition.

'Make the best of things,' the physiotherapist said, and gave him a big hug.

'Make the best of things,' Johansson said, with a nod and a smile. Easy for you to say, he thought. I'm free, he thought. He felt free as well. Bright and clear in his head. No worries, no angst, not even the slightest trace of anxiety.

After that came his doctor, now also his own personal informant, Dr Ulrika Stenholm, who this morning looked so tired that she could very well be taken for a woman of forty-four.

'I don't know what's wrong with me,' she sighed. 'First time in months I get a bit of peace and quiet and I barely managed a wink of sleep all night. Thinking about the kids, dreaming about the kids, calling their dad and waking him.'

'Well, it's hardly that bloody surprising,' Johansson interrupted. 'If you're going to sit and play the piano half the night, then start drinking red wine and listening to other people playing the piano.' Get yourself a decent bloke, he thought.

'Do you know what?' Ulrika Stenholm said. 'Sometimes, you really worry me. You're sure you're not sneaking out of here at night and spying on me?'

'Thanks for the invitation,' Johansson said. 'But no, I'm not. A fat pensioner in a white nightshirt dragging a drip-stand behind him standing there with his nose pressed against your window in the middle of the night? No, definitely not.' He shook his head. 'I reckon even you might have spotted someone like that.'

'Do you know what?' she said, with a smile. 'You can be very funny, when you're in the mood. Talking to you cheers me up.'

'I know,' Johansson said. 'So what do you think about all the practical arrangements, then?'

Already done, according to Ulrika Stenholm, who had spoken to Pia earlier that morning. Pia had sorted

159

out everything at home. She was also up to speed when it came to check-ups, new appointments, tests and daily visits to see the physiotherapist.

'Apparently, one of your former colleagues is coming to collect you,' she said. 'He's going to bring your clothes. He's coming in his car, but you're entitled to a taxi, as you might already know.'

'That'll be my best friend,' Johansson said, and felt someone or something touch his heart when he said it. 'We've known each other since we were at Police Academy together. Almost fifty years ago. He was one of the people who worked on Yasmine's case, by the way. I was on the National Police Board at the time.'

'On Yasmine's case?' she said, looking at him in surprise. 'But that's great, isn't it? Has he been able to help, then?'

'He brought me some old papers to read through.' Johansson nodded towards the files on the table next to the bed. Has he been able to help? Sort of, he thought.

'Great,' Ulrika Stenholm said as she put her hand in the pocket of her white coat and fished out her mobile. 'Okay, looks like it's time to go.' She shook her head. 'I've got to rush.'

'Look after yourself,' Johansson said, and held out his left hand towards her. What a fucking job the woman has, he thought.

'You look after yourself,' she said, giving him his second hug of the morning. 'I've told them to give you a hand packing your things. But I'm afraid I do have to rush.'

Wonder what it is? Johansson thought. Even though your face is drooping to one side, they're still crazy about you.

*

160

Five minutes later Jarnebring marched into his room. He walked straight over to the bed and emptied out a bag of clothes.

'Up you get then, lad,' he said. 'You can't just lie here letting your youth pass by.

'Pants, T-shirt, shirt, socks, shoes and trousers. And the longest belt I could find,' he went on, gesturing with his whole hand. 'It's sunny out, twenty degrees, so you're not likely to freeze your arse off.'

'About bloody time,' Johansson said, sitting up with some effort.

'Stop whining,' Jarnebring said. 'Do you want me to dress you, or shall I just stand in a strategic position to stop all those beautiful nurses seeing you?'

'Sit down on that chair over there and shut up, and I'll do the rest.'

Half an hour later they were standing in the car park beside Johansson's very own car.

'I thought I'd give it a try while your brother sorts the paperwork out,' Jarnebring said.

'You've bought my car,' Johansson said, not the least bit surprised, as he knew his eldest brother as well as he did his best friend – or himself, for that matter.

'Yep. There's some document you need to sign. I've got it with me, so we can do that once we get back to yours.'

'Okay. And what about me, then?'

'What do you mean, you?' Jarnebring shrugged his broad shoulders.

'Am I expected to walk everywhere from now on, or what?'

'Apparently, you're getting one exactly the same, but an automatic. And a few other bits and pieces

161

your brother told them to add until you get your arm sorted out.'

'Okay,' Johansson said. He had never been interested in driving. Less so now than ever. *I wonder what Bo had to stump up for my car?* he thought.

33

Wednesday afternoon, 21 July

'Aaah,' Jarnebring said, sighing with contentment as he pulled away from the car park. 'Twelve cylinders, 450 horsepower,' he explained, nodding towards the long, black bonnet.

'If you say so,' Johansson said. 'It goes fucking fast if you put your foot down,' he added. Whatever anyone might want that for, when the highest permissible speed was 120 kilometres an hour, now that blue lights and sirens were a thing of the past for men like him and Jarnebring.

'What do you want to do?' Jarnebring asked. 'Straight home, or shall we take a detour out into the field first?'

'Ear to the ground,' Johansson said. High time I saw it with my own eyes, he thought.

'Then let's start with Yasmine's mum's flat, down in the centre of Solna,' Jarnebring suggested. 'It's only two minutes away.'

'Drive to Äppelviken,' Johansson said. 'I want to see the house where she lived with her dad. I know Solna,' he explained. Besides, it wasn't there it happened, he thought. Why, he didn't know, not yet, just a feeling, but it was strong enough for him. It had always been good enough in the past. Back when he was a different person to the one he was today.

'Okay.' Jarnebring reached out his long right arm and pulled on the safety belt that Johansson had forgotten, even though the car was bleeping at him and a red light was flashing on the dashboard.

'Thanks,' Johansson said. 'We're in no hurry,' he added, just to be on the safe side.

Nice, safe driving; no rush, no stress. Out from Karolinska Hospital, left along the edge of the cemetery, left at the first roundabout on to the Solna road, then right on the first slip road on to the southbound E4, then right again towards Bromma and Äppelviken, and twelve minutes later Jarnebring pulled up at the junction of Äppelviksgatan and Majblommestigen.

'Somewhere around here was where that witness thought he saw the red Golf,' Jarnebring said, pointing towards the first house on the right-hand side. 'This is Majblommestigen.' He waved his large hand at the little cul-de-sac. 'About one hundred metres long, a dead end, with a turning circle at the top of the slope. Yasmine, her father and his new partner lived in the house at the top, Majblommestigen 10, on the right from where we're sitting.' He raised his hand again.

'And the car was parked down here, where we are,' Johansson said. 'Parked outside the house where we're parked. Majblommestigen 2. Here, by the junction?'

'According to the witness's first statement, yes,' Jarnebring said. 'Then the silly sod started to wobble, and in the end he wasn't sure about anything. Nor were we.'

You pushed him too hard, Johansson thought. He got worried when he realized what he said he'd seen, and suddenly a load of journalists showed up and started ringing at his door.

'Things weren't made any better when all the hacks started hanging around his house, playing at being interviewing officers,' Jarnebring said, as if he could read Johansson's mind.

'I can imagine.' Johansson was already thinking about something else.

Wooden houses from some time between the First and Second World Wars, in red, yellow, white and blue, even pink, but not so garish as to upset the neighbours. Contemporary wooden details, porches, verandas; painters and blacksmiths who knew what they were doing and took the time to do it well. Picket fences, neatly clipped hedges, mature, leafy gardens with flowerbeds and fruit trees and smart lawns. One or two of the houses even had raked gravel paths between the gate and front door. A well-kept area, extensions, renovations, pious restorations throughout the years. Well-behaved, well-off middle-class residents and, in recent years, a few neighbours who were considerably wealthier, in line with the increase in the value of the houses.

The house at the top of the road where Yasmine had lived was not the biggest, but not the smallest either. Red with white details, a freshly painted façade, some of the painters' equipment still on the drive, loosely covered by a tarpaulin.

'Do you know if she still lives here?' Johansson asked. 'The father's ex-girlfriend, I mean.'

'No,' Jarnebring said. 'I heard she sold up and moved out the following summer. Yasmine's dad left just a month or so after it happened. I can imagine that it made things pretty hard for them.'

A house that had gained new memories, Johansson thought. Memories that made it impossible for the people who had lived there to remain.

'Do you want to get out and take a look?'

'No,' Johansson said, shaking his head.

'Not that I'm an expert on child-killers, but I promise to eat my old police helmet if it happened out here,' Jarnebring declared, and he turned the car with confident movements of the wheel. 'This area feels completely wrong.'

'So where did it happen, then?'

'If you ask me, I'm pretty sure someone picked her up when she was on her way back to her mum's again. The poor kid was probably tired, tired and upset. This isn't the sort of area where people murder little girls,' Jarnebring repeated as they glided slowly down the road.

'Can you stop here at the corner?' Johansson asked.

'Sure,' Jarnebring said.

This house was considerably larger than the others on the street. Blue, with a hipped tiled roof, a projecting porch held up by two white pillars, the upper storey jutting out above. An imposing flight of stone steps led up to the double front doors. A large glassed-in veranda faced the garden at the back. Different owners who had been there a while – perhaps several owners – because if there was one thing Johansson knew without looking in the property register, it was that the woman who lived here when it happened had moved out as soon as she realized what had happened, and that it had happened in her home.

Wonder when she realized? he thought. Maybe as early as the autumn of the same year; it would be easy

166

enough to find out. I wonder where she found Yasmine's hairgrip? That was far from easy to find out, twenty-five years later.

'If you're thinking about moving to a villa, I'd consider taking on your flat,' Jarnebring said. 'Seeing as I've already bought your car, I mean.'

'No,' Johansson said. 'I like living on Södermalm.'

'You've got stuck with your ear to the ground,' Jarnebring said with a grin.

'No. I just thought you might like to take a look at the crime scene.' Johansson nodded towards the big, blue house.

III

*Eye for eye, tooth for tooth,
hand for hand . . .*

Book of Exodus, 21:24

34

Wednesday afternoon, 21 July 2010

At first, Jarnebring made do with a nod. Initially towards the big house on the other side of the road, then at Johansson.

'What makes you think that?' he asked. 'That this is the crime scene?'

'The pillow. Well, the pillow and the pillowcase,' Johansson replied. He seemed submerged in his own thoughts. 'That was when I first realized.'

'The pillow? And the pillowcase?'

'Yes, although there were other things. The red Golf – I have a feeling it was parked just there. The whole setting, if I can put it like that.'

'The pillow, the pillowcase, and a red Golf. The whole setting?' Should I be pleased or worried? Jarnebring thought.

'Well, there's a lot more. But it's mostly just feelings. The woman who lived here, for instance.'

The woman? The woman who lived here? Okay, I'm getting seriously fucking worried now, Jarnebring thought. Where the hell did she come from?

'I don't suppose you feel like explaining?' he said.

'Later,' Johansson said. 'I'd like to go home now.'

*

Home at last, he thought as he stepped across the threshold into his home on Wollmar Yxkullsgatan, leaning on his best friend, admittedly, but largely under his own steam.

'Let's go and sit in my study. Then I can prop myself up on the sofa. Just give me my stick and I'll be okay.'

'It's no problem,' Jarnebring said. 'If you'd rather—'

'Just do as I say,' Johansson interrupted. 'Get me a glass of water. If you want something to eat, there's bound to be loads in the fridge. Pia's good at that. But I'll be fine with just a glass of water.'

Home at last, he thought, once he had managed to sit down on the sofa, not without effort, and had arranged his legs the way he usually had them. The same sofa, the same corner of the same big sofa where he must have spent thousands of hours over the years, reading, watching television, having little afternoon naps, or just thinking. The room now also contained a large bed that Pia had bought for him, positioned against the short end of the room – with a load of electrical features that he looked forward to trying.

Jarnebring brought over a chair and sat down opposite him. On the table between them he put a large bottle of mineral water, a bowl of fruit and two glasses.

'You don't want a sandwich as well?' Johansson asked, nodding at the tray.

'I'm not hungry. But I am seriously fucking curious.'

'Calm down,' Johansson said. 'All in good time. I'm just working out what order to explain things.'

'I suggest you take it in whatever order a simple constable could understand.'

'Of course,' Johansson said. 'You remember the feather and the two white threads that the pathologist found in the poor girl's throat and between her teeth? Indicating that she was smothered by a pillow covered by a white pillowcase?'

'Yes, I believed that,' Jarnebring said. 'Everyone did. Even that fat little bastard Bäckström bought the idea of the pillow.'

'The problem is that it wasn't an ordinary pillow. Not an ordinary pillowcase, either. It was stuffed with eiderdown and the pillowcase was made of linen.'

'Hang on a minute,' Jarnebring said, raising his hand to be on the safe side. 'The wife and I have got loads of down-filled pillows at home in our humble abode. We've even got down pillows at our place in the country. Which is even more humble. Well, you know that, you've been round ours. Both here in the city and out in the country.'

'I know,' Johansson said, 'but I'm not talking about standard down pillows, or ordinary cotton pillowcases.'

'No, you're talking about—'

'If you could just shut up for a minute and stop interrupting the whole time, I'll explain the difference between an ordinary down-filled pillow and an ordinary white cotton pillowcase, and the pillow our perpetrator used to smother Yasmine.'

'I'm listening,' Jarnebring said. He leaned back and folded his hands over his flat stomach.

The whole thing was really pretty simple, according to Johansson. The stuffing of most so-called down-filled pillows was mainly feathers. Feathers and a bit of down from farmed birds, usually ducks and geese that were bred for the purpose. The main producers of feathers and down for pillows were based in Asia, and the country that exported most was China.

Ordinary pillowcases, with the exception of the most basic and cheapest ones, were made of cotton. Almost all pillowcases were made of cotton, not linen.

'So what you're trying to say is that this pillow was pretty damn unusual,' Jarnebring said with a grin.

'Have you got any idea what a pillow like that would cost today? If you even managed to get hold of one, that is. A pillow stuffed with eiderdown with a pillowcase of the finest linen?'

'Not a clue,' Jarnebring shook his head.

'Twenty thousand, thirty thousand, maybe even more. If you wanted a duvet to match, you're probably looking at a hundred. A hundred thousand, I mean. That's if you could actually find any pillows and duvets like that now.'

'I hear what you're saying,' Jarnebring said. 'Who the fuck would pay a hundred grand for a pillow and a duvet?'

'Not your average child-killer,' Johansson said. 'Not someone like John Ingvar Löfgren, Anders Eklund or Ulf Olsson. None of the others either, for that matter. And not even Yasmine's murderer, the sensitive and considerate paedophile described by Professor Sjöberg.'

'You've lost me now,' Jarnebring said. 'You're going to have to explain.'

'It wasn't his pillow,' Johansson said.

Jarnebring considered this for almost a minute. Then he nodded to Johansson, straightened up on his chair, leaned forward and nodded again.

'I'm listening.'

'Margaretha Sagerlied,' Johansson said. 'Is that a name you remember?'

174

'Doesn't ring any bells,' Jarnebring said. 'Who's she?'

'She cropped up in your investigation. Widow, seventy-one years old at the time of the crime, former opera singer – posh old lady, if I can put it like that. Died in '89. Considering that her husband was twenty years older than her – he died in 1980, by the way, at the age of eighty-five – and bearing in mind what I've heard about the woman in question, I'd say she had a fair bit of money. That was her house we stopped in front of. When Yasmine was murdered she was living at Majblommestigen 2. She was away when it happened. Left a few days before and got back about a week later. She was ruled out of the investigation fairly early. By Bäckström, of course.'

'I understand. I get it now.' Jarnebring suddenly looked delighted.

'Splendid,' Johansson said.

'So we can forget her bloke. Far too old. And dead. What about children or grandchildren?'

'A problem. Neither she nor her husband appear to have had any.'

'None born on the wrong side of the blanket, as they used to say?'

'No,' Johansson said. 'I can't find any, and I'm of the opinion that there aren't any illegitimate children, or grandchildren, at all. On his side or hers. It must be some younger, male acquaintance of hers. Someone you missed.'

'Well,' Jarnebring said. 'I don't think you should get too hung up on that confused witness who said he saw the red Golf. After all, he withdrew his statement altogether.'

'Sure,' Johansson said, shrugging his shoulders. We live in a free country, he thought.

'But I buy the idea of the pillow,' Jarnebring went on. 'There were a fair number of rich people living in the area, you know. Quite a few with sons of the right age. I see what you're thinking. Nice parents, nice little sons. We might well have missed someone there.'

'Forget them,' Johansson said. 'The red Golf was parked where the witness first said it was. The old woman's house is our crime scene: Majblommestigen number 2. Can you pass me that bag over there?' he said, pointing. 'The one with my stuff from the hospital. The one with your files in it.'

'Sure,' Jarnebring said. 'But you're not very likely to find anything we missed in those files.'

'No,' Johansson said. 'You missed something else that I was thinking of showing you.' The sort of thing you miss doesn't usually end up in a folder, he thought.

After some difficulty he found the plastic bag containing the red hairgrip. He fished it out with his working left hand and passed it to Jarnebring.

'Do you recognize this?' Johansson said.

The look in Jarnebring's eyes suddenly changed. They were narrow and wary as he carefully held the bag up in his right hand.

'Yes,' he said. 'I'm definitely with you now, so you'd better bloody well explain yourself.'

35

Wednesday afternoon, 21 July

Johansson merely shook his head.

'Later,' he said.

'What's wrong with now? That hairgrip caused us a lot of problems. A hell of a lot of problems.'

'Later,' Johansson repeated. 'Why did the hairgrip cause you problems? Because you never found it, did you?'

'That was the problem. Yasmine had long, black hair. Maybe twenty centimetres below her shoulders, and she always used to wear it tied up with a hairgrip or band of some sort. She had loads of different hairgrips. If she wanted to look really good she used to ask her mum to do her hair for her. I even saw a photograph where she's got it in that Farah Diba style. You know, the woman who was married to the Shah of Iran.'

What's she got to do with anything? Johansson thought. Married to the Shah of Iran, Reza Pahlavi; he remembered that.

'Yes, I'm listening,' he said.

'It was our colleague Sundman, the one who lived next to the mother, who put together the first description. He did it the night she disappeared, along with her mother. According to that description, she had her hair tied up with a red plastic hairgrip in the shape of one of those little monkeys—'

'Monchhichi. A Monchhichi.'

'Exactly,' Jarnebring said, holding up the inventory of Yasmine's clothes and other belongings. 'Sundman was a perfectly sound officer, and when we found her his description matched almost exactly. As you'll recall, the perpetrator had put her clothes and other things in a parcel of their own. They were found wrapped in two plastic bags a couple of hundred metres from the body.'

'I remember,' Johansson said.

'It was all there. Even her two rings and her watch. Her local-transport pass, everything. Everything except the hairgrip that her mother and Sundman claimed she'd had with her.'

'How was she dressed?' Johansson asked.

'White leather moccasins – Indian shoes, I think they used to be called in those days. White socks, white underpants. Pale blue jeans, a pink T-shirt – the one she changed into after she'd spilled her drink at her mum's – a small Adidas rucksack, also pink, the same colour as the T-shirt. She'd tied her jacket around her waist. A thin blue one from Fjällräven, then her watch, two rings, transport pass. In her rucksack she had a mixture of things. A magazine, chewing gum, a bag of throat sweets, her purse, also pink, made of leather. I have a vague memory that her mum told me during one of the interviews that red and pink were Yasmine's favourite colours.'

'And it all matched the inventory?'

'Yes,' Jarnebring said. 'Everything matched, with the exception of the hairgrip.'

'So what did you think?'

'Our first thought was that she'd forgotten to put it on, like the necklace with her keys on it, when she changed her damp white blouse for the pink T-shirt. Everything else was there, after all, so why would the perpetrator have kept her hairgrip? If anything is ever missing in a case like this, it's usually the victim's underwear. So the general idea was that she'd forgotten to put it on. Just like she'd forgotten her keys. Bäckström was convinced that was the case. He couldn't understand the problem. So we never followed it up.'

'I see,' Johansson said. 'So why wasn't the hairgrip found in the bathroom, then? Seeing as her keys were there.'

'Exactly. Anyway, Sundman was certain she'd been wearing it when she went past him towards the underground.'

'She *was* wearing the hairgrip. You're holding it in your hand.' I've already given it back to her, he thought.

'I hear what you're saying,' Jarnebring said. 'I'm even inclined to believe you. Which makes me seriously bloody worried. How the hell could you have got hold of it twenty-five years later? Because you surely haven't been sitting on it all this time until that blood clot prompted a pang of conscience?'

'No cause for concern,' Johansson said. 'I got it yester-day.' It was yesterday, wasn't it? he wondered.

'You got it yesterday. Who from?'

'An anonymous source,' Johansson said. 'Don't worry. Your unidentified perpetrator isn't my source, so there's no need to worry about that.'

'So who is it, then?'

'For the time being, an anonymous informant, and because you and I have exactly the same thoughts about those, you can stop going on about who it is. Anyway, give me the hairgrip back.'

Jarnebring shrugged, handed the hairgrip to him, apparently somewhat reluctantly.

'You'll have to excuse me, Lars,' he said. 'Correct me if I'm wrong. You have a stroke. You end up in the Karolinska, and while you're in there for a fortnight an anonymous source appears and hands over a hairgrip that a little girl was wearing when she was murdered twenty-five years ago.'

'More or less,' Johansson said with a nod. She thanked me when she got it back, he thought.

'If you only got it yesterday,' Jarnebring said, 'I can't help wondering why you started going on about this case a week ago.'

'It's not at all strange,' Johansson said. 'My anonymous source needed time to find it. She didn't even know what she was looking for.' Bo isn't his usual self, he thought. Seems to have lost his edge.

'I don't agree with you. This is probably the strangest story you've ever told me, and I can only assume that you've got a damn good explanation.'

'I have,' Johansson said. The best one going, he thought.

'So what is it, then?'

'Divine providence.'

36

Wednesday afternoon, 21 July

Before they parted they dealt with a number of practical issues. First, Johansson signed the papers handing his Audi over to his best friend, but he felt far from comfortable as he did so.

'Are you sure this is such a good idea?' he asked. 'You're letting yourself in for some fairly steep monthly repayments.'

'Don't worry,' Jarnebring said. 'Your brother promised I could buy myself out.'

'Just out of curiosity, what did he want for it?'

'Two hundred.'

'Wow. That doesn't sound like my brother.' Wonder if he's had some sort of crap going on in his head, too? he thought.

'I've promised to take on a bit of chauffeur work, running simple errands for an old acquaintance. Isn't that the point of being retired?'

'Sounds good,' Johansson said, already thinking about something else. 'You don't fancy calling in on Herman and asking if I can look at everything he's got about that opera singer in your old investigation?'

'Margaretha Sagerlied.'

'That's it. That was her name. And all the records of the door-to-door inquiries you conducted.'

'That was all done in June and July '85. With some follow-ups in August, and later that autumn, once people had got back from their holidays. That's a lot of paper. But sure, I'll sort it out.'

'Is there anything I've forgotten?' Johansson asked.

'That red Golf you won't let go of. There's a whole box of printouts from the vehicle registry and the records of any owners who stood out. Previous convictions, or people living nearby.'

'That, too,' Johansson agreed.

'You'll have it tomorrow. Anything else I can do for you?'

'Yes, you can get out of here. I was thinking of having a little nap.'

'Is that wise? I was thinking of waiting until Pia got home. I can go and sit somewhere else, if you like.'

'Okay, okay.' Johansson was tired, all of a sudden. No energy, he thought. Have to sleep. His headache was already hammering at his temples.

'I'll go and sit in the kitchen,' Jarnebring said. 'Shout if you want anything.'

'I just thought of something. Do you think it's possible to solve a twenty-five-year-old murder case if you're forced to lie on a sofa the whole time?'

'We'll just have to take another trip out into the field,' Jarnebring said with a smile. 'We can take the sofa along if you like. No need to worry on that count.'

'Hmm,' Johansson said. It ought to be possible, he thought. That bloke, the one who was Sherlock Holmes's elder brother, he could have done it. Whatever his name was, he thought.

Then he fell asleep.

37

Wednesday afternoon, 21 July

It was the smells that woke him. The smells of the food she was cooking for him, then her hand gently stroking him on his cheeks and temples. It made the pain in his head disappear.

'Jarnebring,' Johansson said. 'Is he still here?'

'Don't worry,' Pia said. 'I threw him out an hour ago. I've made you something to eat,' she added, nodding towards the large tray she had put down on the table beside the sofa.

Home at last, decent food at last. Maybe not the meal he would have chosen for himself, but still from a different, better world than the one in which they had chosen to build a huge health-service kitchen. A lukewarm salad with brown rice and fried salmon, just pink enough in the middle. Perhaps a little too much salad to be entirely to his taste, but at least it had asparagus and mushroom. No beer, wine nor even a sneaky vodka, of course, but the chilled mineral water was good enough. And proper coffee. A double espresso, with warm milk on the side.

You're alive, Lars Martin Johansson thought. So stop feeling sorry for yourself.

'You're far too good to me, Pia,' Johansson said. 'If you were the main character in an everyday novel of our times, your sisters in the arts sections of the press would rip you to shreds for betraying the feminist cause.'

Now I recognize you, she thought. 'And if it had been the other way round?' Pia said. 'What if I'd been the one who got ill?'

'That would probably be just as bad,' Johansson said.

'For better or worse,' Pia said, raising her glass.

'For better or worse,' Johansson repeated.

'Do you feel up to going through some practical details?' Pia asked when they'd finished eating.

Johansson made do with a nod. He felt a sudden anxiety, the source of which he couldn't trace. Things were the way they were, after all. What had happened was irrevocable. But it was still possible to do something about what was yet to come.

The best solution for all parties, according to Ulrika Stenholm, and even for her patient and Pia Johansson's husband, would have been if Johansson had been transferred to a care home specializing in aftercare and rehabilitation of patients like him.

'Out of the question,' Pia had said, shaking her head. 'He'd never agree to that.'

'Do you think it might be possible to reason with him? We might only be talking about a month or so.'

'I'm not even going to try,' Pia had said. What the hell is the woman suggesting? she'd thought.

'In that case, there'll be quite a lot of toing and froing. And he'll need supervision. He's got the right to ambulance transport, but I'd be surprised if he could get much home care. Especially seeing as it's summer and people are away on holiday.'

'Give me the times of his appointments and who he needs to see, and I'll sort that out.'

'And of course there are a number of private alternatives. But I'm afraid that's where we are. Don't be cross with me, Pia, but that's all I can offer.'

'I'm not cross,' Pia had said. 'But I'm seriously pissed off that you've got the nerve to suggest putting him in a care home. You've had him as a patient for a couple of weeks now, but you don't seem to have given any thought to the sort of person he is.'

'Sorry,' Ulrika Stenholm had said. 'I didn't mean to make you unhappy.'

'I'm not a bit unhappy. Just give me his appointments and who he needs to see, and I'll sort out the rest.'

When Pia spoke to her husband about it, she didn't mention that part of her conversation with his doctor.

'I spoke to your doctor, Ulrika Stenholm. She's happy for you to carry on being her patient. Or I can organize another one. There are several at Sophia Hospital who are excellent. We use them at the bank.'

'What for?' Johansson said, surprised. 'There's nothing wrong with Stenholm, is there?' Besides, we're working on a case together, he thought.

'In that case, you've got an out-patient appointment with her on Monday.'

'Good,' Johansson said. I wonder what they fell out about? he thought.

'And you'll need help during the day as well. I've sorted that out. We use a private care company at the bank when things such as what you've suffered happen.'

'Good to hear,' Johansson said. 'That you take care of your cashiers, I mean.'

'Really,' Pia said. 'Do you know what?' She leaned forward and took his hand. Smiled at him.

'No,' Johansson said. 'What?'

'You're starting to sound just like my husband.'

'I'll end up better than him after this five-star bean-counter treatment,' Johansson said.

'I've spoken to the girl who'll be helping you. Her name's Matilda, and she's known as Tilda. She's coming tomorrow morning, when I'm still here.'

'Okay,' Johansson said. 'So what's wrong with her, then?'

'There's nothing wrong with her. She's twenty-three years old, pretty, energetic, happy and positive. Studied healthcare at high school. Trained as a personal assistant.'

'Come off it,' Johansson said. 'What's wrong with her?'

'Well, she looks like most young people do these days.'

'What do you mean?'

'She's got a few tattoos on her arms, that sort of thing.'

'That sort of thing?'

'Rings in her ears, too.'

'Bloody hell,' Johansson said. 'Why do kids today insist on scribbling all over themselves? In my day, only criminals and sailors had tattoos. And that Danish king whose name I've forgotten.'

'But, apart from that, she seems like a really sweet girl.'

Johansson didn't seem to be listening.

'If little Alicia showed up like that, looking like a bit of old carpet, ready to stick a curtain rail through her face, I'd soon have something to say about it.'

'That's just what young people are like these days,' Pia said dismissively; she had been in the sauna with

186

Johansson's eldest grandchild and clearly knew more about her than her grandfather did. 'On a different matter . . .'

'Yes?' Johansson said.

'What are you and Bo up to? Is it some old case?'

'Yes. An old murder investigation. Unsolved. One of those ones that us police officers – some of us – have trouble letting go of.'

'God, how exciting,' Pia said, and looked like she really meant it. 'Can't you tell me what it's about? Is it one of your old cases?'

'No,' Johansson said. 'Definitely not. My old cases were usually solved when I let go of them.'

'Sorry,' Pia said. 'You're tired, you should get some sleep.'

'No,' Johansson said. 'I want to test-drive my new bed.'

Then he fell asleep. Hypnos had summoned him. He smiled amiably at Johansson. Then he put the green poppy seedhead in Johansson's good hand before taking him firmly by the arm and leading him into the darkness.

38

Thursday, 22 July

For the first time in a long while, Johansson slept his usual eight hours but, instead of feeling alert and rested, he was tired and sluggish. He had a headache when he woke up, so had to add another pill to all the others he was stuffing himself with these days.

You look fucking awful, Lars, he thought as he stared at himself in the bathroom mirror. Unshaven, haggard, and saggy in a very literal sense. He couldn't even think about doing anything about his stubble.

Then Jarnebring showed up just after eight o'clock in the morning. He brought in three large boxfuls of paper and put them down on the floor of Johansson's study.

'Herman says hello,' he said. 'He's sent some sort of application form that you need to sign. The case may have been written off and prescribed, but it's still confidential, so you need official permission to see the files.'

'Okay,' Lars Martin said. 'Have you got a pen?' Left hand, he thought. How difficult can it be? He had written his name so many times that even the other hand ought to be able to manage it by now.

'Nice,' Jarnebring said when he was handed the signed form. 'Lars Martin Johansson, four years old, by the look of the handwriting. Congratulations, by the way. You're now a police researcher.'

'A police researcher?'

'According to Herman, that's the simplest solution,' Jarnebring said. 'Okay, so pretty much anyone can get permission to research whatever they want, just to satisfy their curiosity. That mad professor on the National Police Board, the one who's always talking a load of crap on *Crimewatch*, he approved your application as soon as Herman picked up the phone to call him. That's what I've got here, in case you were wondering. Sends his best wishes, apparently. The professor, I mean. Says you shouldn't worry too much, because he's had his own problems with blood clots and strokes. And several heart attacks.'

'Isn't he dead?' Johansson said. He must be ancient, he thought.

'No, fit as a fiddle, apparently. On his last legs, but they keep going. And, according to Herman, he also says it's high time the bastard was boiled down and turned into glue.'

'Who?' Johansson said. 'Who should be turned into glue?'

'The man who killed Yasmine,' Jarnebring said. Off he goes again, he thought. Completely out of it.

'Oh, he said that, did he?'

'Yes. Those very words, according to Hermansson. Anyway, I've got to dash. That water leak at my daughter's, you know. Looks like I'm going to have to rip the floor up and get it dried out before it starts going mouldy.'

'Those papers,' Johansson said, nodding towards the three boxes.

'They're a right mess. Don't worry about them now. I'll help you when I get back.'

After that Matilda, his new carer, showed up. His wife's description was fairly accurate, because her bare upper arms were black with what looked like coiled snakes. That may have been why Pia had failed to mention all the rings she had in her face: one in her left nostril, two through her bottom lip and three in each earlobe.

I wonder how long my dear wife was planning to hide that from me? Johansson thought. But Matilda did seem cheerful and very perky.

'Okay,' Pia said. 'Time for you to take over, Tilda. You've got my number, just in case.'

'Don't worry,' Matilda said. 'It'll all be fine,' she added reassuringly.

Just like when the kids were little and they were going to a party, Johansson thought. Never forget to give the babysitter your phone number.

Then he ate breakfast sitting on the sofa in his study. Yoghurt, muesli and fresh fruit, coffee and water. Nothing especially worthy of comment. And nothing wrong with the service, either. She even offered to tie his napkin round his neck. Naturally, he declined and did it himself, even though he dropped it twice.

'I was going to ask if you had any special requests?' His personal assistant looked at him inquisitively.

'Special requests?' What the fuck's she going on about? Johansson thought. Special requests?

'Yes, you know, walks, or any particular food you'd like. If you want, we could go for a drive in the car.

Go to the cinema. You name it.' She nodded almost encouragingly at him.

'I'm very fond of peace and quiet,' Johansson said. 'So I'd really like to be left alone.'

'I'll sit in the kitchen and read,' Matilda said. 'That's fine. Shout if you want anything.'

Johansson lay on the sofa and looked at the ceiling. He didn't even want to think about the boxfuls of papers.

Seems quite nice, after all, Johansson thought. And she was pretty. So why the hell did she do that to herself, he thought. And why didn't her parents say anything?

Then he fell asleep. And woke up to find someone gently touching his arm.

'Time to get up,' Matilda said. 'We've got to be at the physiotherapist's in two hours.'

'Two hours,' Johansson said. 'I need fifteen minutes at most to get dressed.' How long can it take to drive there? No more than twenty minutes, he thought.

'I thought I'd smarten you up before we go,' Matilda said. 'Do you think you could sit on this chair?' she said, indicating an armchair she had placed just a metre from the sofa where he lay.

'Yes,' Johansson said. What's the problem? he thought. One metre – does she think I'm completely paralysed, or what?

Then he stood up and sat down on the chair, up and down.

Matilda put a cushion behind his head and wrapped his face in a warm towel. His headache was suddenly gone, as if she had banished it with a click of her long, slender fingers.

'Now, you just sit there for a minute or two, and I'll get the razor and some shaving foam.'

Then she shaved his stubble off. Carefully and without leaving the slightest trace of blood, in spite of the anticoagulants he was on. She removed the shaving foam with another towel which she had moistened with warm water. She gently patted his cheeks and chin dry with aftershave from his bathroom cabinet. She held a mirror up in front of him.

'Go on, admit that there's a slight difference,' she said.

'Yes,' Johansson said. That's as close to sex as I've come recently, thanks to these wretched blood-pressure pills, he thought. 'Thank you, Matilda,' he said.

'Don't mention it,' she said. 'I know people say funny things when they've had a stroke. It's fine. But my friends call me Tilda – in case you were wondering, I mean.'

'Thank you, Tilda,' Johansson said. What the hell's she going on about? he thought.

39

Thursday afternoon, 22 July

Jarnebring appeared after lunch, just as he had promised. Matilda brought coffee, water and fruit for them. Then she shut the door on them so they could be in peace. She just disappeared into the silence that pervaded his big apartment.

'Pretty girl,' Jarnebring said. 'Smart, too.'

'Yes, I suppose so. But all those tattoos and rings – what's the point of that?'

'They've all got them these days,' Jarnebring said with a shrug. 'Adults and children alike. My wife, for instance. She's got two tattoos.' Thank God you've never seen them, he thought.

'I've managed to miss those,' Johansson said. What's going on? he thought.

'Where do you want to start?' Jarnebring asked, nodding towards the boxes.

'You said they were a right mess.' Johansson sighed.

'To put it mildly,' Jarnebring said. 'But I've got a bit of an idea. I can give you a reasonable description of what's in those boxes.'

'Start with the door-to-door,' Johansson said. No headache now. Instead, there was that odd, distanced feeling he'd been getting recently. As if he were on his way somewhere else. 'Start with the door-to-door,' he repeated. Pull yourself together. You've had a shave, you've just done your exercises, you've got over that plateau, been praised by the physiotherapist, and now you're sitting here with your best friend. What more do you want? You're alive, after all, he thought.

In summary: the door-to-door inquiries in the investigation into the murder of Yasmine Ermegan had been a disaster. By the time they got going, a week had passed since she had gone missing and, according to Jarnebring, it was a miracle that he and his colleagues managed to find any witnesses who could place her in the area, let alone on the street where she lived with her dad.

There had been good weather all week, and on the news they were forecasting similar for the weekend. The summer holidays had started, and the affluent middle classes who lived in the neighbourhood were not short of places to go and stay out in the country, or invitations to visit friends and acquaintances. According to one list, fewer than five of the neighbours had been at home on the evening of Friday, 14 June, when Yasmine disappeared. The only ones who were still there were elderly people who had either gone to bed early or were sitting indoors in the cool. Reading, listening to the radio, playing music, watching television . . . anything but seeing or hearing anything that went on outside the walls of the homes that were their castles.

'I don't need to tell you, Lars,' Jarnebring said, 'but from the point of view of door-to-door inquiries, she could hardly have chosen a worse day to go missing.

Friday evening, Swedish summer, school holidays. A nightmare for police officers going door-to-door.'

'I hear what you're saying,' Johansson said with a nod.

Wonder what the perpetrator was doing there? he thought. Late on a Friday evening, late on a summer's evening. Good weather, too. What would he have been doing there? This man who, in all likelihood, didn't even live there. Why wasn't he driving around the city, cruising about in his red Golf and staring at all the little girls playing in their short skirts? Even though it was really far too late for them to be out playing.

'I managed to find our summary of the door-to-door inquiries,' Jarnebring said. 'The list of everyone living in the area when it happened; almost all the properties were private homes – no offices, which was good. But the interviews themselves seem to have ended up in a hell of a mess.'

'As long as we've got the list, it will all work out,' Johansson said. Bäckström probably stuck his fat little fingers in and messed everything up, he thought.

'The search for the Golf is even worse. I couldn't find the summary. There's no back-up printed copy after that computer trouble they had. There must have been one, but it looks like it was lost. The vehicles we managed to track down on the national registry ought to be in the log, though; otherwise, we're buggered.'

Probably ended up in Bäckström's wastepaper basket, Johansson thought.

'We'll have to make the best of it,' he said. 'If the worst comes to the worst, we'll just have to compile a new list.'

'Sure,' Jarnebring said. 'Mind you, I don't believe it. But I've already said that. Even if you don't seem to want to listen.'

'Margaretha Sagerlied,' Johansson said. 'Have you found the interviews with her?' Sometimes I can't help wondering if Bo's the one who had the stroke, he thought.

'Yes,' Jarnebring said. 'Two of them. The first from Tuesday, 2 July, so two and a half weeks after Yasmine went missing. Like most of the others, the old dear was away at the time, and supplementary interviews were conducted about a month later, on Friday, 9 August.'

'I'm listening,' Johansson said.

'I managed to find those interviews with her among all the mess,' Jarnebring said. 'I've put them in the same plastic folder as the summary. Do you want to read them?'

Jarnebring held up a blue plastic folder.

'Why don't you tell me?' Johansson said, shaking his head. I don't feel up to it, he thought.

'The two interviews were conducted by the same officer, Carina Tell. Seriously attractive, must have been twenty years younger than me. Barely out of school. She'd been brought in from Solna, where she worked in Patrol Cars. She was clever, too, properly on the ball, and you should have seen the tits on her—'

'Get to the point,' Johansson said. 'What did the old woman she spoke to say? The Sagerlied woman?'

'She'd been away,' Jarnebring said. 'Left a couple of days before Yasmine went missing. Got home a couple of weeks later.'

'So where had she been?'

'At her place in the country, outside Vaxholm. On Rindö,' Jarnebring said. 'A big old place her husband left her. She used to spend her holidays there with an old friend who also used to be an opera singer.'

'You questioned her as well?'

'What do you take me for?' Jarnebring said. 'Her story matched Sagerlied's, down to the last comma. The friend was actually even older than she was – around eighty, if I remember rightly. Supposed to have been bloody well-known in her day. The friend, I mean.'

'Okay,' Johansson said. 'So what does she say? Margaretha Sagerlied?' Makes sense, he thought. If she spent time with someone who was eight years older than she was, she must have had her reasons.

'It boils down to four things,' Jarnebring said. 'Firstly, she had nothing to say on the matter. Because she was away when it happened.'

'And secondly?'

'Secondly, she knew Yasmine. Little Yasmine had been to see her a number of times. Pretty and pleasant and polite, according to Sagerlied. They even played the piano and sang together. Naturally, she was distraught about what had happened. But she was one hundred per cent certain that it couldn't have happened where she lived. Not in Äppelviken in Bromma, because only decent, educated people lived there.'

'Thirdly, then,' Johansson said. Definitely not where she lived, he thought. That must have been utterly unthinkable for her.

'Male contacts.'

'What about them?'

'There weren't any. No children, no grandchildren, no one else, either. Not on her side, or on her husband's. No younger contacts at all, of either gender. Old friends her own age, both sexes. People from the same background as her. Old singers, people who worked in the opera and the theatre, ex-actors, celebrities from her time, so to speak.'

'For God's sake,' Johansson said. 'You've seen the house she lived in. She must have had a cleaner, at the very least.' Someone who did the washing-up, he thought. In worn, pink rubber-gloves; her employer may have been a bit mean when it came to things like that.

'Officer Tell asked that very question. Like I said, she was on the ball. The old woman said she did the cleaning herself. And, before Christmas, she would employ a cleaning company. Same thing in the spring, when it came to cleaning all the windows and smartening things up before summer.'

'Rubbish,' Johansson snorted. 'What about workmen? Did she ever employ any?'

'She hadn't for several years. The last time they had any work done was when her husband was still alive and they had the gutters and drainpipes replaced. They installed new copper pipes because the old tin ones had rusted. Cost a fortune, apparently. I called Carina yesterday and asked. There was a lot of that sort of thing, reading between the lines. Money and famous names. The old woman had barely been asked about her place in the country before she started going on about its fifteen rooms and two verandas, and how much her father-in-law had paid for it.'

Obviously, Johansson thought. That was exactly what she was like. 'What about home helps?' he said.

'She didn't trust them. Wouldn't dream of having anyone sent by the council in her home. Not after she read in the papers about that Indian who strangled an old woman he was supposed to be helping. The one whose conviction was dismissed on appeal, if you remember?'

Yes, I do remember him, he thought. 'What about the fourth point, then?' Johansson said. 'What was that about?'

'The red Golf that was supposed to have been parked outside her house.'

'What did she have to say about that?'

'Not a thing. She couldn't drive and didn't have a car. No one she knew owned a red Golf. She didn't even know what sort of car it was.'

Not good, Johansson thought. Not good at all. Not when he could no longer see round corners.

'That officer . . .'

'Nina – Carina, Carina Tell.'

'Yes, her,' Johansson said. 'Is she still in the force?'

'Nope,' Jarnebring said. 'She left a few years ago. These days, she's some sort of lifestyle consultant. Very successful, by all accounts. Gives lectures, owns two gyms, personal trainer to half a dozen billionaires, as well as teaching a load of ordinary, fat, wealthy old men like you how to live a healthier life. She's even written a couple of books on how to do it.'

'How do you know that?'

'I know her,' Jarnebring said. 'I called and spoke to her. I told you that.' He gave a satisfied smile.

'How do you mean, you know her?'

'The usual way,' Jarnebring said with a grin. 'It was twenty-five years ago, before I met my wife.'

'You couldn't ask her to call me?'

'On one condition,' Jarnebring said, with an even broader smile.

'What's that?'

'That you don't say anything to Pia.'

'I won't,' Johansson said. Why would I do that? he thought. 'One more thing,' he said. 'There was one more thing.'

'Yes?'

'That second interview, the one Tell conducted five weeks later. What did Sagerlied say in that one?'

'Nothing,' Jarnebring said.

'Nothing?'

'No. Margaretha Sagerlied was the one who called Carina. She wondered how the investigation was going, if we had reached any conclusions. The usual, you know. The way every old dear who lives close to where something awful happened always phones and goes on. The interview was conducted over the phone. There wasn't any reason to go to talk to her at her home. Read it for yourself, if you don't believe me. Anything else you're wondering?'

'I'm tired,' Johansson said. 'Need to have a little nap.'

There he goes again, Jarnebring thought. Seems completely out of it. 'But you're doing fine,' he said.

'I am fine. Just need a little rest.'

'Look after yourself, Lars. See you tomorrow, same time, same place, same old team from Central Surveillance. Do you remember those days? The ten years we spent sitting in the front of the same clapped-out old Volvo?'

Then he leaned forward, put his arm round Johansson and hugged him tight.

'Promise to look after yourself, Lars,' he said.

'I promise.'

Five weeks later, she phones up to ask how it's going, Johansson thinks, staring at the door his best friend had just closed behind him. Gently, so as not to disturb him, as he thought Johansson was already drifting off.

What had happened in that time? he thought. To make her suddenly wonder how things were going? Someone she knew but hadn't thought of, not in that way? Someone who drove around in a red Golf? Or was it to do with a red plastic hairgrip? A red Monchhichi that she had perhaps found under the bed in her bedroom?

Then he fell asleep.

40

Friday, 23 July

Another day in his new life. Breakfast, physiotherapy and Matilda, who was actually going from strength to strength, in spite of all the rings and tattoos.

'What do you want to do now?' she asked when they were on their way home from the Karolinska.

'I'm going to see Jarnebring,' Johansson said.

'It's a few hours before he arrives,' Matilda said. 'Come on, what would you like to do if you were allowed to choose?'

'In that case, I'd like to go swimming,' Johansson said.

'Swimming,' Matilda said, and nodded towards his dangling right arm. 'Is that a good idea?'

'Listen,' Johansson said. 'I could still beat you by half a pool-length with both arms tied behind my back if I had to.'

'Okay,' Matilda said, smiling and shrugging her shoulders.

The Eriksdal pool or the Forgrénska at Medborgarplatsen lay closest, and were Matilda's suggestions. Johansson wanted to go to the Sture baths in the centre of the city, so that's what happened. He had to use the ladder to get into the pool; there was no way he could dive in now, not with a flapping right arm. No energetic crawl, no butterfly. Mostly backstroke with powerful kicks of his legs, helped by one arm. He hadn't felt so good since he got out of his car in front of the best hotdog kiosk in the world to buy a Zigeuner sausage with sauerkraut and Dijon mustard.

'Where did you learn to swim like that?' Matilda asked when they were sitting in the car on the way to Södermalm. 'You're pretty hot.'

'My eldest brother used to throw me in the river back home when I was little. I didn't have a lot of choice.'

'How old were you then?' She looked at him in surprise.

'A year or so,' Johansson said with a shrug.

'Wasn't he worried you'd drown?'

'No,' Johansson said. You don't know my brother, he thought.

After that she made lunch for him. Not quite up to Pia's standard, and still a few too many vegetables, but considering the way she looked, it was nothing short of a miracle.

'Good,' Johansson said, nodding towards his empty plate. 'Where did you learn to cook like that?'

'My brother used to throw me in the river when I was little,' Matilda said. 'I didn't have a lot of choice.'

Then Jarnebring called and asked to be let off that day's visit. The water leak in his daughter's kitchen had turned out to have had unforeseen consequences.

'It's got through to the cellar,' Jarnebring said. 'I'm sorry, but—'

'Don't worry,' Johansson said. 'See you on Monday.'

'Are you sure?' Jarnebring asked.

'Quite sure,' Johansson said. 'Give me a ring if you need any advice about proper plumbers.'

'Can't afford it,' Jarnebring said. 'I've just filled up that car I bought off you. So what are you going to do?'

'I'm going to lie on the sofa and read some old interviews,' Johansson said.

For practical reasons, those ended up being the interviews with Margaretha Sagerlied that Jarnebring had already dug out for him. The idea of poking about among all the bundles in the boxes never entered his head.

The first interview that Officer Tell had conducted with Margaretha Sagerlied was dated 2 July 1985, eighteen days after Yasmine went missing. It had commenced at quarter past two in the afternoon and concluded at five minutes past five. Almost three hours, which was practically unique for a door-to-door interview. All too often you had to make do with the five minutes it took to ring the doorbell and ask if whoever opened the door – if you were lucky – 'had seen or heard anything'. They usually hadn't, and five minutes was normally more than long enough. Carina Tell had been thorough and systematic, and Margaretha Sagerlied both talkative and accommodating. The interview stretched to almost ten pages. It had been recorded on tape, summarized, printed out, read and verified by Margaretha Sagerlied.

There wasn't really anything in the interview that Jarnebring hadn't already told him. One or two details, perhaps. That Margaretha Sagerlied had two cats, for instance. Which she had obviously taken with her when she went to the country. That none of her neighbours had a key to her house. She valued her privacy: no one in the house if she wasn't at home; and the people she socialized with were all of the same age as her. Came from the same background as her. She knew them all well, had known them for many years.

Everything Johansson read annoyed him intensely. Especially since he was unable to put his finger on what it was that was upsetting him. Could she have had a lover, or some attentive cavalier, someone she didn't want to mention? Was she lying, or was it just that she didn't understand what the police were looking for? A younger man. Seen through her eyes, a perfectly ordinary, normal younger man. Someone she knew and trusted, because he wasn't only entirely normal but also educated and sociable, polite and attentive. Nothing like the monster who had raped and murdered little Yasmine.

Johansson barely had time to put the document down before Carina Tell called him on his mobile.

'Carina Tell,' she said. 'I've spoken to your good friend Bo Jarnebring and he led me to believe that you'd like to talk to me.'

'Yes,' Johansson said. 'I don't suppose there's any way you could call in?'

'I can be with you in half an hour,' she said. 'I'm down at the gym. I just need to have a quick shower first.'

'Splendid,' Johansson said. 'Let me give you—'

'I've got your address and the code for the door,' she interrupted. 'See you in half an hour.'

A very efficient woman. And punctual, he thought, when the doorbell rang exactly half an hour later.

41

Friday afternoon, 23 July

'Sit yourself down,' Johansson said, gesturing to the nearest chair. 'You must forgive me if I don't get up to say hello, but I've been a little under the weather recently.' A very attractive woman, Johansson thought. Almost as attractive as Pia.

'Would you like anything?' he added.

'Thanks, I'm fine,' Carina Tell said. 'I understand that you wanted to talk about Yasmine's murder. And that you're particularly interested in the old opera singer I interviewed when we went door-to-door.'

'That's right,' Johansson said. 'I've read both your interviews with her.'

'Just one question,' Carina Tell said, smiling at him. 'To be honest, because obviously I know who you are, I don't really understand why you're interested in this old case. Would you mind explaining?'

'It's mostly a feeling I've got,' Johansson said. 'Tell me, instead, do you remember what Margaretha Sagerlied was like as a person? I never met her, as you'll appreciate.'

'Yes, I remember her. A bit self-obsessed, to put it mildly. She was happy to talk at length about herself, her career as a singer and all the fancy people and celebrities she knew. But what had happened to Yasmine still seemed to have hit her hard. She had tears in her eyes when she talked about her. She described her as a quite enchanting little girl. Yasmine had been round to her house several times. They used to play the piano and sing together.'

'How did she live, then? Tell me what her house looked like. Do you remember?'

'A large villa. Furniture and carpets and crystal chandeliers. Paintings and photographs, ornaments, vases and pot-plants. I remember, we sat in her living room. There were things everywhere. There must have been at least ten large photographs in silver frames of her in different roles she had sung. And there was a small photograph of her late husband. He had to make do with a black wooden frame. It was on the mantelpiece above the open fire. He can't have had an easy life, poor sod. She had two big cats as well. Those creepy, long-haired ones. I've never liked cats.'

'And she'd taken the cats to the country with her?'

'Yes,' Carina Tell said, nodding. 'Naturally, I asked, and I'm fairly sure she was telling the truth. She'd taken the cats with her to the country.'

'No cleaner? No one who looked after the house?'

'No, I spent quite some time asking about that. She was very clear on that point. She did all her own cleaning. Before Christmas and in the spring she got a cleaning company in to go through the house properly, clean the windows and so on.'

'What about the garden?' Johansson said. 'Who looked after that for her? All those damn plants and pots? Who watered them?'

'She did. She was very interested in gardening, and there was nothing to indicate otherwise. She had loads of flowerbeds, and a big fruit garden.'

'She must have had a cleaner,' Johansson said, finding it hard to conceal his irritation. Margaretha Sagerlied wasn't the sort to clean up after herself, he thought. How stupid could you be?

'Why do you think that?'

'From what you're saying,' Johansson said, 'I'm having trouble believing that she was the sort of woman who did her own cleaning, laundry and washing-up – anything like that.'

'Why not?' Carina Tell retorted. 'She was in good health. Lively and mobile. Seemed a lot younger than she was.'

'I hear what you're saying,' Johansson said. 'Listen, she was gone for two weeks. It was hot and sunny pretty much the whole time. She must have had someone to water the pot-plants. Not to mention the flowerbeds and the lawn.'

'I don't recall us talking about that particular detail. But now that you come to mention it . . .'

'Could she have had someone working for her unofficially? And that was why she didn't say anything?'

'I didn't ask about that,' Carina Tell said with a smile. 'If she was using black-market labour, I mean. Stupid of me. I was twenty-three years old. I'd been a police officer for one year. I was sitting there interviewing a smart old lady of seventy or so. Obviously, I should have asked if she made a habit of employing black-market staff.'

Yes, it was stupid of you not to do that, Johansson thought. Incredibly fucking stupid of you.

'Just out of curiosity,' he said. 'That second interview, the one you conducted over the phone?'

'I don't know that it was an interview,' Carina Tell said. 'She was the one who called me. She had a question, I think. I remember asking her if she'd thought of anything else. Anything she wanted to add. But she didn't. Mostly, she wanted to hear how we were getting on. What I wrote up afterwards was mainly just a note to say that she'd called.'

'Did you get the impression that she was poking about?'

'No, definitely not. It was the usual thing with old ladies – anxious, of course, and curious. I remember her asking if we'd found that car we were looking for. The red Golf.'

'What did you say?'

'I said it was no longer an issue. That the witness had changed his mind. That it was no longer of interest to us. She couldn't drive, and didn't own a car. Didn't know a thing about them. She barely knew the difference between a Volvo and a Saab.'

'How did you get round that, then?'

'I was young and ambitious in those days, so when I spoke to her the first time, obviously, I had a picture of a red Golf with me.'

'And?'

'No, it wasn't a car that she recognized. Those of her friends who had cars certainly didn't drive about in such small models. She was very definite on that point. They drove Mercedes and Jaguars and BMWs, things like that. Her husband used to prefer big American cars. That was what she said. He had a Lincoln when he died. I think she was almost offended that I thought she might go

209

about in such a ridiculous little car. That was what she said when I showed her the picture of the Golf the first time. That neither she nor anyone she knew would drive about in such a ridiculous little car.'

'So you were sitting inside her house when you questioned her?'

'Yes, first we sat in her living room and talked, like I said, and before I left she showed me the rest of the house.'

'And you were happy to take a look around?'

'Of course,' Carina Tell said. 'What do you take me for?'

'So tell me,' Johansson said. 'What was it like?'

'Over-furnished, like I said. Things absolutely everywhere. A lot of nice stuff, of course: antiques and carpets and crystal chandeliers and paintings that were probably worth a bit. But because there was so much there, you didn't really pay much attention to any of it.'

'The living room was downstairs, on the ground floor?'

'Yes.' Carina Tell nodded. 'Let's see if I can remember. First, you entered a big hall. Then off to the left was the kitchen and a serving room. On the right was an old library. Her husband had used it as his gentleman's room, or study, she said.'

'And?'

'Straight ahead was a large living room, with a glazed veranda facing the garden. That was where we were sitting when I questioned her. To the left of that was a dining room. It wasn't a bad house at all, very fancy, really. It would cost a fortune today.'

'And upstairs?'

'First, the landing. Straight ahead, above the living room, was a big room that she used as a music room.

There was a huge grand piano in there – I remember thinking that it couldn't have been easy getting it up all those stairs. Next to the music room was her bedroom, with a separate room for all her clothes, a dressing room and a large bathroom. She and her husband had evidently had separate bedrooms when he was alive. I remember that her husband's room and bathroom – he had his own bathroom as well, although hers was at least twice the size – faced the street. Then there was a sewing room and a couple of smaller bedrooms. In total, there must have been eight or ten rooms in the house. Oh, and there was a maid's room behind the kitchen as well. But that had stood empty for years, apparently. When her husband was still alive they had a housekeeper who slept in there, but she left just a year or so after the husband died.'

'Cellar?'

'Yes, there was one. Steps down from the kitchen, but I didn't see it. But she made sure to let me know that was where she kept all her wine.'

'Attic?'

'I didn't see that either.'

'Well, then,' Johansson said. Over-furnished, he thought. Things everywhere. Wine in the cellar, and God knows what up in the attic. Plenty to snoop about in if you were that way inclined.

'So, tell me . . .' Carina Tell leaned forward and smiled at him. 'Why are you so interested in Margaretha Sagerlied and her house?'

'I have a feeling that was where it happened. That that was where Yasmine was murdered, I mean.'

'With all due respect,' Carina Tell said, shaking her head, 'I really, really can't believe that. How can you think that?'

'Mostly just a feeling,' Johansson said, with a shrug.

'Okay. I hear what you're saying. But if that's true, then the woman who lived there, Margaretha Sagerlied, couldn't have had any idea about it. I'm absolutely certain of that. A thousand per cent.'

'I agree with you,' Johansson said. 'She couldn't have known anything about it.' She only realized that later, he thought. And it blew her world apart. 'Nothing else you can think of about the investigation?'

'I actually think about it fairly regularly,' she said. 'For various reasons. One of my clients – he trains at one of my gyms – used to live in the next street from Yasmine and Margaretha Sagerlied at the time it happened. I sometimes see him several times a week.'

'Who's he, then?'

'Retired military – I think he even made it as far as General before he left. He's over eighty. Doesn't seem a day past sixty. Alert and in good shape, still got all his marbles.' For some reason Carina Tell was smiling and nodding at Johansson.

'So what's his name?' Johansson asked. The bastard must have a name, people who go to gyms usually do, he thought.

'Axel Linderoth,' Carina Tell said. 'I'm sure he's in the phone directory, and if he isn't I can get you his number. I've a feeling he was a lieutenant general when he retired. Lieutenant general in Defence Command. I might as well give you my card while I'm here.' She stood up and put her business card on the table.

'Thanks.'

'Feel free to get in touch. I could help you with all that fat you're dragging around, quite unnecessarily.'

'That's very kind of you, Carina,' Johansson said. 'Very kind of you to volunteer, and I promise to consider your offer carefully and in a positive spirit.' And you're very lucky I wasn't your boss back then, he thought.

'Good,' Carina Tell said. 'Say hi to your wife.'

'You know Pia?'

'She comes to the gym. Anyone sensible who cares about their health does.'

And then she left, with a nod and a smile, closing the door behind her. Here you lie, Johansson thought. Alone, fat and out of the game, barely able to roll over on your own sofa. But no headache any more, no anxiety. It was even easier to breathe. I'll get you soon enough, he thought. I'll get you. In spite of everyone who thinks you don't even exist.

42

Friday afternoon, 23 July

Johansson was tired, but he couldn't sleep. He lay there on his sofa, twisting and turning, paddling with his healthy left arm, but he couldn't find any peace of mind. No nap-giving tranquillity. So he had no choice.

'Matilda!' Johansson roared. 'For God's sake, woman!'

She came rushing in like a shot – she must have been standing ready to move outside the closed door of his study; it took a second at most – and Johansson immediately felt much brighter.

'Has anything happened?' Matilda asked.

'No, damn it,' Johansson said. 'Everything's fine. Just doing a test run, that's all.'

'I see. And?'

'Well, seeing as you're here now, I was wondering if you could get hold of a telephone number for me?' He gestured towards the business card that Carina Tell had left on the table.

'It's on there,' Matilda said. 'Carina Tell, her number's—'

'On the back.'

'Axel Linderoth?'

'That's the one,' Johansson said with unexpected warmth in his voice. 'Good girl. He lives in Bromma. Retired army officer.' What do you mean, good girl? he thought. Why am I saying that?

'Okay, boss. Anything else?'

'A triple espresso. The strong sort. No milk.'

'Coming right up,' Matilda said, and disappeared.

Boss, Johansson thought. Why is she calling me boss? She isn't a police officer.

'Do you want me to dial the number for you?' Matilda looked at him innocently.

'Yes, if you wouldn't mind,' Johansson said. That serves you right, he thought.

'Do it yourself,' Matilda said. 'It's important to prac- tise your motor skills.'

Then she walked out and closed the door on him. 'Just shout if you want anything, boss.'

Lively girl. No chance of running rings round her. I need to talk to her about those tattoos, he thought.

Then he dialled the number of the retired general and, as he did so, he thought about what he was going to say. A mixture of white lies, he thought. He'd been a general in Defence Command, so he probably wouldn't mind.

The general answered on the first ring.

'Linderoth,' former Lieutenant General Axel Linderoth said. He sounded like one as well.

'Johansson,' Johansson said. 'I hope I'm not disturb- ing you, but I've got a question. I was wondering—'

'I know what you want,' Linderoth interrupted. 'Carina Tell, my personal trainer, called and told me.'

Not partial to lengthy preambles, then, Johansson thought.

'If it's urgent, then we have a practical problem,' Linderoth said. 'I'm going down to Skåne first thing tomorrow. Playing golf for a week.'

'I can be with you in half an hour.'

'Agreed,' Linderoth said.

'Matilda!' Johansson roared as soon as he had hung up.

Might as well ask her, Johansson thought when they were sitting in the car about to head off to Äppelviken in Bromma to visit a retired lieutenant general.

'There's something I've been wondering,' Johansson said.

'Go ahead, boss,' Matilda said.

'Why do you call me boss?'

'I heard at work that you were some sort of supercop. Head of the Security Police and then head of that other lot – National Crime. Well, before you retired, of course.'

'Oh,' Johansson said. 'So you heard about that.'

'Yes, although to start with, I thought you were like all the rest of our clients. When I saw the way you lived and all that.'

'Like all the rest?'

'Yes, a bean-counter. One of those bonus-junkies who've fallen to earth in spite of their parachutes. I could call you director if you'd rather.'

'Boss is fine,' Johansson said. Smart girl, thought Johansson. Presumably, it was possible to have those tattoos removed.

'Of course, boss. Glad that's sorted.'

'Äppelviksgatan,' Johansson said.

'I know.' Matilda nodded towards the dashboard. 'I've already put the address in the satnav.'

Johansson contented himself with a nod. What's someone like her doing with people like me? he thought. Melancholy, he thought.

An agreeable feeling of melancholy spread through his body. She knew how to drive as well, smoothly and efficiently. Almost like his best friend, when he was in the mood.

'I think it would be best if I stayed in the car,' Matilda said as she pulled up in front of the yellow wooden villa.

'What for?'

'Retired army officer,' Matilda said.

Johansson made do with a nod. We're predictable as well, he thought.

'Here,' she said, and leaned over and popped his dictaphone in the breast pocket of his jacket.

'Then you don't have to worry about taking notes. I've switched it on. The battery's supposed to last at least twenty-four hours. If you don't want him to know you've got it, you can just leave it in your pocket. It will cope with that fine.'

'Thank you,' Johansson said. 'Thanks, Matilda. That's very kind of you.'

43

Friday afternoon, 23 July

'Coffee, juice, water?' Axel Linderoth said, pointing in turn at a steel Thermos flask, a jug of red juice and a large bottle of Ramlösa that he had placed on the garden table where they were sitting, along with two glasses and two white porcelain mugs with the emblem of the armed forces on them.

'Water would be good,' Johansson said. This man doesn't need a uniform, he thought. Slim, fit, suntanned; white cotton trousers and a short-sleeved, red polo shirt. Didn't look a day over sixty. A very fit sixty.

'My then wife and I – I've been a widower for five years – moved here in 1972,' the general said. 'And as you can see, I still live here. Our three sons have long since moved out. Grown men, these days. The eldest is forty-one, the middle one forty, the youngest thirty-nine.'

'Quick work,' Johansson said. Sixteen, fifteen and fourteen years old when Yasmine went missing. Just like that, he thought. He hadn't even had to think about it.

'Yes,' the general said with a slight smile. 'I was almost forty when I had the first of them. My wife, admittedly, was eight years younger than me, but a rapid advance across the terrain was called for if the Linderoth family was to have a future.'

'Were you here when it happened? When little Yasmine went missing, I mean, in June 1985?'

'I was in the Middle East, working for the UN in the Gaza Strip. So I didn't have to deal with your colleagues. My wife and our boys didn't get off as lightly.'

'They were at home,' Johansson stated.

'No,' the former general said. 'They weren't, but it took a fair while for your colleagues to grasp that point.'

'I daresay that was just a regrettable matter of routine that sometimes happens in cases like this. Necessary routine,' Johansson emphasized.

'Apparently so,' the general concurred with a grim expression. 'My wife and sons had gone down to Skåne the weekend before to visit her parents. The boys' grandparents. They got home a few days after that little girl went missing. They had plane tickets, plenty of witnesses down in Skåne – aside from my parents-in-law, I should point out. But that didn't help them in the slightest. One of your colleagues seems to have been a uniquely persistent and stupid individual. A fat little fellow. My wife called me in Gaza in tears. I got angry and called the Chief of Police. He was a good man – we knew each other from his time with the Security Police. He sorted the idiot out, told him to get his act together. So, at long last, my wife and sons were left in peace. What had happened was bad enough in itself – it really was a terrible business – but you probably had to be a police officer to get it into your head that it had actually happened out here.'

It's always Bäckström, Johansson thought.

219

'You don't believe it could have happened here?'

'Certainly not. You only need a pair of eyes in your head to realize that. Wrong area, wrong people. And the only neighbours who were at home at the time were pensioners. More water?' the general asked, nodding towards Johansson's empty glass.

'Thank you,' Johansson said. 'Yes, please.'

'I remember there being a huge fuss about some little red car that was supposed to have been parked here that evening. Over on the corner, by the junction with Majblommestigen,' the general said, gesturing in that direction. 'A hundred metres down the road from where we're sitting,' he clarified. 'Supposed to have been parked outside Johan Nilsson's house.'

'Johan Nilsson?' Where have I heard that name before? Johansson thought.

'Correction,' the general said with a slight smile. 'The house where Johan Nilsson used to live. He was already dead when it happened. But his dear wife, his widow, still lived there.'

'Margaretha Sagerlied,' Johansson said.

'The very same,' the general said. 'Born Svensson, Margaretha Svensson, which is one of many things she preferred not to talk about. In contrast to all the things she loved to talk about.'

'What was she like?'

'Stuck-up, tedious, phenomenally self-obsessed. But her husband was a good man. I both ate crayfish and drank schnapps in his company. He was old enough to be my father, but that wasn't an issue at all. He was a smart businessman, too. Traded in meat and charcuterie, had a big wholesale business out in Årsta and Enskede. And he owned several grocery stores in the city centre.

His wife, the opera singer, wasn't left short, if I can put it like that.'

'I understand that they married late in life?'

'Yes, so Johan told me. About all the years he spent courting her before she finally agreed. And about all the years it took him to realize that he should have spent his time doing something else instead.'

'Was he bitter?' What does that have to do with anything? Johansson thought.

'No, not in the slightest. He was a good-natured man, kind and decent, very generous. But after a few glasses when there were just the two of us, he could be fairly open-hearted.'

'Had he had any previous relationships? By which I mean, did he have any children from previous relationships?'

'No,' the general said. 'He often spoke about that: it was something of a regret to him. He was very fond of my boys, I remember. He couldn't have had it easy, not with that wife,' the general declared with a sigh. 'That red car – I seem to recall my wife saying it was a Golf – I don't think that's anything to get hung up about.'

'You don't think so?' Johansson said. 'Why not?'

'Not bearing in mind who it was who claimed to have seen it. The local nuisance. An officious little man who poked his nose into all manner of things where it had no business. A proper little busybody.'

'What sort of thing did he poke his nose into?'

'Everything,' the general said. 'The school board, the Parents' Association; then he was going to set up some sort of neighbourhood-watch scheme in the area, and organize care of elderly residents, local parties, Christmas festivities. Shared transport for people who wanted to go to church on Christmas Eve but might have had one too many drinks that evening, which was pretty much everyone round here, if you ask me. He used to roam about in the evenings with a huge, black beast of a dog. He was a short, skinny little man, so when you saw them together it looked like the dog was taking him for a walk.'

'Do you remember what his job was?'

'He was some sort of lawyer. I think he worked for the National Audit Office. Terribly exciting, no doubt.'

'Is he still alive?'

'No, he's dead. Died a few years after that business with the little girl. Heart attack, I seem to remember. As so often happens when you spend your whole life worrying about anything and everything.'

'So Johan Nilsson had no children of his own from a previous relationship?' Just drop it, Johansson thought. You've been wrong before, after all.

'No,' the general said.

'His wife,' Johansson said. 'After her husband died, did she have a wide circle of acquaintances?'

'I'm not sure I could say that,' the general said. 'A number of elderly people like herself, from the same background. Cultural personalities, I suppose they were. Mostly, she spent her time alone. She wasn't particularly popular as a neighbour. You used to say hello to her, but that was about it.'

'A big house,' Johansson said. 'She must have had someone to help her? With the house and the garden?'

'When her husband was alive, in Johan's time, they had a housekeeper who lived with them. Quite a lot of parties back then, when they'd hire extra staff. My wife and I went on a number of occasions, despite the difference in our ages. But the housekeeper left as soon

222

as Johan was dead. I think she moved out before the funeral. Why she did that is a matter of speculation.'

'What do you think, then?'

'Margaretha Sagerlied was a difficult woman. She was never particularly pleasant.'

'So, from then on, she looked after herself?'

'Not at all,' the general said. 'She got hold of a new cleaner and factotum more or less immediately. As a rule, they only used to stay for a year or so before leaving. Until she got hold of Erika – Erika Brännström.'

'Erika Brännström?'

'An excellent person, very pleasant, very patient,' the general said with a smile. 'From Norrland. You Norrlanders are made of stern stuff. She must have worked for Sagerlied for several years. Until she, too, moved out. I have a feeling that Margaretha Sagerlied sold the house in the spring of the year after that little girl was murdered. In the spring of '86. I'm fairly sure of that. I was sent back to Gaza in the autumn, and when I got home just before Christmas the house was already for sale. My wife and I actually went to look at it, but it was a bit too expensive, even then, for a man in the service of the crown. Margaretha Sagerlied had already moved into the city centre. She'd bought an apartment in Östermalm, so the house out here was empty.'

'When Margaretha Sagerlied was interviewed – coincidentally, by our mutual acquaintance, Carina Tell – she was adamant that she didn't have any staff. She claimed she looked after everything herself. Why would she say something like that?' Considering how smart she pretended to be otherwise, Johansson thought.

'I suppose Erika was working unofficially,' the general said.

'What makes you say that?'

'Well, she certainly was when she used to help my wife and me with the cleaning,' the former general said.

'Erika Brännström,' Johansson said.

'Erika Brännström,' the general confirmed. 'Her husband had found a new woman and moved in with her. She had two little girls she was raising on her own. She was probably around thirty-five at the time. Must be about sixty now. Lived on Lilla Essinge with her daughters.'

'Do you know if she's still alive?' Johansson asked. She had two little girls, he thought.

'I know she's alive,' the general said. 'I spoke to her as recently as last week. I met her on the tram from Alvik. She was going to visit a friend who lived out in Nockeby.'

'Do you happen to have her phone number?'

'Yes,' the general said. 'I asked if she might still be interested in helping an old man like me with his cleaning.'

'And she was?'

'Yes,' the general said. 'She was. I'll get her number for you. I wrote it in my book, it's in the hall.'

Things are moving along nicely, Johansson thought. The only explanation was, presumably, that it was already too late to make any difference. Erika Brännström, who was Margaretha Sagerlied's cleaner for several years and had two small girls. Wonder who the father was? he thought. This man who's supposed to have left her. Who was he?

224

44

Friday afternoon, 23 July

Home at last. No place like home. Never had been, and all the more so now.

This is going swimmingly, Johansson thought.

He clutched the rubber-pointed stick firmly as Matilda held the door open for him, with a gentle grip on his bad arm, and as soon as he had crossed the threshold he had a brilliant idea. A quite magnificent idea.

'Alf Hult,' Johansson said, nodding to Matilda. 'Alf Hult,' he repeated.

'Alf Hult?'

'Exactly,' Johansson said. 'Alf Hult.'

Friday evening, 23 July

It wasn't just his investigation that was making progress. Even his physical health was improving, day by day. No great strides, just tiny little steps that took him closer to the life he had lived before. But what was going on inside his head was more complicated. Things kept happening up there the whole time, and there was no structure or order to any of it. And there were also the headaches that plagued him as good as daily. One thing at a time, he used to think. One thing at a time.

A beautiful evening. After some persuasion, his wife had agreed that they should eat out on the terrace, the way they always used to on fine summer's evenings when they ate dinner in the city. He walked up the stairs under his own steam. Without his stick, which was mostly just in the way; on his legs, his left hand on the handrail to stop him falling. Pia walked behind him, even though he tried to tell her not to.

'I'll only break your arms and legs if I go arse over tit,' Johansson said. Stubborn as hell.

He's starting to get back to his old self again, his wife thought. Restless as an old horse.

When they were drinking coffee after the meal he told her about the brilliant idea he'd had only a couple of hours earlier.

'I've invited Alf for lunch tomorrow,' Johansson said.

'Alf?'

'Alf Hult.'

'Your brother-in-law?'

'Yes,' Johansson said.

'Is Anna coming, too?' Pia asked, unable to hide her surprise.

'Anna? Which Anna?'

'Your sister. Your youngest sister.'

'Well, of course I know she's my little sister. No, she's not coming. Just Alf and me.'

'I see. I didn't think you could bear to be in the same room as him,' Pia said, recalling a number of Johansson family gatherings.

'That's a bit of an exaggeration,' Johansson said. 'Alf's got a lot of good points. In some respects, he's a completely unique person,' he added, for some reason.

'That's not the impression I've ever got,' Pia said. 'That you were so fond of Alf,' she explained. 'Out of curiosity: why do you want to see him, all of a sudden?'

'I've employed him,' Johansson said. The best idea I've had since I took that detour to Günter's that saved my life, he thought.

46

Saturday morning, 24 July

Alf Hult was a retired auditor. Married to Johansson's younger sister, Anna, the last of Mother Elna and Father Evert's large brood of children. An afterthought, five years younger than the previous child, former head of the National Crime Unit, Lars Martin Johansson.

Alf Hult had spent his career working for the tax office out in Solna, for almost forty years, from the time he gained his accountancy qualification to his retirement. He was successful, and feared, with good reason, by the individuals and legal entities that were the subjects of his audits.

Johansson's eldest brother Evert loathed him with all his heart. According to Evert, Alf Hult was a threat to every form of normal business, and human life in general, and he rarely even needed a drink inside him to vent his opinion on the subject.

Alf Hult wasn't the sort of man to care. He had a hawkish appearance, was tall and skinny, with thinning hair, and in good shape. He was slightly stooped after several decades bent over the attempts of the subjects of his audits to evade their social responsibilities and duties as citizens. He wasn't a coward either and, at his wife's fiftieth-birthday dinner, which big brother Evert was obliged to attend in the name of family unity, he had even given his brother-in-law a gentle reprimand over the coffee and cognac.

'You may think I have a long nose, but to date no one has been able to lead me by it.'

After he retired Alf Hult began to get interested in genealogy. He became passionate about it, applying the same intellect, objectivity and precision that he had previously devoted to his auditing. Because he was as conscientious with his own business as anyone else's, he had also run his own successful one-man family-history business for the past few years. Naturally, he had already investigated his wife's sprawling family. This he had done in his usual way, without sidestepping even marginal historical shortcomings, thereby incurring even more displeasure from the family's two patriarchs, Father Evert and his eldest son, Evert, known as 'Little Evert' until he reached his majority, when his father spoke publicly for the first time about the inevitable.

'From now on I don't want any of you to call my eldest son "Little Evert",' said Big Evert. 'There are now two Everts, and soon enough he'll be the one who takes over.'

You, Alf, can be the Sherlock to my Mycroft, Lars Martin Johansson thought when he had his brilliant idea. Mycroft Holmes, Sherlock Holmes's elder brother, who didn't even have to leave the comfort of his armchair to solve even the most complicated of crimes. What could be more fitting, bearing in mind the fact that Johansson now spent most of his time lying on the sofa in his study? That was as close to the field as he could get under his own steam these days. He noted that he suddenly had no difficulty remembering the name of the elder of the Holmes brothers.

Now Johansson's very own Sherlock was sitting at his right side, former auditor Alf Hult, with his sharp features, leaning forward slightly in the armchair he had pulled over to the sofa so as not to overexert his brother-in-law unnecessarily. Happy to listen, parrying, *toujours*, always ready to counter all forms of dastardly deeds and insidious traps.

'Margaretha Sagerlied and her husband, Johan Nilsson,' Alf Hult said, nodding thoughtfully at his own notes.

'And Sagerlied's old cleaner, Erika Brännström,' Johansson said.

'Not so old, perhaps,' Hult said. 'If your information is correct, she ought to be considerably younger than both you and me.'

'Shouldn't be any problems, should there?' Johansson wondered. 'The only one whose date of birth and ID number I've got is Sagerlied. As far as Erika Brännström is concerned, all I've got is the address and phone number I gave you.'

'No problem at all,' Alf Hult said with a light shake of his head. 'What do you want to know?'

'Everything,' Johansson said.

'Everything,' his brother-in-law repeated. 'Then I ought perhaps to let you know that this sort of thing can quickly get out of hand, in terms of cost.'

'Cost doesn't matter,' Johansson said with a dismissive gesture, as he was the second wealthiest member of his extensive family.

'And you want it within a week?'

'Exactly,' Johansson said. 'Plenty of time for you to smoke your three pipes.' Mycroft smoked cigars, didn't he? he thought.

'Conan Doyle has never been a favourite of mine,' Alf Hult declared. 'Far too much of a romantic for my taste.'

47

Monday, 26 July

Monday. A new week and another day in a life that had almost been lost. Breakfast, physiotherapy and a check-up with Ulrika Stenholm, forty-four years old and without the slightest wrinkle on her smooth, white neck. Neurologist, vicar's daughter. Bore a striking resemblance to a squirrel when she sat and twitched her head of cropped blonde hair.

'How are you getting on?'

'Things are going forwards,' Johansson said. Never mind the constant headache, the tightness in your chest and the seal's flipper you've got in place of your right arm. Stop whining, he thought.

'That's my impression as well,' she agreed. 'That things are going forwards. Your physiotherapist is very pleased with you, by the way. And I heard from Pia that things are working out well at home.'

What would Pia know about that? he thought with sudden bitterness. 'And how are you getting on?' Johansson asked.

'Nothing.' Ulrika Stenholm shook her head. 'I've been through all of Dad's papers now. All the bags and boxes, and I promise I was thorough. I haven't found anything since that hairgrip and the envelope it was in.'

'You must have found something?' Johansson interjected.

'Nothing about Yasmine. A few old programmes about Margaretha Sagerlied singing in Bromma church, a couple of invitations for my parents to have dinner with her back when her husband was still alive, some old photographs that must have been taken when Dad and Mum were visiting her and her husband. One where she's singing in church. I think that was at some Christmas service in the seventies. I put it all in here,' she said, handing him a brown envelope.

'That's all?'

'That's all,' Ulrika Stenholm said. 'How about you? How's it going?'

'It's going well,' Johansson said. 'I'll have him soon.' Why am I saying that? he thought.

'Do you know who it is? Can you tell me who it is?' Ulrika Stenholm had trouble concealing her surprise.

'I promise, you'll be the first to know,' Johansson said. Why am I saying that? he thought.

'You promise?'

'I promise.' I just need to peer round the next corner first, he thought.

'I feel like a fucking traitor,' his best friend said three hours later.

'I'm listening,' Lars Martin Johansson said, even though he had already worked out what this was about.

It was the usual story about marital difficulties and unexpected complications. It had all started with Jarnebring's

233

new car. Quite regardless of the fact that he had got it at half price, they had more pressing expenses, according to Jarnebring's wife. Especially for two middle-aged people who were supposed to live on his police pension and her teacher's salary.

'So what did you do, then?' Johansson asked, even though he already knew the answer.

'I backed down,' Jarnebring said. 'She's booked a last-minute holiday for us, to Thailand, so I'm left looking like an idiot. A romantic holiday, so she can work out if she still wants me. It's only a week, admittedly, but even so.'

'At the height of the Swedish summer,' Johansson said, suddenly feeling the elation that these days seemed to alternate with the headache, the tightness in his chest, his angst, anger and melancholy. Sell the car, he thought.

'Women,' Jarnebring said.

'It'll be fine,' Johansson said. Just promise not to say anything to my brother, he thought.

'I've already spoken to your brother, by the way,' Jarnebring said, as if he could read his thoughts.

'And what did he say?'

'That I should be careful not to let the women take over,' Jarnebring replied. 'Then he recommended some nice places in Thailand.'

Sounds like Evert, Johansson thought.

As soon as Jarnebring had left, Matilda came in with a large cup of tea and a perfectly respectable sandwich. Coarse rye bread, lettuce, sliced tomato, all covered with a generous layer of air-dried ham, and enough to prompt a pang of conscience.

'I haven't been looked after like this since I was little and was off school sick,' Johansson said. Stop whining, he thought.

'Company policy,' Matilda said, then nodded towards the boxes of paper on the floor beside the sofa. 'Is that an old case you're working on? You know you're supposed to be taking things easy and not getting stressed. You've got to learn to chillax a bit.'

'I don't know if I'd call it a case,' Johansson said. 'It's an old, unsolved murder.'

'A murder – cool!'

'Don't be childish,' Johansson said, shaking his head. 'It's not the least bit cool. It's nothing but tragic and miserable. Gruesome, too.'

'I could help, if you like.'

'I doubt that,' Johansson said.

'Why not?'

'The investigation is confidential, to stop inquisitive souls like you from going through it.'

'You don't have to worry about me,' Matilda said. 'I'm not a gossip.'

Not a gossip, he thought. 'Okay,' Johansson said, suddenly struck by another thought. 'Do you know your way around the internet?'

'Not as well as Lisbeth Salander, but I'm not bad.'

Who the fuck is Lisbeth Salander? Johansson thought.

'Maybe you could have a look and see if you can find anything online about someone called Joseph Simon, with a "ph" at the end; otherwise, like it sounds.'

'By all means. You'll soon know everything about him,' Matilda promised, even though she wasn't as good as Lisbeth Salander. 'Is he the bad guy?'

'No,' Johansson said. 'He's a doctor, born 1951. Arrived in Sweden as a political refugee from Iran in 1979. Left Sweden and moved to the USA in 1990. Supposed to be very rich, works in pharmaceuticals.'

'Why are you so interested in him? If he isn't the bad guy, I mean.'

'I want to know how he's dealt with his grief,' Johansson said.

Pia gets home from work and asks how he is.

'Fine,' Johansson replies with a smile. Even though his head aches and his chest feels tight. Even though just a quarter of an hour earlier he took one of those white pills he's supposed to take in emergencies. Because his angst suddenly shook him up as if he were a small child, and his one salvation is the detachment that only a little white tablet can offer him.

'Like a pig in shit,' Johansson lies. 'Come and sit down here. Tell me how you're getting on at the bank, darling.' Why am I saying that? he thinks. Why didn't I just ask how she got on at work?

That evening his brother-in-law rang to tell him that his work was going better than expected and that he hadn't encountered any insurmountable problems yet.

'I've pretty much finished with Erika Brännström and her two daughters,' he said.

'Have you found their father?'

'Yes,' Alf Hult said. 'They've both got the same father. His name is Tommy Högberg, born 1956. Three years younger than Erika Brännström, who was born in '53. The oldest daughter, Karolina, was born in 1975, and her younger sister, Jessica, in '79. Erika never married

236

Tommy Högberg, but they lived together and he acknowledged his paternity of the two girls. Do you want it by fax or email?'

'Fax,' Johansson said. 'Then I won't have to fiddle about with all those little buttons on the computer,' he explained. So he acknowledged paternity, he thought.

'Judging by his taxable income, the father seems a bit of a layabout. Maybe you should check with your former colleagues to see if he's been active in your area of expertise. I wouldn't be at all surprised.'

'Really?' Johansson said. I wonder if Tommy Högberg has anything else he'd like to confess? he thought.

Then he ended the call, and had barely put the phone down before he fell asleep.

48

Tuesday morning, 27 July

As usual, Johannson spent the morning trying to regain his health. When he and Matilda returned from the physiotherapist, she suggested a walk around the block in which he lived.

'I've already done my exercise,' Johansson countered.

'Come on,' Matilda said. 'You can't have too much exercise.'

Reluctantly, he gave in. Too tired to argue. By the time they stepped back through the front door his face was dripping with sweat, even though he had barely walked a kilometre and needed twenty minutes in which to do even that. His heart was pounding in his chest, the pain radiating up over his face and forehead. Matilda glanced at him surreptitiously in the lift. A quick, anxious glance.

'Lie down on the sofa, and I'll get us some lunch,' she said. She held the front door open for him and took a careful grip of his limp right arm as he stepped across the threshold.

That taught you, Johansson thought as she plumped the pillows up behind his back. Better now, he thought. Better now, when he was able to lie down.

'I'm not trying to kill you,' Matilda said. 'But you do need to move occasionally. Are you lying okay like that?'

'Stop fussing,' Johansson said. 'Get me something to eat instead. And give me the message that's come through on the fax.'

Erika Brännström was born in 1953, in Härnösand, where she also grew up. When she was twenty years old she moved to Stockholm and started work as a nursing assistant at Huddinge Hospital. She met Tommy Högberg, who was three years younger than her and had lived in Stockholm all his life. He had studied vehicle technology at vocational college and worked as a car mechanic.

They moved into a flat out in Flemingsberg together. They had two children, Karolina, born in 1975, and her younger sister, Jessica, born in 1979. Four years after the younger daughter was born, in 1983, Erika and Tommy split up. Tommy remained in Flemingsberg and had a son that year with his new partner, who had been born in 1964. She, too, worked at Huddinge Hospital as a nursing assistant. Erika took the daughters with her and moved to Lilla Essinge. She started working part-time at St Göran's Hospital, and there was no sign of a new man in any public records.

Part-time at St Göran's, Johansson thought. In 1983, when she moved into the city with her two girls. In all likelihood, that was when she started cleaning for Margaretha Sagerlied. Her bloke had found a new woman, eleven years younger than Erika, and presumably she needed all the money she could get.

His conscientious brother-in-law had gone on to look into the man who was the father of Erika's children, with the help of public records and his declared taxable income. Two years after fathering his fourth child, in 1985, he was living alone again, at a new address out in Huddinge. Same employer, but his income had dwindled, and was now supplemented by payments from the income-support system.

He started drinking, Johansson thought, with the insight given to someone with past experience of a common professional affliction in the police force. His partner kicked him out. So what does he do? Contact Erika again? Maybe he even tries to visit her at the home of her new employer at her big, fancy villa out in Bromma?

Another year later, something even more drastic must have happened. His income fell by half, but there was no income support this time. At this point in his reading Johansson picked up his mobile and called Superintendent Hermansson at Regional Crime in Stockholm.

'Johansson,' he said.

'Hello, boss. I hope everything's okay, Lars?'

'Never felt better, Herman,' Johansson lied.

'What can I do for you, sir?' Hermansson asked.

'I'd like you to check the records for me. His name is Högberg, Tommy Rickard, born in '56.'

'Just a moment, I'll go and sit down at the computer. Okay, I'm listening.'

'Högberg, Tommy Rickard, born on 16 February 1956, ID number 0539. Last known address—'

'I've got him,' Hermansson interrupted. 'Lives out in Flemingsberg. Diagonalvägen 14.'

'What else?'

'A mixed bag, mostly nonsense, really. Looks like he has trouble holding his drink. First entry is drink-driving

240

in '83, and the latest was the same, drink-driving, 2006. And driving without a licence. He lost that in 1996.'

'Nothing since then? After 2006, I mean?'

'No,' Hermansson said. 'Poor lad was probably worn out. Drink takes its toll. Looks like he was given early retirement on health grounds the year he turned fifty, in 2006.'

'Nothing serious, then?'

'Not really,' Hermansson said. 'He was given a six-month custodial sentence for aggravated burglary in 1987, but the rest is mostly crap, like I said. Three drink-driving convictions, a few instances of driving without a licence, one attempt at insurance fraud, but that was dropped. Violence against a public official. Also dropped. Sounds to me like he got thrown out of the pub. That's the lot.'

'That's it?'

'Yes. So if you feel like explaining—'

'Is he in the DNA database?'

'No,' Hermansson said. 'But we got his other details after the robbery in '87. I have to admit, I'm extremely curious now.'

'We'll take that up later. See what else you can dig up, and we'll talk later on.'

Then he ended the conversation, despite Hermansson's protests, got up from the sofa without any great difficulty, and went out to the kitchen to see how things were going with the lunch he had been promised. Matilda was talking on the phone, hadn't heard him approach. She sounded upset. Johansson stopped and eavesdropped, another bad habit he had picked up at work.

'Yes, but that's not my problem. You promised to pay by Thursday at the latest. I think this is fucking awful behaviour. I can't actually pay my rent, thanks to you. Just so you know.'

Boyfriend, girlfriend, best friend, Johansson thought. Then he cleared his throat, just loudly enough. Matilda lowered her voice. She turned her back to the kitchen door.

'Just so you know,' she repeated. Then she switched her phone off and put it in her pocket.

'Sorry,' Matilda said. 'Food's nearly ready.'

'Boyfriend? Girlfriend?' Johansson smiled amiably, and nodded.

'My crazy mother,' Matilda said. 'She's mad. She drives me round the bend.'

'Don't let her,' Johansson said. 'That could damage my health. I'm hungry. What are we having?'

'Poached chicken with couscous and salad. I've topped it with a healthy dressing that I think you'll like. Then there's a surprise. Do you want to sit in here, or shall I lay a tray?'

'Here,' Johansson said, nodding at the kitchen table. 'From now on, we'll be sitting up when we eat in this household,' he added. A surprise, he thought.

242

49

Tuesday afternoon, 27 July

Matilda had spoken to Pia, who had spoken to his cardiologist, and now the surprise was standing on the table in front of him. A glass of red Bordeaux. At first, Johansson sniffed the glass cautiously. This is what it smells like when you haven't touched a drop for almost a month, he thought. Then he tasted the wine and felt the same peace that only the little white tablets could give him but, this time, it appeared instantly.

'No more than two glasses,' Matilda said. 'That's non-negotiable. Two glasses okay, three glasses a definite no-no.'

'We'll have to find a bigger glass,' Johansson said. He smiled and raised it towards her. 'On a completely different subject: where do you live?'

'Hägersten. A two-room rented flat. No boyfriend. Why do you ask?'

'I'll get to that,' Johansson said. 'What's the rent on something like that? Two thousand a month?'

'Are you kidding?' Matilda said. 'Maybe, if you live in Lapland. I pay six thousand a month. How much do you pay?'

'This is privately owned,' Johansson said.

'I worked that out,' Matilda said. 'I'm not completely stupid. What's the monthly maintenance charge, then?'

'Nothing, actually. The association has a number of retail units that we rent out, and that pays for maintenance. Members of the association don't have to pay for any of the upkeep.'

'Whoever said that life was fair?' Matilda said.

'What do you earn, then?'

'Thirteen a month, after tax. How about you? Unless that's a secret?'

'To be honest, I don't actually know. Pia looks after all that.'

'Why are we talking about this?'

'I happened to overhear part of your conversation,' Johansson said.

'It's not nice to eavesdrop.'

'I know. It's a bad habit I got into at work.'

'I know, I like eavesdropping as well.' Matilda beamed at him.

'Where am I going with this?' Johansson said. Where am I going with this? he thought.

'My rent, how much I earn and the fact that you eavesdrop on people,' Matilda said.

'Quite,' Johansson said. 'You got paid on the 25 July, the day before yesterday. You lent your mum some money, and she promised to pay it back as soon as possible so that you could pay your rent on the last of the month. That's in four days' time. But now she can't, so you haven't got enough for your rent. Out of curiosity, how much did you lend her?'

'Enough for me not to be able to pay the rent.'

'Does that happen often? Her borrowing money from you and not paying it back?'

'Drop it,' Matilda said, shaking her head. 'It's really none of your business.'

'I interpret that to mean it's happened before,' Johansson said. Probably all too often, he thought.

'You can interpret it any way you like, but it really doesn't concern you.'

'As long as it doesn't jeopardize my health,' Johansson said, smiling at her. 'Just say if you need a loan.' What a fucking mother, he thought.

'If I borrow money, I get the sack. Anyway, I don't want to borrow your money, just so you know.'

'Just say if you change your mind,' Johansson said, and shrugged his shoulders.

When he had finished his meal and let his tongue gather the last valuable drops of his second glass, he told Matilda to bring a coffee in to him. Then he went straight to his secret place and, with some difficulty, pulled out his emergency case and relieved it of six thousand-kronor notes, folded them and put them in the pocket of her jacket, which was hanging on a hook in the cloakroom.

'Where did you get to?' Matilda said when she came into his study with the tray.

'Toilet,' he said, with a cheery grin. 'Must have been all that red wine I guzzled.'

'Bound to be,' Matilda said. 'Say when,' she said, and poured warm milk into his cup of coffee.

'Stop,' Johansson said. 'If you'll excuse me, I need to make a call.'

Then he phoned Erika Brännström. A very reluctant Erika Brännström. First, he explained who he was and

245

what he wanted to talk about: the twenty-five-year-old murder of Margaretha Sagerlied's nine-year-old neighbour Yasmine. She interrupted him at once.

'I know very well who you are. Axel – Axel Linderoth called – and told me that you'd probably be getting in touch. I even saw you on television years ago. I know very well who you are, but I don't understand why you'd want to talk to me.'

'About Yasmine, like I said,' Johansson repeated. 'You're the only person I'm aware of who actually met her.'

'What about her parents?'

'Can't get hold of them. They left Sweden over twenty years ago.'

'Fine, but I still don't understand. I can't have met her more than ten, twenty times at most, and, obviously, that must be at least twenty-five years ago.'

'You had two young daughters who were the same age as her. I have a feeling that it might be worth having a conversation with you,' Johansson said. Besides, your daughters are alive, Johansson thought. Grown women, over thirty, regardless of anything else, he thought.

'I've booked to use the laundry room this afternoon,' she said.

'No problem,' Johansson said. 'I'm happy to come over. Shall we say an hour from now?'

'Call before you get here,' she said. 'Promise you'll call before you get here.'

At last, he thought, as he ended the call. Why should it be so hard to volunteer to help the police?

'Matilda!' he roared.

'Boss,' Matilda said. She must have been leaning against the door to his study.

'Fire up the Batmobile,' Johansson said. 'We're going out into the field.' Must be the wine, he thought. No headache, no tightness in his chest, not even any elation. Just calm and focused. Like a man who makes the best of things, hates coincidence and never complicates things unnecessarily.

50

Tuesday afternoon, 27 July

Essinge Brogata, a building dating back to the thirties, a compact two-room flat on the top floor. Two rooms, and a kitchen with a little sleeping alcove next to the dining table. Presumably where Erika slept, he thought, while her daughters shared the smaller of the two rooms. The same flat she had moved into almost thirty years ago, and where her two girls had grown up. Where they had lived with their mother until they moved out to get on with their own lives. He didn't even have to ask. To judge by the decor, and everything on the floors, ceilings and walls, he realized that this was where Erika had spent the past twenty-seven years of her life. A frugal life, a hard-working life; neat, tidy, but with little to spare and no room for material fripperies.

Just like the woman herself. Fit. Lithe movements, alert eyes, strong, suntanned hands – a working woman's hands – and she had clearly been beautiful when she was younger. With a spring in her step, dreams about the future that you could see in her smile and eyes. But she still looks good, Johansson thought, feeling a pang of awareness without really knowing why. She had made coffee without even asking if he might prefer tea. That's what we're like, us true Norrlanders, Johansson thought, as someone, or something, tugged at his battered heart.

'Sugar and milk?' That she *had* asked.

'Black is fine,' Johansson said.

'What do you want to talk about?' she asked.

'Let's take it from the beginning,' Johansson said. 'When you started working for Margaretha Sagerlied.'

The spring of 1983. Her husband had left her for a younger woman, a workmate of hers at Huddinge Hospital. Eleven years younger than her, no more than a child, and already pregnant with her husband's baby. She had worked all this out without even having to ask him. Listening to his lies, observing his angry rages and guilty conscience.

Her boss at the hospital had arranged all the practical details for her. A senior consultant and an opera lover, wealthy, independent of his generous salary, like everyone born with a silver spoon in their mouth. He had sorted out the flat on Lilla Essinge for her. The building was owned by a good friend of his, and she was allowed to live in it rent free if she cleaned the lobby and stairwell once a week and changed a bulb or two when necessary. It had taken him just a day to find her a new job at St Göran's, by calling a friend and colleague. And the job with Margaretha Sagerlied as well. A close friend of him and his wife.

'Naturally, you're wondering if I was sleeping with him,' Erika Brännström said.

'No,' Johansson said. 'Were you?'

'No. He was just a nice person. The sort who makes you feel you can put up with all the other men who aren't like him. Anyway, he was twice my age.'

What's that got to do with anything? thought Johansson, whose wife was twenty years younger than him.

'What did you do for Mrs Sagerlied, then?' Johansson asked. Just between us Norrlanders, he thought.

'Cleaned, washed up, did the laundry, took care of the house and garden. Bought food. Helped out when she had guests.'

'What was she like? To work for, I mean.'

'She wasn't mean,' Erika Brännström said. 'She really wasn't mean, but she was very pleased with herself. If I'd had the stomach to sit and listen to her stories the whole time, I could probably have been a lady's companion instead, then I wouldn't have had to wash and clean.'

'Demanding?'

'You had to wheedle your way round her, agree with her and then do what you were going to do from the start.'

'Unkind?'

'Definitely not. She was self-obsessed, but she wasn't unkind. She could be demanding if you approached her the wrong way. She didn't have any children, of course. She used to talk about that a lot, actually – the fact that her career had stopped her having children. That was her big regret: that she got married so late, to a man who was much older than her.'

'What about your children?' Johansson said. 'Did she meet them?'

'Oh, yes, lots of times,' Erika said. 'Every time one of them had a cough or cold and couldn't go to preschool. Or at evenings and weekends when I was helping her with something, when it made sense for all of us to sleep at hers. You have children yourself?'

'Yes,' Johansson said.

'So you know what it's like to have small children.'

'More or less.'

'I can imagine,' Erika Brännström said. She smiled slightly and stirred her coffee once more.

'What was it like when you had the children with you, then? With Mrs Sagerlied, I mean?'

'It was absolutely fine,' Erika said. 'They adored Aunt Margaretha. They played the piano and sang and put on plays and dressed up and I don't know what. I had to keep a grip on things. She spoiled them. Gave them presents that were far too expensive. She used to take them off to NK to buy them presents for Christmas and their birthdays, that sort of thing.'

'What about your husband?' Johansson said. 'Your former husband,' he corrected himself. 'Did he ever meet Mrs Sagerlied?'

Suddenly alert now, he thought.

'No, never. But I can see why you'd ask.'

'How do you mean? Why can you see that?'

'You're a police officer – you must know all about him by now. If we're honest, he's the real reason you're sitting here, isn't he?'

'Actually not,' Johansson said. 'I was going to talk about Yasmine but, seeing as you've worked out why I'm curious about your husband, perhaps you could tell me about him, anyway?'

'Well, there isn't really anything to hide. Tommy was a slob. He drank too much. He already did when we first met, when he was only eighteen. I was the girl from the country, and presumably easy prey, even though I was a few years older.'

'He drank too much?'

251

'Too much partying; he was far too fond of the ladies. I'm pretty sure he was seeing other women the whole time he was with me. Eventually, he started to develop a serious drink problem, but by then I'd already taken the girls and left him.'

'He never made any attempt to contact you?'

'No, he barely got in touch at all during those first years. I had to talk to him on the phone a few times about his maintenance payments, but it was hopeless. I ended up going through a solicitor, and after that the money was deducted straight from his wages. That meant I didn't have to phone and nag him, which was just as well. He was lazy, he drank far too much, like I said, but there was no harm in him. Obviously, I know about the silly things he got involved in. I know he even went to prison for a while. There was some burglary racket going on at his work and he got caught up in it.'

'What about his daughters? Didn't he want to stay in touch with them?'

'When my successor, which is how I usually think of her, when she told him to get lost, he tried to establish contact. But it never worked. He kept promising things, but nothing ever turned out the way he said. Just a load of empty promises, and lots of crying from two upset little girls. When they were older they tried to stay in touch with him. Of course, that didn't work either. I don't think either of them has seen anything of him in the past ten years. Tommy was a child. A child who drank. He never grew up.'

'When did you last see him?'

'I only saw him once unofficially after I left him in '83. That was a few years later. He came to my work, to

252

St Göran's. He wanted to borrow money. I agreed. A few hundred kronor. Naturally, I never got it back.'

'Apart from that, then?' Johansson said. 'With your solicitor? Or social services? You must have had some form of contact.'

'Maybe half a dozen times in total over the years. I've only met him once when there were just the two of us, and that's when he came to the hospital wanting to borrow money. And I was stupid enough to give it to him.'

'I see,' Johansson said. What a fucking arsehole, he thought.

'I know what you're after,' Erika Brännström said. 'But if you think Tommy had anything to do with Yasmine's death, you're on the wrong track completely. Tommy would never do anything like that. That's just how it is. Tommy was interested in grown-up girls, in women, and they were far too interested in him. Little girls ought to be pretty and happy and not cause trouble. He could barely manage to read them bedtime stories.'

'I believe you,' Johansson said. 'To change the subject: in June 1985, when Yasmine was murdered, what were you doing then?'

'I'd finally got some time off to have a proper holiday, for the first time in several years. Margaretha was going to meet up with a friend and go and stay at her place in the country. As soon as my eldest broke up from school I took the girls and went to stay with my parents. We were there all summer. We didn't get back until the middle of August, just in time for the start of term. My youngest, Jessica, was starting school that year.'

'My colleagues never got in touch with you, wanting to talk to you?'

'No, why would they want to do that? I know they spoke to Margaretha, because she told me. But why would they have wanted to talk to me?'

'Yes, quite,' Johansson said. 'Yasmine,' he said. 'Tell me about her.'

Yasmine moved into the house at the top of the road in the spring after Erika had started working for Margaretha Sagerlied. Together with her father and his new partner. It wasn't long before the little girl was visiting her employer.

'She was pretty – really pretty – a charming little girl, lively, happy and very theatrical. Not a little spoiled, either. So it was love at first sight between her and Margaretha. There was nothing wrong with her father, either, if I can put it like that.'

'What was he like?'

'Big and strong, very fit. Dark. Very handsome. And he was a doctor as well. Margaretha was very taken with him. She invited him and his partner to several parties. She was a doctor, too. I know that, the first time I saw them together – Yasmine's dad and his new partner – was at one of Margaretha's parties. I remember thinking to myself, I wonder how long that's going to last.'

'You thought that?'

'He was like a magnet. All the women, no matter what age they were, they all wanted to go over and talk to him.'

'The fact that he was an immigrant, from Iran, that didn't make any difference?'

'No, Margaretha wasn't like that at all. Quite the contrary. Nor were any of her friends. Yasmine's dad looked like a taller, younger, more handsome version of the Shah. And who wouldn't want to be Farah Diba? I don't suppose I'd have turned him down either.'

'No?'

'No, but as he never asked, I didn't have to worry about that. I don't think he was the sort who socialized with servants. He was charming and polite, but I'm pretty sure he didn't really spare much of a thought for people like me.'

'Yasmine,' Johansson said. 'Did she ever meet your daughters?'

'I did think about that,' Erika said. 'When it happened, I thought about it. They never actually met. They might have said hello to each other at some point, but they never played together. Considering what happened later, that was probably just as well. I didn't have to answer a lot of difficult questions, if I can put it like that.'

'Yes, dear God,' Johansson said. 'What sort of person could do something like that to a little girl?'

'I thought people like you knew that?' Erika said in surprise. 'Isn't it your job to know that sort of thing?'

'Yes,' Johansson said. 'But understanding it is a different matter.'

'I know what you mean,' Erika said. 'That's why there's no reason for you to worry about Karolina and Jessica's father.'

At some point during the autumn of 1985 Margaretha Sagerlied decided to sell the house in Äppelviken and move away.

'I have an idea it was sold in the spring of 1986,' Johansson said. 'About nine months after the murder.

Do you know why she wanted to move, all of a sudden?'
She's like she was before, now, he thought: wary. Very
obviously wary.

'I'm not sure you could call it sudden. It was almost a
year later, after all.'

'Well,' Johansson said. 'You don't sell a house like that
overnight. And I believe the estate agents started showing people round in the autumn.'

'I don't think it's odd at all,' Erika Brännström said.
'She'd talked about it for a while, saying the house was
too big for her, that she was getting old, that she wanted
to move into the city and was thinking of buying a
small apartment in Östermalm so she could be close to
everything.'

'The house was too big?' The house that was her
museum, Johansson thought. A memorial to her life.
Not a chance.

'Yes, she'd talked about it for quite a while. She definitely had.'

'What about what happened to Yasmine? You don't
think that could have influenced her? After all, she used to
go and play round there. Considering what happened,
those can't have been particularly pleasant memories.'
Why are you lying to me? he thought.

'No,' Erika Brännström said, shaking her head. 'I can
see what you mean, but that certainly wasn't something
she ever mentioned.'

'You helped her to move, if I've understood correctly,
cleaning up afterwards, and so on?'

'Yes,' Erika said. 'She'd bought an apartment in
Östermalm, on Riddargatan. I helped her to move
in there.'

'What about after that?' Johansson said.

'How do you mean?'

'Did you stay in touch with her? Presumably, she wanted you to carry on helping her?'

'No,' Erika said. 'One of the reasons she wanted to move somewhere smaller was that she didn't want to rely on anyone. And then she got ill. Cancer. She was sick for quite a while before she died, just a couple of years or so after she moved. We spoke on the phone a few times, but that was all.'

'Did she call you, or did you call her?' Why are you lying? Who are you trying to protect?

'A bit of both. I called her, she called me.'

'On a different subject,' Johansson said. 'Her social circle. If I've understood correctly, she mainly spent time with people of her own age. People from the same sort of background as her.'

'Yes,' Erika said. 'With the exception of one or two neighbours, like Axel and his wife, and Yasmine's father and his partner. Children of old friends. Adults, of course, but still around thirty or forty, something like that. The youngest ones, anyway.'

'A direct question,' Johansson said. 'Was there any particular male acquaintance who was close to her? Around thirty years old, or thereabouts? Anyone she used to see regularly?'

'How do you mean? If she was seeing a younger man?'

'No, not like that. Someone she knew well, who helped her, maybe. A relative, an acquaintance, the son of one of her friends.' Why are you pretending to be more stupid than you are? he thought.

'No.' Erika Brännström shook her head. 'There was no one like that. If there had been, I'd have known about it.'

257

'Of course.' Johansson smiled. 'What about your girls? I understand that things have gone well for them.' More a statement than a question this time.

'Yes,' their mother said. 'Things have gone well for them. They're both married, with jobs and children of their own. How do you know that? Both my sons-in-law are perfectly normal, decent guys, in case you were wondering.'

'Naturally,' Johansson said. 'Given that their wives had a mum like you, I mean.'

'Well. It wasn't always easy,' Erika said.

'I can imagine. Okay, then. Is there anything else we ought to talk about? Nothing you can think of?' I'm giving you another chance, Johansson thought. Take it, for God's sake, woman, so I don't have to hurt you when there's really no need.

'No,' Erika Brännström said. 'Well, I've got an awful lot of laundry to do.'

He waited until they were standing in the little hallway and she was about to open the door for him. Then he put his hand in his jacket pocket and pulled out the little plastic bag containing the hairgrip. He held it up towards her. Even though he was practically forcing it upon her, she didn't take it.

'Actually, yes,' Johansson said. 'There was one more thing. You don't recognize this?'

'No,' Erika Brännström said. 'I can see that it's a hairgrip, but it didn't belong to either of my girls.'

'You're sure about that?' Johansson said.

'Yes, quite sure. I don't want to seem like I'm trying to get rid of you, but I've—'

'Think about it,' Johansson said. 'You've got my number. Think about it. Call me if you change your mind.' He nodded to her.

Scared now, scared eyes; she hadn't snapped at him, hadn't got angry the way she would have been if what he had just said were wrong and nothing but an unfair accusation. I wonder where you found it? Johansson thought as he stood in the lift on his way downstairs. Must have been about the same time you noticed that a sheet and pillowcase were missing, possibly also a pillow, he thought. Some time in early autumn, 1985, when you did a thorough clean of the house after the holidays.

51

Wednesday, 28 July

More or less at the same time that Johansson's best friend was putting on his bathing trunks and going for a late-evening swim in the Indian Ocean, Johansson was lying on the floor of his study, having almost knocked himself out. But before that, quite a bit had happened.

When Matilda served him his morning coffee, she asked if she could speak to him in private.

'There's something I need to talk to you about,' she said. 'If that's okay.'

'Go for it,' Johansson said, smiling obligingly. Well aware of what was coming.

'When I got home yesterday evening I found six thousand-kronor notes in my jacket pocket. I don't suppose you know anything about that?'

'No,' Johansson said, shaking his head. 'I don't know what you're talking about.'

'I'm serious,' Matilda said. 'I can't accept money from our patients. Not as gifts, or loans. So that's why—'

'Stop going on,' Johansson interrupted. 'I haven't the faintest idea what you're talking about.'

'We'll have to talk about it later, then.'

'I'm afraid I'm unlikely to know any more about it then,' Johansson said with a cryptic smile.

'I'll be talking to Pia about it, just so you know.'

'I think you should definitely do that. But I'm afraid she probably won't know any more than me.' Women, he thought. 'Now you'll have to excuse me,' he said. 'I need a bit of peace and quiet before you start carting me round to see all the white coats.'

'Yes, we're seeing your cardiologist today as well,' Matilda said. 'Before we go to see the physiotherapist.'

'My cardiologist,' Johansson said. 'What an honour. My own neurologist, my own cardiologist, my own physiotherapist, and my own babysitter.' All he was really missing was a life of his own, he thought.

First, the appointment with Johansson's cardiologist, a small, fit man in his fifties with a bald head and alert brown eyes. The same expression in his eyes as the squirrels of his childhood before he squeezed the trigger and extinguished the light in their heads. His cardiologist also had the good judgement not to keep twitching his head the whole time. He simply sat there, smiling amiably, as he listened to Johansson's chest, lungs and heart, examined the results of his ECG, and just looked at him in a more general sense.

'It's like this,' Johansson said, thinking that it was just as well to have it over with. 'I've worked as a police officer all my life. I'm used to hearing things straight, and I'm sick of all the bullshit from you and your colleagues. I want to know how I am, and the reason I want to know is because I think I'm in a pretty wretched state. I'm not one for complaining, either. So just tell it to me straight out.'

'Okay,' his cardiologist said. 'Your heart has taken a serious battering over a lot of years,' he said. 'Your readings are poor. What worries me most is your blood pressure. We've got to get that down. Medication will help, but you have to lose weight, get more exercise and take things much easier. You've got to stop getting stressed, stop worrying and stop getting excited. Is that plain enough?'

'Yes,' Johansson said. 'Should I be taking care of any practical arrangements, just in case?'

'If you do as I tell you, you can probably wait a while before drawing up a new will.'

'Good,' Johansson said. Make the best of things, he thought. Make the best of what you've got when you haven't got any choice.

After his exercise session his physiotherapist got the same question.

'Look at this arm,' Johansson said.

Then he raised his right arm in front of him, opened and closed his hand, stretched his right forefinger out.

'Elk-hunting season starts in a month,' Johansson went on. 'I've hunted elk since I was a small boy. Will I ever be able to hunt again with this arm? Hold a rifle with it? Will I be able to pull the trigger with my right forefinger? Right now, I have hardly any feeling in my fingers, and I can't even hold up my newspaper in the morning.'

'It's going to take time,' she said.

'What does that mean?' Johansson said. 'A year? Five years? Never?'

'It's impossible to say but, like I've said to you before, you mustn't think like that, because—'

'Thank you,' Johansson interrupted. 'Let me tell you, I'm seriously fed up with everyone telling me how to think.' And not think, he thought.

What's the point of a life that consists merely of counting down the days to the end? Johansson thought as he sat in the car on the way home. What sort of life is that?

'You'll have to excuse me if I'm nagging,' Matilda said. 'But it's about that money.'

'Yes, you really are fucking nagging,' Johansson replied. 'And I'm feeling really shit, so if you could shut up, I'd be grateful if you'd just drive me home. Otherwise, we can stop here and I'll call a taxi.'

'Sorry,' she said. 'Sorry, I didn't mean to upset you.'

Now you've made someone else unhappy, Johansson thought.

'What's the point of a life that consists merely of counting down the days to the end? What sort of fucking life is that?'

'You'll get better,' Matilda said. And patted him on the arm. 'You'll soon be back to normal. I promise.'

He ate his lunch alone, half lying on the sofa. He couldn't even think of sitting on a chair at the same table as his babysitter. No wine, either. He just shook his head when she asked.

His head ached and his chest felt tight. I can't do this, Johansson thought, and got up from the sofa to go to the bathroom to swallow one of the little white pills that could take him away from everything. He'd taken only a couple of steps when the floor suddenly lurched, his legs gave way beneath him and the walls started to spin.

He flailed with his right arm in a vain attempt to find something to hold on to, then fell flat on his side as everything went black in front of his eyes.

'Lie still,' Matilda said, kneeling beside him. How did she get here? he thought.

'Can you hear me? Can you move your legs? Try to flex your feet. I'm going to call for help,' she said.

'Like hell you are,' Johansson said. 'Help me up on to the sofa instead.'

'You need to lie still.' Matilda held her left hand to his chest as she pulled out her mobile with her right hand. 'I'm calling Pia,' she said. 'Just take it easy.'

'Like fuck you are,' Johansson said. Then he pushed her away with his left arm. 'If you call her I'll kill you.'

She didn't say anything, just shook her head and walked out of the room, closing the door behind her.

It took him over five minutes to heave himself up on to the sofa. A sofa that was only a few metres away. When he finally got there, the door flew open and his eldest brother marched in.

'Lunch at Gondolen. Pia called. What the hell is going on?' Evert asked. He wasn't prone to using extraneous words when time was short.

'There's not a damn thing going on,' Johansson said. 'I fell over, that's all.'

'Don't talk crap,' Evert said, and at that moment Matilda came back into the room.

'I think he got up too quickly, his blood pressure dropped and he got dizzy and fell. I don't think he—'

'If you could just shut up and leave so I can have a quiet word with my brother,' Evert said, gesturing in her direction with his hand.

When Evert gestures with his hand even Superman shits himself, Johansson thought, suddenly feeling unfathomably cheerful in spite of the pain in his chest and side.

Evert moved a chair and sat down.

'Do you want a glass of water?' he asked.

'Get me a cognac,' Johansson said. 'A large one.'

'Fine,' Evert said, with a nod of approval. 'Of course you shall have cognac. I think I might have a Scotch.'

Then they sat and talked. In peace and quiet, man to man, elder brother to younger, as Evert sipped his whisky and Johansson his cognac.

'You can't go on like this – you can see that for yourself,' Evert said.

'Really?' Johansson said. 'I had actually worked that out for myself. Any suggestions gratefully received.'

'You can borrow my lad. I'll bring him over; he can help you. The lad who works on the estate for my wife and me.'

'Your lad?'

'Yes,' Evert said. 'It seems a trifle unnecessary for you to fall and kill yourself at home in your own apartment.'

'So what's wrong with him, then?' Johansson said. 'Your lad?'

'There's nothing wrong with him,' Evert said, shaking his head. 'He's big and strong, far from stupid, and he does as he's told.'

'Nothing wrong with him at all?'

'No,' Evert said with a broad grin. 'Sometimes when I offer him a vodka he starts going on about wanting to join the police but, apart from that, he's perfectly normal.'

'What about you, then?' Johansson said. 'Don't you need him?' With all those horses and dogs, and the farm, the woodland and the hunt, he thought.

'I daresay I'll cope.' Evert snorted. 'Right now, you're the one we need to get sorted out.'

'Okay,' Johansson said. 'That's very kind of you.'

'Shake my hand,' Evert said. 'High time you pulled yourself together. It's only a month before the elk season starts.'

'To the hunt,' Johansson said, nodded and raised his glass.

52

Wednesday evening, 28 July

Dinner with Pia. They ate in the kitchen. They couldn't sit on the terrace, because it was raining, which was perfectly appropriate, given how he felt.

'How are you feeling?' Pia asked. 'You frightened the life out of me today, you know that?' She ran her hand over his hopeless one as it lay on the table.

'No, I didn't,' Johansson said, instantly annoyed at what she had said. 'I told that little tattooed bitch not to call you, but she ignored me. I asked her to help me up on to the sofa again, but she ignored that as well.'

'You have to understand that she had to. She had to call. She did it because she cares.'

'No, I don't understand. I hear what you're saying, but I don't agree with you, and I'm seriously bloody fed up with everybody thinking for me. That applies to you, too, by the way.'

'You're having a hard time right now,' Pia said. 'I understand that, but you still have to appreciate that we only want to help you.'

This is pointless, he thought, his anger slipping away, exhaustion shoving it aside.

'I spoke to your brother,' Pia said. 'I think his idea sounds excellent. It would make me feel a lot calmer. There's more and more to do at work now that people are getting back from their holidays, so I thought he could stay in the guest bedroom for a while.'

'Lovely that the two of you are in agreement,' Johansson said.

'I think you're being unreasonable now, Lars. And I also talked to that doctor who came to have a look at you. Nothing broken, but you sprained your ankle, and you've got a lot of bruising. You've got to take it slowly when you stand up. If you get up too quickly you'll only get dizzy and fall.'

This can't be happening, Johansson thought.

'There's one thing I'm wondering,' he said. 'I feel bloody tired. I have a feeling that might be because I am bloody tired. Is it okay if I go and lie down, or what?'

A forced smile now. Her hand had stopped. 'I'll help you,' she said.

'No,' Johansson said. 'You bloody well won't. I'm going to put myself to bed. I'm going to have a wash, brush my teeth, take all my wretched bloody pills, and then I'm going to bed. All on my own.'

He nodded to her. She'd stopped smiling. And had pulled her hand away.

Then he did everything he said he would. He concluded by taking another of the little white tablets and a sleeping pill. He fell asleep the moment his head hit the pillow, in spite of the ache in his side and the fact that he was having trouble breathing.

53

Thursday morning, 29 July

The moment he opened his eyes that morning Johansson decided to regain control of his life. He woke before six, the way he always used to before he had been laid low and brought face to face with his own mortality. He limped out to the toilet, showered, shaved, brushed his teeth, took his pills, drank two glasses of water, put on his dressing-gown, fetched the morning paper, limped back to his study, lay down on the sofa and began to read the paper. His head began to ache as good as instantly, and he tossed the newspaper aside. When Pia came in and asked if he wanted breakfast, he merely shook his head. He had his eyes closed, and couldn't have offered her a better chance for a reconciliation. Not if he was going to regain control of his life. Regardless, she just walked away.

He must have dozed off after that, because the next thing he remembered was hearing his wife talking to Matilda out in the hall before she came into his room, bent over him and ran her fingers down his left cheek. And whispered:

'Look after yourself, darling. See you this evening.' Then she left; he heard the front door close behind her, no more to it than that. More angry than worried, he thought, and then he must have fallen asleep again.

Then Matilda was standing there. Smiling happily, as if the previous day hadn't happened.

'Up you get, boss,' Matilda said. 'We've got to go and see the physiotherapist.'

'What do you mean, "we"?' Johansson said, shaking his head. 'You go,' he said. 'I'll give it a miss. Ask if she can do something about those tattoos. Who knows, maybe you can get rid of them by exercising?'

'Don't be silly,' Matilda said. She even tilted her head, the way his neurologist did as soon as he didn't fulfil her expectations.

'I was thinking of going for a walk on Djurgården,' Johansson said. 'Then I'm going to have lunch in a restaurant. If you want to drive me, that would be good. If not, I can call for a taxi.'

'Okay,' she said with a shrug. 'I'll drive you. Let me know when you're ready.'

Johansson got dressed carefully. White linen trousers, blue linen shirt, yellow linen jacket. To match his mood, and the sunlight shining in through his window. He took his time and noticed Matilda sitting in his living room glancing at her watch when he walked straight past her without taking the slightest bit of notice of her. He decided instantly to push the front line a bit further forward. If they want a child, they can have a child, he thought.

'You can calm down,' Johansson said. 'I need to make a phone call before we leave.'

Then he took out his phone and called Hermansson's mobile.

'Johansson,' Johansson said. 'There are a few things I'd like you to do.'

'I'm listening, boss,' Superintendent Hermansson said. Three years of retirement were as good as blown away by Johansson's tone of voice.

'How are you getting on with Högberg?'

'I did a broad search for him. The boys in Surveillance have taken a few pictures as well. Doesn't look too sprightly. They took them when he stumbled out of his local bar last night. Rather the worse for wear, if I can put it like that.'

'Good,' Johansson said. 'Not that the last twenty-five years matter too much. The question is more what he looked like back then. See if you can send me the photographs from when he was arrested and had his prints taken.'

'Of course,' Hermansson said. 'Patrik was going to bring them over to you as soon as he finishes his shift. Low profile, you know. Trying to keep it in the family.'

'What do you mean, "low profile"?' Johansson said.

'Well,' Hermansson said. 'The case is prescribed now, after all. We've just got to be a bit discreet about it, that's all.'

'What a load of crap,' Johansson said. 'Send someone to get a DNA sample from the bastard. If you're right, he's probably out cold right now. You just have to ring on his door. His DNA is all we need.'

'I hear what you're saying, boss,' Hermansson said. 'Let me think about it. As I've said, we're talking about a prescribed case, and I'm not exactly keen to have the judicial ombudsman breathing down my neck.'

'Don't bother, then,' Johansson said. 'I'll call someone else instead.'

'Hang on, now, boss. Lars, for God's sake, don't be like that. We've known each other a fair while now, haven't we?'

'Sometimes I worry about you, Herman. If it was Högberg who killed Yasmine, you can't seriously believe that was the last time he did anything like that?'

'No,' Hermansson said. 'I hear what you're saying. I'll make sure we get a DNA sample as soon as possible, though how on earth I'm going to manage that, I don't know.'

'Why don't you send your son-in-law?' Johansson suggested. 'I'm sure he could do it straight away. If Högberg refuses to open his mouth, just stick the swab up his nose.'

'Okay, boss.'

'Good. And then I'd like you to get it prioritized by the National Forensics Lab.'

'Hang on, hold your horses,' Hermansson said. 'I spoke to them yesterday regarding another case, a current murder we're dealing with here at Regional Crime. Two Russians, shot and dumped out at Biskopsudden. Three weeks at the earliest, they said.'

'Who's in charge?' Johansson said. 'At the lab?'

'That woman, the one who was head of the National Police Board in your day.'

'Good,' Johansson said. 'Call her and give her my regards. Tell her you want this done at once, within six hours of them receiving the sample at the very most.'

'Sure,' Hermansson said. 'I hear what you're saying. I'll make sure it gets done.'

'Excellent,' Johansson said. 'I look forward to seeing your son-in-law.'

Then he put his mobile into the breast pocket of his jacket, picked up his stick and limped out into the hall.

Matilda was sitting on a chair, waiting for him. She smiled weakly.

'The first day of your new life,' she said, shaking her head. 'Where do you want to go?'

'Just drive, and keep your mouth shut, and I'll make sure you get all the information you need on the way,' Johansson said. Back on the road again, he thought.

Johansson showed the way, gesturing with his left hand as they went, crossing the junction at Slussen, along Skeppsbron, past Gamla Stan, past the Grand Hotel, along the quayside on Strandvägen, past the American Embassy and the Kaknäs Tower, across the little bridge over the canal to Djurgården. Yellow sun, blue sky, gentle white clouds, like the down on the breast of an eider duck in mating season, the same sort of down that was more than good enough to smother a nine-year-old girl. Stockholm at its most beautiful, showing its finest side to the onlooker.

'Stop here,' he said.

No objections this time. She stopped the car without saying anything.

'I was thinking of walking back towards the city,' Johansson said. 'I'll see you at that old inn at the bottom of the funicular railway at Skansen.' What the hell's the name of it? he thought. It was gone, all of a sudden, even though he must have eaten there a hundred times in the days when his life was normal.

'Ulla Winbladh's,' Matilda said.

'Exactly. See you at Ulla Winbladh's. In an hour or so.'

Only then did she look at him. Then she nodded.

'Okay,' she said. 'See you at Ulla Winbladh's.'

Then she got back in the car and drove off.

*

273

To start with, he felt almost buoyant: there were no tricky hills; he just walked along the edge of the canal, alone, at his own pace. After a quarter of an hour or so he began to feel a bit tired. He sat down on a bench, wiped the sweat from his brow, took several deep breaths with his eyes closed as he felt his blood pressure go down. After a while he stood up to go on, slowly, carefully, so that his blood pressure had time to keep up, to stop him falling arse over tit for no good reason.

After another fifteen minutes he was almost half-way. He was breathing more easily now, sweating less. Another bench, time to rest, and all he was missing was a flask of coffee and a chunky sandwich filled with slices of Falun sausage. Perhaps also the sharpness of a September breeze against his cheeks and chin. A stump to sit on, a view of the river back home and the low bark of a Swedish elkhound that had just spotted an elk.

You're alive, Lars Martin, Johansson thought, as he walked into the inn at the appointed time.

'What do you think about grilled char with warm salad?' Matilda suggested, already sitting there with the menu.

'Don't let me stop you,' Johansson said. 'I'm going to have pork chops with potato pancakes, a cold Czech pilsner and a large vodka.'

54

Thursday afternoon, 29 July

Once he was home again, he lay down on the sofa in his study and told Matilda to bring him a cup of coffee and a bottle of mineral water. He felt brighter than he had for a long time. No headache, no tightness in his chest. Best to make the most of it, Johansson thought, and pulled out the brown envelope Ulrika Stenholm had given him a few days before. It was also reassuringly thin for someone who had been told to take it easy and not get stressed.

A number of concert programmes for performances by Margaretha Sagerlied.

Christmas concert in Bromma church. Standard repertoire, Johansson thought, without really knowing much about the subject.

Concert in Spånga church. Clearly a more mixed repertoire, Johansson thought, without really knowing much about that either.

Mozart at the Drottningholm Palace Theatre. Everyone knows about that, Johansson thought, despite never having set foot in the place.

Half a dozen photographs, immediately more rewarding to someone like him, because they suddenly put faces to a number of people he had never met, spoken to or even seen pictures of.

A signed photo of Margaretha Sagerlied – a young and very beautiful Margaretha Sagerlied – taken in 1951, according to the photographer's stamp on the back. The only reason it had ended up in the hands of Ulrika Stenholm's father many years later had to be that she had given it to him. Or, rather, to him and his wife, Johansson thought. She was pictured in half-profile against a dark background, her head tossed back, eyelids partly lowered, an almost scornful smile and – half a century later – a dramatic expression that didn't work at all. Carmen, Johansson thought. Was that how she saw herself?

Another photograph. 'Crayfish party, 1970, at Margaretha and Johan's', Johansson read on the back. 'Our host, Johan, my dear wife, Louise, our charming hostess, Margaretha, and myself', he read on the line below. Clearly Daddy Vicar's writing, Johansson thought. Two men in smoking jackets flanking two women in fancy party dresses, all of them with crayfish-party hats on their heads, the wide-bowled champagne glasses of the time and cheerful smiles. Wonder who took the picture, Johansson thought. Who cares? he thought, seeing as the photographer, assuming he was a man, would also have been far too old fifteen years later.

To the right of the photograph was a man of about seventy with thinning hair and a flushed complexion; he was big and burly and his expression was jovial. Beside him was a woman who looked half his age and could have been Johansson's neurologist's twin sister. Then the charming hostess, who looked younger than her fifty-six years when the picture was taken. A head taller than Ulrika Stenholm's mother, beaming into the camera, raising her glass and with her left arm around the man next to her. Daddy Vicar, Johansson thought. Thin, not much hair, open, regular features, a friendly, almost shy smile. A wise and good man, judging by his appearance. Possibly slightly embarrassed by the arm round his waist, he thought, then put the photograph down as his mobile started to ring.

'Johansson,' Johansson said, seeing as he usually responded since he had retired by giving his surname, instead of just grunting at the caller.

'Hello, Lars,' his brother-in-law said. 'Alf here. I hope all's well with you?'

'Constant pain,' Johansson said. Because who the hell bothers to lie to a man like Alf Hult? he thought. 'How are you getting on with our opera singer and that old butcher she was married to?'

'I was just about to let you know.'

'Tell me,' Johansson said. 'I'm listening.'

They were both childless, according to all public registers on the matter, and, for once, Alf Hult was inclined to believe that this was actually the case.

'No kids out of wedlock?' Johansson said.

'Not all families can afford things like that,' Alf Hult said with a discreet cough.

'Anyone else, then? Young men of the right age, nephews, cousins, anyone else?'

None of them either, according to his brother-in-law. Neither Johan Nilsson nor Margaretha Sagerlied had any siblings.

'Johan Nilsson was a third-generation meat-trader. He was born in 1895, died 1980. His father, grocer Anders

Gustaf Nilsson, was born in 1870, and his son, Johan, was his only child. Anders Gustaf died in 1950, by the way. Johan's grandfather, on the other hand, had a whole brood of children. Eight of them, if I've counted right – three boys and five girls – but none of them seems to have produced any male descendants of the right age.'

'What about her, then?' Johansson said. 'Sagerlied?'

'To make it nice and easy, she was an only child as well. She was born Svensson; her father was a furrier in Stockholm and her mother a housewife. Lower bourgeois, as they probably said in those days. At the risk of disappointing you, there's not much joy to be had there either. No close male relatives. Margaretha Sagerlied, born Margaretha Svensson, changed her name in 1937 when she was twenty-three years old. That was two years before she got a permanent job at the Stockholm Opera.'

'Got to give the right impression,' Johansson said, for some reason.

'Yes,' his brother-in-law agreed. 'If only you knew what problems that sort of name change can cause people like me. I could tell you stories from my time at the tax office that would make your hair stand on end, even a man of your background.'

'I don't doubt it,' Johansson said. What do we do now? he thought.

'So, what do we do now?' Alf Hult said.

'We'll have to dig deeper,' Johansson said, having just decided.

'Maybe the man you're looking for isn't a family member at all. Assuming there are any, of course.'

'Maybe not,' Johansson conceded.

'If there are any relatives, we'll find them,' Alf Hult said. 'You don't have to worry on that point.'

'Of course not,' Johansson said. If there are any, he thought, and ended the call.

Unless you've got the whole thing wrong, because you had a blood clot in your brain when it was actually your heart that was going wrong, he thought.

Then he fell asleep on the sofa. He woke to find Matilda leaning over him, gently nudging his shoulder.

'You've got a visitor,' she said. 'A police officer. Says he's got some documents for you.'

'Does he have a name?' Johansson said.

'Not that he told me,' Matilda said, smiling as she said it.

'How do you know he isn't lying, then?' Johansson said. Patrik Åkesson, P-2, he thought.

'It's written across his forehead,' Matilda said, grinning at him. 'Just like it is on yours and your best friend's, that huge guy who looks like a wolf.'

Not written across his forehead, Johansson thought. It's in his eyes. Like all good officers. Like his best friend, like he himself, like all the former colleagues who were just like him and Jarnebring. The friendly, watchful expression that could only mean that you were in trouble if you didn't behave. You'd find yourself in handcuffs, being told to keep your mouth shut, or kicked in the backside. Or worse, depending on the circumstances.

'Sit yourself down,' Johansson said. 'I've told the maid to bring us coffee.'

'Sounds good,' Patrik Åkesson said.

'So tell me, P-2. Enlighten an old man. Have you found anything on our drunk, Högberg?'

'My father-in-law phoned and hassled them this morning,' P-2 said, smiling for some reason.

'I can imagine.'

'So Högberg, Tommy Rickard, has given a DNA sample. My colleagues and I just happened to be passing,' he said, with a smile and a shrug.

'What did he think about that?'

'No objections at all. He was very accommodating. A bit tired, perhaps – he'd evidently had a late night – but once we managed to shake some life into him there were no problems. The super was going to send it to the National Lab at once. Apparently, we'll get the results by tomorrow, at the latest.'

'I can imagine,' Johansson grunted. 'Have you got a picture of him?'

'Of course,' P-2 said. He dug through his papers and handed over a custody photograph from 1987, taken by the Stockholm Crime Unit when Tommy Högberg was arrested on suspicion of aggravated burglary. Frontal, right and left profiles, and, despite the circumstances, he was smiling at the camera.

Curly, dark hair, regular features, white teeth, a broad smile. Tommy Högberg, ladies' man, Johansson thought.

'What do you think, boss? Is it him?' P-2 said, nodding inquisitively at the photograph in Johansson's hand.

'I doubt it,' Johansson said, shaking his head. Too weak-willed and a bit too stupid, to judge from his eyes, he thought. 'Time will tell,' he added with a shrug of his shoulders. Fairly soon, he thought.

'If it does turn out to be him, I'd be happy to go and bring him in,' Patrik Åkesson said, with a look in his eyes that didn't bode well for Tommy Högberg.

'Prescribed,' Johansson said. 'Not as simple as that,' he said, for some reason sounding just like P-2's father-in-law, Superintendent Hermansson of the Stockholm Regional Crime Unit.

'He must have done other stuff,' P-2 said. 'Men like that never stop, do they?' he said with sudden vehemence. 'We'll find something. You only have to pick up the phone and I'll go and bring him in. I'll rip his arms and legs off if he puts up a fight.'

Goodness, Johansson thought. Now where have I heard that before?

'There's nothing you want to tell me?' Johansson said.

'Has Herman said anything? My father-in-law, I mean?'

'No,' Johansson said. 'But I'd be happy to listen to you.'

'Our youngest girl, Lovisa, was at that fucking nursery out in Tullinge. We lived there at the time. Four years ago, now. You must have seen it in the papers. There was a huge fuss in the media, even though social services tried to hush it up.'

'It's not ringing any bells,' Johansson said. 'Remind me.' Someone must have deleted loads of stuff from my head, he thought.

'They'd employed a male trainee who was studying to be a preschool teacher. He'd only been there a couple of months when they worked out that he'd been . . .'

Patrik Åkesson fell silent, swallowed, leaned forward in his chair, his hands hanging between his knees as he clenched and unclenched them.

'Abusing the children?' Johansson said.

'Showing them his cock and asking them to touch it while he fiddled with them. Right in the middle of the nursery. Took his chance when he helped them go to the toilet, and not a single one of the other staff had a fucking clue what the bastard was up to. Until the manager caught him with his trousers down. After three months, even though he'd probably started on day one. Blind as fucking bats.'

'Your daughter,' Johansson said.

'No,' P-2 said. 'This particular one was only interested in little boys. So not Lovisa. She was the wrong sort, thank God. On that occasion she was the wrong sort.'

'It can't have been easy,' Johansson said. It must have been hell, he thought.

'No,' P-2 said. 'It's not easy to have to take a four-year-old girl for a gynaecological examination. Not to mention all the hours she spent talking to a load of psychologists who just sat there nodding their empty heads.'

'Time will tell,' Johansson said. 'And if it was him, then obviously we'll find something.'

'If we don't, we could always make sure that we do, anyway,' Patrik Åkesson said. 'I think I'll skip that coffee. Hope you don't mind, boss,' he said, and stood up.

'Of course not,' Johansson said. 'Look after yourself. And, just in case, I don't want you doing anything stupid.'

'I promise, boss,' Patrik Åkesson said. 'I promise,' he repeated. 'You have my word on that.'

That evening, after dinner with Pia, when he was lying on the sofa in his study, alone with his thoughts, his mobile rang. Alf, the old stalwart, the Einstein of genealogy, has found him, Johansson thought.

'Johansson,' he said.

'Herman,' Superintendent Hermansson said. 'I hope I didn't wake you?'

282

'No,' Johansson said. 'Have you found him?' Not exactly Einstein, he thought.

'Afraid not. I got a call from the lab a little while ago. No match for Tommy Högberg in the Yasmine case. Nor with any other case, for that matter.'

'Well, then,' Johansson said. For some reason, Erika Brännström's face popped into his mind.

'You'll get him next time.'

'Yes,' Johansson said. Of course I will, he thought. Wonder what she's frightened of? A hardworking Norrlander with hands marked by years of toil. Two daughters who are doing well in life. Unlike Yasmine, who would have been the same age as them if she'd been allowed to live, and for whom things would doubtless have gone even better. In a material sense, at least.

'Promise to call me,' Hermansson said. 'That I'll be the first to know.'

'Of course,' Johansson said. 'We'll stay in touch.'

Once I've found him, I'm certainly not going to tell either you or your son-in-law, he thought as he put his phone down. A moment later it rang again.

'Yes,' he said. Someone else who wants to rip someone's arms and legs off, no doubt, he thought.

'Evert,' Evert grunted. 'Your big brother. Perhaps you remember me?'

'And what does my big brother want?' Evert must have ripped loads of arms and legs off in his time, Johansson thought. Tons of them in the People's Park in Kramfors alone.

'Our lad will be with you on Saturday,' Evert said. 'But I've already arranged that with Pia, so there's nothing for you to worry about.'

'So why are you calling, then?'

283

'There was something I forgot to say.'

'What's that?'

'About the lad.'

'Oh,' Johansson said. I knew there was something fishy about this, he thought. 'I'm listening.'

'He's Russian.'

'He's Russian,' Johansson repeated. 'Does he speak any Swedish, then?' Evert's sending me a bastard Russian, he thought.

'Of course he does,' Evert said. 'He's lived here almost fifteen years, for God's sake.'

'How old is he, then?'

'He was born in '87, came to Sweden when he was a young boy. Ten years old, something like that. Before that he was in a children's home in St Petersburg, and I daresay he didn't have much to laugh about there.'

'But you'll vouch for him?'

'Of course I will. He's a good lad, not remotely spoiled, unlike my own children.'

'What's he like, then, as a person? If you had to describe him?'

'Like me,' Evert said. 'He's good. He's like me.'

'Does he have a name?' Johansson said. I'm going to end up with my own Little Evert, he thought. All I had to do was have a stroke first.

'Maxim – Maxim Makarov. You know, like that ice-hockey player. The disgustingly talented bastard who used our lads in the Three Crowns as marker buoys, back in the day. He's called Max for short, by the way.'

'Sergey,' Johansson said. 'The ice-hockey player. His name was Sergey Makarov.'

'Who knows, maybe that was his father?' Evert chuckled.

'Was there anything else?'

'No,' Evert said. 'Actually, yes, one more thing. He's bringing your new car with him. Same as before, but with an automatic gearbox.'

'Thanks,' Johansson said. His very own Little Evert, who was going to be living with him and Pia. In the home that up until recently had been his castle. What the fuck is going on? he thought.

55

Friday morning, 30 July

'Have you got a moment?' Matilda asked. 'There's something I thought we could get out of the way before we go to see the physiotherapist.'

'Sure,' Johansson said, putting the newspaper down. Just as well, he thought, because whenever he tried to read his head started to ache.

'It's about that Joseph Simon you asked me to check out on the internet.'

'Did you find anything?'

'Loads,' Matilda said. 'There's no end of stuff.'

'Try to give me a summary.'

'Okay,' Matilda said. 'Born in 1951 in Tehran. Came to Sweden as a refugee in 1979, together with his wife and young daughter. His name back then was Josef Ermegan, and he was a trained doctor. He worked as a researcher and doctor at the Karolinska Institute in Solna. Swedish citizen in 1985. Divorced the same year. Changed his name to Joseph Simon a year later. Left Sweden in 1990 and moved to the USA: he had a green card before he even stepped off the plane. He became an American citizen in 1995 – apparently, it's unusual for that to happen so quickly. Especially these days, after

9/11, but of course this was before that. But you already knew all that, didn't you?'

'Yes,' Johansson said. 'But I'm wondering what happened after that.' You could say what you liked, but she certainly wasn't stupid, even though she did look like that, he thought.

'There were three things that struck me.'

'I'm listening.'

'Firstly, he seems to be incredibly rich. I repeat,' she said with a smile, '*incredibly* rich. He's a big name, a really big name, in the pharmaceutical industry. Owns or controls loads of drugs companies, and even a number of IT firms active in that area. He recently sold one that had developed some sort of software that means they don't have to experiment on animals. All the mice, rats, rabbits, chimpanzees, cats and dogs, you name it, that they usually kill. Have you got any idea how many animals the drugs industry and cosmetics companies kill every year?'

'No,' Johansson said. 'How many?'

'Several hundred million, according to their own figures, and over a billion according to other independent sources. The company he sold has come up with some computer-simulation program that means they can save almost twenty per cent of the test animals. Not because rabbits are cute or anything like that, but because Peter Rabbit costs them a hundred kronor before they're finished with him and can chuck him in the bin.'

'So how much did he get for the company?' Johansson asked.

'He got 1.7 billion dollars. Almost 13 billion Swedish kronor, just like that. When he started it seven years ago, he invested only a few million in it. Dollars, that is.'

'In other words, he seems to have made a bit of money over the years,' Johansson said.

'Yes, boss. He's made a fuck of a lot of it. He's on that list, too. Has been for years.'

'What list?' Johansson said.

'The one of the five hundred richest people in the world.'

'How much is he worth, then?'

'Last year his personal fortune was estimated at between 12 and 15 billion. Dollars, that is.'

Drop dead, Evert, Johansson thought. If he changed all that into Swedish money he could fill a swimming pool, and even old Scrooge McDuck could go fuck himself.

'And secondly?' Johansson said.

'Secondly, he seems to be running some kind of crusade against paedophiles and child molesters.'

'What kind of crusade?' Johansson asked. 'How does he run it? I can't imagine he goes running after them with a sword?' Not such a bad idea, he thought. A big, swarthy Persian with a fez and scimitar, meting out a bit of cold, biblical justice to men like John Ingvar Löfgren, Ulf Olsson and Anders Eklund, a millennium on.

'He does, actually,' Matilda said. 'Well, as close to that as he can get, anyway.'

'How do you mean?'

'All sorts of ways,' Matilda said. 'He set up a foundation – way back, in 1995 – called Yasmine's Memorial Foundation. He and his businesses have pumped hundreds of millions of dollars into it since it was set up.'

Tax deductible, Johansson thought. Tax deductible for him and his companies. Not that that mattered when it was also 'good for business' in the country he lived in, and probably even better in the industry he was in. Whatever difference that makes, he thought. Seeing as Joseph Simon had lived alone for twenty-five years with that fire burning in his heart and head the whole time, a fire he could now afford to throw any amount of fuel on.

'That's just an accounting error to someone like him,' he said. 'What do they actually do? The foundation, I mean?'

'Mostly, they seem to run campaigns. They run adverts against paedophiles and child molesters absolutely everywhere. Television, radio, newspapers, internet, ordinary old-fashioned books, even. Political campaigns, basically.'

'How's it been going, then?'

'Very well indeed,' Matilda said. 'In the USA these days, anyone convicted of sexual assault of a child is obliged to tell the police their address whenever they move. And where they work, what their phone number is, their car's registration number, who they're living with, their families, kids, anyone else who lives there – you name it, whatever. That applies in almost all the American states now. It doesn't matter where you served your sentence and were released. Or if you were only fifteen and were found guilty of sleeping with a girl who was fourteen, and that it was her crazy father who handed you in. But that's just the start, only one part of the whole package.'

'What else is there, then?'

'The local police can also decide where you're allowed to go and who you're allowed to see. You can't go near any nursery, preschool, school, swimming pool or sports centre where children and young people go. Or anywhere else where you might succumb to temptation. You only have to drive past the same school twice in one afternoon and you could end up back in prison.'

'What's the third thing, then?' Johansson said. It's just like it soon will be here, he thought. But only on the internet and in the evening tabloids so far. And no one seems to care.

'He hates Sweden,' Matilda said. 'There isn't a single interview with him where he doesn't throw a load of shit at Sweden. And the interviews are almost always about completely different subjects – about his business, usually. But that doesn't make any difference. He always finds a way to make a detour and land a few more blows on his old adopted homeland.'

'Anything else?' Johansson asked. How come we never read about that over here? he thought.

'I've got something like twenty pages for you.'

'I shall read them with great interest,' Johansson said. As soon as my headache lets me, he thought.

'He's also very good-looking.'

'In what way?'

'A real hunk,' Matilda said. 'I mean, he's sixty, or something like that. But he looks more like fifty, at most. He looks like your best friend. Well, physically, anyway. Not his eyes.'

'Not his eyes.'

'Not like a wolf.' Matilda smiled. 'This is a man who's suffered,' she said. 'Not someone who's just helped himself. And a lot of us girls find that attractive. Guys who've been through the mill but are still standing. They're pretty hard to beat, actually.'

'So?' Johansson said. He was sixty-seven and had never been particularly good-looking, but his looks had been steadily improving until very recently, something like a month back. 'What's your point?'

'I'm twenty-three,' Matilda said. 'If Joseph Simon asked, then if he's the man he seems to be, and even if he didn't have a penny in his pocket, well, woohay!'

'What do you mean, "woohay"?' Johansson asked.

'I'd be on my back in an instant, or whatever position he wanted.'

'Really?' Johansson said. Which might well explain the tattoos and piercings, he thought.

'Yes,' Matilda said. 'I would. Anyway, I've got a question.' She nodded towards the boxes that were still on the floor of the study.

'Yes,' Johansson said. 'I'm listening.' Even though he already knew the answer to the question.

'The girl in those boxes, that's his little daughter, isn't it? Yasmine?'

'Yes,' Johansson said. 'That's his daughter, Yasmine.' These days, she lives in boxes on the floor of my study, he thought. And all I've managed to do so far is give her back her hairgrip.

'Good luck,' Matilda said. 'I hope you manage to catch the man who did it. And that you tell me when you know who it is.'

'Why?' Johansson said. So you can rip his arms and legs off, and boil him down to make glue? he thought.

'So I can scratch his eyes out,' Matilda said. 'Just stick my fingernails in and dig them out. Just like that, plop, plop.'

291

56

Friday afternoon, 30 July

In the car on the way home from the physiotherapist, Johansson sat in silence to start with, wondering whose fault it really was. Whose fault it was that even normal, decent people, usually perfectly normal and even respectable people, kept offering to kill someone they had never met in the most gruesome ways.

If I'd been given this case back in the day, then obviously the perpetrator would have been behind bars within a month and, apart from the unavoidable occurrence that we couldn't have done anything about, at least we would have escaped all the rest of it, Johansson thought. The murderer would have disappeared into collective forgetfulness just like John Ingvar Löfgren, Ulf Olsson and Anders Eklund. They lived on only inside the heads of anyone who had been close to their victims, and all the victims men like Löfgren, Olsson and Eklund hadn't managed to kill, the ones who were allowed to live on with their lifelong suffering. Not like the rest of us, who had enough distance to be able to move on. But instead Evert Bäckström had been put in charge of the case, and it had turned out the way it always turned out when Bäckström was supposed to do something.

But it isn't only Bäckström's fault, he thought. Maybe it's partly that crazy police chief's fault. The man who thought he could be a detective even though he didn't know his way round the most basic interview, still less how to get anything useful out of it in the process. Or the chief of police's best friend, the publisher who got robbed and seriously beaten up for taking the wrong person home, losing both his wallet and Rita Hayworth's old evening dress into the bargain. And who, as the icing on the cake, was allocated Evert Bäckström as the person who would see to it that he got earthly justice.

Hardly Ebbe Carlsson's fault either, he thought. The fact that he blabbed to his best friend was hardly that odd, considering all the indignities Bäckström had subjected him to.

Maybe it wasn't Bäckström's fault at all, he thought. Maybe it was actually his fault, for failing to keep the force clean of men like Evert Bäckström, the force that was his family, despite the occasional cuckoo like Evert Bäckström. The same organization in whose upper echelons he had spent the last twenty years of his police career.

'I've been thinking about something,' Johansson said, nodding towards his chauffeur, Matilda.

'I'm listening, boss.'

'What you said earlier,' he said. 'About scratching out the eyes of the man who murdered Yasmine. Would you really do that?' Think about this carefully now, he thought.

'If it had been my own daughter,' Matilda said. 'If men like you had let him get away?'

'Yes,' Johansson said.

'Then I'd do it.'

'I hear what you're saying.'

'I understand why you're asking.'

'How can you?'

'Because I think you're going to find him,' Matilda said. 'I'm pretty certain that you're going to, actually. So you're worried I'm going to find out who it is and get something like a hundred million for letting Yasmine's dad know what his name is and where he lives.'

'Would you do that?' Johansson asked. You wouldn't be alone in that, he thought.

'No,' Matilda said, shaking her head. 'That's the boundary. If it had been my own daughter, okay. I swear to you, I'd make mincemeat of him. But otherwise, no.'

'Why not?'

'There are boundaries. You should know that.'

'I know,' Johansson said. Boundaries you never cross, he thought. Boundaries you can't bring yourself to cross, because that would make you a worse person than the people who are so terrible that you can't even kill them.

'Just make sure he gets sentenced to life. Then it'll be fine, and you won't have to worry about people like me.'

As soon as Johansson got home he called an old friend of his brother Evert. Someone Johansson knew as well, seeing as they usually went hunting together. A prominent freelance journalist who had been covering the business world for almost forty years and who knew most of what had been going on in the sphere of human life that constituted his area of expertise and was far from afraid to speak out when necessary.

'I'm calling because I've got a question,' Johansson said. 'I hope I'm not disturbing you?'

'Good to hear from you, Lars. No, definitely not. You could never disturb me. How are you?'

'On top of the world,' Johansson lied.

'So we'll see each other for the elk hunt as usual?' his good friend said.

'I certainly hope so,' Johansson said. 'There's something I've been wondering.'

'Doesn't cost anything to ask.'

'Joseph Simon. Is that anyone you know?'

'Yes, I'd even venture to say that I know him better than most people. I knew him back when he lived in Sweden. I wrote an article about him in the early eighties. He and his uncle, who was a professor at the Karolinska, had a private business on the side. They used to analyse blood samples, urine, faeces – anything the health service would throw at them. Must be thirty years ago now.'

'How did it go?' Johansson asked.

'It turned out very well indeed,' his hunting partner said. 'Hence my interest, and the resulting article. Do you know, an ordinary shit can be worth its weight in gold if someone gets it into their head that it contains bacteria that shouldn't be there. Or anything else, for that matter. Or too much or too little. But no matter.'

'How would you describe him? Simon, I mean,' Johansson said. 'In one sentence,' he added.

'In one sentence?'

'In one sentence,' Johansson said. Can't be that hard. After all, you're a journalist, he thought.

'In one sentence. Then I'd put it like this: if there's one person on this planet that I don't want to fall out with, in any serious sense – and I don't mean about business, but feelings and personal relationships – then it's Joseph Simon. Not at any cost.'

'What would happen if you did?'

'Then he'd probably be capable of killing me. I presume you know what happened to his little girl, Yasmine?'

'Yes, of course. But hang on a moment,' Johansson said. 'You mean he could seriously get it into his head to get rid of someone like me?'

'Despite the fact that you used to be head of both the Security Police and National Crime, you mean?'

'Yes.'

'If it turned out that you were involved in his daughter's murder, then he'd definitely do it. Even if you were the president of the United States, he'd have a serious attempt at it. Joseph is a man with infinite resources and, if you ask me, there are one or two American paedophiles who have already been made very painfully aware of that. Without ever having heard of or read about his daughter, Yasmine. Or her father.'

'Really?'

'I was looking on the internet recently,' the journalist said. 'Around the time when Yasmine's murder passed the statute of limitations, and in conjunction with the new legislation abolishing the statute where murder is concerned, I don't know if you read it, but *Svenska Dagbladet* printed an article comparing the murder of Olof Palme with that of Yasmine. And the fact that Palme's murder will never be prescribed, whereas the murder of a little girl like Yasmine already is, because it was three weeks too old when the new law came into force. Even though there's DNA evidence that could convict a perpetrator no matter how long it takes to find him. I mean, if there are any cases that eat up ordinary people from the inside, it would have to be the sexually

296

motivated murder of small children. We're all parents, after all.'

'I see what you mean,' Johansson said. Every parent's worst nightmare, he thought.

'I uncovered a lot of interesting things. Do you know, for instance, how many paedophiles were murdered in the USA last year?'

'No.'

'Over three hundred. That number comes from the FBI, if you were wondering, so it wasn't just snatched out of the air. These murders have even got their own category in the States: they're called paedophile-victim-related murders. More than three hundred in the past year. Do you know how many of them have been solved so far? With their murderers being prosecuted?'

'No,' Johansson said.

'Three,' his friend said. 'In one case, the perpetrator was released because of an illegal search of his home. A hillbilly from the South, and a local jury. And guess who paid for the million-dollar lawyer who represented the idiot? You guessed it. That foundation Joseph set up in memory of his daughter.'

Yasmine's Memorial Foundation, Johansson thought.

'What about the second one?' he asked. 'What happened to him?'

'That was even more straightforward. He was himself a victim. So he was given a probationary sentence and released into the community. He'd cut off the perpetrator's, or rather the murder victim's, cock and shoved it in his mouth. This was in New York, where the law tends to be applied relatively fairly.'

'The third case?'

'Secure psychiatric care. But an appeal has already been lodged and is due to be considered shortly. The defendant is currently out on bail.'

'But this isn't Joseph running about the streets trying to get justice?'

'Why on earth would he do that? He gives a billion a year – Swedish kronor, I mean – to people who'd do it for nothing. Who would even pay to do it, if they were given a name and address. Often people who themselves have been the victims of abuse.'

'Really?' Johansson said.

'And he's caught the mood of the moment, the Sweden Democrats have just made it a big issue in this autumn's election, saying that we should have the same legislation they've got in the USA, where all information about paedophiles and others found guilty of sexual offences are in the public domain and open to everyone. A similar law was passed in Poland last year. And a dozen other EU member states, including Denmark, are preparing similar legislation.'

'I hear what you're saying,' Johansson said. What am I supposed to do about that? he thought.

'Excuse my curiosity,' his friend said. 'Obviously, I don't think for a moment that you had anything to do with the murder of his little daughter, but I can't help being curious. I don't suppose that you and your colleagues have been sitting on the identity of the perpetrator? The man who raped and strangled little Yasmine?'

'No,' Johansson said. 'Absolutely not. I just happened to look at the case when it passed the statute of limitations.'

'That's a relief,' his hunting partner said. 'That's a relief,' he repeated. 'Because Joseph would give his right

298

arm to find out. You could be as rich as your brother if you told him the name of the man who did it. And if he didn't get it, he'd demand far more than that of you if he was convinced that you knew and didn't want to tell him.'

'Well, that's all academic,' Johansson said. 'See you at the hunt.'

Silly fucker, he thought as he hung up. Crapping himself over nothing. Murdering the US president? Christ, who the hell do these people think they are? Do they really think they can do whatever they want just because they've got a bit of money? Anyway, what the hell has happened to your head? he thought. Why can't you just keep your mouth shut?

57

Friday evening, 30 July

That evening he had a talk with Pia. Asked her a direct question. A man-to-woman question, an older-man-to-a-twenty-years-younger-wife question, if you like.

'There's something I've been wondering,' Johansson said. 'Quite a few things, actually.'

'In that case, you've come to the right place, Lars,' Pia said with a smile.

'How many adult men do you think would be able to do it with a child? I'm talking about ordinary, normal blokes like me or Evert or your dad or your brothers – pretty much anyone at all, really.'

'None,' Pia said, shaking her head. 'Not if we're talking about normal men. No normal man or person has sex with a child.'

'I believe you,' Johansson said. 'And I'm not asking for my own sake. What about all men, then?'

'One per cent or so, maybe,' Pia said. 'One in a hundred, one in fifty, or maybe even forty. Assuming we're talking about children. Not twelve-year-olds, not young girls who've just got breasts and hair between their legs. Which is fairly easy to shave off, of course, if you're that way inclined.'

'How many is that, then?' Johansson said.

'Far too many,' Pia said. 'Go and have a look on the internet if you don't believe me. Apparently, those sites get tens of millions of hits each week. Discreet visitors, not page hits, because then it would be hundreds of millions.'

'I've already done that.'

'A question,' Pia said. 'Those boxes,' she continued, nodding towards the boxes on the floor of his study.

'Yes,' Johansson said. 'What about them?'

'They contain the investigation into the murder of little Yasmine Ermegan, don't they?'

'Yes,' Johansson said. 'How do you know that?' That that's where Yasmine lives, he thought.

'I had a look inside them, of course. Who do you take me for?'

'Ah. You had a look.'

'As long as it doesn't kill you.'

'How do you mean?'

'When you find him,' Pia said. 'Because I'm absolutely convinced that you will. As long as it doesn't come at the cost of another stroke or a heart attack.'

'No,' Johansson said. 'You don't have to worry about that.'

'So what will you do then?' Pia asked. 'Once you've found him, and when someone like you can't do a blind thing about him because it's too late, according to some law that's so screwed up you'd have to be a lawyer to come up with something so utterly fucking stupid. So incomprehensibly stupid that any thinking, feeling person can only shake their head at the idiocy of it. Pardon my French.'

'I won't have to do a damn thing,' Johansson said. Once I've found him, it will already be too late, he thought. When I find him, everyone else will do it for me.

58

Saturday morning, 31 July

'Lars,' Pia called. 'There's someone at the door. Can you get it?'

'What for?' Johansson called from the sofa, where he was lying with his newspaper, for once without a headache.

'I'm on the toilet,' she shouted.

I didn't think female bank directors went to the toilet, Johansson thought. Then, with some effort, he got to his feet, picked up his stick and limped out into the hall to open the door. He didn't even look through the peephole first, seeing as it didn't really matter that much, given the way he felt these days. If it came to it, he could probably administer a couple of well-aimed blows with his stick.

'I'm Max,' said Maxim Makarov. 'Your brother Evert sent me.'

Little Evert, Johansson thought. Where the hell did Evert manage to find him? I didn't think they made them like this any more.

'Come in, Max. You're very welcome indeed.' Your very own Little Evert, he thought. After sixty years, you've got your very own Little Evert, and one who's going to be living with you and your wife. 'Come right on in, Max,' he said, suddenly inexplicably elated.

Pia seemed more seriously delighted in their new lodger. She served up grilled steak for lunch. Johansson was permitted a small piece with nothing but salad, whereas Max shovelled down a mountain of fried potatoes with three generous spoonfuls of Pia's homemade garlic butter on top. Johansson was allowed his two glasses of red wine. Considering the amount that was being dispensed in his vicinity, this felt mostly like a sympathetic sop. It was measured precisely by the centilitre by his wife when she had her back to him. Two glasses of red wine and a glass of mineral water, while Max drank at least a litre of freshly squeezed orange juice. He's going to eat me out of house and home, Johansson thought.

'You enjoy your food,' he said, with an innocent expression.

'It's great,' Max said, nodding at Pia. 'Thank you. It was really great.'

'Just say if you'd like some more,' Johansson said.

'Thank you,' Max said, 'but—'

'There's dessert as well,' Pia interrupted, firing a warning glance at her husband. 'And I've made fruit salad for us.'

After lunch Johansson went and lay down on the sofa in his study while Max helped his wife to clear away the remnants of their meal. Not only did he have a healthy appetite, but he was evidently very amusing as well, Johansson thought, the second time he heard Pia laugh out loud in the kitchen. And the bastard also moves without making any noise, he thought, when Max suddenly appeared in the doorway. Short and broad as the door of an old grain store on the ancestral farm. Not a sound when he moved.

'Sorry to disturb you, boss,' Max said. 'Is it okay if I call you boss, boss?'

'That's absolutely fine,' Johansson said. 'Just out of interest, what do you call my brother?'

'Evert,' Max said, looking at Johansson in some surprise. 'Everyone does,' he added.

'And what does he call you?'

'Max,' Max said. 'Or Mackan.'

'What would you like me to call you, then?'

'Max is fine. Or Mackan. Whatever you prefer, boss.'

'How tall are you?' Johansson asked.

'One metre, seventy-four.'

'Weight?'

'About a hundred, a hundred and five, something like that. It depends how much exercise I do.'

'Are you strong?'

'Yes. At least, I've never met anyone who was stronger.' He was evidently surprised by the question.

'The reason I ask is that the other day I got a bit dizzy and ended up on the floor in here, and it took me a hell of a lot of effort to drag myself up on to the sofa again. I weigh one hundred and twenty kilos, you see.' A bit more than a hundred and twenty kilos, he thought.

'No problem,' Max said. 'One hundred and twenty isn't a problem at all. But I thought we could start by swapping that stick.' He nodded towards Johansson's rubber-tipped stick. 'You won't get any balance if you have to hold it in the wrong hand, boss.'

'Really,' Johansson said.

'If you'd care to stand up, boss, I'll show you.'

304

Johansson did as he was asked, while Max pulled a tape measure from his pocket and measured the distance from his right armpit down to the ground.

'A crutch would be fine,' Max said. He put the tape measure away and smiled in confirmation.

'The problem is that I'd have trouble holding it,' Johansson said, showing his weak right arm. 'The crutches they gave me at the hospital are too short. I can't hold them.'

'That can be fixed,' Max said. 'Trust me, I'll sort that out. One other thing, boss – I brought your new car with me. If it's okay with you, boss, I thought we might take it for a spin?'

'Did you, now?' What an odd lad, Johansson thought. Unquestionable, somehow.

It was the same model as his last car, the one his brother had more or less given away to his best friend, but with an automatic gearbox and a load of electronic gadgetry that was supposed to make driving easier for him.

'You can open and close the driver's door with the remote, boss,' Max said, demonstrating. 'The seat adjusts automatically as soon as you sit down. As does the belt. It starts automatically when you press a button. This one, boss.' He pointed to the dashboard. 'Automatic gears. Driving with your left hand and right foot is a piece of cake.'

'Excellent,' Johansson said. It was black, too. Men like him – the way he was in the prime of his life, anyway – always drove in black cars, he thought.

As Johansson glided down the street, just gliding with no specific destination in mind, the tightness in his chest eased. It was easier to breathe, as well, and for the first time in almost a month he was the one sitting behind the wheel. Back on the road again, he thought. Another little step towards a normal life. He didn't even think about the two glasses of wine he had drunk with his lunch.

59

Sunday, 1 August

When Johansson came into the kitchen on Sunday morning his wife was packing a picnic basket.

'What's going on?' he asked.

'We're going to the country,' Pia said. 'The cottage has been empty for almost a month now, and there's loads I need to do.'

'Which "we"?' Johansson asked. 'Going to the country, I mean?'

'You and me and Max.'

'As long as I don't have to do any cleaning,' Johansson said. 'I'm not feeling that great, as I'm sure you appreciate.'

'You've never done any cleaning,' Pia said. 'So there's no need to worry.'

What's she saying? Johansson thought. I've definitely done some cleaning.

When he got in behind the wheel Max and Pia exchanged a quick glance, but neither of them said anything. Johansson said nothing either and, as soon as he got out on to the main road to Norrtälje, he pulled over and stopped at a bus stop.

'Someone else can drive now,' he said, without elaborating. 'I can sit in the back. So I can relax for a while.'

Then he changed places with Pia, and he must have dozed off, because when he woke up they were already parked in front of their country cottage out on Rådmansö.

'We're here now,' Pia said. 'How are you feeling?' She smiled at him to hide the concern in her eyes.

'Fine,' he said. No headache any more, he thought. Two days without a headache: a new record. The tightness in his chest had also eased. But he was tired, actually more tired than before he fell asleep. Tired and miserable for some reason he couldn't put his finger on. Pull yourself together, he thought.

'I feel fine,' he reassured her. 'Better than I have for a long time,' he added. 'I was thinking I might go for a dip.'

Neither of them had any objection to that, not even when he limped out on to the jetty, mustered all the strength he had in his legs and dived head-first into the water, his right arm flapping, even though he had taken a firm grip on it with his left hand. He sank slowly towards the bottom, putting up no resistance and fighting a sudden urge to take a deep breath and just let go. Instead, he held his breath for as long as he could before kicking his way back up to the surface. Easier now, he thought as he inhaled. Easier now.

After that they had lunch. Max offered to clear up. Neither Pia nor Lars Martin raised any objection. Pia lay back on a sunbed with a newspaper. Johansson sat on a chair beside her and read the file that P-2, Detective

Inspector Patrik Åkesson from the Stockholm Police rapid-response unit, had given him when he last saw him, and in passing told him what had happened to his daughter at her preschool. Or didn't happen, to take a more positive view of things.

On top of the bundle was the new, more extensive DNA analysis that the Cold Cases team had asked for six months ago, when they were planning to have a last crack at the Yasmine case before it was prescribed. Then they received an email the same day about an as yet unknown perpetrator, or possibly perpetrators, who had murdered an overly conscientious prosecutor out in Huddinge. He had been shot through the head as he stepped out of his front door to let the family dog out, thus depriving his two young children of their father, and potentially solving a tricky problem for his wife, who had been wanting a divorce for the previous six months because he worked far too much and spent far too little time with her and the children.

Then those in charge of the police redeployed their forces. The regional police chief in Stockholm called a press conference and appeared on radio, television and in the rest of the media. This wasn't just a horrifying murder of a good and conscientious prosecutor and father of two little children, she explained. It was also an attack on the whole of the justice system, planned and carried out by highly organized criminals. All imaginable resources would be utilized to solve the murder, and when she said this she didn't spare a thought for a nine-year-old girl who had been raped, murdered and trodden into the mud not far from Skokloster Castle in Uppland twenty-five years before.

The investigation into nine-year-old Yasmine's murder had been 'put on ice until further notice'. That was what Superintendent Kjell Hermansson at Regional Crime in Stockholm was told by his boss, and a week later he carried the boxes containing everything about Yasmine's case out of his office and put them in the group's storeroom. The same Superintendent Hermansson who also happened to be the father-in-law of Detective Inspector Patrik Åkesson. It was a small world they lived in, and even smaller for those citizens who also happened to work as police officers.

Those boxes were still standing there when the case was prescribed, the same boxes in which little Yasmine, nine years old when she was raped and smothered, had been laid to rest for the previous twenty-five years.

Then one day, out of the blue, Kjell Hermansson's old boss, Bo Jarnebring, appeared and asked to borrow them on behalf of a good friend. Not just any friend, either.

'Lars Martin wants to take a look at the case,' Jarnebring explained to Hermansson.

'Bloody hell,' Hermansson said, unable to contain his surprise. Why didn't he get in touch earlier? he thought.

'Why didn't he get in touch earlier?' he said out loud. 'It's too late to do anything about it now.'

'You know what Lars Martin thinks about Cold Cases,' Jarnebring said with a wry smile.

'Yes, I've got a pretty good idea,' Hermansson said with a sigh.

Fresh in his memory, even though it was almost ten years ago, was the veritable massacre to which the then head of the National Crime Unit had subjected him and his colleagues at a national symposium for senior officers from around the country who worked with cold cases.

'So he had to wait until he had a stroke before he got the idea,' Jarnebring said with a chuckle.

Naturally, Lars Martin Johansson knew nothing of these thoughts and this conversation as he sat there reading what had turned out to be 'the last shot at the Yasmine case'. An utterly pointless, almost spasmodic shot from the long arm of the law. A new, more extensive DNA analysis, from the sperm left in Yasmine's body and on her clothes by the perpetrator over twenty-five years ago.

'Anything interesting?' Pia wondered, putting her newspaper down and looking at her husband the second time he grunted out loud to himself as he read.

'Sort of. I'm reading a DNA analysis,' he answered. 'Sperm found in the Yasmine case,' he explained. 'It says here that they're more than ninety per cent certain that it comes from a perpetrator of Nordic origin, probably Swedish – from central Sweden, even – and without any traces of foreign DNA, in an ethnic sense,' he went on. These DNA boffins are getting pretty remarkable, he thought. Soon they'll be able to fax through a portrait of the bastard as well.

'That sounds interesting.'

'Not to me,' Johansson said, shaking his head. I could have worked that out, he thought. He had figured that out long before he had any idea where the crime scene was.

'Really?' Pia said, and smiled. I recognize him again now, she thought.

'Yes.' Johansson said, already thinking about something else.

'I've emptied the fridge, carried the rubbish out, hoovered and done most of the cleaning,' Max said. 'And I've made some coffee.'

He doesn't make a sound, the bastard, Johansson thought.

In his left hand Max was holding an oblong tray with three glasses, three coffee mugs, a flask, a bottle of mineral water, a jug of milk and a large bowl of fruit. He held the tray by its edge, squeezed between the thumb and fingers of his left hand, as he moved the table that stood between them. With his right hand, same grip, no trace of a wobble.

I believe you, Johansson thought. You don't know anyone stronger than you.

'I thought I might drive home,' Johansson said a couple of hours later when they were about to get in the car.

Neither Max nor Pia said anything, they just nodded, didn't even sneak a glance at each other.

The last summer, Johansson thought as he pulled out on to the main road between Norrtälje and Stockholm. The last summer. But before that I'm going to hunt elk, he thought.

That night he dreamed. About Maxim Makarov, a Russian-born refugee who came to Sweden from a children's home in St Petersburg when he was ten years old, and who for good reason didn't know anyone who was stronger than him. About the sensitive but still faceless paedophile who may have brought them together.

'Wake up, boss,' Max said, as he gently shook Johansson's shoulder. 'What do you want me to do to him, boss?' he asked.

Then he held the child-killer out towards Johansson, who was lying on his side in bed. Holding him right up, without his hand shaking at all, squeezed in a thumb grip like a tray of coffees. The paedophile just hung there. While Maxim Makarov held him up in his left hand, he just hung there, eyes closed, head lolling, his body not moving at all.

'Let me think,' Johansson said. 'Let me think.' Then he woke up. Sat bolt upright, his heart pounding like a steam hammer in his chest.

60

Monday, 2 August

Monday. A new week, a new day. Another day in Lars Martin Johansson's new life, his life as a patient. His wife, Pia, went to work while he was still in bed, half asleep, far too tired even to talk to her when she leaned over him and ran her fingers across his forehead.

Matilda served him breakfast on a tray on the table next to the sofa in his study. A healthy breakfast, with soured milk, fruit and muesli, a boiled egg and a cup of strong coffee, as a concession to his past life. Beneath the morning paper he found an envelope containing twelve 500-kronor notes.

Hope she gave the old bag a kick up the backside, Johansson thought, the old bag being Matilda's mother, who had broken the fourth commandment and done to her daughter what she would never have done to herself.

'Matilda,' Johansson said when she came to take his breakfast tray away. 'You don't know anything about this, do you?' he said, holding up the envelope.

'Not a clue,' Matilda said, shaking her head. 'Better check you haven't lost a tooth.'

'Lost a tooth?'

'The tooth fairy. Thanks, by the way,' she said as she pulled the door closed behind her.

Two employees, and staff problems already, Lars Martin Johansson thought, having not so long ago been boss of more than a thousand police officers. When they were getting in the car to go to the physiotherapist, Johansson got in the driver's seat, but when Matilda went to get in next to him Max simply shook his head.

'In the back,' he said, gesturing towards the back seat with his thumb.

'Why?' Matilda said. 'Is this a boys' thing, or what?'

'You're welcome to sit in the front,' Max said with a smile. 'On one condition.'

'What?' Matilda said.

'That you're a qualified driving instructor,' Max grinned.

'Like you are!' Matilda said.

'But I'm stronger,' Max said, and smiled again.

'Stop squabbling, children,' Johansson said, suddenly feeling better than he had in ages. So in the back seat sat the tooth fairy, a bit grumpy, but that would soon pass, and in the seat next to him a former Russian orphan who had never met anyone who was as strong as him.

The session with the physiotherapist was nothing special. No unexpected reverses, no progress either, but, quite regardless of this, Johansson's good mood refused to budge.

'Time for lunch,' Johansson said. 'Call Ulla Winbladh's and ask if they can do some stuffed cabbage leaves with cream sauce, new potatoes and lingonberry jam.' He nodded at Matilda in the rear-view mirror.

'I don't doubt they can,' she said, raising her eyebrows and looking up at the roof.

'Good,' Johansson said. You can say what you like, but that girl isn't stupid, even if she has made a right mess of herself, he thought.

'Maybe the cream sauce isn't a good idea,' Max said, squirming in his seat.

'Listen carefully, Max,' Johansson said, changing lane without indicating and choosing to ignore the taxi behind him that suddenly flashed its headlights and blew its horn at him.

'Listen carefully,' he repeated. 'A real man can have only one boss, and if he says cream sauce, then cream sauce it is.' No matter what my wife has tried to tell you, he thought.

'Understood, boss,' Max said.

'So would you mind giving that bastard the evil eye,' Johansson said, nodding towards the taxi that had pulled up alongside him, a wildly gesticulating taxi-driver behind the wheel.

'Understood, boss,' Max said. He wound the window down and waved his clenched fist at the taxi-driver.

'Sensible fellow,' Johansson said as he watched the taxi brake and pull in behind him. No flashing head-lights, no horn, no more gestures. Just like forty years ago, when he used to share the front seat with his best friend, looking for crooks and cruising up and down the streets, kings of the world. He hadn't felt this good since he'd stopped and talked to P-2 and his colleagues in the rapid-response unit in front of the best hotdog kiosk in Sweden, up on Karlbergsvägen.

*

As soon as he got back he lay on the sofa and had a little afternoon nap. He woke when Matilda came in and checked on him.

'Are you awake?' she asked.

'Yes,' Johansson said. So a cup of coffee wouldn't go amiss, he thought.

'You've had a letter,' she said, holding out a white envelope.

'Oh. Is it from the tooth fairy?'

'No,' Matilda said. 'But it does look a bit mysterious.'

'What do you mean, "mysterious"?'

'The post came two hours ago,' Matilda said. 'There's no stamp on this. No sender's name. Just your name: Lars Johansson. Someone must have put it through the letterbox.'

'Open it, then,' Johansson said, waving his weak right arm to encourage her.

'Really mysterious,' Matilda said, holding up a sheet of A4 that was folded in two.

'What does it say?'

'A name. Staffan Leander. Just a name. That's all. Staffan Leander.'

'Staffan Leander,' Johansson repeated.

'See for yourself,' Matilda said, handing him the sheet of paper.

'How long has it been since you drove me to Lilla Essinge?' Johansson asked.

'That was last week. Tuesday. Almost a week ago.'

Erika Brännström, Johansson thought. Suddenly she was sitting there on the chair in front of him, hands clasped in her lap, with those wary eyes of hers. Hands marked by hard work, he thought. Erika, who had two young daughters the same age as Yasmine.

61

Monday afternoon, 2 August

Just an idea, a fleeting thought, but he had to do *something*, after all. With some effort, he managed to drag the box containing the many hundreds of records from the vehicle register over to the sofa. He picked out the ones at the top. Leafed through them, put them back and pulled out a fresh bundle from the bottom of the box. There's no order at all, everything's all mixed up, Johansson thought, and put those back as well. Precisely what happens when a number of colleagues each decided to dig about for whatever he or she was looking for twenty-five years ago, and without a computerized summary that could give him a clue when he approached the same task twenty-five years later.

Max, Johansson thought. He picked up his mobile and called him. He certainly wasn't going to shout for him. And he had no intention of asking Matilda, who was doubtless sitting on watch outside his door. God knows what might have happened to her with a mother like that, Johansson thought. No plop, plop; definitely no eyes plopping out with the help of a pair of long, red fingernails, he thought.

'Can you come here?' Johansson asked.

'I'm sitting in the kitchen, boss,' Max said, barely able to conceal his surprise.

'Then get a move on.'

Twenty metres at most, but still ten seconds: why the hell did it take him so long? Johansson thought.

'What can I do for you, boss?' Max asked.

'Sit yourself down,' Johansson said, nodding towards the chair closest to the sofa he was lying on.

'I'm listening, boss,' Max said as he sat down.

'A direct question, Max. Are you the sort of person who can keep his mouth shut?'

'Yes,' Max said. 'I don't know anyone who's better at that.'

'Not a word,' Johansson said. 'Not even to Evert. Is that understood?'

'Yes.'

'Good. In this box here are hundreds of records from the vehicle register. People who owned a red Golf about twenty-five years ago. In June 1985, to be precise. Can you see if you can find an owner called Staffan Leander,' he said, giving Max the sheet of paper Matilda had given him.

'How many are there?'

'Hundreds,' Johansson said. 'Thousands, maybe. Loads.' How the fuck should I know? he thought.

'Is there a list of them?'

'Nope,' Johansson said. 'Because some daft bugger managed to lose it.' Twenty-five years ago, he thought.

'Oh, I see,' Max said. 'Is it okay if I take them into my room?'

'Of course.' Johansson nodded towards the closed door. 'On one condition. That you don't—'

319

'I know,' Max said, and grinned.

Max came back just over an hour later.

'How did you get on?' Johansson asked. 'Did you find anything?' Stupid question, because he could already see the answer in Max's eyes.

'No Staffan Leander. No other Leanders either.'

'You're quite sure?'

'Hundred per cent,' Max said. 'There were just over seventeen hundred vehicles, if you were wondering, boss. The most recent model of Golf from 1982, up to 1986, because that year's model was released in June 1985. There are loads of registered owners whose first name is Staffan, but none with the surname Leander. Almost half are company cars, hire cars or owned by leasing firms. Are you quite sure this Leander couldn't have been driving one of those, boss?'

'No,' Johansson said. 'You might very well be right.' And, in the worst-case scenario, I might have got everything completely wrong, he thought.

62

Tuesday, 3 August

In the morning he got a new crutch. It stretched from his right armpit all the way down to the floor, an extended arm with a pistol grip that supported his bad right hip and stabilized his upper arm. A crutch he could hold with no difficulty at all.

'Did you make it yourself?' Johansson asked.

'Contacts,' Max said. 'I used to play ice-hockey. I limped about with one like that myself.'

'Thank you,' Johansson said.

Then his brother-in-law called him on his mobile.

'I think I've found something,' Alf Hult said.

'You do, do you?' Johansson said. 'Tell me.'

'I was going to suggest that I come over, because it's rather complicated. Unless you're busy, of course.'

'I'm never busy,' Johansson said. 'If you like, I can offer you lunch?'

'See you in an hour. The bus leaves in fifteen minutes,' Alf said. He lived out in Täby and, according to his brother-in-law, Evert, had never taken a taxi, not even to his own wedding.

*

Half an hour later Matilda knocked on the door.

'Ye–es,' Johansson said. He had been lying on the sofa reading J. D. Salinger's posthumous *American Reflections*, which had been published in English a couple of weeks earlier. According to the quote from the *New York Times Literary Supplement* on the dust-jacket, it was 'a ferocious indictment of all the -isms that have not only killed the American dream but also transformed highly comprehensible and private neuroses into a national trauma'.

That told them, he thought. And now they couldn't argue with him about it.

'Physiotherapist,' Matilda said, pointing at her watch.

'Cancelled, I'm afraid,' Johansson said, waving his book as a deterrent. 'I'm expecting an important visit. From my brother-in-law.'

'Will he want lunch?' Matilda asked.

'Of course,' Johansson said. 'I think he prefers fish. He's the cautious sort. Run down to the market hall at Medborgarplatsen and see if you can find some fresh salmon.'

Matilda nodded and disappeared, just as Johansson had another idea. Baltic herring, he thought. Fresh Baltic herring with crushed potatoes, a touch of vinegar, a cold Czech pilsner, a—

'Or fresh Baltic herring!' Johansson yelled after her. Wonder if she heard? he thought as the front door slammed shut.

Alf is a uniquely long-winded bastard, Johansson thought half an hour later. First, his brother-in-law had insisted on shaking his hand, even though Johansson was lying on the sofa and had made do with waving at him. Then he arranged the table between them, adjusted his chair, and only then did he pull a thin sheaf of papers out of his battered brown briefcase.

'You said you'd found something,' Johansson said. Wonder if he's messing me about? he thought. Trying to raise my hopes so he can whack the price up.

'Yes,' Alf said, cautiously clearing his throat. 'That's quite right. I've discovered that Johan Nilsson had a hitherto unknown half-sister. You know, the chap who was married to Margaretha Sagerlied.'

'What's her name?'

'Vera Nilsson, born on 21 October 1921. Died on 10 March 1986. If you're wondering why I didn't find her earlier, it's because her relationship to Johan Nilsson isn't apparent from the population register. According to that, her father's identity is unknown. Father unknown: an almost classic element of Swedish population records,' Alf Hult said, looking almost delighted.

'So how do you know they were related?' Johansson asked. She had been twenty-six years younger than her half-brother, he thought.

'That emerges from a will Johan Nilsson signed in November 1959,' Alf Hult said. 'Just a couple of months after his father died. Anders Gustaf Nilsson, the grocer, died on 15 September that year. His son, Johan, signed a new will exactly two months later, on 15 November 1959. It was submitted and registered at Stockholm District Court.'

'Really?'

'So it wouldn't be too presumptuous to assume that Anders Gustaf only told Johan about his sister when he was on his deathbed.'

'Better late than never,' Johansson said. 'You're quite sure?'

'Quite sure,' Hult said. 'In the will Johan Nilsson signed in November 1959, he leaves a sizeable portion of his assets to, and I quote, "my beloved half-sister Vera Nilsson", end of quote.'

'"A sizeable portion",' Johansson said.

'Approximately a tenth of his collected assets, and, according to my rough calculations, that ten per cent is roughly equivalent to half the amount Johan Nilsson inherited from his father, Anders Gustaf. It's worth noting that Anders Gustaf died without having made a will. He was a widower, so everything was passed on to his only son and heir, Johan.'

'How much money are we talking about, then? How much did he leave his sister?'

'About three hundred thousand kronor. Which of course was a lot of money in those days. About a couple of million today, after inheritance tax, so a considerable amount. As well as a number of valuable possessions. Among them a very valuable painting by Leander Engström, *Wanderer and Hunter*. Painted in 1917. Sold relatively recently in Bukowski's spring auction of 2003, when it went for three and a half million. In the will, it was valued at fifteen thousand.'

'A Leander Engström,' Johansson repeated. Another Leander, but as a first name this time, he thought. Dead since the 1920s. He himself owned a mountain landscape by the same artist. It hung in his living room.

'Vera Nilsson is an interesting person,' Alf said.

'In what way?'

'Amongst other things, she was the daughter of a cousin of her and Johan's father, Anders Gustaf.'

'Common enough in those days,' Johansson said with a grin.

'Well,' Alf Hult said, and cleared his throat. 'The Nilsson family had its roots in the Stockholm area, so things may have been a little different to northern Ångermanland. In any case,' he went on, clearing his throat again, 'Vera Nilsson gave birth to a son in the autumn of 1960 – on 5 October 1960 – at the age of thirty-nine, which was fairly old for those days. His father, too, was "unknown", so history seems to have repeated itself. In July that year Johan Nilsson gave his sister an early inheritance, equivalent to the amount he had bequeathed to her the previous year. The most likely explanation is that in August 1960, just a month later, he married Margaretha Sagerlied and, immediately before the wedding, made a new will that replaced the one from November 1959. So first he gives his sister her share of what he inherited from their father, then he makes a new will, leaving all his assets to his new wife. His half-sister isn't mentioned at all in the new will. He marries Margaretha Sagerlied and, when he eventually dies twenty years later, the whole of his estate passes to her.'

'This son,' Johansson said. 'Vera Nilsson's illegitimate son. What's his name?' I knew it, he thought.

'Staffan Leander Nilsson,' Alf Hult said. 'Leander is his middle name, and one can only speculate as to the reason for that. Born on 5 October 1960. I've got his ID number here.'

'Is he still alive?' Johansson asked. Staffan Leander Nilsson, he thought.

'Yes, he's alive. Single, no children. His most recent address is out in Frösunda, in Solna. Gustaf III's Boulevard, number twenty. From his birth right up to 1986 he lived right in the centre of the city, at Birger Jarlsgatan 104, the same address as his mother, Vera

Nilsson. That's the big HSB housing association block between Birger Jarlsgatan and Valhallavägen, if you know the one I mean? In May 1986 he left the country, and didn't return until autumn 1998. Twelve and a half years later.'

'Abroad,' Johansson said. 'Abroad where?'

'Probably Thailand. But I haven't been able to find an address. I'm still grappling with that. When he left the country, he owed a significant amount of tax – several hundred thousand kronor. Among other things, the inheritance tax on his mother's estate. That debt was written off after ten years. So he had good reason to want to stay out of the way, to put it mildly.'

'How sure are you that he was in Thailand?' Johansson asked.

'Fairly sure. He seems to have had a share in a hotel project in Pattaya.'

Thailand, Johansson thought. Must have been paradise for someone like him in the late eighties. Probably still was, come to that.

'So, to summarize,' Alf said, 'his mother dies on 10 March 1986. A couple of months later her son leaves the country, after receiving his inheritance as her only heir. She doesn't appear to have left a will. According to probate, her estate amounted to just under a million, but if you ask me I'd guess at double that. He only returns to Sweden twelve and a half years later.'

'Okay, this is the situation,' Johansson said, sitting up on the sofa. 'This Staffan Leander Nilsson—'

'Yes?' Hult said, and nodded.

'I want to know everything about him. Absolutely everything.'

'Then that's what I'll find out.'

'Can you excuse me for a moment?' Johansson said.

'Of course.'

Then Johansson picked up his new crutch and, without any difficulty at all, went out into the hall and into the guest bedroom, where his very own Little Evert was sitting in front of his computer with headphones on as he played something that looked suspiciously like an unusually violent game.

'Boss,' Max said, taking the headphones off.

'Can you have another look at that box?' Johansson said, pointing at the box of vehicle-registration details Max had left on the bed. 'See if you can find a Staffan Nilsson, or a Staffan Leander Nilsson, born on 5 October 1960.'

'Just a moment,' Max said. He stretched out his long arm and pulled out a thin bundle of printouts held together with a paperclip. 'Just a moment,' he repeated, leafing through the documents.

'I put all the Staffans together,' he explained. 'There are about thirty of them, actually.'

'Very sensible,' Johansson said. The lad's far from stupid, he thought.

'Here he is,' Max said, holding out one of the records. 'Staffan Nilsson, born on 5 October 1960. Back then, he was living on Birger Jarlsgatan, number 104, here in Stockholm. On 5 July 1985 he was registered as the owner of a new Golf GTI, 1986 model. A red Golf. Bought directly from the main dealer, Volkswagen Sweden.'

'You don't say?' Johansson said. 'You don't say?' he repeated, taking the proof of registration.

Now, you bastard, thought the former head of the National Crime Unit, Lars Martin Johansson, having learned to hate coincidence at an early age. Once doesn't count, but twice is two times too many. I've got you now, he thought, and even though he told himself that he had to take it easy if what he had suspected all along turned out to be the case, he felt an instant and quite unreasonable hatred.

'Are you okay, boss?' Max said, gently touching his arm.

'Fine. Absolutely fine,' he said, and nodded. What do I do now? he thought.

IV

Eye for eye, tooth for tooth, hand for hand, foot for foot . . .

Book of Exodus, 21:24

63

Wednesday morning, 4 August 2010

Regular routines, as far as possible. On the days when his
body wasn't tormenting him in a more tangible way he
would eat breakfast in the kitchen, but today he ate sitting
on the sofa in his study. He had had a headache since he
had woken up. Then his chest started to feel tight, anxiety
grabbed hold of him and he was forced to save himself
with another little white pill. Then he must have dozed
off for a moment, because Hypnos had been lurking in
the gloom of his study, head tilted, with his fine fair hair,
just like a child's, and his gentle smile, as he held out the
hand containing the green poppy seedhead to him.

Half an hour later, he felt better. So he got out his
laptop, put it on his knees and decided to come up with
a plan of how to proceed. In the prime of life, he used
to write that sort of thing on Post-it notes that he would
stick on his desk at work, but that was out of the question these days.

In the prime of life, you even used to write little
memos, Johansson thought. Now he couldn't write leg-
ibly with his right hand. But he could use it to hold the
computer on his lap while he tapped at it with the fingers of his left hand.

'Actions', Johansson typed at the top of the screen. Then a new line: 'Continue mapping Staffan Leander Nilsson, born on 5 October 1960,' he wrote. Then another new line: 'Compile biography of Nilsson, Staffan Leander.' When he had got that far Matilda came in and looked pointedly at her wristwatch.

'Physiotherapy,' Matilda said. 'Time to get moving.'

'Give me five minutes,' Johansson said. 'Manpower: one plus four,' he wrote. Me, Johansson thought. Plus his best friend, Bo Jarnebring, his brother-in-law, Alf Hult, then Matilda and Max. But no one else, definitely not former colleagues like Superintendent Hermansson or his son-in-law, who might have trouble keeping a cool head if things heated up.

I've been in charge of considerably worse investigative teams, he thought. Then he switched the computer off, put it on the table and got up from the sofa where he had been lying.

When they were in the car on the way home from the physiotherapist, Max made a suggestion.

'I've been giving some thought to the elk hunt, boss, if you've got a moment?'

'I've got a moment,' Johansson said. What else would I have time for? he thought. Except poking about in an old, prescribed murder case, stuffing myself with pills and counting down the days of what was, until just a month ago, a dignified and even a good life.

'I've spoken to a gunsmith,' Max said. 'Explained about your right hand, boss. Could you manage to feed a new cartridge in using the breechblock, boss?'

'Yes,' Johansson said, because he had secretly been practising this during the past week.

'So it's your trigger finger that's the problem?'

'Yes,' Johansson said. 'I don't have any real feeling in it.'

'According to the gunsmith, we can get round that,' Max said. 'He's done that before for another customer. He had the same trouble as you, boss, so he made it possible for the customer to fire with his left index finger by adding a new trigger towards the front of the body of the rifle.'

'Really?'

'If you can hold the butt against your shoulder with your right hand and take aim, it ought to work.'

'What the hell are we waiting for?' Johansson said. At last. Now we're getting somewhere, he thought. Somewhere that looked at least vaguely reminiscent of the life he had always led up to now.

64

Alf phoned Johansson before lunch and was at his front door an hour later.

'Tell me,' Johansson said as soon as his brother-in-law had sat down and taken out another sheaf of papers from his worn brown briefcase.

'A bit of a mixture,' Alf said, pursing his thin lips. 'You remember that painting I told you about? *Wanderer and Hunter* by Leander Engström, the one Vera Nilsson was given by her half-brother, Johan, which he in turn had inherited from their father, Anders Gustaf Nilsson?'

'Yes,' Johansson said. 'What about it?'

'It was sold in Bukowski's spring auction in May 1986. Went for almost a million kronor, after deductions. The seller just happened to be Vera Nilsson's son, Staffan Nilsson – before the details of her will had been settled, in case you're wondering.'

'They don't care about that sort of thing, do they?' Art dealers, he thought.

'Probably not, probably not,' Alf agreed. 'I could tell you a thing or two about the art market, if you wanted to listen. I've brought a picture of it, by the way. It's a fine painting,' he said, handing a large colour photograph to Johansson.

Wanderer and Hunter, the subject evidently having a rest by a lake when Leander Engström's brush caught him. A mountain landscape in red and blue, green and grey, fading away in the background, the translucent air indicating the chill of autumn, which could be nothing but a sign of approaching winter at that time of year. He had leaned his gun against a rock. His prey – a couple of ducks and a hare – were slung over a tree branch. The man himself was sitting by a fire he had just made, reading a book.

Wanderer and Hunter. Hard to imagine a better title, Johansson thought.

'One million for the painting,' said Alf Hult, former tax-office auditor. 'His mother also owned a couple of apartments on Birger Jarlsgatan, which her son sold at more or less the same time as the painting, apparently with the help of a power of attorney that was set up just a week or so before she died. A highly irregular business.'

'So how much did he get in total?' Johansson interrupted.

'I'd say a couple of million. One million for the painting, seven hundred thousand for the flats, and the rest made up of savings and shares which he seems to have sold at the same time.'

'He sold the whole lot,' Johansson said. 'Before his poor mum was even cold.'

'Yes,' his brother-in-law agreed, pursing his lips. 'That seems to be a reasonable summation.'

'So he didn't bother to pay any tax, ran off to Thailand and bought a hotel,' Johansson said, suddenly thinking about his eldest brother.

'Yes,' Alf sighed. 'That's what he did. But you'll have to be a little patient when it comes to that bit. I'm still waiting for information about that hotel project he seems to have been involved in.'

'What else has he done, then? Before he went to Thailand, I mean?'

'All the things young men usually get up to. Seems to have been rather idle. I've also found a couple of forged certificates.'

'Really?' Johansson said. Now we're getting somewhere, he thought.

'It was when he was applying for a job back in the early eighties – incidentally, I'll be coming back to that job. He declared that he'd graduated from high school in 1979. From the Norra Real School here in Stockholm. After that he claimed to have studied economics at university – in Uppsala, of all places. Two terms of business economics, one of national economics, one of statistics, an introductory course in law. Taken together, approximately three-quarters of a bachelor's degree.'

'But he hadn't?'

'No,' Alf said. 'He did attend Norra Real, but he left high school after just three terms, without graduating. And he never seems to have been enrolled as a student at Uppsala.'

'The cheeky rascal,' Johansson said. 'Where did he do his national service, then?'

'He got an exemption. A medical certificate: scoliosis – severe problems with his back, apparently.'

Not when he raped Yasmine, he was thinking. 'Anything else?' Johansson said.

'I've also tracked down a foundation. A couple of years after her husband, Johan Nilsson, died, his widow, Margaretha Sagerlied, set up a foundation.'

'What's it called?'

'Margaretha Sagerlied's Foundation for the Support of the Operatic Arts,' Alf said, and sighed, for some reason.

Who'd have thought it? Johansson thought. 'Tell me,' he said.

65

Wednesday afternoon, 4 August

When Johan Nilsson died and his wife inherited his estate, she used five million kronor of her considerable inheritance to set up a foundation that would support the 'Operatic Arts'. Young singers and musicians could apply to it for grants to help fund their education or research trips, or to arrange concerts. The foundation also awarded an annual prize of twenty thousand kronor, the Margaretha Sagerlied Award, for 'Most Promising Young Soprano of the Year'. The foundation began its work in 1983. Its chairman was a highly respected Stockholm lawyer and opera enthusiast, while the finances were managed by the foundations department at the SE Bank.

'That Sagerlied seems to have been a regular latter-day Jenny Lind,' Johansson said, having made himself comfortable on the sofa, hands folded over his stomach, and feeling better than he had done in a very long time.

'Yes, perhaps.' His brother-in-law sighed. 'Sadly, there was only a brief period of harmony, if I can put it like that.'

'Why?' Johansson said. 'Five million was a lot of money in those days, wasn't it?'

'That wasn't the problem,' Alf Hult said. 'Unfortunately, Margaretha Sagerlied employed her closest – indeed, only – relative to look after the practical details. I'm talking about the young Staffan Nilsson, of course. After just a couple of years the foundation was more or less obliged to shut up shop, as a consequence of some highly dubious affairs he got the foundation mixed up in.'

'How could that have happened? I thought set-ups like that had a pretty rigorous system of controls.'

'They usually do,' Alf agreed. 'One of the main reasons for that is that foundations have serious tax advantages, so there's always a risk they'll be exploited. When Margaretha Sagerlied chose to employ her only close relative, Staffan Nilsson, the chairman of the foundation pointed this out to her. And that there was a risk that it would be seen as a way of giving him various tax-related benefits. That was also why the chairman requested a CV from him, so it could be demonstrated that he had been appointed on his merits and not merely because he was a family member to whom Margaretha Sagerlied wanted to give unwarranted privileges.'

'But he fabricated his qualifications,' Johansson said.

'Yes, insofar as I've been able to check them. According to his own description, he was a very industrious young man who had various summer jobs while he was still at school, but I haven't been able to look into that, for practical reasons. I have the CV here, if you're interested,' Alf said, holding up a plastic sleeve containing the document.

'Put it on the pile,' Johansson said. Probably lies from beginning to end, he thought.

'At first, the foundation appears to have worked as intended, in accordance with the statutes and deeds of any foundation. Margaretha Sagerlied's prize was awarded each year for the first three years, until 1985. Apart from that, grants and donations to a total value of about a hundred thousand kronor were distributed each year. Together with the other costs – payments to board members, Staffan Nilsson's salary, rent of a small office on Linnégatan in Östermalm – the foundation's annual expenditure amounted to approximately three hundred thousand kronor.'

'Six per cent of its capital. That sounds quite high, if you ask me,' Johansson said.

'They got a good return on their capital in the first year; in fact, the foundation actually made a surplus, in the order of a hundred thousand kronor.'

'But then everything went wrong.'

'As early as 1984, if you ask me,' Alf Hult said. 'Unfortunately, they tried to compensate for this by making risky financial investments, and this is where the supervision broke down. Both internally and at the bank, which of course was supposed to monitor that side of the foundation's activities.'

'So how much ended up in the pockets of young Mr Nilsson, then?'

'Not much, as far as I've been able to see. It was, to all intents and purposes, a case of genuinely bad investments. Anyway, to cut a long story short, an additional six-monthly audit was conducted in the summer of 1986, when it was discovered that more than half of the foundation's capital had been used up. But, by then, young Mr Nilsson had resigned and departed for a then unknown destination.'

'What happened after that?' There was a lot going on in the first half of 1986, Johansson thought.

'Since then, the foundation has been slowly dwindling. Its working capital is a couple of million, as it has been more or less since Margaretha Sagerlied died. The foundation still awards grants, and that prize Mrs Sagerlied set up, but the total amounts to less than a hundred thousand kronor each year. Taking into account the foundation's running costs, its total out-goings per year are about two hundred thousand. Its capital is gradually shrinking by a couple of per cent each year, and has been for many years now.'

'But she made no attempt to refill the coffers?' Johansson said. 'When she popped her clogs, I mean.'

'Margaretha Sagerlied was still a very wealthy woman when she died. The estate was valued at over ten million kronor after tax, and that was in 1989. The foundation didn't get a single krona.'

'Who got it, then? All the money?'

'Margaretha Sagerlied made a new will in October 1986. That's four months after the audit of the founda-tion, when its precarious financial state was revealed. She chose to leave almost all her money to various charities working with children and young people. The Church's Children's Fund, Save the Children, the children's sec-tion of the Red Cross.'

'And young Mr Nilsson?'

'Not a krona. But her former cleaner pops up again. Erika Brännström, who I'm sure you remember, received five hundred thousand kronor. Money which, according to the will, was to be used to pay for her two daughters' education.'

'Who'd have thought it?' Johansson said. Money as penance, an indulgence for another person's crimes, he thought. Or, at worst, a bribe in return for silence.

Margareta Sagerlied's life must have been a living hell in the years before she died, he thought.

'Erika Brännström,' Alf Hult repeated. 'If you're interested, I could find out more about her as well. Both she and her daughters are still alive; I've checked. She's about sixty now; her daughters are in their thirties. You've already had that information, in fact.'

'No,' Johansson said. 'Never mind her.' What I want to know about her isn't anything you can help me with, he thought. 'Anything else?'

'There is, actually,' his brother-in-law said. 'It's about Staffan Nilsson's mother, Vera Nilsson.'

'What about her?'

'Like I said, she died on 10 March 1986. Without a will, which, from a legal perspective, isn't terribly interesting, seeing as her only son was also her only heir. But the circumstances surrounding her death are interesting. Particularly for someone like you. Given your professional background, I mean.'

'Really?' Johansson said. Now we're talking, he thought.

66

Wednesday afternoon, 4 August

Vera Nilsson, sixty-four years old, was found dead in her home at Birger Jarlsgatan 104 in Stockholm on the morning of 11 March 1986. The person who found her was her son, Staffan, who lived in a smaller flat in the same building.

Vera Nilsson was lying on the sofa in her living room. She was wearing pants, a bra, her dressing-gown and slippers. On the coffee table was an empty half-bottle of whisky, half a dozen empty cans of export-strength lager, a large bottle of vodka, approximately half full, an empty mineral-water bottle, a similarly empty fizzy-drink bottle and a tumbler containing a mixture of vodka and carbonated grapefruit drink. An empty jar of strong sleeping pills and a similarly empty jar of tranquillizers were found in the bathroom. But no suicide note, or any message to that effect, was found.

The bed in the bedroom was untouched, made up with clean sheets, but otherwise, the two rooms and the kitchen of the small flat made a cluttered and dirty impression. Drawers had been pulled out, their contents emptied on to the floor, the clothes from two wardrobes were piled on the floor, and someone seemed to have made a right mess of the cupboards and drawers in the kitchen, hunting through the food and household products.

Because the circumstances surrounding Vera Nilsson's death were unclear, to put it mildly, her body was sent to the pathology lab in Solna for a post mortem, and the crime unit of the Stockholm Police had conducted a forensic examination of her flat, with 'suspicious death at home' written on the first page of the report.

According to the post-mortem examination of her body, Vera Nilsson had died of poisoning, a combination of large quantities of sleeping pills, tranquillizers and alcohol. The level of alcohol in her blood was approximately three parts per thousand, and the level in her urine not much lower. Because there was no evidence of more long-term alcohol abuse, these were very high figures for a woman of her age and physical condition.

The pathologist had taken his time and, when his verdict was delivered one and a half months later, he began by stating that he couldn't rule out criminal activity, but that most of the evidence pointed towards suicide. This was also his ultimate conclusion. Vera Nilsson had taken her own life. He regarded it as improbable that anyone could have poisoned her without her knowledge. The drugs she had taken simply tasted too unpleasant for their taste to be hidden by strong spirits, beer or soft drinks. He also regarded it as unlikely that anyone had forced her to take them. There were no injuries on her body to suggest that she had been subjected to violence or physical force.

But at one point in the post-mortem report he did note one disturbing fact. During the post mortem a number of factors suggested that Vera Nilsson had lain dead in her flat for more than twenty-four hours by the time she was found.

Because her son, who found her at about eleven o'clock on the morning of 11 March, claimed to have spoken to her over the phone at seven o'clock the previous evening, this raised at least one question. The pathologist was unable to rule out the possibility that she had died on the evening of 10 March, even if various factors uncovered during the post mortem suggested otherwise.

'Hang on, now, Alf,' Johansson said as soon as his brother-in-law had finished. 'How do you know this?'

'In an unusually propitious case of serendipity, I happen to have a contact at the undertakers who conducted Vera Nilsson's funeral. He's a member of the same genealogical society as me,' Alf said. 'We both happen to be on the committee, in fact. So, his firm took care of all the practical details after Vera Nilsson's death. Apart from dealing with the issue of probate and the funeral, they also cleared out her flat and put her son in touch with a firm of auctioneers which undertook to sell her belongings. The post-mortem report was found when they were clearing out the flat.'

'I see,' Johansson said. 'So why did he keep it?' Must have been sent to the son after the investigation was concluded; how on earth had that happened? he thought.

'My acquaintance knew Vera Nilsson,' Alf said, clearing his throat slightly. 'I don't know if I mentioned it, but Vera worked as a maîtresse d' at a restaurant not far from her home. My acquaintance often used to have both his lunch and dinner there, so that was how they got to know each other. He thought it rather odd that Vera should have committed suicide. He describes her as a happy, positive person, so that was why he took a copy. I assume he gave the original to her son, together with all the other papers they found when they were clearing the flat.'

'But your acquaintance never contacted the police?'

'No,' Alf said. 'He didn't. The police had evidently concluded that it was a suicide and, when it came to the son, the undertakers were supposed to be acting on his behalf and safeguarding his interests, so he left it alone.'

'And the findings of the investigation into her death? He didn't happen to find that? My colleagues must have written a report.'

'Nothing like that,' Alf said, shaking his head. 'But I assume that you're the man to track it down, if such a thing exists. This isn't the sort of thing I usually have to deal with in my genealogical work. But I suppose that, if the report still exists, it ought to be held by the regional archive in Stockholm.'

'Bound to be,' Johansson said. Or in an old cardboard box in the basement of police headquarters, he thought.

'In case it's any use to you, there's a copy of the post-mortem report among these papers,' Alf Hult said, tapping his skinny forefinger on the sheaf of papers he had put on Johansson's coffee table.

'It will all work out,' Johansson said. It will all work out, he thought.

67

Wednesday evening, 4 August

That evening, Johansson had dinner with Max. Italian, ordered from a nearby restaurant. Pia was out at an official bank dinner. It was the first time she had left him in the evening since he got out of hospital, and he more or less had to push her out of the door before she finally left.

'Are you sure you'll be all right?' Pia said when she was standing in the hall in her coat.

'For God's sake, dear,' Johansson said. 'Are you worried Max is going to mug me, or what?'

So he ate dinner with his very own Little Evert. Venison stew and pasta, the healthy sort, which wasn't half as nice as the sort he usually ate; with mineral water. While Max laid the table Johansson sat on a chair leafing through the newspaper and watching him work.

'I want red wine,' Johansson said, putting the evening paper down and nodding towards the wine rack. 'Open something Italian. That one with the black label,' he added, to be on the safe side, out of consideration for Max's doubtless limited knowledge on the subject.

'Of course, boss,' Max said.

*

After the end of the meal Max went and sat in the living room, where he turned the television on and watched a Spanish football match. Johansson lay down on the sofa in his study, with the firm intention of finishing the rest of the bottle that Max had opened for him.

Let's see, said the blind man, Johansson thought, picking up the latest bundle of papers his brother-in-law had left him.

First, he read the post-mortem report. There was strong evidence to suggest suicide, and the only thing that had really caused the pathologist any trouble was the precise time of Vera Nilsson's death.

Hardly surprising, Johansson thought. The little bastard probably needed twenty-four hours to search her flat to make sure she hadn't left any notes or papers that could mess things up for him.

Then his faithful companion, his headache, made its presence felt, and he moved on to a more aimless leaf-through of old probate papers and excerpts from the population register. In the middle of everything he found the CV that Staffan Nilsson had fabricated when he applied for the job of running his aunt Margaretha Sagerlied's foundation, having been forced to do so by its chairman, a lawyer with a fondness for formalities.

At the top, the date when the document had been composed: 'Stockholm, 15 April 1983'.

Then the heading: 'Curriculum Vitæ of Staffan Leander Nilsson, born 5 October 1960'. But no ID number, which was probably just as well, given what Johansson's brother-in-law had said about the veracity of the document.

At the bottom, the CV had been signed by Staffan Nilsson: 'The undersigned hereby solemnly attests on his honour that the information provided above is in entire accordance with the truth.' The signature was a little florid for a young man of twenty-two, and the concluding flourish certainly didn't show any sign of a lack of self-confidence.

Between the heading and the concluding signature was Staffan Nilsson's summary of his life.

His education started in 1967, at the Engelbrekt School on Valhallavägen in Stockholm, and, nine years later, in 1976, its opening stage concluded. He started high school that autumn, at Norra Real on Roslagsgatan in Stockholm. Both schools were located close to Birger Jarlsgatan, where he and his mother lived.

He spent three years at high school, specializing in economics, and in the spring of 1979 Nilsson claimed to have graduated. In the autumn of the same year he started a degree course in economics at Uppsala University, where he spent two years before 'taking a sabbatical to gain practical experience' for a year, apparently at Ericsson's headquarters in Stockholm. By the autumn of 1982 that particular experience was behind him, whereupon he embarked on a 'sabbatical term of linguistic study', which he spent in 'England and France'. In January 1983 he returned to Sweden, where he intended to 'conclude his studies towards his degree in economics at Uppsala University'.

So much for the formal part, solemnly attested on his honour.

The following section dealt with the various summer jobs and other employment he had had during the course of his studies.

Such an industrious little bastard, Johansson thought as he began to read.

At the age of sixteen, his first summer job had been as a 'chef's assistant' at the Strand Hotel in Stockholm. The following summer he was a 'waiter' at the Mornington Hotel, and the two summers after that an 'assistant receptionist' at the same establishment. He passed his driving test in the autumn of 1979, and spent the summers of 1980 and 1981 working as an 'executive assistant and acting restaurant manager' of the restaurant at Skokloster Castle and Museum outside Sigtuna.

Who'd have thought it? thought the former head of the National Crime Unit, Lars Martin Johansson, as he put down the mini-biography that Staffan Nilsson had himself compiled, two years and two months before Yasmine Ermegan was found raped, murdered and hidden in the reeds, just a couple of kilometres from his old workplace.

68

Thursday afternoon, 5 August

Another day in Lars Martin Johansson's new life. First, a glass of water to wash down the now vital medication that he laboriously picked out of the little red plastic box with his left hand. Then into the shower before he ate his healthy breakfast, consisting, as it did, mainly of yoghurt, fruit and muesli.

Then he read the morning paper, lying on the sofa in his study, without a headache, even though he ploughed through the news, the finance section and the arts supplement. Feeling overconfident, he therefore embarked upon the sudoku, which had been part of his daily routine in his old life. Two minutes later, his headache was back.

He tossed the newspaper aside and settled back on the sofa, trying to focus his gaze inward and regain a sense of calm. Deep breaths, trying not to think about anything at all, following all the advice in the little book about meditation and inner peace that his eldest grandchild had given him.

How in the name of all that's holy can you think of nothing? Johansson thought. It's a contradiction in terms.

'You've got a visitor,' Matilda said. 'It's your best friend. You know, the alpha male.'

The previous evening, Jarnebring had returned from his romantic holiday in Thailand – a thin, fit and suntanned Jarnebring, with a wolfish glint in his eyes, and no sign of a twenty-hour flight.

'I've just spoken to the lad Evert sent you,' Jarnebring said, nodding towards the closed door. 'I presume he's more pleasant than he looks.'

'He's a quite excellent young man,' Johansson said. 'He's kind and pleasant, he isn't stupid, and he does what I tell him.' Unlike everyone else, he thought.

'So how are you getting on?' Jarnebring asked.

'With what?'

'With Yasmine,' Jarnebring said.

'Splendidly,' Johansson said. 'I've found the perpetrator, just as I promised you. He's still alive, and all that remains to be done now is sorting out a few formalities.'

'Because it's you, I believe you,' Jarnebring said. 'Tell me.'

'His name is Staffan Leander Nilsson, born on 5 October 1960. Single, no children, lives in Frösunda, out in Solna. I don't have any information about his work, but I get the impression that he's got a finger in all sorts of pies. A variety of activities, you might say.'

'Stop fucking with me, Lars. You know very well what I mean. How did you find him?'

'Internal detective work. It wasn't even particularly hard. Just before I fell asleep last night I even got it into my head that that little fat nightmare Evert Bäckström would have found him if he'd received the same tip-off that I got three days ago.'

'For God's sake, Lars,' Jarnebring said. 'Think about what you're saying. I mean, I was part of that investigation as well.'

'And if you'd received the same tip-off, I'm convinced that you wouldn't have needed more than two or three days.'

'So what do we do now, then?'

'Good question,' Johansson said. 'I was thinking of taking a look at the bastard. Getting hold of his DNA, which ought to be a formality, seeing as I know we're going to get a match for him. But what do we do after that? Good question. The case is prescribed, after all, and, if I've understood correctly, that means that we're simply supposed to forget he exists.'

'For God's sake, Lars,' Jarnebring said. 'You can't mean that?'

'No,' Johansson said. One thing at a time, he thought.

'So what do we do now?'

'We make sure that it definitely is him,' Johansson said. 'Even I have been known to be wrong.' But I'm not this time, he thought.

'At the risk of being annoying, what do we do?'

'I thought we might start by digging out the investigation into Staffan Nilsson's mother's death.'

'I'll talk to Herman,' Jarnebring said. 'He'll—'

'Without talking to Herman,' Johansson interrupted. 'From now on, we don't talk to anyone but each other. You and me, no one else, and definitely no former colleagues.'

'I understand,' Jarnebring said. 'You've heard what happened to Herman's granddaughter?'

'Yes,' Johansson said. 'Her dad, P-2, told me.' The same Patrik Åkesson who probably saved my life, he thought.

'So don't worry,' Johansson added. 'There's no way I'm going to let the bastard get away. The lawyers and the other well-meaning fools can shove the statute of limitations where the sun doesn't shine.'

'Good,' Jarnebring said. 'Give me Nilsson's mother's name and I'll set to work.'

'Everything you need is in that plastic sleeve there.' Johansson pointed at his coffee table. 'And because I trust you implicitly, I've even written down how I worked out what happened.'

'Just out of curiosity,' Jarnebring said, 'who was your informant?'

'You get everything but the name of my informant,' Johansson said, with a stern expression. There have to be some limits, he thought.

69

Friday, 6 August

While Johansson was sitting in the kitchen having his lunch, Jarnebring phoned him on his mobile.

'All right?' Jarnebring said.

'Excellent,' Johansson said, even though his head ached and the tightness in his chest was making it hard to take deep breaths. 'I'm sitting here eating fried herring,' he said. Fried Baltic herring with new potatoes. Sometimes, you just have to be grateful, he thought.

'Don't bother to save me any,' Jarnebring said. He was a notorious meat-eater. 'I've found that report.'

'That was quick,' Johansson said, barely able to conceal his surprise.

'Had a stroke of luck. See you in half an hour.'

As usual, Johansson was lying on his sofa when Jarnebring walked into his study, shut the door behind him, sat down and put a thin plastic folder on the coffee table.

'The investigation into the death of Nilsson, Vera Sofia, born in 1921,' Jarnebring said. 'Conducted by the old crime section in Stockholm. Circumstances unclear, according to the initial report.'

'Where did you find it?' Johansson said, thinking that it had happened suspiciously quickly, bearing in mind their agreement not to involve any former colleagues in their endeavours.

'I had a real stroke of luck, like I said. Do you remember that old medical officer, Lindgren? Tall, skinny, spoke in a whisper, could never look anyone in the eye, completely mad, if you ask me?'

'No,' Johansson said. 'I don't remember that one.' They're all mad, surely? he thought.

'It suddenly occurred to me that his dissertation was about suicides. He kept nagging me when he was working on it, asking if I had any interesting cases for him.'

'And?' Johansson said. Get to the point, he thought.

'Turns out that Vera Nilsson was one of the cases he looked at. He found her in one of the boxes they had at the forensic medical centre out in Solna.'

'Excellent. So what do you make of Mrs Nilsson's death, then?'

'Suicide. I took a look at it while I had an expert in the vicinity – I had coffee with Lindgren. According to him, it was an obvious suicide, despite the absence of a note. Large quantities of sleeping pills and a serious amount of alcohol. Her heart gave out. Organ failure, all that. Read it for yourself,' Jarnebring said, passing him the investigation.

'My head hurts,' Johansson said. 'But I'm happy to listen.' There was bound to be a letter, he thought. And her son had decided to keep it under wraps.

'Her son was the one who found her, our very own Staffan Leander Nilsson. He was questioned when the initial report was set up. Very briefly, by the first patrol on the scene. He said he'd tried to call his mother several times, and even rang at her door. No answer. So he got worried. He said they had pretty much daily contact and that he lived in the same building as her. Naturally, he had keys to her flat, so he let himself in. He found her dead on the sofa and called the police at once.'

Remarkable, he thought. 'Was that the only time he was questioned?' Johannson asked.

'No,' Jarnebring said. 'A week later, once Forensics had turned up and done their thing, he was called in for an interview, to establish what had happened, because Forensics reacted to the fact that the flat seemed to have been searched. They hadn't come across anything properly suspicious, but enough for them to think it a bit odd.'

'So what did little Staffan have to say about that?'

'He said in the interview that his mother had been very depressed for the past year. Apparently, it started when she gave up work the previous summer. She started to drink heavily. According to her son, she could be seriously drunk several days a week and, on a number of occasions when that happened, she became extremely confused.'

'Who'd have thought it?' Johansson said.

'Quite,' Jarnebring agreed. 'If she'd worked out that it was her son who raped and murdered little Yasmine, she can't have been feeling great.'

'No, hardly. Which of our colleagues in Crime was in charge of the investigation?'

'Alm,' Jarnebring said with a grin. 'More commonly known in the violent crime unit as Woodentop. It was actually his boss, Fylking – you remember, Superintendent Pisshead – who dropped the investigation. No crime, according to Fylking, and, seeing as they

357

were up to their eyes in the murder of our beloved prime minister, no one raised any objections. And, as I said, I'm inclined to share that opinion.'

'Nothing else?' Johansson asked, waving the papers he had been given in a desultory way.

'There was an old friend of hers, used to work with her, who got in touch with the police. She's the one who called a week or so after Vera Nilsson killed herself. Said she found it very hard to believe that Vera would have committed suicide. And she didn't buy the idea that she'd started drinking like a fish. According to this friend, Vera had always been careful with alcohol. She wasn't a teetotaller, by any means, but she was very moderate in her habits. She described her as cheerful and positive, pretty much the ideal workmate during the time they worked together.'

'Did they still see each other, then? Before Vera Nilsson killed herself?'

'Ongoing contact over many years. At work, of course, but also privately. Alm pushed her on that point, and she said that Vera Nilsson had seemed more worried than usual over the previous few months. She had even asked her why but got no real explanation. Her friend said in the interview that she more or less assumed that it was something to do with Vera's son. According to the friend, he'd always been idle and useless. A source of constant worry to his mother. The last time they spoke, again according to the friend, was on the phone a few weeks before Vera Nilsson died.'

'I see.' Johansson sighed.

'So what do we do now?' Jarnebring asked.

'I need to think,' Johansson said.

'Lars, for God's sake. Pull yourself together!'

'Have you got any better suggestions, then?'

'How about we stop beating around the bush? Get a DNA sample from the bastard and, if we get a match, we don't have to do any more reading.'

'I hear what you're saying,' Johansson said. 'Let me think about what to do over the weekend.'

'Okay,' Jarnebring said. 'If you change your mind in the meantime, just give me a call. And we'll head out into the field, hit the streets, put our ears to the ground.'

Need to think, Johansson thought. How the hell am I supposed to do that with a head that starts aching like a bastard the minute I try?

70

Saturday, 7 August
After breakfast Pia went off into the country to pick mushrooms with her best friend.

'Try not to get into any mischief, now, boys,' Pia said, kissing her husband on the lips and giving Max a motherly hug.

'We promise,' Johansson said, already looking forward to a serious, old-fashioned long lunch with his very own little lad. Perhaps I should call Jarnebring, too? he thought.

Jarnebring thought it sounded like an excellent idea. Such a good idea, in fact, that Max was welcome to go and pick him up from home. Two hours later, they were sitting in the car on the way to what Johansson usually called 'his country inn', which, very practically, happened to be located on the island of Djurgården in Stockholm.

'You look brighter today, Lars,' Jarnebring said, giving his shoulder a comradely pat.

'I know,' Johansson said. Nag, nag, nag, he thought.

*

Johansson ordered a starter, main course and dessert. Mostly to tease his companions. Max looked uncomfortable but had the good manners not to say anything, but his best friend did not suffer from any such inhibitions.

'Sometimes, I can't help thinking that you're trying to kill yourself,' Jarnebring said, nodding towards the plates containing Johansson's starter.

'How do you mean?' Johansson asked innocently, as he spread a large dollop of mustard and dill mayonnaise across his salted salmon on toast.

'The salmon is fine, but that mayonnaise is the kiss of death for someone in your state. What the hell's happened to your short-term memory, Lars? It's only a month since you almost died because you're always stuffing your face with crap like that and refusing to take any exercise.'

'A month ago no one was asking me how I was or commenting on what I ate,' Johansson said. 'Now that's all I hear. People talking to me like I'm a child.'

Then he took a large mouthful of his salmon and toast, wiped some sauce from the corner of his mouth with his forefinger and, to underline his point, licked his finger, before drinking half his vodka and rinsing it all down with a gulp of beer.

'Where were we? Oh, yes,' he said, and raised his hand before Jarnebring had time to say anything. 'If you can't treat me as an adult, gentlemen, then I suggest you take your wretched salad and grilled beef and go and find another table, so that I can have a bit of peace and quiet while I eat.'

Max seemed fully occupied with his salad and made do with a nod, and Jarnebring shrugged and, evidently, decided to change the subject.

'Max,' Jarnebring said. 'Evert told me you're thinking of joining the police. How old are you?'

'Twenty-three,' Max said.

'Then it's high time. Lars and I were twenty-one when we started at the Police Academy.'

'I never graduated from high school,' Max said. 'I left school at the end of year nine.'

'You can sort that out easily enough,' Jarnebring said, seeing as he himself had been accepted thanks to his sporting merits, despite atrocious grades from the junior school where he had abandoned his academic studies after just eight years.

'Maybe,' Max said. 'But that's not the real problem.'

'I understand,' Jarnebring said. 'I've hit a few idiots in the past. And quite a few after I joined the police. Plenty more, actually.'

'But you were never in a children's home,' Max said.

'No. But I'm bloody good at telling the difference between good people and bad. You're good, Max. That's what counts.'

'What kind of bollocks is this?' Johansson interrupted. 'The world is mostly ruled by shitheads. So, Max, give us the important facts about you, the way you see it. Tell me who Max is.'

'Where do you want me to start?' Max asked. Faint smile, calmer now, his sturdy lower arms resting on the table.

'At the beginning,' Johansson said. 'And, you, Bo – you keep quiet.'

'Okay.' Max smiled. 'Well, my name is Maxim Makarov, and no, I'm not related to the great Sergey.'

Maksim Makarov was born in Leningrad in 1987, a Leningrad that four years later reverted to its original name in tsarist Russia: St Petersburg. In those days, he still spelled his name with 'ks' rather than 'x'.

'Mum worked as a doctor, Dad was a chauffeur and bodyguard for one of the local Party bosses. He earned four or five times as much as Mum. In the Soviet Union, being a doctor was a typically low-paid job. It still is, I think. Unless you were a member of the Party and managed to grab yourself a hospital when we liberated ourselves.'

'There, you see?' Jarnebring said. 'Don't get too hung up on studying.'

'Shut up, Bo,' Johansson said. 'Go on, I'm listening,' he continued, nodding at Max.

Max's parents split up soon after he was born. When he was two years old, in the autumn of 1989, and the foundations of the Soviet empire were beginning to tremble, his mother sneaked through one of the cracks and went to a medical conference in Tallinn. Once she was there, her Estonian friends helped her to get to Finland. There, other contacts took over and got her on board a boat to Sweden. She applied for political asylum in Sweden two days after leaving Leningrad, having left her little son in the care of his grandparents.

'So I was left with Grandma and Grandpa,' Max said.

'What about your dad?' Jarnebring asked, in spite of Johansson's warning glance.

'No.' Max shook his head. 'I can't have met him more than ten times. He isn't even a face to me. Anyway, he got shot when I was four. He went to pick his boss up at his home and they were shot as they came out through the door. Dad, his boss and their driver. There was a full-blown war going on in Leningrad in those days.

Comrade Kalashnikov, and then there was all the money the Party bigwigs wanted to keep to themselves.'

'Can't have been much fun,' Jarnebring said, even though his best friend looked like he was going to groan out loud.

'It didn't really make any difference to me,' Max said. 'After all, we didn't know each other. I suppose I thought it was quite exciting, having a dad who'd been shot. So it didn't really matter. Grandma was a good woman. Grandpa was a good man. But then things got worse, until nothing was good at all.'

'What happened?' Johansson asked.

'First, Grandpa died. He was old, he took part in the Great Patriotic War, and he was already retired by the time I was born. He had a heart attack and died, just like that. I was five at the time. The following year – the day I turned six, I remember – my grandmother died. Also of a heart attack. She collapsed in the kitchen just as she was about to serve my birthday cake. So I ended up in the children's home. I was there for four years. I came to Sweden when I was ten.'

'What was it like, then?' Jarnebring said. 'The children's home?'

'I've tried to forget it,' Max said, looking at Jarnebring through narrow eyes as he clasped his big hands together. 'I don't think any of us really wants to hear about that.'

'Your mother,' Johansson said, to change the subject. 'Why didn't she try to get you to Sweden earlier? If I've understood correctly, she'd been here for several years. Presumably, she had a residence permit and a job by then?'

'Yes,' Max said, nodding. 'To start with, things went really well for her. She was given a residence permit

364

and got a job. She worked as a doctor in Sundsvall Hospital – she got the job when she'd only been here for a year or so, in fact. Then she met a new man, a Swede, and had children with him. I've got two half-siblings, a nineteen-year-old brother and a sister who's eighteen. Things have gone well for them: my half-brother's at university, studying computer science, and my sister's in her last year at high school.'

'A direct question, and sorry if I'm being repetitive,' Johansson said. 'Your mother? Why didn't she make sure that you got to Sweden?'

'I suppose she wasn't that bothered,' Max said, shrugging his shoulders. 'A new life, new man, new kids. I don't really want to talk about that. Anyway, it didn't matter, not at first. I was fine while I was living with Grandma and Grandpa.'

'Let's change the subject,' Johansson said.

'Everything went wrong for her,' Max said, in a toneless voice now, merely presenting the facts. 'She started to drink, her bloke left, taking my half-brother and sister with him. She got fired from the hospital because of her drinking, and for stealing drugs. She used to sell them, apparently, out in the city. To a load of addicts. She ended up in psychiatric care, then at a rehab centre, and that was when she finally remembered about me.'

'Correct me if I'm wrong,' Johansson said. 'So it was her therapist who came up with the good idea of getting you over here? As part of your mother's treatment plan?'

'Yes,' Max said, smiling at Johansson. 'You're quite right, boss. I couldn't have put it better myself. It only took a year or so until I was able to move in with the mother I hadn't seen in eight years. By then she'd got both a flat and a new job. She worked as a care assistant in the rehab centre she'd been in. Gave lots of lectures and classes. And she'd got it together with the psychologist who was with her when she came to get me from the children's home. Obviously, I couldn't speak a word of Swedish, but Mum refused to speak Russian to me.'

Interesting woman, Johansson thought. 'And as soon as you got here everything went wrong again,' he said.

'I was a ten-year-old Russian kid stuck in a junior school in Sundsvall. By the time I was fourteen I looked the way I do today,' Max said. 'So I kind of found my place.'

'What about your mum and her new man? How did that work out?'

'Mum did a repeat performance. First, she—'

'I get it,' Johansson interrupted. 'What happened to you, then?'

'First, I was put in a foster home. I was there until I hit fifteen. Up in Timrå, north of Sundsvall. They were decent people, it wasn't their fault I ended up back in a children's home. I was a nightmare back then. I was in and out of the home loads of times until I turned eighteen, then, when I was discharged for the last time, my care worker found me a job. That was with Evert, at a building firm he owned in Sundsvall. Most of the work involved doing up his own properties. I've worked for him ever since. For the past year at the farm where he lives.'

'So what did my brother say, then?' Johansson said. 'The first time you met him, I mean.' Stupid question, he thought.

'I can still remember,' Max said with a smile. 'More or less exactly, in fact. He said that if I didn't stop fucking about and start behaving like a normal, sensible person, he'd personally see to it that all I wanted would be to get back to that fucking children's home over in fucking Russia among all the fucking bastard Russians.'

'Sounds like Evert,' Johansson said.

'Evert's not a man you fuck with.' Max smiled meaningfully. 'And he's also the best person I've ever met. He speaks very well of you, by the way, boss.'

'For the same reason that he always speaks well of you, Max,' Johansson said seriously. 'Bo?' he added, nodding at his best friend. 'Anything else you've been wondering?'

'Your mother, Max. What's happened to her?'

'She's dead,' Max said. And shrugged his shoulders. 'She died seven years ago. Cancer of the liver. It's funny, really, because I was sixteen at the time, but I can hardly remember what she looked like. Same with Dad, but I was only four when he left, and hardly ever met him.'

Must have felt like a release for you, Johansson thought. 'Bo,' Johansson said. 'That little blonde waitress over there, the one you've been staring at for the past five minutes . . .'

'What about her?' Jarnebring said.

'Get her over here so I can have a glass of red wine to go with my meatballs,' Johansson said.

'There's one thing I've been wondering about, boss,' Max said a couple of hours later, once they'd dropped Jarnebring off and were heading back to Södermalm.

'I'm listening,' Johansson said.

'This business with the police, me applying to join the police, I mean. Is that very likely, really? That they'd accept someone like me?'

'No,' Johansson said. 'But, if it's any consolation to you, you won't be missing out on anything.'

'Just as I thought,' Max said, with a nod.

When they got home Johansson lay on his sofa and fell asleep as good as instantly. He woke up to find Max gently touching his arm.

'Yes,' Johansson said.

'Your wife rang, boss,' Max said. 'She wanted to know how you were, and asked if it was okay for her and her friend to spend the night in the country.'

'What did you say, then?'

'That everything was fine.' Max smiled. 'That you were fine, boss. That everyone was fine.'

'Good,' Johansson said.

Then he must have dozed off again. Without dreams this time, and he only woke up when it was getting light outside the windows of his room. His head ached; he had forgotten to take his pills. He went out to the bathroom and rinsed his face with cold water. He took a few extra pills, just to be on the safe side. Then he went to bed and fell asleep again.

71

Sunday, 8 August

Sunday was a bad day, and it wasn't made any better by his suspicion that this was not unrelated to the previous day's long lunch. The only good thing about it was that Pia wasn't expected back until the afternoon, so he had time to sort himself out. He called her on her mobile. Not because he missed her but to assuage his guilty conscience. She sounded happy. There had been more mushrooms than she had expected, and it made sense to make the most of the opportunity.

The tightness in his chest was making it noticeably harder to breathe properly, and his headache refused to budge. At first, he sought refuge in routine. He took his pills, had a shower and a shave. Then he went into the kitchen to get his breakfast. Max came in while he was at it. He had trouble concealing his concern as he cast a surreptitious glance at Johansson.

'How are you, boss?' he asked.

'Could be better,' Johansson said. 'But it'll be fine. How about you?'

'Fine,' Max said. 'Nothing to worry about. If you sit down, boss, I'll sort out some grub.'

*

Then Max took over as Johansson took the easiest way out. He went into the bathroom and swallowed another little white pill, then an extra headache pill, the strong sort, before going to lie down on the sofa in his study and letting Max bring his food in to him on a tray.

Johansson drank coffee, mineral water, freshly squeezed orange juice and a large glass of yoghurt. Then his headache eased and his chest, heart and lungs relaxed, making it easier to breathe.

'How are you feeling, boss?' Max asked, as he stood in Johansson's study, gesturing towards the tray containing the remnants of his meal.

'Stop fussing, Max,' Johansson grunted. 'Give me that book over there instead.' He pointed. 'The thin one with the blue cover.'

'German,' Max said. 'You read German, boss?'

'Yes,' Johansson said. 'But I was much older than you when I learned to speak German.'

'I can barely speak Russian any more,' Max said with a gentle smile.

'I've got it in Swedish, too, if you're interested. *Der Richter und sein Henker*. Or *The Judge and His Hangman*. Friedrich Dürrenmatt, the man who wrote it, was from Switzerland, an artist as well as a writer. Died twenty years ago. An excellent writer and a fine artist,' Johansson said, who liked to know where he stood with the people in his life, even those he hadn't met.

'I don't read a lot of books,' Max said. 'I spend most of my time on my computer.'

'Reading's rarely wrong,' Johansson said. 'If a book's bad, you usually find out pretty quickly, and then you just chuck it in the bin. If it's good, it can give you something to think about, and if it's really good then reading it can even make you a better person. I've read this one several times.'

'I think I get it,' Max said. '*The Judge and His Hangman*. What it's about, I mean. Let me know if you want me to do anything, boss.'

'Like what?' Johansson asked.

'That fucking paedo,' Max said. 'That Nilsson, the one who killed that little girl.'

'No,' Johansson said. 'I was thinking of dealing with him myself.' So you've worked that out, then, he thought.

Max said nothing, just shrugged his shoulders. Then he picked up the tray with his left hand, nodded and disappeared, silently, in spite of his size. He shut the door behind him, leaving Johansson alone with his thoughts.

No, Johansson thought as he put the book down an hour later. Not even if I was on my deathbed. No headache now, just tired, and then he fell asleep. Wonder what happened to him in that children's home? he thought before he dozed off.

When he woke up Pia was at his side.

'I was starting to get worried,' she said. 'Do you have any idea how long you've been asleep?'

'Yes,' Johansson said. Have to go to the toilet, he thought. The pressure on his bladder was extreme, even for a real man.

'Would you like any lunch, three hours late?' Pia asked, and began to get up.

'I've got to go to the toilet,' Johansson said. 'Sit down. There's something I want to talk to you about.'

No questions. She just nodded and sat back down. Wise woman, doing as I say for once, Johansson thought.

'I'm listening,' Pia said when he came back.

'I've found him,' Johansson said, and for some reason he nodded towards the boxes of papers on the floor of his study.

'Is he still alive?' she asked.

'Yes,' Johansson said. 'He's alive, and I don't think he's exactly been tormented by guilt about what he did to Yasmine.'

'Dear God, that's terrible. Incomprehensible. What sort of person could do something like that and then live with himself afterwards?'

'Yes,' Johansson said. 'It's not a very edifying story.'

'Does anyone else know?'

'I've told Bo,' Johansson said. And the world's strongest children's-home boy has worked it out for himself, Johansson thought. Maybe Matilda, too, he thought. Plus, all the former colleagues who would get there, sooner or later, once they realized that the perpetrator was hidden in their old boxes, lying there in his burrow while the dogs sniffed round above his head.

'What are you going to do now, then?'

'I don't actually know, which is why I'm asking my beloved wife for advice,' Johansson said with a weak smile. Why did I say that? he thought. To smooth it over, make what was unbearable possible to live with?

'Well, you can't just let it go, Lars. I mean, that would be terrible. That wouldn't be you, Lars.'

'In a purely formal sense, I can't do a damn thing. For the past month or so he's been as free as a bird. Yasmine's murder has been prescribed since 21 June, twenty-five years after her body was found. The only hope is that he's done something that isn't prescribed yet, something I can get him for. But, to be honest, I'm not sure I really believe that's very likely.'

372

'And if you talk to the media . . . ?'

'If I go to the media, he's a dead man. I doubt he'd even have time to sue me before some nutter killed him. Open season,' Johansson said, with a crooked smile.

'You know who her dad is,' Pia said. 'Yasmine's dad, I mean.'

'Yes,' Johansson said in surprise. 'But I had no idea that you did.'

'Oh, I know. Anyone who works in financial services knows who Joseph Simon is. When I realized what you were up to, I went online and refreshed my knowledge. It's an absolutely hideous story.'

'My very own Nancy Drew,' Johansson said, and, as he said it, it didn't feel at all wrong to try to smooth things over.

'So what are you thinking of doing, then?'

'I don't know. I don't know,' he repeated. 'I don't want that bastard's blood on my hands. I don't know if I can handle being covered in that sort of crap.'

'If there's anything I can do to help . . .'

'I'm afraid there isn't. I need to think,' he said, shaking his head.

'As long as it doesn't kill you.'

'No,' Johansson said. 'That would be silly.' Then he put his arm round her and hugged her, with his right arm, which, in spite of the tightness in his chest and his aching head, felt stronger with each passing day. All in good time, he thought.

72

Monday morning, 9 August

Monday morning, and a very perky Matilda came into his study before he had even finished his breakfast.

'That Joseph Simon,' Matilda said. 'The man you asked me to google, boss.'

'Yes,' Johansson said. 'What about him?' When have I ever asked anyone to google something? he thought.

'He had a wife back then, Yasmine's mother. Her name was Maryam Ermegan. Also from Iran. They got divorced in 1986, the year after Yasmine was murdered.'

'I know,' Johansson said. 'What about her?'

'I googled her as well. Over the weekend, I didn't have anything better to do.'

'Tell me,' Johansson said.

A few years after the murder of her daughter, Maryam Ermegan converted to Islam. She wrote a number of articles in Swedish newspapers in which she defended Islam's view of women and contrasted it to the liberal, Western view with its practical attitude towards the emotional and sexual liberation of women from their husbands and families. She claimed that this was not about making men and women equal but merely a way to make them easier prey for all Western men, for the entire male collective, and without any shared ties to faith and morality, history and kinship. And, over and over again, she used her daughter's fate as an example of something that could never have happened in her former homeland, Iran.

In the autumn of 1995, ten years after her daughter was murdered, she took part in a televised debate about the Islamic view of women, its oppression of women, the use of headscarves, female genital mutilation, honour killings and all manner of other things which may or may not have had anything to do with the subject. Maryam caused a scandal on live television when she tried to tear out the hair of the Christian female presenter. Naturally, it had been the main news in the following day's evening tabloids.

'She was completely mad. I was sure she was going to kill me,' the 'shocked' presenter told *Expressen*'s reporter.

One month later Maryam left her adopted homeland and returned to Iran. Six months later *Dagens Nyheter* sent a reporter and a photographer to write an article about her and her new life. They never managed to contact her because she had vanished without trace, and that ended up becoming the subject of the article. Was she keeping out of the way of her own volition or had an unforgiving totalitarian regime done away with her?

Neither the Swedish Foreign Office nor the Swedish Embassy in Iran had been able to shed any light on the issue. Because she had surrendered her Swedish citizenship before she left Sweden, the Foreign Office in Stockholm was unable to do anything. For them, Maryam Ermegan was 'a closed case, beyond Swedish jurisdiction', and the Swedish ambassador in Tehran had no comment to make when questioned about her.

This was entirely natural, because Maryam Ermegan 'was, as a result of her current nationality, an internal matter for Iran and the Iranian authorities'.

'Do you think they murdered her?' Matilda asked inquisitively. 'All those ayatollahs?'

'I don't know,' Johansson said. What difference does it make? he thought, seeing as Maryam's life had, to all intents and purposes, ended on the morning of 22 June 1985, when the Solna Police rang on her door to tell her that they had found her daughter. That she was dead and had in all likelihood been murdered. They had spared her the details. The evening papers hadn't been as considerate.

'You don't know,' Matilda said. 'What do you mean, you don't know? Is it just that you don't care, or what?'

'Oh,' Johansson said. 'I do care, very much. But it's what happened before that concerns me most. Maryam Ermegan's right to human life.' Not to have to suffer what she would never have thought of subjecting anyone else to, he thought. All the things that people like him were supposed to protect her from. Or at least make sure she got justice on the occasions when they failed.

'I get what you mean,' Matilda said. 'This is just too much. Now that I come to think about it, I could kill that bastard.'

'Out of curiosity,' Johansson said. 'Nothing ever happened to you when you were growing up? A friend, some man who abused you? Tried to get the better of you, wrestled you to the ground, or worse?' Now we're there again, he thought.

'All girls have to put up with that,' Matilda said, clearly surprised. 'Well, maybe not all, but most of us,' she went on. 'People like me, anyway.'

376

'Tell me,' Johansson said. Good job Pia can't hear you, he thought.

'Years ago, when I was just an ordinary teenager, I was at a party with a load of friends. There was one boy from my class – a friend, there'd never been anything like that between us – he lost it completely and dragged me into a room and fucked me in the mouth. He said if I didn't do it, he'd kill me.'

'So you did it,' Johansson said.

'Yes,' Matilda said, rubbing her shoulders. 'Anyway, I was almost as drunk as he was. And he was twice as strong as me.'

'What did you do after that?'

'Nothing,' Matilda said. 'What do you think I should have done? Told the cops and make myself the school drama queen? I didn't have a dad. Or any big brothers. No one who could beat the shit out of him.'

'But that's the only time?' Johansson said.

'You're kidding, aren't you?'

'No,' Johansson said. 'I'm listening.'

'All the times a guy just won't stop, just keeps on pushing and pushing, until you can't bear it any more and decide to clench your teeth and get it over with. You've never done anything like that?'

'No,' Johansson said. 'I haven't, actually.' I definitely haven't, he thought.

'I believe you,' Matilda said. 'You're the sort who gets given things. You don't have to ask for them. You should be very fucking grateful for that. It's not that common, you know. It would have been cool to have met your mother.'

'My mother was a very good woman,' Johansson said. Elna was a good person, he thought. Good enough to let him choose his own life. She was always there but never stuck her nose in. Once or twice, maybe, in emergencies, when he was still a child, but never otherwise.

'You don't have to tell me that,' Matilda said. 'It's written all over you. You had the sort of mother who did everything for you, without turning you into a mummy's boy. Take another example, your best friend. He's never needed to push for it either. His problem was probably keeping up with all the girls who wanted him.'

'I hear what you're saying,' Johansson said. 'But what happened to Yasmine – nothing like that has ever happened to you?'

'Flashers,' Matilda said with a shrug. 'They're all over the place. Old men who rub against you when you're standing on a train at rush hour, lads at the bus stop wanking while they pick their noses. The first time was at preschool, when I was five. There was a right fuss. Teachers, parents, cops. Everyone. It seemed to go on and on. My friend and me thought it was really horrid. And exciting.'

'I see,' Johansson said. What the hell am I supposed to say? he thought.

'That business with Yasmine,' Matilda said. 'And all this really has to stay between the two of us.'

'Everything stays between the two of us. No need to worry about that.'

'Good,' Matilda said. 'I believe you. My mum's always been a bit crazy – new men all the time, that sort of thing. My family, when I was growing up, was made up of my mum, my sister, who's three years older than me, then me, and then all of Mum's blokes, who kept moving in and out of the flat.'

'Can't have been easy,' Johansson said. Hardly surprising she looks the way she does, he thought.

'Yeah.' Matilda shrugged. 'There wasn't really much wrong with any of them, and Mum was happy enough. She kept falling in love, and when it ended she'd get really depressed, and then it was time for the next one. The only time she got really mad was when one of them got it on with my sister.'

'How old were you then?'

'I must have been about ten, my sister thirteen. It was during the summer. We were on holiday from school, Mum was working as a nurse, her new man was unemployed, lived in our flat.'

'So your mum was a nurse?'

'Yes, lots of odd shifts. Anyway, that summer, Mum's boyfriend got together with my sister. She was thirteen, he was about thirty, she and I shared a room, so I had to pretend to be asleep.'

'She was thirteen,' Johansson said. Intercourse with a minor, he thought. Not that that really has anything to do with it.

'Yes, but she had tits and hair between her legs. Really big tits, actually, even though she was only thirteen. I know it's hard to believe when you look at me, but she did. And she had a huge crush on him. He never tried anything with me. My sister would have killed me. He pulled my duvet off once and looked at me, but no more than that. He said I needed to grow up a bit first. I think he was basically okay, deep down. Never violent, nothing like that. He drank a lot, smoked a bit of weed, but he was never violent.'

'So what happened?' Johansson asked. Wonder how Pia's getting on at the bank? he thought.

'Mum caught them at it. Properly at it. She lost it completely and everything kicked off. She threw him out, she was furious, chucked all his stuff off the balcony. She was furious with my sister, furious with me, too. For not saying anything.'

'Did she report him?' Johansson said.

'No.' Matilda shook her head. 'She went on a last-minute holiday to Greece instead. Mum met a new bloke. So did my sister. Mum and my sister made it up; it only took a week. They're pretty similar, at least when it comes to men.'

'And what did you do?' Johansson asked. 'That summer in Greece?'

'Don't really remember,' Matilda said. 'No boyfriend, anyway. I was still very young. I suppose I spent most of my time in the pool with the other kids.'

'Is this sort of thing common? I mean, among young people of your generation?'

'Well, hello, boss! Time to wake up! Suburban kids born in the eighties – no happy nuclear family for us. When I started junior school there were three kids in the whole class who lived with both their parents, out of more than thirty of us. Two-storey duplexes and more money than you can count . . . You and I come from different planets, boss.'

'I hear what you're saying,' Johansson said, and for some reason found himself thinking about his own children and grandchildren. That doesn't apply to them, he thought. At least they live on the same planet as me.

73

Monday afternoon, 9 August

In the afternoon Jarnebring appeared, to show what he had come up with so far. He began by giving Johansson a bundle of freshly taken surveillance photographs of Staffan Leander Nilsson.

'Where did you get these from?' Johansson asked suspiciously.

'Don't worry,' Jarnebring said with a grin. 'I took them myself. I took the opportunity to do a bit of surveillance on the bastard yesterday. One go in the morning, then again in the evening. There's a pizzeria on the other side of the road to where he lives. He seems to be a regular there. I had a word with the chap who owns it. Little Nilsson usually eats there several times a week.'

'You had a word with the owner. Just like that,' Johansson said, leafing through the pictures. Looks perfectly normal, he thought. Pleasant, even. He looked younger than someone about to turn fifty this autumn. Just under average height, a comfortable weight, neither fat nor thin, regular facial features, short, dark blond hair, turning grey at the temples, well-dressed, but not ostentatiously so: jeans, red polo shirt, blue summer jacket. What were you expecting? he thought. A black cloak and pointed teeth?

'Just like that,' Jarnebring said. 'I haven't lost my touch yet, if that's what you're worried about. The owner's a Turk, nice and helpful. When Nilsson came out I went in. I thought I'd grab the glass he'd been drinking from but I wasn't quite fast enough. Doesn't look like he smokes or uses chewing tobacco. It could take a while for a couple of pensioners to get hold of any DNA from someone like that. So I took the opportunity to have a quick word with the owner instead. Ordered a beer. Said the customer who'd just left looked familiar. Thought he was someone I used to work with at a haulage company where I work. Who do you take me for, Lars?'

'So what did the Turk say, then?' Johansson said. You haven't changed, he thought.

'Quite a lot. That his name is Staffan Nilsson. That he was a regular, a good bloke, always calm and well-mannered. That I must be mistaken about him working for a haulage company. According to him, Nilsson is an estate agent. Time-shares, houses, hotels in Thailand. Supposed to have some similar project up in Åre. Good contacts, helped his younger brother get a flat out in Solna. Not free of charge, as I understood it, but nothing extortionate either. In short, a decent bloke.'

'A perfectly ordinary, decent Swede,' Johansson said. No drooling, oversized child, no half-crazy conspiracy theorist with violent tendencies and peculiar sexual tastes, not even a fat, bald, retarded lorry-driver from the backwoods, he thought.

'Exactly,' Jarnebring said. 'A perfectly normal, middle-aged Svensson.'

'What else have you got?' Johansson asked.

'A fair bit.' Jarnebring handed over a bundle that was considerably thicker than the one containing only photographs.

'You got Gun to run a check on the bastard,' Johansson said in an accusing tone of voice. 'I thought we'd agreed not to drag any former colleagues into this?'.

Gun, who had been a civilian employee with the Stockholm Police for over thirty years, had spent the better part of her life helping his best friend with the sort of office-based detective work that Jarnebring tried to avoid whenever he could. And had probably been secretly in love with him for just as long.

'Gun doesn't count,' Jarnebring said. 'Christ, she's as likely to talk as the Great Wall of China. Not a crack in that façade, not even a loose brick.'

'I can tell you've never been there,' Johansson said. 'So what did Gun have to say, then?'

'See for yourself,' Jarnebring said.

'My head hurts.' Johansson put the folder down. 'Tell me instead.'

Gun had done all the things she usually did. She looked for Staffan Leander Nilsson in every database that could be imagined to have anything to say about him, from his birth up to the day he encountered Jarnebring, even if he didn't have any idea who he was walking past when he left his local pizza restaurant.

'To take the most important facts first,' Jarnebring said. 'He's lived at his current address since the area was built fifteen years or so ago. That was around the time he returned to Sweden from Thailand. He owns his flat, by the way. No wife or kids. But he does have a passport, a driving licence and a car. One of those little Renaults, a couple of years old. Supposed to be environmentally friendly. No red Golf any more.'

'Has he got any convictions, then?' Johansson asked.

'Never convicted, charged, or even identified as a likely suspect. But there are a number of notes on file. Cases that were dropped.'

'Such as?'

'He gives the impression of being a bit of a fraudster,' Jarnebring said. 'From the late eighties there's an old suspicion of tax evasion – aggravated tax evasion, even. It was written off a few years later; couldn't be proved. That would be when he was hiding out in Thailand and the boys in the fraud office couldn't be bothered trying to find him. You can't get an extradition warrant for crap like that, not even if you know where whoever it is lives and our foreign colleagues just have to go and pick them up.'

'I know,' Johansson interrupted. 'Anything else?'

'A couple more fraud cases. One involving a sublet flat that he's supposed to have sold on the black market but never handed over. The complainant withdrew the charge. Then there was someone who'd put money into some hotel project and thought he'd been ripped off, but that case was dropped as well. It's not clear why.'

'That's all?' Johansson said.

'No. There's one more file, and this is where it starts to get interesting.'

'What is it?'

'Six years ago, in 2004, our colleagues who work with child porn up at National Crime did a sweep of the internet and picked up a hell of a lot of paedophiles. The sort who sit there downloading child porn and exchanging

384

information with each other. One of the men who got caught was Staffan Leander Nilsson.'

'You don't say?' Johansson said. 'How did that investigation turn out, then?'

'The main perpetrator got several years in the clink. Almost all of them were found guilty. All except little Nilsson, whose case was dropped by the prosecutor.'

'Why? Had he bought a flat off him on the black market?'

'The prosecutor fell for his story,' Jarnebring said. 'Our colleagues didn't, and, before you ask, no, I haven't spoken to any of them. I've read the preliminary investigation and the interviews with Nilsson; he was questioned four times, and the last time the prosecutor sat in. It was after that interview that the case against him was dropped, but there's no doubt what our lads thought about the whole thing. The prosecutor bought Nilsson's story. They didn't. No proper police officer would have.'

'What did he say, then? What was his story?'

'Nilsson claims that he rented a room to a Moroccan immigrant. He said his name was Ali Hussein, and he met him in a gay bar in Gamla Stan.'

'A gay bar? Nilsson isn't gay, is he? Is that what he was trying to make out? That he's gay?'

'He was asked about that, if he was homosexual.'

'And what did he say?'

'That he couldn't see what that had to do with anything. That his sexual inclination was his private business.'

'Who'd have thought it?' Johansson snorted. 'What else did he say, then?'

'According to Nilsson, Hussein must have used Nilsson's computer to surf for porn without his knowledge. He claimed he kept his codes and passwords on a piece of paper in his desk. He was both angry and upset with Mr Hussein. Very upset; he thought it was appalling.'

'I can only imagine,' Johansson said. 'So what did Ali say?'

'Sadly, Ali never said anything, because our colleagues never managed to get hold of him. According to Nilsson, this was probably because he was in the country illegally. He himself had begun to suspect as much after a few months, but when he asked Ali about it, his response, funnily enough, was to pack his things and move out of the flat. He took all he owned and disappeared that same day.'

'For Christ's sake,' Johansson said. 'What kind of prosecutor would fall for a story like that?'

'Nilsson was able to provide a rental contract. Signed by landlord Staffan Nilsson and tenant Ali Hussein. A standard contract, where he undertakes to rent one room of his four-room flat for six months. Ali left halfway through, apparently, without even paying the contractual month's notice.'

'So what sort of things had Ali been downloading?'

'Almost only young girls. A few young boys, but only if they played a key role in proceedings. It was all about the little girls. Young girls being subjected to sex and violence. A lot of violence, taken from sites like Young Girls in Correctional Facilities, The Strict Teacher, the Children's Camp, Children for Sale, A Little Jewish Girl's Story. About as bad as you can imagine. Both as child porn, and as violent pornography. All that kind of crap.'

'I hear what you're saying,' Johansson said. 'People like him, who have sex with little girls. So that's why Nilsson claimed to be gay? And that whatever was on his computer wasn't his thing at all?'

'What do you think?'

'I think the same thing you do,' Johansson said.

'Heterosexual paedophile. Sadist. Nilsson gets turned on by forcing himself on little girls. And likes to beat them about a bit before he does so.'

'And the prosecutor dropped the case?' What happened to the sensitive paedophile? Johansson thought.

'Yes,' Jarnebring said with a grimace. 'Maybe because of the aliases Ali Hussein used online. Hussein the Caliph, Master Ali, the Arabian Slaveowner. Total harem fantasy. Plenty of evidence that the perpetrator would be someone like Ali Hussein.'

'For God's sake,' Johansson said. 'Did our colleagues knock on doors in the building? Talk to Nilsson's neighbours? Find anyone who'd ever seen Mr Hussein? Anyone other than Nilsson who could confirm that he actually existed?'

'No,' Jarnebring said. 'I don't suppose they thought of it. Probably hadn't got time either. The sentence for this sort of thing wasn't very heavy back then; it was mostly just fines.'

'Anything else?' Johansson asked.

'Like I said before, I'm picking up a fraud vibe. Director Staffan Leander Nilsson is registered as the owner of a total of three small businesses. Staffan Leander Holding Ltd, which in turn is listed as the owner of Leander Thai Invest Ltd, and Staffan Nilsson Property and Hotels Ltd.'

'Do the companies have any money?'

'Not according to Gun. No real money, mostly hot air. Nothing to make your brother Evert salivate, anyway. They're all registered at Nilsson's home address. Apart from Nilsson, who's listed as the sole proprietor, two other people appear on the companies' boards. According to Gun, they're probably people who work for his accountants. A bit dodgy, but not illegal.'

'Has he got any money, then? What does the bastard earn?'

'Less than you, Lars. Considerably less,' Jarnebring said with a broad grin. 'So there's nothing to worry about there. Compared with you, he's a pauper, and he'd be less than a fly-shit on your brother's desk. A few hundred thousand kronor a year, judging by his self-assessment tax declaration. Some of that comes from a pension insurance policy that his mother took out thirty years ago, by the way. Her son was listed as the only beneficiary.'

When her brother, the grocer, died, Johansson thought. Vera Nilsson, decent, hardworking, honest. The good mother, who ended up with a child-killer for a son.

'With the interest that's built up over the years, that amounts to a reasonable sum now. He gets about fifty thousand per year from that alone. Until he dies, if I've understood it right.'

'Hang on,' Johansson said. 'That sort of thing only pays out after you reach fifty-five, doesn't it?'

'Don't ask me. In his case, it might have been earlier because he was registered as retired last year. Whiplash injury. Someone drove into the back of him at the roundabout at Gullmarsplan. The other driver's insurance company had to cough up some serious money.'

'Is that everything?' Johansson asked. A whiplash injury on top of his scoliosis – he really has had it tough, he thought. Wonder how much he fleeced the insurance company for?

'Yes, more or less. I might have missed something. If I have, you'll find it in Gun's file.'

'I hear what you're saying,' Johansson said. Paedophile, sexual sadist, child-killer, still active. Given that Johansson had been a hunter all his life and had shot thousands of innocent animals, it wouldn't be the end of the world if he got a bit more blood on his hands.

Now he's got that look again, Jarnebring thought. All of a sudden, he looks like he's miles away. 'What do you say, Lars?' he said. 'Shall we go for a drive this evening and take a look at the bastard?'

'Yes,' Johansson said. I want to take a look at him first, he thought. I need to take a look at him first, then I need to talk to him. And then I need to do something.

74

Monday evening, 9 August
When Pia got home from the bank, her husband, his best friend, and their new helper, Max, were already standing in the hall, ready to leave.

'I see the boys are off to cause trouble,' she said. 'Don't forget your packed suppers and flasks. I hope you've got some warm clothes with you? It's only thirteen degrees outside, and I don't want Lars catching a cold.'

'Take care of yourself, darling,' Johansson said. 'And don't worry.'

Jarnebring started to give orders out in the street before they got into the car.

'Max, you're driving,' he said. 'Lars, you sit in the front, and I'll get in the back. That'll make it easier if I need to take pictures from different angles. Any questions?'

'No questions,' Max said.

'No questions,' Johansson repeated.

'Let's saddle up, then,' Jarnebring said with a stern expression. 'Off we fucking go,' he added, to be on the safe side.

'What do you have in mind, Bo?' Johansson asked. Wonder how soon I can have a sandwich? he thought. He was already starting to feel a bit peckish.

'We'll start as usual,' Jarnebring said with a grin. 'By making a nuisance call to the bastard.'

'You or me?' Johansson asked. No sandwich, he thought.

'I thought I might do the Skåne version,' Jarnebring said. 'Have you heard the Skåne version?'

To the point of exhaustion and in every possible form, Johansson thought.

'The first time was probably forty years ago,' he said. 'I have a feeling it was autumn 1975, when we were putting together a map of the brothels.'

'Unless you've got any special requests, I thought I'd go with Larry from Ängelholm – you know, the one who's a bit indecisive.'

'I was hoping for Börje,' Johansson said. 'Börje from Kristianstad. The one who's stupid and easily annoyed.'

'Unnecessary to scare the bastard.' Jarnebring shook his head, pulled out his mobile and dialled the number of Staffan Leander Nilsson's home on Gustaf III's Boulevard out in Frösunda.

Staffan Nilsson answered on the third ring. There followed a confused conversation that lasted two minutes before Nilsson ended it by putting the phone down.

'Nilsson,' Staffan Nilsson said, sounding rather formal.

'Yes, hello,' Jarnebring said, in a broad, whiny Skåne accent. 'This is Larry. How are you, Staffan? Well, I hope.'

'Sorry,' Nilsson said. 'Who did you say you were?' Still formal, but wary now.

'Larry. You know, Larry Jönsson. We met when you came down to mine for the Farmers' Cooperative meeting, in Ängelholm. I promised to get in touch when I was in the area, and it just so happens that the wife and I are in Stockholm, so I thought—'

'I'm afraid you've got the wrong number,' Nilsson said coolly. 'You've called the wrong number.'

'Wrong number? Isn't that Staffan Nilsson in Solna, works for Bilia? Bilia in Haga Norra – that's where it is, isn't it? Larry, Larry Jönsson. We met at mine back in the spring—'

'You've got the wrong number,' Staffan Nilsson repeated. 'My name is Staffan Leander Nilsson, and I'm afraid we've never met.' Judging by his tone of voice, he had already decided Larry Jönsson was an imbecile.

'Well, I never,' Larry said. 'Listen, I can't help wondering—'

'You'll have to excuse me,' Staffan Nilsson interrupted. 'I'm a bit busy. I'm meeting a friend for dinner.'

Then he hung up.

'Nice,' Max said, with a cheery grin.

'Larry's an old classic,' Jarnebring said. 'When Lars and I used to work in Surveillance in the seventies, we used to get him to call the girls and ask them about prices and what services they could offer.'

'And it worked,' Max said, shaking his head.

'This time it certainly seems to have done.' Jarnebring pointed at Staffan Nilsson, who was just emerging from the door of his building one hundred metres further up the street, setting off towards his local restaurant.

'And he wasn't lying,' Jarnebring said, when Nilsson walked into the pizzeria thirty seconds later, said hello to the owner and sat down on a stool at the bar.

'Not this time, anyway,' Johansson said. 'Even if his friend doesn't seem to have turned up yet.'

'What do we do now?' Max asked, switching the engine off.

'Now we wait,' Jarnebring said. 'Surveillance is mainly about sitting and waiting.'

Just like hunting, Johansson thought. Hunting is waiting. Waiting for something that almost never happens, yet has to happen.

'Just like hunting,' Max said.

Bloody hell, Johansson thought. He can't have learned that in the children's home.

'So you know that?' he said. 'Did Evert teach you about that?'

'It's in my blood,' Max said with a shrug. 'But Evert usually takes me, if we're talking about elk and hares and so on. Woodland birds.'

Sounds like it, Johansson thought.

'Are you any good, then? At hunting, I mean?'

'I've never met anyone who was better,' Max said, and shrugged again, leaning back, with his huge hands resting in his lap.

They sat in the car and waited for almost an hour and a half. Max sat motionless, staring fixedly at the man sitting at the bar inside the pizzeria, fifty metres from the car. He said nothing at all, barely responded when spoken to. His watchful, deep-set, grey eyes were like narrow arrow-slits protected by the bulging edges of his

393

eye-sockets; there wasn't a blink, not a single movement of his set face, as he stared at their prey.

Staffan Nilsson looked at his watch increasingly often, made a call on his mobile after five minutes, put it back in his pocket thirty seconds later, finished his glass of red wine. He ordered another glass, made another attempt with his mobile five minutes later. It looked like he left a message before putting his phone back in his jacket pocket. He looked agitated now. Worried, impatient. Then he stood up and said something to the man behind the bar, finished his second glass of wine, got a third, then took a menu and went and sat at a small corner table where he had a good view of the entrance to the little restaurant.

'He's a cautious bastard,' Johansson said. 'Picked the same table I would have done.'

'Something must have happened to his friend,' Jarnebring said.

'Is there any chance of getting a sandwich?' Johansson said. 'And a cup of coffee?' he added.

'Coming right up, boss,' Jarnebring said, sounding just as cheerful as he always used to when they were out on similar jobs back in the day. 'What do you think, Lars? Shall I wander in and try to sneak out with his glass?'

'Don't bother,' Johansson said. 'There are only five customers in there. We'll have to wait until there are a few more people, at least.'

Nilsson's food arrived, along with a fourth glass of red wine. He tried making two more calls while he ate. After half an hour he beckoned the waiter, who took his plate and empty glass away. He returned shortly afterwards with a cup of coffee and a fifth glass of wine.

'The bastard's a serious drinker,' Johansson said unhappily as he peeled the plastic from his third sandwich.

'You're just jealous, Lars,' said Jarnebring, who hadn't yet touched their packed meal. 'You'll have to ask Max to sort out a decent three-course meal next time. A sneaky vodka, cold beer, some decent red wine, the whole lot.'

'I think it might be time to move,' Johansson said. 'It looks like he's about to leave.'

Nilsson got to his feet and, with his coffee cup and empty glass in his hands, went over and put them behind the bar, then got his wallet out to pay.

'I'm changing position,' Max said, starting the engine, then driving one hundred metres up the road. He pulled up just as Nilsson came out of the door and headed towards his building.

'Wonder what happened to his friend?' Johansson said, sounding like he was thinking out loud.

'Her mum probably wouldn't let her out,' Jarnebring said with a grin. 'It's past eight o'clock, after all. Little girls ought to be in bed by now.'

Five metres from his front door, Nilsson stopped. He looked at his watch, then carried on walking, past the door, faster now.

'Where's the bastard going now?' Jarnebring said.

'To move his car,' Johansson said, seeing as – unlike his best friend – he had lived in the centre of the city all his adult life and had had to call in favours for parking offences on numerous occasions. 'My guess is that he's going to move his car.' Before he settles down at his computer and starts looking at porn on behalf of some new tenant, he thought.

*

Two minutes later Nilsson had moved his car to the other side of the street, got out, crossed the road and disappeared inside the building where he lived.

'Bloody hell,' Jarnebring said. 'If we'd been on duty, we could have stopped the bastard, got him to blow into the breathalyser, filed a report, kept the plastic tube and everything would be sorted.'

'There are other ways to sort it,' Max said.

'We're going to take it nice and gently,' Johansson said. 'This character isn't likely to disappear.' Wonder if it was such a good idea to bring Max along? he thought.

'What do we do now?' Jarnebring asked. 'Call it a night?'

'If you gentlemen want to sit here half the night, don't let me stop you. But I was thinking of going home, having a ham omelette and drinking a couple of glasses of red wine.'

'Sounds good,' Max said, and nodded.

'Then that's what we do,' Jarnebring said. 'Home, James. We can have a bite to eat and talk about where we go from here. While little Nilsson is having a wank in front of his computer.'

Wonder who he was waiting for? Johansson thought before he fell asleep.

75

Tuesday, 10 August

Personal hygiene, breakfast and the first meal of the day, then the daily visit to see the physiotherapist. On this particular Tuesday there was also a check-up with his very own cardiologist, first an ECG, then ultrasound and blood pressure, then finally, a heart specialist, who shook his head unhappily.

'Seeing as you like hearing things straight, I can say that I've had patients who've been in a better condition than you,' the doctor said, giving Johansson a friendly nod.

'I daresay,' Johansson said. 'And one or two who've been rather worse?'

'The problem is that they're pretty much all dead,' the doctor replied. 'You've put on two kilos since I last saw you. I interpret that to mean that you're ignoring my advice about diet and exercise. Your blood pressure is even worse than last time, so now I'm going to have to increase the medication to lower it. You need to realize that this is a very short-term solution. Eat healthily, get some exercise, avoid stress. Is that really so difficult to understand?'

'Don't ask me, you're the doctor,' Johansson said. 'Not me.'

'That's not the impression I'm getting. What's so wrong with following my advice?'

'What sort of life is it if you're just counting down the days to the end?' Johansson said, getting to his feet.

Max drove them home to Södermalm. He cast a few surreptitious glances at Johansson. He didn't say anything until they were parked outside the house on Wollmar Yxkullsgatan.

'How are things, boss?' Max said.

'Fine, Max. How about you?'

'I get the impression that I'm feeling better than you, boss.'

'Rubbish,' Johansson said. He smiled and patted him on the shoulder. 'Let me know if you fancy a bit of arm-wrestling.'

Max didn't smile. He just looked at him. Then he shook his head. 'Let me know if there's anything you want me to do, boss,' he said.

'That's kind of you.'

'I know how it feels to have something eating you up from inside,' Max said.

After lunch Johansson went and lay on the sofa in his study. Matilda plumped up his cushions and brought him a large bottle of mineral water in an ice-bucket. She tilted her head to one side and looked at him. 'Shout if you want anything else,' she said.

'Stop fussing,' Johansson grunted.

Then he fell asleep. He woke up to find Pia sitting by his side, stroking his cheeks and forehead with her fingers.

'What did the doctor say?' she asked.

'Tip-top form,' Johansson said. 'Tip-top.'

'Are you sure?' Pia said with a gentle smile.

'Wouldn't dream of lying to you,' Johansson lied, sitting up on the sofa without any great difficulty. My right arm, he thought. At least my right arm is getting better and better by the day. Probably looking forward to the elk hunt, just like its master, he thought.

'Do you feel like talking?'

'Of course,' Johansson said. As long as we don't talk about me, he thought.

'I've been thinking about what we talked about the day before yesterday. About the man who murdered Yasmine,' Pia said.

'What about him?'

'Assuming everything else was the same, if this was about one of your own children, or one of your grandchildren, what would you have done then?'

'I'd have killed him,' Johansson said. 'In the Old Testament way. Eye for eye, tooth for tooth.' And I'd have counted the blows as I did it, he thought.

'That's not the impression I got when we talked about it. I was hoping—'

'That's because we weren't talking about me,' Johansson interrupted. 'For me, hatred is a matter of distance. But if it gets too close, then . . . If anyone were to harm you, or the children or our grandchildren, then there's no other way out. Would I be capable of killing someone like that? Yes, definitely.'

'For my sake?' Pia said.

'"For your sake". How do you mean?'

'Well, for my sake I hope you choose a different solution.'

399

'Don't worry,' Johansson said, taking her hand. 'I promise to think very carefully before I do anything.'

'You wouldn't consider just letting it go? I'm worried about your health.'

'Never,' Johansson said. 'How would it look if someone like me let go of something like this? Where would that leave us? Neither you nor I would want to live in a world like that.'

76

Wednesday, 11 August

Alf called before breakfast and asked if he could invite
Johansson to lunch. Bloody hell, Johansson thought.
It'll be interesting to see how much he charges for that
when the invoice finally arrives.

'I've found a few things that I think you might find
rather interesting,' Alf said. 'About Staffan Nilsson's
time in Thailand in the late eighties, early nineties.'

'Really?' Johansson said. Interesting, he thought.

'It turns out that I had an old acquaintance who
was very familiar with Nilsson. We're members of the
same order, and he's also a member of my club, Stora
Sällskapet. He was involved in the same hotel project as
Nilsson towards the end of the eighties, but he's a very
particular fellow. Slightly older than you and me, lived
over there for many years, for long periods at a time.
He sold most of his assets after the tsunami; I think he
has only a very small share left now. If you don't object,
I was going to suggest that you meet him. I thought
it would be better for you to hear it straight from the
horse's mouth, so to speak.'

'By all means,' Johansson said. 'So what have you told
him? About my interest in Nilsson?'

'I told him Nilsson had asked if you were interested in investing in a number of new projects in Thailand. That you had asked me to find out what he's like, both as an individual and as a potential business partner. All very discreetly, of course,' Alf said, and cleared his throat quietly.

'Excellent,' Johansson said. 'Where and when?'

'May I suggest the club? One o'clock today. The worst of the rush tends to have died down by then, so we'll be able to sit there in peace and quiet.'

When Johansson stepped through the doors of Stora Sällskapet's dining room on Blasieholmen in Stockholm at exactly one o'clock, it was very clear that the 'worst of the rush' had died down. In one corner sat an old duffer in a three-piece suit, picking at a dish of herring as he read *Dagens Industri* and took small sips of what had probably been a large glass of vodka when he started. In the opposite corner sat Johansson's party: his brother-in-law Alf and a somewhat older man who bore a striking resemblance to Alf – tall, thin, slightly bent-backed, with thinning hair and a fetching suntan. He wore a blue blazer bearing the emblem of the Royal Swedish Yacht Club, grey linen trousers and highly polished brown shoes. Apart from them, the room was completely deserted, with the exception of an elderly waiter who had taken up position beside the door to the kitchen.

'A pleasure to meet you at last, Lars Martin,' his new informant said, smiling with his eyes, his mouth and his nice white teeth as he held out a sinuous, suntanned hand. 'My wife has a god-daughter who's in the police, and she lives with one of your former colleagues, so I've heard plenty of stories about you over the years. I'm Carl – my friends call me Calle; Calle with a "C". It will be a pleasure to offer you lunch.'

To offer me lunch, Johansson thought. Well, that explains that, he thought, glancing at Alf, whose mind seemed to be elsewhere.

'Thank you, Calle,' Lars Martin Johansson said, patting his arm warmly, because his right hand still wasn't any good for shaking – his punctilious brother-in-law had no doubt already explained what had happened. 'My friends call me Lars,' he said. And if you call me Lasse I'll kill you, he thought.

'Your god-daughter,' Johansson added as he sat down with some difficulty and leaned his crutch against his chair. From the corner of his eye he saw the waiter hurry over to help him. 'Your god-daughter, what's her name?'

'A young colleague of yours,' his new friend said. 'Susanne Söderhjelm. She worked with you for a while when you were head of National Crime. She's currently living with one of your closest associates from that time, Police Superintendent Wiklander. But perhaps you already knew that?'

So they finally got it together? High time, Johansson thought. It's a small world. Must call Wiklander. We've barely spoken since I left, he thought.

'Two quite excellent colleagues,' Johansson declared. 'Very competent.' Watch yourself now, he thought.

'With such a boss to advise them, how could they have turned out otherwise?' Carl said, with another smile. 'Alf and I have just ordered beer, seeing as it's still summer, but if I can tempt you with anything else you'd be very welcome. I was thinking of ordering a dry Martini to go with lunch.'

'Sounds good,' Johansson said, nodding affirmatively at the waiter, who had the good sense not to try to remove his crutch.

'Splendid,' his host said. 'In that case, we'd like another beer and two properly chilled dry Martinis, my special recipe. So be careful with the Martini. Very careful. A little splash will do nicely.'

'Of course, Mr Blomquist,' the waiter said, and gave a slight bow. 'Please, gentlemen, just let me know when you're ready to order food.'

Kalle Blomquist, Johansson thought. But with a 'C', and probably at least one 'Q' and 'U' as well. No matter, it was a fine moniker, seeing as Astrid Lindgren's books featuring a young detective of that name had both influenced his choice of career and shaped his life at a time when he was still running about in short trousers with permanently scabby knees on a farm in northern Ådalen.

Half an hour and a dry Martini later, when they each had a dish of soused herring in front of them, Johansson's new friend got straight to the point.

'Your brother-in-law, Alf here, told me that you have recently been approached by Staffan Nilsson,' Calle said. 'Some property project in Thailand that he wants you to invest in.'

'I've never met this Nilsson,' Johansson said, shaking his head as he sprinkled some chives on his herring. It glistened plump and silver, looking extremely appetizing as it lay there beside the yellow-white new potatoes. 'He's sent me a lot of information,' he went on. 'I was asked to take a look at it by my brother, Evert. I'm on the board of the family's property-investment business, and he didn't himself have time to look into it. It's a

404

combination of time-share apartments and housing, both wholly and part-owned, with shared facilities, a hotel, restaurant, staff – the works. In Khao Lak in Thailand. I have to say, I don't even know where that is. The total cost was a couple of hundred million, and we've been invited to invest ten per cent,' Johansson said without difficulty, because he had spent half an hour after his trip to the physiotherapist studying the papers Gun had given his best friend.

'If I were in your shoes, I'd be very careful with that man,' said the master-detective's namesake. He emphasized the point by shaking his head and raising his silver fork in a warning gesture.

'Really?' Johansson said. 'Go on.' A witness is someone who has something to say, and this one was doing so with a degree of style, he thought.

A word of warning – not that his new acquaintance was familiar with the project that Johansson and his brother had been invited to invest in. Anyway, he himself had sold his assets in Thailand several years ago, immediately after the tsunami, and these days he visited the country only as a tourist, in the company of his wife, children and grandchildren. He still had a house to the north of Khao Lak, which he shared with his family. A wonderful country, wonderful climate and, not least, wonderful people, but still – a word of warning. Staffan Nilsson, or Staffan Leander Nilsson, or Staffan Leander, as he also styled himself, wasn't the sort of man one would choose to do business with, regardless of anything else.

'Really?' Johansson said again. 'What's the problem? Describe him to me. Like I said, I've never actually met him. I haven't even spoken to him on the phone.'

'Lazy, incompetent and a fraud,' Johansson's new friend said. 'You don't want to touch a man like Nilsson, not even with the longest barge-pole,' he went on.

'Really?' Johansson repeated once more.

In the mid-eighties, Carl Blomquist had used a sizeable portion of the money he had made on the Swedish stock market in previous years to buy a majority stake in a hotel project on the east coast of Thailand, on the bay near Koh Samui, in what was at the time a largely unexploited area: virginal, beautiful in an exotic sense that was hard for Swedes even to imagine. It was also a new concept, because it was aimed at families with children – people from the middle class, in younger middle-age, people who wanted sun and warmth, peace and quiet, good food that was just exotic enough, not too spicy, and one or two umbrella-bedecked cocktails to drink with the wife while the resort's child-minders and play-leaders looked after the next generation.

'Not a load of twenty-year-olds living it up, no discotheques or bars full of whores or any of the things that people still associate with holidays in Thailand, regrettably,' Carl Blomquist said as he poured HP sauce on the Biff Rydberg that had just been presented to him.

'How did Staffan Nilsson come to be involved in the project?' Johansson asked, poking suspiciously at the steak with horseradish which he ought, on closer inspection, to have avoided.

'My partner and I were looking for co-investors. We didn't want to take on the entire project ourselves. So the bank helped us. It was them – I was with the SE Bank at the time – who introduced us to young Nilsson. I say young Nilsson, because he must have been a good twenty years younger that my partner and I. Not even thirty, if I remember rightly.

'He was charming, pleasant. And he had money, too – even offered a couple of million he had inherited from his mother. Sadly, we allowed ourselves to be persuaded and let him come on board,' Carl Blomquist went on with a sigh.

'A shame,' Johansson agreed.

'Unfortunately, we made an even bigger mistake than that.'

'You did?' Johansson asked, trying not to sound too eager as he did so.

'Even before he joined us, he had told us that he was thinking of emigrating to Thailand, of leaving Sweden for good. It was the year Palme was murdered – early summer 1986 – and you didn't have to be a right-wing voter to think that Sweden was heading to the dogs, so he wasn't the only one having that sort of thought. Anyway, he was thinking of moving to Thailand and starting up or buying a share in a business in the hotel and restaurant trade. Setting himself up and making a future in a new country. My partner and I thought this sounded very appealing. Our impression was reinforced by the fact that he had excellent references – and we did check – in the hotel and restaurant industry. He spent his summers working in hotels and restaurants when he was still at school. Long before he started to study economics at Uppsala. I seem to recall him saying that he specialized in the economics of the hotel trade.'

'So you employed him,' Johansson said. 'To look after the whole project.' You certainly put a lot of bloody effort into checking his references, he thought.

'My partner and I had a lot to deal with here at home, and we'd recruited good local staff in the area, everyone from the Thai colleague we appointed as MD, right the way down to the serving staff. But we couldn't help thinking that it would make sense to have a Swede on site, so to speak. Someone to represent us, act as our liaison. So young Nilsson was appointed deputy MD and finance director.'

'But it went wrong?' Johansson said, pushing the remains of his greying steak aside. I'll have to have a decent dessert instead, he thought.

'Well, it did take a while. He turned out to be utterly incompetent when it came to the finances, so we worked that out relatively quickly.'

'He was stealing from you?' Johansson asked.

'Yes, although that didn't come as any great surprise. Not in that business. And he wasn't really stealing more than anyone else. No, there were other things that were considerably worse. When we discovered the inadequacies – to put it mildly – of his financial management, we replaced him and let him concentrate on the hotel and restaurant side of the business, particularly the service end, which was designed to appeal to our type of clients: ordinary families with children.'

'What happened?' Johansson asked, even though he already knew the answer.

'To start with, it went very well. He organized plenty of activities for the children: aqua-aerobics and excursions, treasure hunts by boat out to the islands, theatrical performances and courses in Thai dancing – anything and everything.' Carl Blomquist shook his head.

'So what was the problem?'

Director Carl Blomquist, the master-detective's namesake, if you were prepared to ignore the spelling, took a sturdy mouthful of red wine before managing to say what his new acquaintance had been waiting for.

'He was only a young man, of course, charming, handsome. He seemed perfectly normal. A mother-in-law's dream, really. When I heard that we had received complaints from guests saying that he had fiddled with their children – well, their little girls; he didn't seem at all interested in the boys – I practically fell off my chair.'

'That's awful,' Johansson said. 'What did you do?'

'We did what people always do. Hushed the whole thing up and paid people off. It cost a fair bit, unfortunately, but we didn't have any other option. We even employed extra security guards to make sure he didn't come anywhere near the complex.'

'So he was never prosecuted? The police never found out what he was up to?'

'In Thailand, back in those days?' Carl Blomquist said, and shook his head. 'I'm afraid you can forget that. Millions of dirty old men from Western Europe used to show up each year to have sex with young girls. The only thing that was unusual about Nilsson was that he was half the age of all the others. Dear God, Lars. In those days – and I don't know what it's like now, but I can't bear to think about it – poor peasants from the north of Thailand used to sell their children. They sold their own children for less than you'd pay for a puppy back home. They would end up in brothels or bars in Bangkok and the other big tourist resorts. There weren't many who ended up working as maids in hotels. And I daren't even think about what share of the takings ended up in the pockets of the local police. The police in Thailand weren't like you and your colleagues back home in Sweden.'

'Do you have any idea what he did after that? Nilsson, I mean? After you fired him?'

'I heard a few things. There were a lot of Swedes over there, so there was quite a bit of talk. Not least about Staffan Nilsson. Seems like the first thing he did was buy a share of a couple of whore-bars – the sort with little girls – in Phuket. That was probably what he did with the money he stole from us. I think those bars were his main source of income. He had a souvenir shop, too, apparently. Also in Phuket.'

'Does he still have any assets over there?' Johansson asked.

'The last I heard was that he'd had a serious falling-out with his Thai associates and had moved back to Sweden again. Had to, pretty much, from what I heard. Dear God, that must have been at least ten years ago. When Alf told me he was still involved with projects in Thailand, it came as a total surprise to me. I thought he pulled out years ago.'

'Well, thank you very much,' Johansson said. High time he went to the toilet and switched off the little recording device before it started to bleep in his breast pocket, he thought.

'Don't mention it,' Carl Blomquist said, raising his glass. 'I presume this conversation will go no further than this table?'

'Of course not,' Johansson said. 'Discretion is a point of honour,' he said, raising his glass.

410

77

Thursday, 12 August

In the afternoon Johansson had a check-up with Dr Ulrika Stenholm. After the usual squeezing and hammering, she passed on greetings from his physiotherapist, who was happy with his progress, and from his cardiologist, who wasn't.

'I can't say that I'm particularly happy either,' Ulrika Stenholm said, then tilted her blonde head. 'Your readings could be much better. How are you really, Lars?'

'You shouldn't be asking me that – you're the doctor, not me. Anyway, how are you?'

'Well, naturally, I'm curious about the other thing,' she said, craning her long, thin neck. 'About Yasmine, I mean.'

'That's going very well indeed,' Johansson said. 'I've found the man who did it.'

'What? You're not kidding, are you?'

'You don't kid people about things like this.'

'Who is it, then? Is he still alive?'

'He's at the peak of fitness, if you ask me.'

'I have to say, this comes as something of a shock.'

Yes, you look rather taken aback, Johansson thought. No longer curious, more like frightened, he thought.

'Well, it's good to have it done and dusted,' he said vaguely.

'But I don't understand. Your colleagues, twenty-five years ago, there were loads of police officers working on this case, for several years. Without any success. Then you show up, and after a month – it's no longer than that since I told you – twenty-five years later, say that you've found the man who did it.'

'That's partly thanks to you,' Johansson said. 'So thank you for that.' Lucky for you that it wasn't little Bäckström who turned up in your department, he thought. Always assuming that a massive boil on the arse could cause a blood clot in the brain.

'You've got to tell me who it is,' Ulrika Stenholm said. 'What a terrible business.'

'That's a bit tricky,' Johansson said. 'Because the case is prescribed, of course, so in a purely legal sense that means that nothing can be done about it now. With that in mind, I'm not sure it's such a good idea for me to go round telling people his name. I'm assuming, by the way, that this conversation, and all our conversations on this subject, will stay strictly between the two of us.'

'You don't have to worry on that point, Lars. I haven't breathed a word to anyone. Dear God, this is terrible. There must be something that can be done? I mean, someone like that. There must be some way of punishing him?'

'That would be down to the good Lord,' Johansson said. 'As far as worldly justice is concerned, I'm afraid we've already lost him.'

'But there must be something you can do?'

'I'm still thinking about that,' Johansson said. 'I hear what you're saying, and I'm thinking about it.' But you

412

probably shouldn't hope for too much on that score, he thought.

The best idea would have been for you to keep your mouth shut, Johansson thought as he sat in the car on the way home. She looked terrified, poor thing, he thought.

'How did you get on with him? With the doctor?' Matilda asked once he was safely installed on the sofa in his study.

'Lady doctor,' Johansson said. 'Dr Stenholm's a she. Fine, thanks. It went absolutely fine. She's very pleased with me.'

'Don't lie to me,' Matilda said. 'Do you know something? You're just like a big child,' she said, shaking her head.

'Double espresso,' Johansson said. 'With a jug of warm milk on the side. And a little ham sandwich would be nice.'

'Forget it,' Matilda said. 'You can have the coffee, but on one condition.'

'What's that?'

'That you pull yourself together and start looking after yourself.'

'I promise.' Johansson said.

Matilda's a good girl, Johansson thought as he watched her go off to make his coffee. But it's a fucking disgrace that she's got all that scribbling all over her body. Mind you, given the mother she's got, I should probably be grateful she hasn't taken to cutting herself.

78

Thursday evening, 12 August

Pia had an evening meeting at the bank and had hardly made it out of the door before Johansson decided to use his new-found freedom to pay a surprise visit to Erika Brännström.

'Fire up the engine, Max,' Johansson said. 'I'm going out to talk to a witness.'

'Right you are, boss,' Max said.

Max stayed in the car once Johansson had explained things to him. Sensitive situation and all that, and some conversations had to stay between two people. If they happened at all, that is.

'It might take five minutes, might take an hour,' he said. 'So stay nearby and I'll call you on my mobile.'

'What's his name?' Max said. 'In case,' he added with a slight smile.

'It's a she,' Johansson said. 'Woman in her sixties. Her name's Erika Brännström, and she lives on the third floor.'

'Okay,' Max said. 'Give me a call if you want me.'

*

Johansson did as he had been taught. The problem was that it had been more than twenty years since he last did it. First, with a considerable amount of effort, he crouched down and gently opened Erika Brännström's letterbox in order to hear better. There's someone in the flat, he thought. A radio was on, easy listening from the sound of it, and in the gap between two songs he even heard her humming the last lines of 'Dancing Queen' by Abba.

Well then, Johansson thought, and straightened up to ring the doorbell, but suddenly everything went black and the floor where he was standing turned into a trapdoor. He crashed into her door, bounced back and fell flat on his backside. Which, all things considered, was much better than last time. And he didn't even have to ring the doorbell. Ten seconds later Erika Brännström opened the door, looked at him and shook her head. Judging by the look on her face, she found the sight amusing.

'Were you thinking of sitting there all night?' she asked.

'You should know,' Johansson said. 'One Norrlander to another.'

'Take it easy as you get up,' she said, taking a firm grip of his healthy left arm and helping him to his feet.

'Thanks,' Johansson said.

'Coffee?' she asked.

'A cup of coffee would be lovely.'

Five minutes later they were sitting in her living room, drinking coffee. At first, Erika Brännström sat in silence, just looking at him. Not remotely hostile, more intrigued, and possibly slightly anxious. Not for her own sake, apparently, but his.

'You've never considered looking after yourself?' she said, shaking her head. 'You're even fatter than you were last time I saw you.'

Where have I heard that before? Johansson thought. 'It's not that easy,' he said. 'Let me tell you, it's not that easy.'

'A stubborn, restless man like you. Don't try to tell me you couldn't do it. You've got it too easy, that's what it is. Unless you just don't care, of course.'

'I promise to make an effort,' Johansson said. 'I've got a few questions, if you don't mind?'

'Probably best to get them out of the way, then. Before the neighbours start to wonder what's going on. I imagine it's that hairgrip that's bothering you. The one you thought belonged to Yasmine.'

'Yes,' Johansson said. We might as well start with that, he thought.

'It wasn't me who found it,' Erika said. 'It was Margaretha. Some time in the autumn, after that terrible summer when little Yasmine was murdered. Margaretha found it under her bed when we were cleaning in advance of her move. She gave it to me, asked if it belonged to Karolina or Jessica. My daughters, but you know that. Why she asked, I don't know, seeing as they had short hair at the time.'

'So what did you say?'

'I said it wasn't theirs. It wasn't until much later that it occurred to me that it might have been Yasmine's. That wouldn't have been all that odd, actually, given that she sometimes played round there several times a week. And she used to run about pretty much as she liked. Jessica

and Karolina were a bit better behaved. Besides, I was the one who had to tidy up after everyone. So I used to keep an eye on them.'

'Did Margaretha have any ideas of her own? Did she think it might be Yasmine's?'

'No,' Erika Brännström said. 'She never asked. But you didn't have to work in the health service to tell that she wasn't feeling great, which was hardly surprising, as she'd been so fond of the girl.'

'No,' Johansson said. 'The idea that something like that could have happened to the child of one of her neighbours must have come as a great shock to her.'

'If I've understood you correctly, it was actually much worse than that,' Erika Brännström said.

'How do you mean?' Johansson asked, even though he knew exactly what she was thinking.

'That she was murdered in Margaretha's home,' Erika Brännström said. 'While I was up at Mum and Dad's in Härnösand with the girls, and Margaretha was at her summer cottage out on Rindö. That's what you think, isn't it?'

'Not think,' Johansson said. 'I'm fairly certain that's what happened. In Margaretha Sagerlied's bedroom, if you're wondering. I've thought that all along.'

'That explains a thing or two.'

'Such as?'

'When we were putting together the inventory before she moved – because most of the contents were going to be sold – I thought there was one sheet and one pillowcase missing. She had a dozen of each; they were a gift from her husband when they got married. Finest-quality linen. Embroidered with her initials: MS.'

'What did you think at the time?'

'I don't think I thought anything. The last thing I would have thought is that anything could have happened inside Margaretha's own home. That was completely out of the question. If I thought anything, it was probably that they'd gone astray in the laundry at some point over all those years. Maybe she'd taken them out to the country, or given one set away. Something like that, I suppose.'

'You never asked?' Johansson said.

'No. Anyway, Margaretha was getting worse and worse. This was some time during the spring, or winter, maybe – after New Year, anyway, in 1986 – when most of her things were sold. I was really worried about her. She seemed so distant the whole time. I was actually very fond of her, in spite of all her idiosyncrasies, you know. And my kids certainly didn't have any complaints. Aunt Margaretha was their great idol.'

'Yes, I can imagine,' Johansson said. No lies this time, he thought.

'Well, then,' Erika Brännström said. 'That really only leaves one thing, doesn't it?'

'What do you have in mind?'

'Staffan Leander, Margaretha's husband's nephew. The son of Johan's half-sister, so Johan was his uncle, Margaretha his aunt by marriage. Yes, that was it,' Erika Brännström said, and nodded. 'Margaretha was his aunt.'

'Staffan Leander Nilsson,' Johansson said. 'Leander is his middle name. To be more precise, his surname is Nilsson.'

'I see,' Erika said. 'Staffan Nilsson. Well, well. When he introduced himself to me, I'm sure he said his name was Staffan Leander. That was also when he told me that Margaretha was his aunt, because I had no idea about that. I thought all her relatives were dead.'

'Tell me,' Johansson said. You should have been a policeman, Lars Martin. You've got this interview thing down pat, he thought.

The first time Erika Brännström met Staffan Leander Nilsson was in the spring of 1984. She was helping out at a big party in Margaretha's house, and that was where they met. The last time they spoke to each other was six months later, in the autumn of the same year, when she called him to have it out with him about what she thought he'd done to her daughters. In between, during the spring and summer of 1984, they saw each other on perhaps ten separate occasions, at most. On two of them he called round to pick up her daughters, the first time, when he and Margaretha were going to take them to Skansen, and the second time, when he and the girls went to Kolmården Wildlife Park.

'He was extremely charming, you know. Funny and entertaining, too. Polite and helpful and all that. Nothing like the bloke I'd been married to.'

'Did he try it on with you?'

'I thought he was at first. But I wasn't remotely interested. He was ten years younger than me, after all, and I was sick of men at the time. But he was very sweet with the girls; he used to play and mess about with them. Nothing like their father, like I said.'

'That didn't strike you as odd?'

'I remember asking him. He said he was an only child; he'd been brought up alone by his mum. Never met his dad. He said he spent the whole of his childhood wishing he had younger brothers and sisters. Preferably younger sisters, to play and muck about with. That was what he used to wish for, apparently.'

'Yes, I suppose that sounds plausible,' Johansson said, even though he had grown up with three brothers and three sisters and spent most of his childhood wishing he were an only child.

'Yes, this was before the big paedophile debate, and the idea that such a nice, pleasant young man might be interested in young girls in that way . . . Well, it was unthinkable. I mean, Jessica, my youngest, was only five or six years old at the time, and her big sister was ten. And the first few times he met them I was there the whole time. We went to the funfair at Gröna Lund once. And we went on an outing to Hagaparken. I suppose I was just happy and grateful to have found a nice young man who wanted a couple of younger siblings he'd never had.'

'When did you start to suspect that there was something wrong?' Johansson asked.

'I don't know,' Erika Brännström said. 'It was mostly just a feeling. That there was something odd about him. That such a young, handsome, pleasant lad didn't have a girlfriend. I know I asked him about that, actually.'

'What did he say?'

'That he'd had several girlfriends, but none of them had lasted very long. He thought girls his own age were too superficial. He just hadn't found the right one yet. I suppose I didn't start to get suspicious until he'd been to Kolmården with the girls. That was when I realized that something must have happened. They were both completely different afterwards. I asked them what had happened, but neither of them wanted to say anything. That was some time towards the end of the summer.'

'So what did you do?'

'I'd spent a lot of years working in the health service, so I talked to a good friend of mine, a colleague. He worked as a paediatric doctor. So he examined them. He already knew them, so it would have been a bit easier for them if anything had happened. But he couldn't find anything physically wrong with them. But he was fairly confident they'd been through something they didn't like, or didn't understand. But at least it wasn't rape or anything like that.'

'That must have been a relief for you. Did you talk to a counsellor about it, at all?'

'Like I said, I talked to my friend. Asked what he thought. He advised against it. He said he thought it was the kind of thing that would sort itself out, and that therapy might actually make it worse. Said he didn't think adults should insist on digging up that sort of thing. At least not if it was only on that sort of level.'

'So you followed his advice.'

'Yes,' Erika Brännström said. 'It wasn't a hard decision, either. I've met so many crazy people in that part of the health service. I suppose I'm a bit of a Norrlander on that score.'

'Very sensible,' Johansson said. 'Staffan Nilsson, then? What happened with him?'

'That was the funny thing,' Erika Brännström said. 'He didn't get in touch for a whole month, whereas before he used to call several times a week, so in the end I decided to call him. I asked him straight out what he'd done with my girls when they were at Kolmården.'

'What did he say?'

'He was shocked; he swore and promised he hadn't done anything, and for a while I even thought he was crying. It sounded like it, anyway. He didn't understand what I meant. He was completely innocent. So I said it was probably best that we leave it at that. And that if he made the slightest attempt to contact me or them again, I'd go straight to the police and report him.'

'That was the last contact you had with him?'

'Yes. Since then I haven't met or spoken to him. I haven't even seen him.'

'Did you mention it to Margaretha?'

'No, I didn't. She would have dropped dead on the spot if I had. If anything, she was even more gullible than I was.'

'I don't think your reaction is unusual,' Johansson said. 'For normal, decent people, the idea that someone you trust could do that is completely incomprehensible. Not least if you're a parent.'

'I'm sure you're wondering if I suspected anything after what happened to Yasmine. That's what's so odd, and I can understand if you don't believe me, but I genuinely didn't. Not that Staffan could have done it. I figured out that it had to be someone with the same inclinations as him, obviously. But the idea that it might actually be him . . . That thought never even occurred to me, because what happened to Yasmine was just so utterly appalling. Completely different to whatever had happened to my girls. Whoever murdered Yasmine had to be a complete monster, and the Staffan Nilsson I knew wasn't like that. He may have tricked them into fiddling with his willy, or something like that. But he hadn't raped and strangled them or anything like that. It was out of the question. It was just too horrible to be possible.'

'I believe you,' Johansson said. 'You're not the first person to think like that.' Nor the last, he thought.

422

'I'm honest, anyway,' Erika Brännström said. 'I just didn't get it.'

'Margaretha Sagerlied,' Johansson said. 'Did you have any contact with her after she sold the house and moved into the city? After you stopped working for her – what? – in the spring of '86?'

'She called me. It was six months later, during the autumn. Asked me to go and see her. We met in her flat. In Östermalm, Riddargatan, if I remember rightly. It was quite a shock, actually. Her whole personality had changed. She seemed pretty confused. Thin as a rake, too. She told me she had cancer. It took me a while to work out what she was talking about. That she was talking about Johan's nephew. I'm fairly sure she thought he'd killed himself. Then she went on at length about my girls, and how I shouldn't worry about them. That there was nothing to worry about. That she was sure nothing had happened. It was terrible.'

'I can imagine,' Johansson said. 'Was that the last time you heard from her?' Time for the big honesty test, he thought.

'While she was alive, yes. Then I read in the papers that she'd died. I think that was in the spring of 1989, and just a week later her solicitor called me to say that she'd left a lot of money to my girls. Five hundred thousand kronor – half a million. Have you got any idea how much money that was in those days?'

'Yes,' Johansson said with a smile. 'I have, actually. About two million in today's money.'

'For me, us, it was a fantastic amount of money. In her will, it said that it was to be used to pay for the girls' education and help them to have good, decent lives. That was exactly what she wrote.'

'And it did?'

'I'll say,' Erika Brännström said. 'Neither of them has any student debts at all, even though they both went to university. Karolina's a physiotherapist, and Jessica has an MBA. They're both married, with children and husbands who are nothing like their dad.

'And there was enough money left over to pay the deposits on their flats when they moved away from home. Nothing remarkable, but still. They own the roofs over their heads, and how many ordinary kids can say that?'

'I'm very pleased to hear it,' Johansson said. 'Lovely to hear that things have turned out so well for them.' Sagerlied must have been going through hell when she tried to buy her way out of what her nephew had done, he thought.

'I've got a question for you,' Erika Brännström said. 'When she said that he killed himself. Is that true?'

'His mother killed herself. In the spring of 1986, I know that for certain. So that's true. He himself disappeared at about the same time. What happened after that is less clear.'

'Are you telling me the truth, now?'

'Either way, there's one thing I think we need to be absolutely clear about.'

'What's that?'

'That the only person responsible for what happened to Yasmine is the man who murdered her. And certainly not you.'

'So why do I keep thinking I should have got in touch with the police after that trip to Kolmården?'

'You can rest assured on that point,' Johansson said. 'They wouldn't have done a thing about Staffan

Nilsson if you'd called and said you suspected he was a paedophile. They may well have thought that you were mentally ill. Because you don't imagine he'd have just given in and confessed?'

'You're a good man, Johansson,' Erika Brännström said. 'Do you know what?'

'No,' Johansson said. 'I don't. What don't I know?'

'Since I met you that first time, I've thought about what happened every single day. Wondering if I could have done anything to prevent what happened to Yasmine. Could I have saved her life? I don't think so, but of course I can't be certain. Could I have helped you to get hold of him? I don't think so. I couldn't get it into my head that it might have been him. And as for the idea that it could have happened in Margaretha's home, that thought never even entered my mind.'

'I haven't actually said that he was the one who did it,' Johansson said.

'No, you haven't. But that's because you're a good man. You're being kind to me. That's why you're saying the things you have.'

'So you say.'

'Yes. I know that you know it was Staffan Leander – or Staffan Nilsson – who murdered Yasmine. And I'm absolutely certain you're right. But I have no idea how you worked it out. I certainly didn't. I'm also certain that he's still alive, and that you know where he is. He hasn't killed himself. The fact that his mother did is presumably because she suddenly realized what had happened. If I'd had a son who had done something like that, I'd probably have killed myself, too. And there's one more thing I understand. Even if I didn't think it was true at first when I read it in the paper.'

'What's that?'

'That it's too late for him to be punished for what he did. Because of some weird law that you have to be a lawyer to understand.'

'Yes,' Johansson said. 'That's how it is. If a case has passed the statute of limitations, the perpetrator can no longer be punished.'

'There's one thing I was thinking of asking you,' Erika Brännström said.

'What's that?'

'That you make sure he gets his punishment.'

'I promise to do my best,' Johansson said.

'Good,' Erika Brännström said. 'If you're going to look decent, respectable people in the eye, you have to be a decent, respectable person yourself. And it isn't easy for a good person to keep evil at bay, and sometimes you have to be just as evil back. Then you might be able to carry on as normal. But you understand that, seeing as you're a Norrlander.'

'I wasn't thinking of killing him, if that's what you mean,' Johansson said.

'No, I certainly hope not, because that's not what I want either. But you'll manage to come up with something that even us decent people can live with.'

'Did it go okay, boss?' Max asked when they were sitting in the car on the way back to Södermalm.

'It went very well indeed,' Johansson said. In spite of the subject matter, he thought.

'Good to hear,' Max said. 'Just let me know if there's anything I can do.'

'I promise,' Johansson said. The easiest way out, he thought. Let Max or someone like him beat Staffan

426

Nilsson to a pulp. Eye for eye, tooth for tooth, all the way down to his little feet in his doubtless very shiny shoes.

'Max,' Johansson said. 'What do you think about stopping on the way and grabbing a burger?'

'No,' Max said, shaking his head. 'I don't think that's a good idea.'

'You're not the slightest bit tempted?'

'I am,' Max said. 'But given that Pia would kill me, I think it's a really bad idea. You'll have to forgive me, boss, but that's how it is.'

'What do you think about knocking up a nice salad when we get home, then?'

'I think that sounds like an excellent idea,' Max said. 'You can't go wrong with a nice salad.'

79

Friday, 13 August

On Friday evening Jarnebring and Max made another attempt to get a sample of Staffan Nilsson's DNA. First, they made another nuisance call to his landline. No answer. Not even an answer-machine. Then they called his mobile, using the number Gun had provided. No answer there either, and they had no intention of leaving a message.

As they were already out, they decided to go round to his home to check the situation. His car was in its usual place. Neatly parked, locked and alarmed, as usual.

Then Jarnebring went into the building where he lived. Tried listening outside the door of his flat. Not a sound. He went back down to the street. Went into the building opposite, where the stairwell had a decent view into Nilsson's flat. No lights on, no television on, no sign of human activity at all.

'Do you think he's done a runner?' Max asked when Jarnebring returned to the car.

'No,' Jarnebring said. 'I'm not getting that feeling.' If only I were still on the force, with an active case on my hands, he thought. A murder case, at that, with the usual complement of officers to take care of the practical details, then I wouldn't have to sit here and speculate. 'Let's call it a night. We'll do a quick circuit of the local bars, then we'll call it a night. Unless something comes up, of course.'

'There's no way he's done a runner,' Johansson said when Max was standing in front of the sofa in his study, giving a report of the evening's activities.

'If you say so, boss,' Max said.

'He's not the type,' Johansson said, shaking his head. 'He's not the type to commit suicide, because he's far too fond of himself. And he's not the type to leave his car behind, if he had done a runner. He'd have sold it first. People like him are mean. Which is often very useful for people like me when we want to lock them up. They're often a bit slow off the blocks.'

'You're a wise man, boss,' Max said.

'Yes,' Johansson said. 'For the time being, I'm wiser than you, but that's not your fault.'

'Why not?'

'All the crap you went through when you were a young lad. All the crap that wicked grown-ups subjected you to when you were too small to be able to defend yourself against them. All the stuff that wasn't your fault but which is still governing your life. The day you get over that will be the day when you're as wise as me.'

'Good to hear,' Max said.

'Yes,' Johansson said. 'So there's no need to worry on that score. And because you're on your feet and I'm lying down, and Pia's chatting to her friends on her computer, I was wondering if you could go into the bathroom and get the case containing my pills?' So I can shut my head up and breathe like a normal person, he thought.

'No problem,' Max said.

When he came back two minutes later Johansson was already asleep. Max sat down on the chair beside him. Listened to his snoring. He sat there for two hours, mainly to reassure himself that his boss would still be there when he woke up in the morning. Then he went into his room and closed the door behind him. He lay down on his bed without even kicking his shoes off.

The boss is a good man, Max thought. A bad man is eating him up from inside. I have to help him, so he doesn't die on me, he thought.

Then he fell asleep. He slept as silently as he moved when he was awake. Slept with his eyes half open, the way he always had, without ever being aware of it.

80

Saturday, 14 August

On Saturday, 14 August, Bo Jarnebring made yet another attempt to acquire a sample of Staffan Nilsson's DNA. More actively this time. He went early in the morning, let himself into the building where Nilsson lived with the help of the entry-code Gun had given him, seeing as she, unlike him, was still employed by the Stockholm Police and could find such things out without difficulty. Once he was in the lobby, he stole Staffan Nilsson's copy of *Svenska Dagbladet*, which was sticking out of his mailbox, in the hope of forcing him out of his flat to take an early-morning walk.

An hour later Nilsson appeared down at the front door dressed in pyjamas, slippers and dressing-gown, and, even though he couldn't hear him, Jarnebring could tell he was swearing about his missing newspaper.

At first, he tried to pinch the neighbour's copy of *Dagens Nyheter*, but because Jarnebring was a conscientious man when it came to the various forms of police provocation, he had made sure to push every other morning newspaper as far inside their recipients' mailboxes as possible. Nilsson made a number of further attempts before finally giving up, getting in the lift and disappearing back up to his flat on the third floor.

Ten minutes later he emerged on to the street dressed in trainers, shorts and a jacket and set off towards the next block and the nearest convenience store, which not only sold newspapers, cigarettes and a variety of groceries but also offered customers the chance to consume a simple breakfast. Jarnebring felt his hopes rise as he strolled down the street to take up a better position.

Staffan Nilsson bought a copy of *Svenska Dagbladet*, a cinnamon bun and a cardboard cup of coffee. He took the whole lot and went straight back to his flat, leaving Jarnebring to curse him out loud.

In the absence of better options, he checked Nilsson's car, but it was just as locked and alarmed as it had been on every other day he had checked it to see if he could get hold of anything of forensic interest.

The bastard doesn't even seem to lose any hair, Jarnebring thought unhappily, as he inspected the front seat and headrest through the side window. Well, quitters never win, he thought, as he returned to his own car. He parked so he could see the windows of Nilsson's kitchen and living room and kept watch on the front door while he leafed through his freshly stolen newspaper.

After another two hours of fruitless waiting, he gave up.

On his way home he called Johansson on his mobile and told him about his early-morning travails.

'The bastard doesn't even seem to lose any hair,' Jarnebring said.

'Probably what happens if you don't smoke or use chewing tobacco,' Johansson said.

'You don't think it's time to make a call to our colleagues out on patrol? Before he moves his car next time? We could probably get him for drink-driving as well. Give him a little appetizer before we shove the main course up him?'

'No,' Johansson said. 'I don't. Well, if you'll excuse me, I'm going to have my breakfast.'

81

Sunday, 15 August

'Your friend and I were thinking of doing some more surveillance on the paedo, boss. See if we can't get hold of a bit of DNA,' Max said.

'Sounds good,' Johansson said. 'Good luck.'

'You don't want to come along, then, boss?'

'No.' Johansson shook his head. 'I was thinking of lying here and staring at the box. The television, I mean,' he added, seeing as he wasn't sure how much slang a young man like Max might have picked up in the course of his short life. 'Thought I might watch an old eighties flick I've got on DVD.' He must know what a flick is, surely? he thought.

'What's it about?'

'It's quite interesting, actually,' Johansson said. 'It's about a story Jarnebring and I were involved in when we worked in Spain in the seventies. A right mess, really. A Minister of Justice hanging out with prostitutes. But the film's good.'

'Have a nice, quiet evening, then, boss,' Max said.

'You too. Say hello to Bo, and good luck.'

'Thanks.'

*

Even though it wasn't a bad film, Johansson fell asleep in the middle of it, perhaps because he seemed to be able to fall asleep at the drop of a hat these days, regardless of what was going on around him. He woke up to find Max leaning over him, gently nudging his left shoulder.

'It's done,' Max said.

'What?' Johansson said, sitting up on the sofa. 'What's done?'

'That business with the DNA, I sorted it,' Max said, holding up a two-litre freezer-bag containing what looked like a used paper napkin.

'What the hell have you two been up to?' Johansson asked, taking the bag containing the napkin.

'Bo's entirely innocent,' Max said.

'What do you mean, innocent?'

'He couldn't make it,' Max said. 'He had to help his daughter with something.'

'I see.'

'So I went off on my own.'

'You did, did you?'

'It was just like when you were there, boss,' Max said. 'First, he came out and went over to the restaurant, and sat there and had a meal. Only this time he didn't make any calls. He ordered a pizza and a bottle of red wine. A whole bottle, which he finished.'

'Then what?'

'Then he went to move his car, because it's Monday tomorrow. The thing I don't understand is why he doesn't park it in the right place to start with. Well, that's his problem, not mine. I followed him. As soon as he started to reverse I walked out behind him, so he couldn't help driving into me.'

'He drove into you?' What the hell's the lad saying? Johansson thought.

'Yes, he reversed into me, but it didn't matter. Nothing to make a fuss about. When he realized what he'd done he opened the door and asked if I was okay.'

'What did you do, then?'

'I walked up to him and yanked him out. Asked what the fuck he thought he was doing. Told him he was drunk and shouldn't even be driving. He started to argue, so I gave him a slap across the nose. Then I pulled out a napkin I had in my pocket and wiped him down. Said he ought to be a bit more fucking careful before he thought about driving drunk. That he could kill someone if he wasn't careful.'

'You hit him? You hit him on the nose?' This can't be happening, Johansson thought.

'With my hand open,' Max said, holding up a right hand that was even bigger than Johansson's best friend's. 'An open hand across the nose. Anyway, he'd already run me over.'

'Across the nose?' The lad's done this before, Johansson thought. He knows the difference in punishment for an open hand and a clenched fist, he thought.

'Best place if you want someone to start bleeding without hurting them badly,' Max said, shrugging his shoulders. 'If I'd hit him in the jaw or eyebrows he could have died. I could have fractured his skull without him even shedding a drop of blood.'

'You didn't do anything else?' Johansson asked. He's considerate as well, he thought.

'No,' Max said. 'I just walked away.'

'I sincerely hope he is still alive.'

'Of course he is,' Max said. 'A little nosebleed never killed anyone, did it?'

'No,' Johansson said. 'You didn't think you had any other options, then?'

'No,' Max said. 'I could hardly go into the restaurant and give him a slap. With loads of witnesses and all that. I hope you're not mad at me, boss.'

'No. I'm afraid to say that I'm not. Not if what you're telling me is what really happened.' I can think of at least two people who'd adopt you on the spot, he thought.

'There's no need to worry, boss,' Max said. 'I'm not lying. Only bad people lie. I've never needed to.'

No, Johansson thought. Why should you need to? 'Just one question,' he said. 'Do you always go round with a paper napkin in your pocket?'

'Always,' Max said. 'In case I need to blow my nose or something. Was there anything else you were wondering, boss?'

'No,' Johansson said. 'But there might be something I ought to say.'

'What's that?'

'Thank you, Max,' Johansson said with a nod. 'Thank you very much. And next time you decide to solve a problem for me, I'd appreciate it if you asked me for permission first.'

'Of course,' Max said.

Must call Bo, Johansson thought. He suddenly felt inexplicably elated, as if someone had removed the strap that had been constricting his chest and stopping him breathing properly. No headache, either. Just free. At last, he thought.

82

Monday, 16 August

Johansson had made up his mind what to do before falling asleep the night before. The Security Police can deal with the practical side of things, he thought. You could think what you liked about the Security Police, but they knew how to keep their mouths shut. If he sent Max's bloody napkin to one of his many contacts in the regular Crime Unit, he was more than likely to find himself reading about it in the paper at pretty much the same time as the test results came through. He didn't even want to think about the consequences of that, and didn't need to, seeing as they were bleeding obvious.

I need to talk to Lisa, Johansson thought. Lisa Mattei, his youngest and most talented colleague during his last ten years in the force, who had moved with him from the Security Police to National Crime. She had returned to the Security Police after he retired. These days she was a Deputy Police Commissioner on the staff of the Director General, despite being just thirty-five years old.

On Monday morning Johansson cancelled his appointment with his physiotherapist and called Lisa Mattei instead.

'Johansson,' Johansson said when she answered.

'Lars,' Lisa Mattei said. 'Good to hear from you. According to the latest news in the staff room, you're improving by the day.'

'I'm fine,' Johansson said. 'Lars', he thought. What happened to 'boss'? Are we close friends, all of a sudden?

'Is there something I can help you with?'

'Yes,' Johansson said. 'And, practically enough, I think you may be the only person who can. It's urgent, too.'

'I can see you in an hour,' Mattei said. 'How long do you think it will take?'

'Fifteen minutes,' Johansson said. Little Lisa's grown up, he thought as he hung up.

A reserved, very fit blonde, well-dressed, respectable, pleasant appearance. Lisa Mattei in one sentence, Johansson thought as he stepped into her office. She was obviously pregnant now, judging by the size of her stomach. Little Lisa is properly big now, he thought.

'Lars,' Lisa said. 'It's really good to see you. Can I give you a hug?' she asked.

'Okay,' Johansson said, and leaned forward to make it easier for her to put her arm round his back. 'Do you know what sort it is?' he went on, nodding towards her round stomach as soon as he had sat down.

'A girl. I couldn't wait, so I asked them to tell me,' she said.

'And her dad? Is he a police officer, too?'

'Not remotely. He teaches film studies. Works at the university.'

'Good to hear,' Johansson said.

'What can I do for you, Lars?'

439

'I need to get a DNA sample tested. It's a sensitive subject. If we get a match, I don't want it to leak out.'

'What's the case?'

'The unsolved sexually motivated murder of a nine-year-old girl twenty-five years ago, now prescribed.'

'Yasmine Ermegan?' Lisa Mattei stared at him.

'Yes,' Johansson said.

'You've solved it for us?'

'Yes,' Johansson said. 'I'm pretty certain I've found him. And he's still alive.'

'I can't help being curious,' Mattei said. 'What made you take an interest in Yasmine's murder? It wasn't one of your old cases, was it?'

'I needed something to do while I was in hospital.'

'You haven't changed, Lars,' Lisa Mattei declared.

'Maybe,' Johansson said. 'To be honest, I've felt better. This is his DNA, and a hairgrip that I believe belonged to the victim,' he said, putting his two plastic bags down on her desk.

'Blood,' Mattei said, holding up the bag containing the paper napkin.

'Yes,' Johansson said. 'Sometimes you have to make the most of things. We can deal with that later.' He shrugged.

'And this hairgrip was Yasmine's?'

'Yes,' Johansson said. 'Not that I think there's anything on it, but from a purely academic perspective it's probably worth a try. I've got a question. Can this be regarded as a security matter?'

'If we get a match, then yes, definitely. I presume you know who Yasmine's father is?'

'Yes,' Johansson said. 'What about as things stand now?'

440

'What are friends for?' Mattei said with a smile. 'Besides, this is where I work,' she added.

'Let me know,' Johansson said, and stood up. 'And take care of yourself.' He nodded towards her bulging stomach.

'You, too, Lars,' Mattei said.

After lunch a thought struck Johansson. He quickly weighed up his options. Decided to break one of his own rules. He called one of his old contacts at Solna Police and began by asking a direct question.

'Toivonen,' said Superintendent Toivonen from the Crime Unit in Solna.

'Johansson,' Johansson said.

'Bloody hell,' Toivonen said. 'How are you?'

'Fine,' Johansson said. 'Are you still good at keeping your mouth shut?'

'Better than ever,' Toivonen said. 'You only get more and more tired as you get older. I can barely be bothered to talk to myself any more,' he clarified. 'What can I do for you?'

'Can you check if you received a report of an incident yesterday evening? Frösunda. The parking spaces near the square. About ten o'clock. Assault.'

'Just a moment,' Toivonen said.

It took five minutes, but he got an answer.

'Sorry it took a while,' Toivonen said. 'Computer trouble,' he explained. 'Had to check with the officer who's looking after the case. What do you make of this, then? Aggravated assault. The plaintiff, a Staffan Nilsson, born 1960, was mugged just before ten o'clock last night when he was heading home to go to bed. He'd been for a meal at a nearby restaurant.'

'Aggravated assault?'

'Yes,' Toivonen said. 'The perpetrators, at least two of them, according to the plaintiff, possibly three, were the usual sort, going by his description. They took his gold-and-steel Rolex, a gold note-clip containing twelve thousand kronor in notes, the gold chain he had round his neck and a signet ring in white gold he was wearing on his left hand. Total value around one hundred and fifty thousand kronor. Frankly, he was asking for it if he was wandering about with all that on him. Or else he's just got fucking good insurance.'

'Witnesses?' This is getting better and better, Johansson thought.

'None who saw what happened. An elderly couple who were out for an evening found the victim immediately afterwards. He was sitting on the pavement, bleeding from the nose. They called 112. The first patrol arrived five minutes later. The meat-wagon arrived just after that.'

'Surveillance cameras?'

'No, none where it happened.'

'How is the victim, then?'

'He was discharged from hospital last night after they patched him up. Fractured nose. Nothing too serious. Is it someone you know?'

'Who?'

'The victim?'

'What victim?' Johansson said.

'I understand,' Toivonen said. 'Take care.'

So how do I use this? Johansson thought.

83

Monday evening, 16 August

That evening Lars Martin Johansson, sixty-seven, had a conversation lasting over an hour with Maxim Makarov, twenty-three. A personal conversation in which Max talked about events in his life which were almost unbearable to talk about. It was Johansson who got him to do this, and whether it was right or wrong of him was a question to which he would never know the answer. It all began innocently enough, mostly as an attempt to forge a bit of simple, human contact. Possibly even an attempt to joke about serious things.

Johansson asked Max to make him some tea. It was a relatively risk-free enterprise, asking a Russian to make tea, regardless of gender. The sort of tea that Johansson liked, not that English dishwater. Russian tea. Then they sat down in the study and Johansson told him that Staffan Nilsson evidently hadn't merely had his nose slapped and then wiped afterwards, in a way which could hardly have been beneficial to his pride. He had also been mugged of his note-clip, money, watch, the gold chain round his neck and the signet ring on the little finger of his left hand.

'He's lying,' Max said. 'He wasn't wearing a gold chain. But I do remember the ring and watch.'

'I believe you,' Johansson said. 'Besides, you're a very bad match with his description of his attackers. Two, possibly three, perpetrators, none of them much like you if I understood correctly.' By now Staffan Nilsson ought to have filed a report with his insurance company too, he thought.

'It wasn't easy,' Max said. 'I have trouble with people like him.'

'I'm glad you didn't kill him,' Johansson said.

'For your sake, boss. I let him live for your sake.'

The lad seems completely out of it, Johansson thought.

'Tell me about the children's home you were in,' Johansson said. 'Sometimes it can be good to let out a bit of pressure. Anything you say will stay inside this room.'

'Okay,' Max said.

It's 1993. Maksim Makarov is six years old, and he has just lost his foothold in life. His grandmother has died, and he's been left on his own, with no close relatives to feed him and give him a bed to sleep in. No adult hand to cling to for a bit of comfort. That leaves the children's home: a home for him and children like him.

The old stone city of St Petersburg, where the River Neva flows into the Gulf of Finland, 5 million inhabitants, squeezed into an area a third the size of Stockholm. The commissars of the Soviet state and the relative order they created have been replaced by voracious capitalism and a vicious free-for-all, even if the individuals concerned are largely the same.

444

Ordinary people are suffering; wages and pensions are paid late or not at all. There is a sudden torrent of goods that only a minority can afford. The price of bread, potatoes and everything else people use to fill their stomachs keeps on rising. Crime is growing to epidemic levels. Members of a new lumpen proletariat have made the streets and squares their home. Police vans no longer appear every morning and evening to cart them off to the police cells of the people's republic, where they were once given water, thin gruel, bread and a bucket to vomit, piss and shit in. Nothing like that now. The Soviet welfare state has ceased to exist, and free enterprise has taken over.

This applies even to people like Max, and all the lonely children who have no adult hand to guide them through life. But there is the children's home, which at least offers three meals a day, a roof over their heads and beatings at any hour of the day for anyone who doesn't behave or has simply wet themselves. There is still the hope of being adopted. Of getting a new mother and father who will take them away, to a new life in capitalist heaven, at a safe distance from the despair of St Petersburg.

'I grew up in Grazdanka,' Max said. 'It wasn't a lot like Östermalm, exactly. Where all the rich people live, where Evert's office is,' he explained.

'Is that in the suburbs?' Johansson asked. Despite having visited St Petersburg both before and after the collapse of communism, he didn't really know his way around.

'There are hardly any suburbs in that city,' Max said, shaking his head. 'It's not like here. Petersburg is a stone city; Grazdanka is a slum. The building where I lived with Grandma and Grandpa had an outside toilet. For a while there was a children's home in almost every block. It's better now. The worst is over. I don't think the staff in the homes are allowed to sell children any more. I think Putin put a stop to that.'

The sale of children used to follow the same rules that applied to the sale of most other goods. The price was set according to supply and demand, and customers obviously had the expected preferences when it came to something like a child. They should be as young as possible, healthy, of course, pleasant, and as pretty as possible. Girls were more in demand than boys.

'So you were left on the shelf?' Johansson said with a wry smile.

'Guess,' Max said, smiling back. 'I looked the way I do now, just a much smaller version.'

'So there were never any offers?'

'Once, a fat old Finn started poking and prodding me,' Max said. 'His wife was even fatter. So I jumped up and punched him. Guess if I got beaten after that. I had to sleep on my front for the rest of the week.'

The children's home where Max lived for four years was an old, abandoned hospital that had been patched up and turned into a home the year before he ended up there. There was space for three hundred children and twenty staff, mostly women. The children were sorted according to the usual principles. Infants and toddlers at the bottom, children between six and twelve on the next floor, where boys and girls were sent in different directions at the top of the stairs. The older children were on the top floor, and as soon as they turned fifteen it was time to find another home.

'When you grew hair on your balls, or round your fanny if you were a girl, you were moved to the top floor. If Mum had waited another year, I'd have ended up there, too. Once you got there, you were finished.'

'I can imagine,' Johansson said.

'I had a number of older friends who lived up there. They're all dead now. Drink, meths, solvents, heroin, crime. You got chucked out of the home straight on to the street. One of my best friends – he was four years older than me – he smuggled a bottle of methanol in and drank the lot. He died in the home that night. Thirteen years old.'

'Did you get any kind of education? You must have gone to some sort of school?'

'Sure,' Max said. 'In the building next door. You were taught to read, write and count, but most of it was practical. You worked in a workshop, basically. I spent a whole year nailing pallets together. The last year I was there. Before that I washed dirty glasses and peeled potatoes. That was the staff's perk: anything we did, they got to trouser. And they couldn't make any money from us being taught how to read.'

'"Trouser"?' Johansson asked.

'Stick the money in their own pockets,' Max explained. 'We worked for loads of customers. Restaurants, small workshops, ordinary shops, building firms. They used to turn up with a truck and dump a load of rubble in the yard. Then we'd run out and start pulling out nails, sorting the wood and putting it into piles. Knocking mortar from old bricks. There we were, a load of Russian kids. It was like that film with the seven dwarfs. But they worked in a mine, didn't they?'

447

'Yes,' Johansson said, and sighed. What could he say? he thought. That he used to sit in the kitchen back home at the farm, splitting kindling long before he started school, while his mother bribed him with chocolate and whipped cream and freshly baked cinnamon buns.

'There wasn't really anything wrong with us paying our way,' Max said, as if he could read Johansson's thoughts. 'But we were basically the staff's slaves. If they couldn't make money from selling us to rich Westerners, then we had to work. If we did learn to read and write, that was just a façade to cover what the staff were really doing.'

'It can't have been easy,' Johansson said. I have to say something, he thought. That I used to sit by the stove in the kitchen splitting kindling? That I had to mound up the potatoes and harvest hay when I was a lad?

'There was worse, I'm sure – kids who had it much worse, I mean,' Max said, and shrugged. 'But what I've told you wasn't the worst of it. Worse things went on.'

'Tell me about that,' Johansson said.

'I'm not sure you want to hear that, boss.'

'We'll see.'

'Okay.' Max shrugged again. 'I had a best friend, a girl, actually; she was a few years older than me. We arrived at the home at more or less the same time. She got there a couple of months before me. We already knew each other; we used to live in the same block. She was like my big sister. Her name was Nadjesta. Nadjesta Nazarova.'

Maybe this wasn't such a good idea, Johansson thought when he saw the expression in Max's eyes.

'If you feel up to it,' Johansson said. 'Tell me about Nadjesta.'

84

Monday evening, 16 August

Nadjesta Nazarova was three years older than Max. She lived in a house across the yard, in the same block as him. She shared the yard with him and the hundred other kids of a similar age who grew up in the same block. Who her father was was unclear; her mother's boyfriends were grown-up men she never got to know. They weren't all nice. Her mother died a couple of months before his grandmother.

'What did she die of?' Johansson asked. 'Nadja's mother?'

'She fell off some scaffolding, drunk as a skunk. Died instantly.'

'What the hell was she doing up a load of scaffolding?'

'She worked there,' Max said with a smile. 'She was a builder, used to plaster the outsides of buildings. We're talking Russia here, boss.'

'I hear what you're saying,' Johansson said.

When Max ends up in the children's home at the age of six, Nadja, nine years old, is already there.

'She ended up being my big sister,' Max said. He nodded to himself, no longer thinking about Johansson, who was lying there on his sofa.

'We ended up in the same section. Different rooms, though, seeing as I was a boy and she was a girl, but we spent most of the time together. In the evenings, when everyone else had gone to sleep, she used to sneak in and cuddle me,' he said. 'Whisper to me, tell me stories, whisper in my ear until I fell asleep.'

'So what happened?' Johansson said, even though he had already worked out the details. He could even see it in his mind's eye.

'Nadja was really pretty,' Max said. 'Even though she was nine, there were lots of people who wanted to adopt her.'

'But she stayed with you,' Johansson said. Bloody hell, he thought.

'Of course, because she'd promised to take care of me until we were old enough to escape and move into a house that only we knew how to find. We'd get married and have children who we'd kiss and cuddle the whole time. Once a Swedish couple came, and they were willing to pay any amount to get her, and they seemed pretty normal, actually. He was some sort of director, his wife was a teacher; they lived in Västerås. I'm pretty sure of that. Västerås,' Max repeated. 'Västerås in Sweden, of all places.'

'What happened?' Johansson asked.

'I was sure it was over. It's all over now, I thought. But then Nadja faked a hysterical attack, went mad and thrashed about on the floor, and tried to scratch out the eyes of the woman from Västerås. The staff had to drag her away and lock her in the office. The couple from

Västerås picked another kid instead, a poor little thing who didn't say a word. So everything was okay. You can imagine how relieved I was.

'But then she got hair between her legs,' Max said. 'And then it really was all over. For real.'

Nadja hit puberty before she turned twelve. Grew breasts and hair in her crotch. Like all the others, she was sent to the home's doctor for her first gynaecological examination. And, just like all the other pubescent women that he thought were attractive enough, she had her first sexual experience.

'He fucked her,' Max said, with a faraway look in his eyes. 'He fucked all the girls in the home as soon as they grew pubes. All the kids knew about it. None of the adults who worked there had a clue. At least, that's what they said when the cops showed up. Nadja shut herself off completely. It was like I no longer existed. She didn't want to talk to me any more. She didn't even look at me. She just went round like a zombie.'

'The police,' Johansson said. 'Why did they show up?'

'Nadja died that night,' Max said. 'The last time he fucked her. He spent all his time in his room. And he got her drunk first. So she wouldn't scream when he did it. He must have drunk a whole litre himself. Vodka. The fuel that has always driven Mother Russia. Then he fell asleep. Just passed out. Nadja had been strapped down in the chair where the girls had to sit when they were examined. She'd fallen asleep, too, or passed out. I don't really know.'

'How do you know all this?' Johansson said. Why can't you ever keep your mouth shut? he thought the moment he said it.

'I was the one who found her.' Max stood up with a jerk, his thin, bony face as white as a sheet, expressionless. 'Excuse me, boss,' he said, pressing his clenched fist to his mouth and rushing out.

'Okay,' Max said when he returned ten minutes later. 'Where were we?'

'You said you were the one who found her,' Johansson said.

'Yes. I got up to go to the toilet, in the middle of the night. The toilet was next to the doctor's office. I don't know how, but suddenly I just knew. The door was locked, so I grabbed a fire extinguisher and smashed it open.'

Nine years old, Johansson thought.

'Nadja was already dead,' Max said. 'Not that I realized it at the time, because I tried to shake her awake. Apparently, she'd drowned in her own vomit. The doctor was lying there asleep, flat out on the floor, completely out of it. I went and got the fire extinguisher and hit him in the head with it. I only had time to hit him once before the other staff showed up and wrestled me to the floor. Then the cops came.'

'What happened after that, then?'

'He left,' Max said. 'That was pretty much all that happened. If you're wondering, boss, his name was Aleksander Konstantinov. He was the doctor at several children's homes. The first time I was put in a secure children's home in Sweden, under paragraph 12, I ran away. I got the boat to Finland, then the ferry to St Petersburg. I was planning to put an end to it, give him one last message from me and Nadja.'

'How old were you then?' Johansson asked.

'Sixteen,' Max said. 'But I already looked the way I do now, so that was no problem.'

'Did you get hold of him, then?'

'No,' Max said. 'I did my best, but he'd died the previous year. He got drunk, fell into the Neva and drowned. That's probably the second-biggest sorrow of my life.'

'I understand,' Johansson said. After Nadja, he thought.

'No,' Max said. 'With all due respect, boss, you're a good man. And a good man like you can't really understand any of this. You never will, boss, and you should be fucking grateful for that. I understand from Evert that you were brilliant at locking up murderers when you were in charge of the police, boss. That doesn't count. What I'm talking about is something completely different. When you asked me to check that registration number from the vehicle registry, the one belonging to that paedo Staffan Nilsson, who murdered that little girl, I almost started to believe in God,' he went on.

'Why?'

'To start with, he was born in 1960, the same year as Dr Konstantinov. And there was a physical resemblance, too. I found a picture of Nilsson on the internet. Not a new photograph, exactly, but they looked similar. Could have been brothers. Maybe that's what they are, anyway. Men like Konstantinov and Nilsson. The sort of men who fuck little girls to death – they're brothers. The moment before I gave Nilsson that slap across the nose, I actually believed that there is a God. A God who had given me Staffan Nilsson in place of Aleksander Konstantinov, who sadly managed to go and drown himself before I got my hands on him.'

'I'm glad you didn't kill him.'

'With respect, boss,' Max said, 'just as I was about to do it, it struck me that he actually belongs to you, boss. That you were the one who found him, so he belongs to you, not me. And that's something I can't change.'

85

Tuesday, 17 August

'You've got a visitor, boss,' Matilda said, nodding towards Johansson as he lay on his sofa, relaxing after lunch.

'Jarnebring,' Johansson said. What's so hard about phoning first? he thought irritably.

'*Nyet*,' Matilda said, for some reason. 'No wolves in sight. And little Max is in his room, playing computer games. Your best friend is probably at home chewing on the bones of some poor sod he ran into out in the city. This is much better, though.'

'How?'

'A girl. A young, pretty girl. Well, fairly young, anyway.'

'Is she as pretty as you?' Johansson asked, suddenly in that mood.

'Maybe,' Matilda said. 'She's a different type, certainly.'

Lisa Mattei, Johansson thought, and suddenly felt completely calm. Calm, and slightly distant, the way he usually felt when he took one of those little white pills, which he probably did far too often.

'Lisa Mattei,' Matilda said. 'Says she knows you, boss. Says you know what it's about. I hope she's not disturbing you.'

*

'Sit yourself down, Lisa,' Johansson said, gesturing towards the armchair closest to the sofa. 'Can I offer you anything?'

'A cup of tea would be nice,' she said, nodding at Matilda.

'And a double espresso, no milk. Can you shut us in, as well, please?' Johansson asked, waving his hand in the general direction of the kitchen.

'How are you, Lars?' Lisa Mattei said, sitting down and modestly crossing her legs. The hem of her blue skirt fell just below her knees. 'You look even brighter than when I saw you yesterday,' she said.

'I'm in tip-top condition,' Johansson said. And you're never going to call me boss again, are you, not now you're all grown up? he thought.

'What a lovely room.' Lisa Mattei looked round at the bookcases.

'Never mind all that, Mattei,' Johansson said. 'Get to the point.'

'Okay.' She looked at him with a serious expression. 'For the first time since I met you, which must be more than ten years ago now, I was actually hoping that you'd turn out to be wrong. That even you had made a mistake for once.'

'But I hadn't,' Johansson said. Who does she take me for? he thought.

'No,' Lisa Mattei said. 'That was stupid of me. The DNA in the blood on that paper napkin you gave me matches the DNA found in the perpetrator's sperm from Yasmine's murder. According to our experts, the chance of it being someone else's are less than one in a billion. And they even managed to get a DNA trace from the hairgrip. Microscopic fragments of skin on the inside of the clip.'

'And?'

'Yasmine Ermegan,' Mattei said, and the moment she said it she put her right arm protectively across her stomach.

86

Tuesday, 17 August

'I've got a number of questions, as I'm sure you can appreciate,' Lisa Mattei said. 'I hope you don't have any objections?'

'Of course not,' Johansson said. 'Go ahead.'

'The first is actually from the scientist who isolated the DNA sample. The blood on the napkin. He thought it was blood from the nose, which would be rather unconventional in a situation like this.'

Whoops, Johansson thought. 'What made him think that?' he said.

'Nostril hairs in the blood – three of them, to be precise. The result of energetic treatment of a bleeding nose, according to our expert. So I can't help being a little curious.'

'Nothing serious,' Johansson said, shrugging his shoulders. 'Delaying any longer would have been hazardous, and one of my colleagues got a little impatient. Asking him to stick a cotton-wool bud in his mouth wasn't really an option, as you'll appreciate.'

'There are other ways,' Lisa Mattei said. 'Without necessarily rousing his suspicions.'

'He doesn't smoke or use chewing tobacco. There's a chute for rubbish in his building. He's careful about locking his flat, and his car is kept locked, alarmed and very clean. When he's in a bar having a drink, he never leaves his glass on the table. Jarnebring spent a week watching him, without success.'

'You could have called me.' Lisa Mattei gave a slight smile.

'I know. I could have called lots of former colleagues from my time in the business. The lads in the rapid-response unit could have done it in fifteen minutes, regardless of the amount of blood plasma required. I chose not to do that. You don't have to worry. The bastard is still alive, and in good health. Considerably better health than me, if you're wondering. He lives a very comfortable life, in spite of what he did to that poor girl twenty-five years ago. So there's no need to worry about him.'

'I'm not at all concerned about him,' Mattei said. 'I assume you've already found out almost everything about him?'

'I've found out the usual,' Johansson said. 'Within the natural limitations that come with being a pensioner these days, and taking into account the fact that I've avoided talking to former colleagues who can't keep their mouths shut. And that I had a stroke not all that long ago.'

'Can you tell me his identity? That would make things a lot easier for me, as I know you realize.'

'Negative, not as things stand at the moment. Come back in a week when I've had time to think.'

'No criminal record?'

'Not in Sweden, anyway. Is he still active as a paedophile? I'm quite convinced that he is. Has he done anything else? Almost certainly, but nothing that comes close to what he did to Yasmine. You and your colleagues probably shouldn't start hoping that I've found a hitherto unknown serial killer for you.'

'I've uploaded his DNA on to our international network,' Mattei said, 'in case you're wondering, and you're the only person who knows about that. I did it just before I came here.'

'Then we'll just have to keep our fingers crossed and hope that something crops up that way,' Johansson said. 'Try the usual places where people like him go to ground. Thailand, the Philippines, Mexico, Central America, Russia, the Baltic states, the southern Balkans. I'd start with Thailand, if I were you. But I think you can forget about Sweden and our Nordic neighbours. I haven't been able to come up with any unsolved sexually motivated murders of young girls that match. No girls going missing or other extreme paedophile activity either.'

'I'm in complete agreement with you on that point,' Lisa Mattei said with a smile. 'I checked that yesterday, as a matter of fact. One more question. How would you describe him, in social terms?'

'Swedish, middle-aged, single, no children, neither successful nor a failure, makes a living from various activities in the property industry. And, if you're wondering, he looks perfectly normal. Nice, even, to be more precise. Let me put it like this – we're not dealing with another Anders Eklund.'

'I understand precisely.' Lisa Mattei sighed, for some reason.

'So do I,' Johansson said. 'If this were to leak out, bearing in mind who Yasmine's father is and what we know about him, I venture to suppose that you would have a potentially explosive political problem to deal with.'

'Don't worry about that,' Lisa Mattei said. 'I've already informed the Director General.'

'What did he say?'

'He sends his regards and hopes you get well soon. If you're thinking about coming back to work, you just have to give him a call. Essentially, he thinks the same as you. That Joseph Simon should be regarded as such a formidable adversary that our perpetrator deserves the attentions of the forces defending the Swedish constitution.'

'One final question,' Lisa Mattei said, as she got to her feet and gestured towards the boxes of documents on the floor of the study.

'Okay,' Johansson said. One final question before I have yet another headache pill, he thought.

'How long would it take me and my colleagues to find him?'

'Longer than a week, anyway. So you can save yourself the bother.'

'I'll take that as a promise,' Mattei said, 'that you'll get in touch in a week's time and tell me who he is.'

'On the condition that you and your bloody comrades don't try to spy on me,' Johansson said, and smiled.

'I'd never dream of spying on someone who can see round corners. And if any of my colleagues were to come up with such a ridiculous idea, I promise to set them right immediately.'

'Look after yourself, Lisa,' Johansson said, nodding towards her protruding stomach. Wonder if I'll get to see her kid? he suddenly thought.

'You look after yourself, Lars,' Lisa Mattei said, suddenly serious. 'Remember, you'll soon have a christening to go to.'

Then she leaned over and gave him a hug.

Go now, he thought, as he felt his throat tighten. Go now, before I burst into tears.

V

Thine eye shall not pity: life shall go for life, eye for eye, tooth for tooth, hand for hand, foot for foot . . .

Book of Deuteronomy, 19:21

87

Wednesday, 18 August: Day 44

High time to get something done, Johansson thought when he woke up that morning. High time to make contact with Staffan Nilsson. High time to make him an offer he couldn't refuse.

Killing Nilsson, cleaning up afterwards and then getting on with his life would, naturally, have been easier, in purely practical terms. He had all the knowledge and resources he needed, and evidently no shortage of willing hands. But it was an unthinkable idea, and an impossible act, despite the wave of emotions raging through the people around him, and even inside him. It was easy enough to dismiss the idea when it came down to it, because in his world there was no end that could justify that sort of means.

Hanging him out to dry in the media and letting the ensuing lynch mob do the job for him was also out of the question. As was contacting Yasmine's father and letting him deal with the whole thing in his capacity as principal mourner, with all the support he could find in the Old Testament's rules about justice.

Nor could he just sweep the whole thing under the carpet and move on. The fact that evil emerged victorious on so many occasions was bad enough, but letting it get away with such an easy victory as this was unthinkable. Not this time, because it was he who bore the ultimate responsibility – and if he was to be able to get on with his life, he needed to be able to do so at peace with himself and his conscience.

That left talking to the bastard and getting him to realize what was best for him, Lars Martin Johansson thought.

After breakfast he called his eldest brother to ask for his help with a number of practical details. Recently, Evert's concerns about his welfare had become more and more time-consuming, and it had taken him more than five minutes before he was able to get to the point.

'I need to ask for your help,' Johansson said. 'There's a bastard I need to lay a trap for.'

'Then you've come to the right man,' Evert grunted. 'How much money are we talking about?'

'None at all,' Johansson said. 'This is worse than that.' You haven't changed, he thought.

'You don't want to tell me about it?'

'No, maybe later. Once it's all over.' Assuming everything goes the way I hope, he thought.

'I'd like to borrow your office,' Johansson went on. 'It's all about making a credible impression,' he explained. So he doesn't suspect anything and run for the hills, he thought.

'You don't even have to ask,' Evert said. 'After all, it's your office as well. Have a word with Mats, our number-cruncher.'

'Thanks, brother,' Johansson said.

*

Then Lars spoke to Mats. Mats Eriksson was half Johansson's age, had an MBA and was deputy MD of the group of companies owned by the Johanssons. Mats was responsible for the details, Evert for the big ideas which brought in the big money, and Lars sat on the board as a representative of both his own interests and those of the rest of the family.

'It's to do with an invitation to invest in a property venture in Thailand. Hotel, time-share apartments, houses, associated services. All the usual. I'll courier the project proposal to you, and I want you to arrange a meeting on behalf of Johansson Holding Ltd with the company in charge of the project.'

'What's it called, then?'

'Leander Thai Invest Ltd. The man in charge is called Staffan Nilsson, and he's the person I want to meet.'

'Staffan Nilsson,' Mats said. 'Hang on, are we talking about Staffan Leander Nilsson?'

'Yes,' Johansson said. 'And it's vital that I get to see him in person.'

'Does Evert know about this?'

'Yes,' Johansson said. 'Why do you ask?'

'Because I know who Staffan Nilsson is,' Mats said.

'So do I. You don't think I'm stupid, do you? I need a plausible reason to meet the man. Do you think you can arrange that for me?'

'In that case, I understand. Do you want me to be there?'

'Yes, definitely,' Johansson said. 'But I don't want you to say a word about me and, specifically, nothing about my background, just that one of the proprietors will sit in on the meeting.'

'Then I'll check my diary,' Mats said. 'I understand.'

'Don't bother,' Johansson said. 'I want to meet him tomorrow, or the day after at the latest. I want you to be there, but you don't have to worry about my schedule. I can do either day.'

'I'll sort it out. I'll call as soon as it's arranged.'

'One more thing,' Johansson said, as a thought struck him. 'It's important that we host the meeting. In our office. No lunch, none of that nonsense. And I want him to come on his own, too.'

'I don't think we'll have any trouble with that part,' Mats Eriksson said. 'Staffan Nilsson is the sort who has his office in his pocket, and his colleagues are easily counted. I'd never dream of offering a man like him lunch, so you don't have to worry. Coffee and mineral water will be more than good enough.'

'Thanks,' Johansson said. Cocky little sod, he thought.

Half an hour later Mats Eriksson called back.

'It's all arranged: a meeting here in the office on Friday at 1 p.m. If that's okay for you?'

'Yes,' Johansson said. 'See you the day after tomorrow.' Back on the road again, he thought, and suddenly his headache was gone.

Then he put all of Staffan Nilsson's colourful brochures in an envelope and called Max in.

'Something I can do for you, boss?' Max asked.

'I was going to ask you to take these papers and drop them off at Evert's office here in Stockholm. It's on Karlavägen—'

'I know where it is,' Max said. 'In Östermalm, where all the rich people live.'

468

88

Thursday, 19 August

When he woke up that morning the tightness in his chest was bearable, and he didn't have a headache. As he leaned over the washbasin and rinsed his face, it occurred to him that it was high time he had a shave. You look a bloody mess, Johansson thought with a grimace as he looked at himself in the bathroom mirror. But he didn't feel like doing it just then.

When he sat down in the kitchen to have breakfast, Matilda made the same observation.

'Are you planning on growing a full beard, boss?' Matilda said.

'Disguise,' Johansson said, having just been struck by an idea that may not entirely have been an excuse for his lethargy in the face of his condition and his crumbling body.

'Disguise?'

'Secret mission,' he explained. 'Seeing as I shall soon be embarking upon a secret mission, I thought I should change my appearance.' Not such a silly idea, he thought, considering all the times he'd appeared on television before he retired. And considering the fact that Staffan Nilsson seemed to be an alert individual, and no doubt particularly alert when it came to people like Johansson. And, not least, considering the fact that, back in the days when they worked in Surveillance for the Stockholm Police, he and Jarnebring used to disguise themselves as taxi-drivers, road workers and hotdog sellers.

'I can sort that out for you,' Matilda said. 'I can disguise you so that not even your best friend would recognize you. All you need is a pair of sunglasses, the right clothes and a load of oil in your hair.'

'No tattoos,' Johansson said. Best to make that point very clear, he thought.

'Not even a tiny ring in your ear?' she said with a smile. 'Don't worry, boss.'

Must be forty years ago now, Johansson thought. Back then, he had been a hotdog seller outside Johanneshov ice-hockey stadium, when he and Jarnebring were on the trail of a notorious flasher who had evidently chosen to combine his interest in hockey with his inner compulsion to wave his willy about.

Jarnebring was ruled out of being a hotdog seller. Even then, he looked so terrifying that no one would have dared approach his stand, let alone ask for extra mustard and ketchup.

But it hadn't been a problem for Johansson at all.

'Can I have some extra mustard?' asked the willy-waver, moments before Jarnebring appeared behind him and grabbed him in a headlock.

'Where do you want it?' Jarnebring asked.

Then they cuffed him, called for a patrol car to cart him off to jail and spent the rest of the evening watching Brynäs walking all over Djurgården down on the ice.

470

Memories, Johansson thought. At least I've still got some of my memories left, he thought.

'Hello there, boss!' Matilda said. 'Hello! Earth calling . . .'

'Sorry,' Johansson said. 'I was miles away.'

Then he went to see his physiotherapist. Not a place for any more thoughts or memories. Just physical effort: new, enforced routines, a daily and bitter reminder of a life lost. After that he went for a walk with Max. Neither of them said anything at all, because neither of them felt any need to do so. Calmer now, he thought, taking deep breaths as he walked.

Then he had lunch. He held back from his two glasses of red wine, so he could save them for dinner with Pia. And Max, of course, who nowadays functioned as the child of the house, even though he looked the way he did and – unlike ordinary children, and everyone else, come to that – moved without making any sound at all.

While Johansson was lying on the sofa in his study, thinking about how best to make Staffan Nilsson an offer he couldn't refuse, his phone rang. An unexpected call, with a surprising message.

'Hello, boss,' said Superintendent Hermansson from Regional Crime in Stockholm. 'I hope I'm not disturbing you, boss?'

'No,' Johansson said.

'And I hope all's well with you, boss?'

'Muddling on,' Johansson said. Get to the point, you sycophantic bastard, he thought.

'We've got a complication,' Hermansson said. 'I'm afraid I need those files about Yasmine that we lent you, boss.'

471

'What for?' Johansson asked. 'I've only just got them.' Something must have happened, he thought. Something that wasn't only dependent upon Hermansson's desire to satisfy his and his son-in-law's curiosity.

It was a complicated business, according to Hermansson. The member of the National Police Board in charge of research had been in touch. Evidently, a renowned group of researchers from Northwestern University outside Chicago in the USA had contacted him: they were planning to conduct a large comparative international study of violent sexual attacks against children and, consequently, wanted access to the police investigation into the murder of Yasmine Ermegan, among others.

'Apparently, it's part of a UN project dealing with trafficking,' Hermansson said. 'You know, when they sell women as sex slaves, sometimes even children.'

'I hear what you're saying,' Johansson said. 'But what does that have to do with Yasmine?'

'Looks like they've been given a grant to expand the project to look into paedophiles who have killed young children as well. The investigation's going to cover both Europe and the USA.'

Who'd have thought it? thought Johansson, who had learned to hate not only coincidence but also other mysteriously synchronous occurrences.

'So, if you don't mind, I thought I'd call in and pick up those boxes containing the investigation,' Hermansson said. 'I certainly don't want to put you to any bother. The simplest solution is probably if I just call in with my son-in-law.'

472

How thoughtful of you, Johansson thought. 'I'm afraid I'm busy this evening,' Johansson said. 'So it would have to be tomorrow.'

'That'll be fine, absolutely fine,' Hermansson said. For some reason, he seemed unable to conceal his relief.

'Give me a call tomorrow morning,' Johansson said.

The moment he put the phone down, he realized what was going on. You've started to lose your edge, he thought. How had his best friend described her? A young, attractive blonde? A young, attractive blonde who was only nineteen years old that summer twenty-five years ago when Yasmine Ermegan was raped and murdered.

89

Thursday evening, 19 August

It hadn't been particularly difficult to find out her home address; it was in the phone directory. And Matilda was still there, so he got her to make a nuisance call so as not to alarm her unnecessarily.

'She's at home,' Matilda said. 'Sounded like my sister usually sounds when she's trying to put the kids to bed before settling down in front of the telly.'

'Max,' Johansson said, 'you and I are going out.' He nodded towards Max, who was leaning against the windowsill with a blank expression on his face and one of the sports drinks he seemed unable to live without in his hand.

He nodded back, then went out.

'What shall I tell Pia?' Matilda said, for some reason glancing at the stove.

'Dinner will have to wait,' Johansson said. 'I'll be home in a couple of hours. You know what?' he added, looking at Matilda. 'Why don't you stay and eat with us, then you and Pia can have a bit of wine before Max and I get back?'

'Waiting for the boys,' Matilda said tartly. 'Where have I heard that before? Sure, boss.'

'Excellent,' Johansson said. 'Waiting for the boys.'

Waiting for the boys, he thought. The simple and obvious act that was supposed to have enslaved the women of the Western world since the Stone Age, but because he himself had grown up on a farm in northern Ångermanland in the forties and fifties, he had never really understood what all those bourgeois women were going on about. Elna wouldn't have done either, he thought. His beloved mother had her hands full all the time, and never spent a minute waiting for anyone. Least of all any of the men she was surrounded by.

Karolinska Hospital had opened in 1940, but the doctors' residences were only built in the early fifties: three large villas for the hospital's senior consultants and professors who preferred to live close to their work, a dozen terraced houses for the junior doctors who hadn't yet reached the pinnacle of their careers. All constructed according to a typically English design, with solid workmanship, of bricks and mortar, with generous gardens and areas of greenery, and quietly tucked away between Solna cemetery to the north and the sprawling hospital to the south.

Naturally, she lived in one of the terraced houses – in keeping with the times, and doubtless with her finances and everything else that dictated the terms of lives such as hers, Johansson thought.

'There's nothing to worry about,' he said, smiling at Max. 'I'm just going to see a little lady.'

'Watch your back, boss,' Max said, smiling back.

'Johansson,' Ulrika Stenholm said with obvious surprise when she opened the door. 'What are you doing here? I don't usually see patients at home.'

'I'm not here as a patient. We can do this inside, or we can sit and talk in my car,' he said, gesturing towards the big, black Audi where a motionless Max sat behind the tinted glass.

'Come in,' she said. 'I haven't put the boys to bed yet,' she explained. 'Has something happened?'

'Don't ask me,' Johansson said. 'You know better than I do.'

Five minutes later she had moved her two boys out into the kitchen. Five and six years old, by the looks of it, and just as blond as their mother. She had to bribe them with ice-cream and computer games before she got them to settle down.

Bookshelves from floor to ceiling, worn but high-quality carpets on the floor, prints by Peter Dahl on the walls, a sofa, an armchair with a foot rest, a coffee table, a large grand piano and a music centre that took up half the room. All of it expensive when it was bought, but many years had passed since then – she had probably inherited it from her parents. Except the Dahls, Johansson thought. Judging by their subject matter, they weren't the sort of thing that a man of the Church of the older generation would have hung on his walls. Still less given to his daughter, he thought.

'Has something happened?' Ulrika Stenholm asked as she sat down on the sofa opposite him. 'Can I get you anything, by the way?' she added. 'A cup of coffee, perhaps?' She was anxious: so anxious that she didn't have time to tilt her narrow, pale-skinned neck.

'No,' Johansson said. 'I don't want anything. But I would like you to tell me about your relationship with Yasmine's father. I suggest that you start with the weekend twenty-five years ago when his daughter was murdered, while you were out in the archipelago fucking each other's brains out.'

As soon as he said that the white flame that had been burning brightly in his head was turned down and he could suddenly breathe properly again. And at that moment Ulrika Stenholm clapped her hands to her face and burst into tears.

Typical, Johansson thought. Exactly the sort of thing people like him were incapable of steeling themselves against.

'Sorry,' Ulrika Stenholm said. 'Sorry, but I never actually thought you'd find him. The man who murdered Yasmine, I mean.'

'Tell me,' Johansson said. 'And stop snivelling,' he added, handing over the paper napkin that he, with the same degree of forethought as his little helper, had put in his pocket before he left home.

Ulrika Stenholm had graduated from the New Elementary School in Bromma in 1984. She was eighteen years old, had excellent grades, and consequently had no problem getting in to read medicine at the Karolinska Institute in Stockholm. After her first year she got a summer job at a private medical laboratory owned by Joseph Ermegan and his uncle. The same Joseph Ermegan who would soon change his name to Joseph Simon and move to the USA because his daughter had been murdered.

He had been her tutor on her course in medical chemistry. She worshipped him, as did all the other female students. After the end of the course he asked if she would be interested in a summer job. Naturally, she said yes, and slept with him on the second day at her new place of work.

'He was the love of my life,' Ulrika Stenholm said as she dried her tears. 'My only love, actually.'

'What happened next?' Johansson asked.

Then her life had been struck by lightning. It had been blasted into pieces so small that they couldn't even be gathered together, taking with them any idea of staying with the man she was with at the time, the great, all-encompassing love of her life. But she also had a boyfriend with whom she had just moved in. He was a schoolfriend, two years older than her, also planning to become a doctor. He was doing his national service that summer, the way all medical students had to in those days, just in case the worst happened and the Russians invaded. All the male medical students' female colleagues were left to fend for themselves.

'He's the father of my boys,' she said, craning her long, thin neck and nodding towards the closed door to the kitchen, where the children were. 'We got married three years later. But it was actually fifteen years before I got pregnant. Three years after that we were divorced. I just couldn't bear to carry on pretending.'

'What does he do, then?' Johansson asked, even though she had already told him.

'He's a consultant at Huddinge Hospital,' Ulrika Stenholm said. 'A professor of internal medicine. He's remarried. Has two little kids with his new wife. We share custody,' she added.

'And then what?' Johansson asked.

It was as if the love of her life had been beaten to the ground. He refused even to talk to her. He slammed

478

the phone down when she did finally pluck up the courage to call him. She tormented herself every day with the thought that it might not have happened if she and Yasmine's father hadn't escaped from the city that weekend, the weekend when all the things that would change her life took place.

'If . . . if we hadn't gone, she'd be alive today,' Ulrika Stenholm said, and started to cry again.

'What sort of nonsense is that?' Johansson said, because he wasn't very well disposed to that type of self-reproach or hypothetical argument. Besides, he was still very angry with the woman he was talking to.

'Pull yourself together now. If you hadn't gone with him, he'd just have found someone else who would,' he said.

For ten years – at least ten years – she had blamed herself every day for what had happened to Yasmine. And she didn't have anyone she could talk to about it either. Not her boyfriend. Not her dad, who would have been shocked, for the same reasons that would have left her fiancé in pieces. Not her mum, seeing as she would only have told her father at once. Not even her older sister, who had just left home and broken off relations with her parents after telling them that she was now living with another woman. As man and wife should live, according to Daddy Vicar, but certainly not the way a woman should live with another woman, least of all his elder daughter, who had thus rendered any further contact impossible.

'After ten years I stopped thinking about it every day,' Ulrika Stenholm said, blowing her nose on the paper napkin Johansson had given her. 'In the end I only thought about it occasionally. And then I had children. And I thought that was what life was supposed to be like. My husband was happy, and I hadn't so much as spoken to Joseph on the phone since the summer when it all happened.'

'What about your dad, then?'

'When Dad told me about that confession, barely a year ago now, it was as if my life had been turned upside down again. Just when I had finally found some peace. I didn't understand it. I thought for a moment that he was trying to punish me, that he had known what I'd done all along but hadn't said anything all those years. And that now, on his deathbed, he wanted to punish me by telling me that he had been told who murdered Yasmine. But that he couldn't say who because it had been told to him in the confidentiality of confession.'

'Is that how it was, then?' Johansson said. 'Did he know? Did he want to punish you?'

'No,' Ulrika Stenholm said, shaking her head. 'He didn't. Not a chance. My dad wouldn't do something like that. If he'd found out what had gone on between me and Yasmine's father, he'd have talked to me – that would have been the first thing he did. It was just another one of those horrible coincidences in my life. Dad had no idea what I had been through. He was labouring under his own torment, for the same reason I was. But neither of us knew that the other was struggling.'

I believe you. Coincidence, striking both of them. The exceptional instance when a coincidence was just that. 'So when you met me, then,' Johansson said, 'what were you thinking?'

'At first it was just a whim,' Ulrika Stenholm said. 'I mean, I'd heard all the stories my sister had told

480

me about you. Not that I believed them – Anna has always been a hopeless romantic, and I'd tried to rid myself of that part of my character. But, all of a sudden, there you were. I don't know, it was like Dad was talking to me from beyond the grave. Telling me that the Lord moved in mysterious ways. It's happening again, I thought. First me, then Dad. And then you showed up.'

'I hear what you're saying,' Johansson said.

'I've never lied to you,' Ulrika Stenholm said, shaking her head. 'I had no idea it was about Margaretha Sagerlied. I didn't even know she lived in the same road as Joseph, even though I was there the night Yasmine went missing, before we left the city. I took a taxi round to his. It picked me up from work; he'd booked it for me. Then we got in his car and drove off to the country. That hairgrip – I realize now that it was Yasmine's. But I had no idea it was the one she was wearing the night she was murdered. And if it hadn't been for you, I would never have found it.'

'Really?' Johansson said. I believe you, he thought.

'I swear,' Ulrika Stenholm said. 'It's completely true.'

'When did you call your old boyfriend, then?' Johansson said. 'When did you phone Joseph Simon?'

'The day you told me you knew who it was, who murdered Yasmine. It was the first time I'd spoken to him in twenty-five years.'

'That was a stupid thing to do,' Johansson said. 'It was a very stupid thing to do. You should have talked to me instead.'

'Sorry,' Ulrika Stenholm said. 'Sorry, I didn't realize.'

'Call him again. Tell him to get over here as soon as possible so that I can talk to him. I'm in no fit state to travel,' he said. Anyway, a man like Joseph Simon has probably got a private jet, he thought.

'Are you sure? You promise to talk to him?'

'On Monday,' Johansson said. 'If he can get here on Monday, I promise to talk to him.'

As soon as he was back in the car he called Mattei. From his mobile to her mobile, and, because Mattei was Mattei, she answered on the first ring.

'I need to see you. Preferably right away,' Johansson said. 'We've got a problem.'

'Then I suggest you come to my office,' Mattei said. 'I'm still here.'

90

Thursday evening, 19 August

Soon the only thing missing will be the double-headed eagle above the entrance, Lars Martin Johansson thought as he walked into the headquarters of the National Crime Unit on Kungsholmen in Stockholm. The large, marble-clad lobby, the armed security guards in their bulletproof lodge, the airlocks enclosed in matt-polished steel. The guard who spoke to him over the loudspeaker must have been there since his day.

'I've called them,' he said. 'They're coming down to fetch you, boss. By the way, I hope everything's okay, boss.'

'Couldn't be better,' Johansson said, gesturing behind him with his thumb, towards the big, black Audi out on the street. 'That's my car and my chauffeur. Nothing for you to worry about,' he added.

The guard responded by putting his hand over the microphone, opening the little glass hatch above the counter and talking directly to Johansson. 'I get it, boss,' he said. 'Everyone here knows that you're still working in Covert Ops.'

*

Five minutes later Johansson was sitting on the visitor's chair in front of Lisa Mattei's desk. These days, it was almost as large as the one he had left behind three years ago.

'Shouldn't you and your little girl be asleep by now?' Johansson said, nodding towards her bulging stomach.

'We work the same hours, she and I,' Mattei said with a smile. 'Right now she's playing football in her mum's tummy. We'll go to sleep in an hour or so.'

'Like I said on the phone, I'm afraid we've got a problem,' Johansson said. 'And I'm sorry to have to admit that I was the cause of it.'

Then he told her the whole story. From the moment Ulrika Stenholm had told him her story. He left nothing out, apart from the name of the man who murdered Yasmine. He even gave Mattei the name of his informant, even though he hadn't even told his best friend. All the way through, from his first conversation with Ulrika Stenholm to the call he received from Superintendent Hermansson just a few hours ago.

'So now they want my files,' Johansson said.

'Nonsense,' Lisa Mattei said. 'They can forget that.'

'What do we do now?'

'I'll sort it,' Mattei said. 'You don't have to worry at all, Lars. I'll call you as soon as it's done.'

'The security guard in there thought you worked for the Security Police,' Johansson said when he was back in the car.

'That's not so strange,' Max said with a shrug. 'My dad looked just like this, and Grandpa always claimed he used to work for the KGB.'

'What did he do there, then?' Johansson said.

'Professional hit man,' Max said. 'Grandpa always used to say he was a professional hit man.'

'What did you think?' Johansson said. What the hell am I supposed to say to that? he thought.

'I used to think it sounded exciting,' Max said. 'But, obviously, I wasn't very old at the time.'

Pia and Matilda were sitting in the kitchen when he and Max walked in. They were drinking white wine, just as he had told them, the way girls usually did, quite irrespective of any difference in age and income, Johansson thought.

'I thought you said two hours. That's what Tilda told me, anyway,' his wife declared with a pointed glance at the clock above the stove.

'Barely three,' Johansson said sheepishly, checking his watch just to make sure.

'Welcome home,' Pia said. 'You can have a salad of grilled chicken thighs, avocado, beans, tomato and red onion. And, if Tilda is to be believed, you were a good boy and saved your red wine from lunchtime.'

'I love you,' Johansson said. What do you mean, 'good boy'? he thought. Only Elna has ever called me that.

'Just as long as you don't go and end your own life,' Pia said.

'No,' Johansson said, shaking his head. What life? I haven't got a life, not any more. I need to talk to her, he thought.

After dinner he took his coffee into his study to drink it in peace and quiet while Pia, Max and Matilda sat in the kitchen chatting and drinking more wine. Just when he had leaned back on the sofa his phone rang.

'Are you awake, Lars?' Lisa Mattei asked.

'Very much so,' Johansson said.

'I've spoken to our DG. He talked to the NPC, who in turn talked to the DPC. We all agree. The investigation stays with you, and, if you don't have any objections, I thought I might pick the files up tomorrow morning.'

She's all grown up now, Johansson thought. Little Lisa has called the Director General and the head of the Security Police, who called the National Police Chief, who called the District Police Commissioner in Stockholm, and they all did exactly what she told them to do.

'No problem at all,' Johansson said. 'Send someone first thing tomorrow. What do you think about calling her Elna, by the way? After my mother. Your little football player, I mean.' Your very own football player, kicking up a storm in your womb, he thought.

'Actually, Elina is one of my favourite names,' Mattei said.

'What does your bloke say, then?' Johansson said.

'Ingrid. After Ingrid Bergman.'

'Marry me instead, then,' Johansson said. Why did I say that? he thought.

A quarter of an hour later, he was fast asleep. In spite of the cheerful voices from the kitchen. In spite of Hypnos tempting him with a greenish-white seedhead when he was teetering on the boundary between dozing and sleeping. Sorry lad, you're too late, Johansson thought. Then he closed his eyes and fell asleep of his own accord. Without dreams, without any external help from anything or anyone. He simply slept, and woke up the following morning to find Max standing next to his bed and gently shaking his left shoulder.

'There's a couple of spooks who'd like to see you, boss,' he said. 'A bloke and a girl.'

'Who are they, then?' Johansson asked.

'Not that they're anything like my old man, but I still get the impression they work in the same sort of place,' Max said. 'But the Swedish version,' he added.

91

Friday, 20 August

It was two taciturn colleagues from the Security Police: a man in his fifties and a woman some ten years younger. He didn't recognize either from his time as operational head, but the fact that they were aware of who he was – or had been, to be more precise – was obvious.

'We're here to pick up some boxes,' the man said.

'Sure,' Johansson said. 'Hang on and I'll ask Max to carry them down for you.'

Then he took Max with him into the study.

'There's nothing you've forgotten, boss?' Max said for some reason, nodding towards the three cardboard boxes on the floor.

'No,' Johansson said. He had removed all his own contributions and ideas the previous evening, and concluded by extracting the record from the vehicle register relating to Staffan Nilsson's ownership of a red Golf. He had put the whole lot in a folder and locked it away in his safe.

'Okay,' Max said. 'In that case.'

Half an hour after that his phone rang. It was Hermansson.

'What's going on?' he asked.

'Don't ask me,' Johansson said, sounding more irritable than he meant to.

'I've just had a call from the chief of police's office, saying that the Yasmine case is going to be staying with you.'

'Yes,' Johansson said. 'What's funny about that?'

'Well, it seems pretty bloody mysterious to me,' Hermansson said warily.

'It's not the least bit mysterious. I haven't finished with the case. That's all there is to it.'

'So I'd be way off the mark if I were to think that you'd already found him?'

'Found who?'

'Yasmine's killer. I thought we trusted each other, boss.'

'Yes, of course. But there are some things it's probably better not to know about.'

'With all due respect, you'll have to forgive me, boss, but not this time.'

'That's because you don't know what you're talking about, Hermansson. With all due respect,' Johansson said, and ended the call.

First, the usual visit to the physiotherapist, then, as soon as he returned home, he shut himself in his study. He called Mats Eriksson and gave him some brief instructions. Not a word about Johansson's past if Nilsson happened to ask. Johansson was a businessman, a part-owner of the company, brother of the main shareholder, and was on the board. Rich and eccentric and all the other things that made men like Staffan Nilsson salivate with greed. That was all: no more, no less. Mats would also have to do most of the heavy lifting when it came to the conversation, asking all the questions that should be asked in a situation like this. All the classic accountancy questions.

'I shall mostly sit there in silence,' Johansson said. 'So that I don't say anything stupid,' he added. Or get to my feet and beat him to death, he thought.

'I can't help being a bit curious,' Mats Eriksson said. 'He must have done something really terrible.'

'Yes,' Johansson said.

'What?'

'It's so fucking terrible that you really don't want to know,' Johansson said.

Then he had lunch. He took all his usual pills, plus one of the little white ones, and even considered taking a second, to guarantee maintaining enough distance from the man who had murdered Yasmine and who would soon be in the same room as him. He refrained, because there was a risk that he would seem completely detached, and possibly even fall asleep.

'Are you ready, boss?' Matilda asked. 'Ready for the grand transformation?'

'Ready as I'll ever be,' Johansson said. She seems unusually perky, he thought.

Matilda found everything she needed in Johansson's wardrobe. A pair of red trousers Pia had bought him that time she was determined to drag him off for a golfing weekend in Falsterbo, even though he had never held a golf club, and had no intention of ever doing so. A blue blazer with some sort of mysterious crest on the breast pocket that had been there when he got it. Another gift from his wife. A loose, white linen shirt; a silk scarf round his neck; brown golfing shoes with little leather tassels, acquired at the same time as the red trousers.

How the hell can any normal man walk around in this sort of get-up? Johansson thought when he looked at himself in the mirror a quarter of an hour later. Good job Evert can't see me. Or Bo.

'Clothes maketh the man,' Matilda declared, happy with what she saw.

Then she concluded her work by oiling his hair. His normally unruly grey hair now sat like a shiny, back-combed helmet on top of his head. It was considerably darker, too. And he had a completely different facial expression, all of a sudden.

'Very Stureplan. Classic twat hairstyle.'

'Are we done?' Johansson asked.

'Almost.'

Two details remained. First, she rubbed his cheeks with strongly scented aftershave. And, finally, she put a pair of rimless mirrored sunglasses on him.

'Remarkable,' Johansson said when he looked at himself in the mirror. That's not me, he thought.

'Aging director with a penchant for little girls,' Matilda said. 'If you like, boss, I could put a tight top on and come with you?'

'That's a kind offer, Matilda, but if you could just order me a taxi,' Johansson said. He looked like Pinochet, he thought as he got in the taxi. Pinochet towards the end, after they'd taken his uniforms away from him.

He was, intentionally, ten minutes late for the meeting. When he limped in on his crutch Mats Eriksson and Staffan Nilsson were already sitting in the meeting room.

491

'Sorry I'm late,' Johansson grunted. 'The traffic in this city, it really is beyond belief. Sit down, sit down,' he said, waving his good arm as Staffan Nilsson made to stand up and introduce himself.

'You look better with every day that passes, Lars,' Mats Eriksson said with an innocent expression.

'Thanks,' Johansson said. He sat down at the end of the long table and took out his diary and a pen. Nodded from behind his dark, mirrored glasses.

'It's good that you could find the time to see us, Staffan,' Johansson said. No headache now, no tightness in his chest. Just enough distance from his prey. Even his right index finger felt normal.

A smart, respectable prey, he thought. Evil in its most disarming guise. Blue jacket, white shirt, grey trousers, the same type of shoes as him. Friendly blue eyes, white teeth. No sign of swelling or bruising from the slap on the nose administered by Johansson's little helper the week before.

'Thank you,' Staffan Nilsson said. 'It's a pleasure to be able to come and meet you, gentlemen. I'm looking forward to presenting our new project.' He raised the screen of his laptop.

'Splendid,' Mats Eriksson said. He leaned back in his chair and steepled his fingers. 'Why don't you begin, Staffan?'

Staffan Nilsson showed pictures of his Thai paradise. It could be completed within three years but as yet existed only in the form of financial calculations and animated 3D designs of the architects' plans for the proposed resort. Backed up, of course, with the usual photographs of the surrounding landscape: the long white beach, the blue sea, the islands off the coast, the high mountains behind.

'Without wishing to exaggerate, I think it's justifiable to describe the southern coast of Thailand as one of the most beautiful places on the planet,' Staffan Nilsson said, smiling and nodding amiably towards Johansson.

It took half an hour. Mats Eriksson asked all the expected accountancy questions about funding, liquidity, projected profit. And, of course, all the risks that might arise during the process, and how these might be dealt with. Johansson made do with grunting occasionally; he mostly sat and looked at Staffan Nilsson and his body language, his facial expressions, trying to see the thoughts in his head, remaining himself ensconced behind his dark, mirrored glasses and generally eccentric disguise. He believes what he's saying, Johansson thought. He is the very embodiment of the man he's making himself out to be. He doesn't even have to pretend any more. He just switches himself on and off because he's spent his whole life learning to dissemble.

As a result, Staffan Nilsson gave an irreproachable presentation. He had done his homework; he was quietly spoken, likeable. You could have made any amount of money, Johansson thought. If only you'd been normal. If it hadn't been for your proclivities. And the fact that everything in your life is geared towards allowing you to have sex with little girls.

'What do you say, Mats?' Johansson said. 'Time for us to do some serious thinking, wouldn't you say? Let's sit down and crunch some numbers. I think we should book another meeting.'

'It's undoubtedly a very interesting project,' Mats Eriksson agreed. 'But, as you say, we need a bit of time to look into the figures.'

'Thursday afternoon. Or Friday morning,' Johansson said, making a show of leafing through his diary. 'I'm away after that,' he said. 'Elk hunting with my brother.'

'I'm busy all day Thursday,' Staffan Nilsson said. 'But Friday morning would be good.'

'Let's say that, then,' Johansson said. 'Friday, nine o'clock.' After that meeting, you're going to be busy for the rest of your life, he thought.

As soon as he got home to Södermalm Johansson called Mats Eriksson.

'Well, then,' he said. 'What sort of impression did you get of Staffan Nilsson?'

'I was positively surprised,' Mats Eriksson said. 'After everything I've heard about him, I'd go so far as to say that I was very positively surprised. And his proposed project doesn't seem to be entirely without merit either.'

'So now you're thinking of starting to build hotels in Thailand?'

'Strangely enough, no, I'm not,' Mats said.

'Why not?' Johansson teased. 'If it was that good?'

'Because Evert would kill me,' Mats Eriksson said. 'You still don't feel like telling me why you're so interested in Staffan Nilsson?'

'No,' Johansson said.

'Why not?'

'Because you'd probably kill him.'

As soon as he had hung up, Mattei called him.

'Everything okay, Lars?'

'Muddling on,' Johansson said. 'What can I do for you?'

'Staffan Nilsson,' Mattei said. 'Our now prescribed perpetrator. Nephew of Margaretha Sagerlied's husband. To save you the trouble of phoning me in a few days' time.'

'Congratulations,' Johansson said. 'That was quick work.'

'Not too much of a challenge after what you told me,' Mattei said. 'I presume you know that there's an old case against him for child pornography, a case that was dropped?'

'I know. What makes me think that you and your colleagues are bugging Ulrika Stenholm's phone? Since I mentioned her name to you?'

'You'll have to excuse me. I didn't hear that.'

'I don't want to embarrass you, Lisa. I know as well as you do that we don't comment on that sort of assertion but, on Monday morning, as I'm sure you're aware, I'm going to be meeting Joseph Simon at the Grand Hotel in Stockholm. Naturally, I intend to send him away empty-handed.'

'I wouldn't expect anything else,' Lisa said.

'So you can hold back on putting Nilsson under surveillance. He'll be okay for a bit longer. And there's no need for you to listen to me and Simon, either. Save your money; don't waste resources unnecessarily. I promise to behave.'

'As I've said already, I wouldn't dream of bugging you, boss,' Mattei said.

'Good to hear,' Johansson said. At last, he thought. There it was. 'Boss'.

*

495

'What are your plans for the weekend, boss?' Max asked. 'I hear that Pia's going off to some conference.'

'Peace and quiet,' Johansson said. I need to think, he thought.

'Let me know if there's anything I can help you with, boss.'

'You can call Jarnebring and ask if he'd like to have lunch with us tomorrow,' Johansson said. 'Here in the house,' he added. 'So we can talk openly.'

92

Saturday, 21 August to Sunday, 22 August

On Saturday, Johansson had lunch at home with Jarnebring and Max. He had the food delivered from a local restaurant and, as Pia was safely out of the way, he allowed himself and his guests one or two little treats. While they were eating, Johansson told them about the latest developments and his encounter with Staffan Nilsson. But he didn't mention his forthcoming meeting with Joseph Simon. That could wait.

'So, what was he like?' Jarnebring asked.

'If I hadn't known about Yasmine, I daresay I'd have thought him a nice, pleasant chap. He doesn't exactly exude guilt. So he seems to have learned to deal with that.'

'Good thing you didn't take me with you,' Jarnebring said. 'I'd have killed the bastard.'

'Quite,' Johansson said. 'I daresay that's why I didn't take you with me.'

'At least Max has had a chance to take a swing at him,' Jarnebring said, slapping his fellow diner on the shoulder. 'Whoever said that life was fair, eh?'

'That's why Max had to stay at home, too.'

'So what are you thinking of doing, then?' Jarnebring asked.

'As far as I can make out, there are four options,' Johansson said thoughtfully, taking a bite of the splendid Italian salami that his favourite restaurateur had selected as a starter, along with an assortment of sardines, olives and miniature preserved artichoke hearts.

'Which are?' Jarnebring said.

'The first option is just to forget about the whole thing. It's a prescribed crime,' Johansson said, and shrugged his shoulders. 'There are no formal impediments to us simply keeping our mouths shut and getting on with our lives.'

'For God's sake, Lars,' Jarnebring protested. 'You're not serious, are you?'

'No,' Johansson said. 'In my book, there are some things you can't just ignore. This is one of them. Anyway, I don't think that would work, even if the three of us at this table are doubtless capable of keeping our mouths shut.'

'I quite agree,' Jarnebring said. 'Sooner or later, one or other of our former colleagues would work everything out. As you can imagine, there's already a certain amount of talk in the corridors. The man who can see round corners has identified Yasmine's killer. And is refusing to say who it is. All that sort of crap.'

'Option two is to go directly to the media and hang him out to dry. That would be pretty easy, and would at least save time, compared to letting Hermansson or another like-minded colleague figure out who did it.' Because that would no doubt take a while, Johansson thought.

'That wouldn't be particularly pleasant for him,' Jarnebring said.

'No,' Johansson said. 'A number of our criminal gangs already post pictures of ordinary paedophiles on their websites, and when it comes to Nilsson there are doubtless a fair few people who could imagine compensating for the shortcomings of the judicial system.'

Johansson sighed and sipped his wine thoughtfully. Then he popped a large olive and a couple of anchovies in his mouth to help him think better.

'With that in mind, maybe the simplest solution would be to kill the bastard straight off?' Jarnebring said.

'That's the third alternative,' Johansson said, 'and I sincerely hope that you're not thinking of anyone sitting at this table.'

Jarnebring said nothing, just shrugged his shoulders and exchanged a glance with Max, whose mind seemed to be elsewhere.

'You said four options,' Jarnebring said. 'So what's the fourth?'

'Talk to him,' Johansson said. 'Talk to Nilsson. Explain the situation. Offer him the chance to take his punishment. The punishment for what he did to Yasmine would have been life imprisonment. I'm pretty certain of that – actually, completely certain since I met him and had the chance to study him at close quarters. Secure psychiatric treatment wouldn't have been an option in his case.'

'I hear what you're saying,' Jarnebring said with a shrug. 'The problem these days is that he wouldn't even get a rap on the knuckles for what he did to her.'

'I'm getting to that,' Johansson said. 'How we arrange a life sentence for him.'

'I certainly hope we can,' Jarnebring said.

'A life sentence,' Johansson repeated. 'They'd probably let him out after twenty years or so, so I could probably live with that.'

'A life sentence for what, though?' Jarnebring asked. 'The problem is that we can't find any other crap he's done. Sitting there downloading child porn from the internet. What would he get for that? Six months and a slap on the wrist, at most.'

'I'm pretty sure he's been with a number of young girls the same age as Yasmine over the years. If he could just be made to confess that, we're looking at a number of years. Or he could make something up. Take that idiot Thomas Quick, the worst serial killer in the history of Scandinavian crime. He's in his twentieth year in jail now, isn't he? Thanks to his vivid imagination and a number of our colleagues who are even stupider than he is. Wasn't Bäckström involved in that whole business?'

'Bound to have been,' Jarnebring said. 'I hear what you're saying. I was thinking about Nilsson's mother's suicide. That hasn't passed the statute of limitations yet. Whether it was a murder, I mean. Which I don't think it was. She killed herself, for the simple reason that she'd worked out what her little boy had done to Yasmine. So much for his willingness to accept some sort of punishment . . .'

'Regrettably, that does seem to be the case,' Johansson said with a nod. 'He appears to be able to live with a number of things on his conscience.'

'What makes you think he'd change his attitude?'

'I have an idea that I might be able to get him to realize what's in his best interests. Give him the chance to crawl off into the sort of place where they put men like him. Give him a chance to survive, at the cost of the punishment he should have received.' Johansson nodded to underline what he'd just said.

'And if he doesn't get it?' Jarnebring asked.

'That still leaves the first three options. But at least he'll have been offered a choice, which is rather more than Yasmine had.'

'If you want me to do anything, just say the word, boss,' Max said. 'In my book, there are plenty of people like him who've forfeited their right to life.'

'I hear what you're saying, Max,' Johansson said. 'Believe it or not, but it's actually for your sake that I'm asking you not to do it.'

Johansson spent Sunday afternoon doing what people in his home district called 'death tidying', making sure that the not-yet-deceased had his or her paperwork in order when they finally shuffled off this mortal coil. That they, to take just one good example, got rid of anything that might spoil the image of a close and devoted relative.

When he failed to think of anything that he ought to look for, he sat down and wrote a private letter to his wife, Pia, instead, to be kept with his will. When it came down to it, it was all about the idea that keeping things in order was a way of prolonging life. Like all the life-insurance policies that people like him kept taking out, even though they never actually paid out anything while there was any real point in having it.

It was a way of not letting go. In spite of his constant headache and the tightness in his chest that made it hard to breathe. In spite of all the little white pills he kept taking, when flight and detachment were the only options remaining to him.

Wonder if I'll get to heaven? Johansson suddenly thought as he lay on the sofa, where he now spent the majority of his time. I probably should, he thought. He'd never done anything too awful, not even when he worked in the Security Police. Not that he could remember, anyway. In a purely professional sense, he had devoted most of his life to trying to protect and help people who had suffered the most unimaginable horrors.

'Max!' Johansson called.

'Yes, boss,' Max said when he appeared, almost instantly, in the doorway to his study.

Quite astonishing, Johansson thought. You just had to say his name and there he was. I don't even have to sit here rubbing an old lamp. 'Do you believe in God, Max?' he said.

'I don't think there's a God,' Max said, shaking his head.

'Why not?'

'If there was a God, he'd never have left me in that home in Grazdanka. I was only a child. I hadn't done any harm to anyone.'

502

93

Monday, 23 August

At nine o'clock on Monday morning Johannson met Joseph Simon in his suite in the Grand Hotel in Stockholm. Simon himself had called him an hour earlier, when he was on his way to his hotel from Bromma Airport.

'My name is Joseph Simon,' Joseph Simon said. 'I was Yasmine's father. I'm in Stockholm now. I'd like to meet you as soon as you can manage. I'm staying at the Grand Hotel, but if you'd rather meet somewhere else that would obviously be fine.'

'See you at the Grand in an hour,' Johansson said. 'Nine o'clock.'

'Perfect,' Simon said. 'Do you want me to send a car to pick you up?'

'No,' Johansson said. 'I've got my own chauffeur.'

Perfect Swedish, he thought. Only a trace of an accent, in spite of the many years that had passed. That saved Johansson practical worry, seeing as his English left a great deal to be desired these days.

'Max,' Johansson said.

'Boss,' Max said, a moment later.

'We're going out. You're coming with me to meet Yasmine's father.' Just in case, he thought. Taking Jarnebring was out of the question, for historical reasons.

He was physically similar to Jarnebring, Johansson thought when he and Joseph Simon shook hands, but otherwise completely different to his best friend. He looks like the Shah of Iran, he thought, even though he had only ever seen pictures of him.

He was surrounded by the usual entourage that people like him presumably took with them, even on private trips. Four men and a woman. His lawyer, his secretary, three personal assistants, of whom two were bodyguards, to judge by their appearance and the look they exchanged when they caught sight of Max.

'I'm glad you could see me,' Joseph Simon said with a polite gesture to the armchair next to his.

'Well,' Johansson said, 'I felt we should meet. But I'd rather speak to you in private.'

'Of course,' Simon said, and all he had to do to get the others to leave the room was nod towards his secretary. Even Max picked up the message and went out with them.

'Well, then,' Simon went on. 'An acquaintance of mine believes that you have identified the man who murdered my daughter, Yasmine.'

'Yes,' Johansson said. 'That's why I asked her to arrange this meeting.'

'Please don't be offended, but over the years a number of people have contacted me, claiming to know who he is. The man who murdered my daughter. People wanting money from me – the usual lunatics. Sadly, it

504

has never been true, but they have caused me personal suffering as well as practical problems.'

'I know,' Johansson said. 'I know the sort of people you're talking about, but on that point you can rest assured. I have really found him.'

'Of course, I know who you are,' Joseph Simon said with a slight smile. 'But how can you be sure? After all, twenty-five years have passed since it happened.'

'I got hold of a sample of his DNA and compared it to the perpetrator's,' Johansson said. 'The chance of it being someone else is less than one in a billion. That was mostly to confirm to myself that it really was him. To rule out any possibility of a mistake.'

'You'd already worked out that it was him? Without DNA?'

'Yes,' Johansson said. 'If I'd been part of the investigation when it happened, I'm fairly certain that I'd have got him convicted even without any DNA. Of course, we didn't have access to that technology when your daughter was murdered.'

'It's the same with people like me,' Simon said. 'Within my profession, I mean. There are good doctors and there are bad ones. There are some who are so bad that they should never have been allowed to become doctors.'

'Yes,' Johansson said. 'You and your wife were unlucky. The investigation was poorly handled, and my colleagues were unable to give you and your wife the justice you had the right to demand from us. That's one of the reasons why I'm sitting here.'

'Give me his name,' Joseph Simon said.

'Sorry,' Johansson said, shaking his head. 'Because I know who you are, I don't see any possibility of doing that.'

'Why not?'

'Naturally, I can't begin to imagine the suffering you've been through. That would be presumptuous of me. Let me put it like this. If I were you, and the same thing happened to me – if our roles were reversed – then I wouldn't dare trust myself.'

'You're worried that I'd kill him,' Simon said.

'Yes.'

'So there's nothing I could give you in exchange?'

'Nothing,' Johansson said. 'But I was thinking of making a suggestion.'

'What?'

'Suppose we had found him twenty-five years ago . . .'

'Yes?'

'Then he would have been sentenced to life and would have served seventeen or eighteen years before being released. I've already met him, by the way, in case you were wondering. Without him having any idea of who I am and what I know about him. I shall be meeting him again soon. I'm going to offer him exactly that. That he take his punishment.'

'How can you do that?' Simon asked. 'My daughter's murder has already been prescribed. You mean he's done something else apart from that?'

'I can't go into the details,' Johansson said. 'I'm thinking of making him an offer he can't refuse.'

'And if he doesn't take it? What will you do then?'

'Considering the alternatives, I hope he accepts my offer.'

'And if he doesn't?' Joseph Simon repeated.

'Then I'll give you his name,' Johansson said. 'If he refuses to accept responsibility, I'll let you have him.'

'When?'

'At noon on Wednesday of next week, at the latest. You needn't worry about the practical details, because I've already taken care of them. Just give me your phone number, and I promise to call you as soon as I know.'

'I believe you,' Joseph Simon said. 'I'll give you my number. I accept your offer. If he accepts the same punishment he would have received for murdering my daughter. In nine days' time,' he said.

'I can appreciate that it must seem like a long time,' Johansson said. 'Unfortunately, it will have to take as long as it takes.'

'Twenty-five years is a long time,' Joseph Simon said. 'Nine days is no time at all. I have no problem waiting another nine days.'

'Well, then,' Johansson said, getting to his feet.

'If there's anything I can do for you, you only have to say. I'd be prepared to do whatever is in my power to help you,' Joseph Simon said. As he said this, for some reason he glanced at the crutch under Johansson's right arm.

'People like me are the ones in your debt,' Johansson said. 'So don't give it another thought.'

Good job I'm not made the same way as my eldest brother, because then Joseph Simon would be penniless by now, Johansson thought as he sat in the car on the way home.

94

Tuesday, 24 August to Thursday, 26 August

Tuesday, Wednesday, Thursday: the usual routine, tightness in his chest and headaches, dangling right arm, the numb forefinger of his right hand, which, in spite of all the physiotherapist's promises, would remain that way until his last breath. And the preparations, all the practical details he had to sort out before it was time to confront Staffan Nilsson with what he had done to little Yasmine.

'On Friday it'll be time for me to visit the make-up salon again,' Johansson told Matilda.

'Are we still talking about the same character? No need to back it up with a blonde in a very short, black leather skirt and a skimpy red top?'

'That's very kind of you, Matilda,' Johansson said. 'I appreciate the offer, but I think I'll be absolutely fine with a bit of oil in my hair and those dark sunglasses. I'd be very happy if I could wear one of my usual suits.'

'I don't think that would be a problem,' Matilda said. 'Not now that he's already seen you. I doubt he'd even notice, actually. It's like you've already established the character.'

'Excellent,' Johansson said.

'What about the bit about scratching his eyes out, then?'

'I think I could manage that bit all on my own,' Johansson said. 'But there is one little detail I was going to ask you to help me with. If you could get this photograph enlarged?' he said, handing her the one of Yasmine that he'd taken from the police investigation.

'She's very pretty. Beautiful,' Matilda said. 'She's on the internet as well – I think it's the same photograph. Will A4 be all right?'

'That would be excellent,' Johansson said.

On Thursday morning his brother-in-law phoned and asked if there was anything else he could do for him.

'We haven't spoken for a few days, so I interpret your silence to mean that you've got all the information about Margaretha Sagerlied and her relatives that you wanted.'

'I'm more than happy,' Johansson said. 'And I'm looking forward to settling your bill.' That's what he wanted to hear, he thought.

'I listened to her last night – Margaretha Sagerlied. I found an old LP of her singing Tosca with Sigurd Björling, among others – he sings Scarpia, a quite phenomenal baritone – but Sagerlied really isn't bad either. Decent pipes on the woman. And the role seems to have suited her,' said Alf, who was an opera buff.

'Do you have many albums she sings on?' Johansson said, having just been struck by an idea. A detail, but well worth trying, he thought.

'I may have one or two,' his brother-in-law said, with his habitual modesty.

'I don't suppose I could borrow a few of them? The ones with Sagerlied on, I mean. It would be interesting to hear them.'

'By all means.' Alf was barely able to hide his surprise. 'You're very welcome to. Any particular requests?'

'I want anything with her on the album cover,' Johansson said. Who gives a shit what it is? All that stuff sounds the same, he thought.

'In that case, I'd suggest Tosca,' Alf said. 'There's a very striking picture of Margaretha Sagerlied on the cover. And that one might be rather fitting, given your previous occupation.'

'How do you mean?' Johansson asked.

'Scarpia's a policeman,' Alf said. 'Not a terribly pleasant policeman, let me tell you, but Sigurd Björling gives a magnificent interpretation of the role.'

'Excellent,' Johansson said. 'Send it over by courier and put it on my bill. Thank you very much, Alf.' 'Not a terribly pleasant policeman', Johansson thought.

That afternoon he called Mats Eriksson and told him that he wouldn't need to sit in on the next meeting with Staffan Nilsson. That there was no need for him to contact Nilsson and inform him of his absence, but that he should stay out of the way when Nilsson turned up at the office. He also planned to see Nilsson in his brother's room. Mats Eriksson had no objections.

'No problem at all,' Mats said. 'Is there anything else I can do for you?'

'That old record-player of Evert's, is it still in his room?'

'Of course,' Mats said. 'So he can play all his golden oldies for me and the rest of our colleagues at staff parties. You know, "Corinna, Corinna", "Tell Laura I Love Her", "Red Sails in the Sunset".'

*

Well, then, Lars Martin Johansson thought when he and Max arrived at Evert's office at eight o'clock on Friday morning, so they would have plenty of time for the final preparations, before an entirely unsuspecting Staffan Nilsson walked into the office to make a real killing from a rich but gullible hillbilly from Norrland.

95

Friday, 27 August

He sorted out the final preparations himself. The record sleeve with the picture of Margaretha Sagerlied was fully visible on his brother's large desk. The chair where Nilsson would be sitting while Johansson spoke to him and hopefully got him to realize what was best for him ended up at just the right angle after three attempts. His faithful assistant, Max, was already sitting behind the closed door to the next room – just in case Staffan Nilsson decided to be awkward and needed another slap across the nose.

Five minutes to go, Johansson thought, checking the time. Then he began to play the old record featuring Staffan Nilsson's aunt in the title role of the opera. Hopefully, he would manage better than his colleague Scarpia, Johansson thought, having read the summary of the plot on the back of the sleeve the previous evening.

What a lot of shouting, Johansson was thinking five minutes later when a discreet knock on the door warned him that his visitor had arrived.

'Mr Nilsson is here to see you now,' said Gerd, Evert's secretary.

'Sit down, sit down,' Johansson said, waving his crutch first at Nilsson, then at the visitor's chair. 'And would you mind switching the gramophone off, Gerd?' he said, nodding towards her. 'And shutting us in,' he added.

'Wonderful set of pipes she's got, that woman,' Johansson said, nodding towards the record cover.

And you're already sniffing at the bait, he thought.

'It's nice that you think so, Lars,' Nilsson said. 'Especially nice for me, because she was in fact my aunt.'

'Really?' Johansson said. 'Your aunt? Is she still alive, or—'

'I'm afraid not,' Staffan Nilsson said, shaking his head sadly. 'She died in the late eighties.'

Yes, you ought to know, Johansson thought.

'That's a beautiful painting,' Nilsson said, gesturing towards the large landscape hanging on the wall behind the desk.

'It's an Osslund,' Johansson said. 'Late winter in Ådalen, painted in 1910. The view from the family farm. According to the family story, the artist set up his easel on the meadow in front of the house. My grandfather bought it off him on the spot. For one hundred kronor, so the story goes.'

'I was lucky enough to own a Leander Engström in my youth,' Staffan Nilsson said. 'That was one of those Norrland landscapes, too. There was some sort of hunter in it.'

'I see,' Johansson said. Who'd have thought it? he thought as he leaned forward and pulled his sunglasses down on to his nose. 'Well, art and music are all very well, but it's high time we got down to business,' he went on. 'I'm afraid Mats isn't able to join us, by the way, but

I don't think we should let a detail like that get in our way.'

'No, of course not,' Staffan Nilsson said with a smile.

You still haven't got a clue, Johansson thought. You're just sitting there, licking your lips. 'A curious question,' he said. 'How much money are you looking for from me and my brother? Twenty million? Fifty?'

'I usually leave that to my investors to decide,' Nilsson said, still smiling.

'Do you know what? I'm thinking of offering you something that will be worth more to you than all the money in the world.'

'Now I'm definitely curious, Lars,' Nilsson said, smiling even more broadly.

'I'm going to offer you a chance of survival,' Johansson said. 'For at least another fifteen, twenty years, assuming that you take your punishment and sit it out in a Swedish penal institution. I promise to do my best to make sure you end up with people with the same proclivities as you, so your fellow inmates don't kill you.'

He still doesn't get it, Johansson thought. He looks like he's just heard something his mind can't take in.

'I don't understand,' Staffan Nilsson said. 'Is this some sort of joke, or what?'

He gave a nervous twitch of the head towards the closed door, fear beginning to creep into his eyes.

'I'm afraid not,' Johansson said, handing over the photograph of Yasmine Ermegan.

He was almost as white in the face as Max had been when he'd talked about Nadja, a moment before he had to dash out to the toilet, but if Staffan Nilsson ended up being sick on Evert's expensive carpet, Gerd would just have to clean up after him. That would do very nicely as a confession and, in the worst-case scenario, I could always buy my brother a new carpet, Johansson thought.

'I have no idea what you're talking about,' Staffan Nilsson said. He pushed the photograph away. The trap had snapped shut. Fear was now the dominant emotion in his eyes. His head was twisting and turning as those same eyes looked for a way out.

'I'm talking about little Yasmine,' Johansson said. 'She was nine years old when you raped her and smothered her with a pillow in your aunt's bedroom in her villa out in Äppelviken. That was on the evening of Friday, 14 June, 1985. You were there to look after the house and water your aunt's plants while she was away in the country, when suddenly Yasmine rang on the door because she wanted to use the phone to call her parents. Of course, you already knew her. You must have met her on numerous occasions when you visited your aunt. Surely you remember that?'

'I can't believe my ears,' Staffan said, standing up with a jerk. 'Not a single word of that is true. Who told you such a grotesque story?'

'I worked it out all on my own,' Johansson said. 'And, now, I've also been able to compare your DNA with the sperm found on Yasmine's body, so there's really no need for us to discuss your guilt or innocence.'

'Clearly, I've ended up in the hands of a madman, some lunatic private detective. You know, what you've just said is criminal. It's gross defamation, and I won't hesitate to—'

'Shut up before I kill you,' Johansson said, firing him a look that brooked no contradiction. 'You can forget about sneaking out through that door, by the way,

515

because it's locked. If you want to call the police, I won't stop you, but I'd advise against it, for your own sake. Unless you want to find yourself in the evening papers, that is. If it will calm you down at all, you haven't ended up in the hands of some lunatic private detective. I may be retired now, but I spent all my working life as a police officer. Before I retired I was head of the National Crime Unit and, if it's any consolation, sadly, I've encountered hundreds of men like you over the years.'

'Not a word – not a single word – of what you just said is true,' Staffan Nilsson said. His voice was noticeably different now, stressed, hoarse, as if he were having trouble breathing. His eyes kept darting round the room, landing on everything except Johansson.

'I can appreciate that you're terrified,' Johansson said. 'I wouldn't be feeling too great if I'd raped and murdered Joseph Simon's daughter. If anyone has been able to disturb your sleep during all these years, I daresay it's him, Yasmine's father, with all his hundreds of billions, and the knowledge of what he and his associates would do to you the day he caught up with you.'

'I have no idea what you're talking about,' Staffan Nilsson said, even though the look on his face was saying something completely different.

'Don't lie,' Johansson said. 'Besides, I'd like you to shut up for two minutes and listen to my offer. Listen very carefully. This is what is usually called a once-in-a-lifetime offer. An offer you can't afford to turn down.'

As long as he doesn't shit himself, Johansson thought. Nilsson was drooping in his chair now, his head sagging, suddenly miles away.

'I met Yasmine's father a few days ago,' Johansson said. 'He wanted me to sell you to him. I turned him down, so he still doesn't know who you are. I explained to him that I wanted to talk to you first, to give you a chance to take your punishment. To go to the police and clear the decks. Tell them about all the little girls you've slept with, all the ones you've raped or drugged before you had sex with them. All the ones you simply had to pay for before you had sex with them. I'm convinced that would be enough to warrant a two-figure custodial sentence. Failing that, you could always say you murdered your mother. Fortunately, her case hasn't yet passed the statute of limitations, unlike Yasmine's.'

'I didn't murder my mother! This is completely insane.'

'I don't think you murdered her either,' Johansson said. 'I'm actually convinced that she committed suicide as soon as she worked out what you did to Yasmine. But I'm just as convinced that a court would find you guilty of murder if, for instance, you were to tell my colleagues that she'd threatened to tell the police about you, and that you decided to poison her by tricking her into taking lots of sedatives and drinking lots of alcohol. That it was you who murdered Yasmine, because they'll work that out pretty much instantly, and that your mother threatened to give you away. A story like that would solve any problem regarding your motive. And that's without even taking into account all the money you stood to inherit.'

At least he's hearing what I'm saying now, Johansson thought, even though he's having to cling on to the arms of the chair to stay upright. But his head is still lolling, and his eyes keep darting about.

'To sum up,' he went on. 'Either you do as I say, and, if so, I want to know as soon as possible – by

517

noon on Wednesday of next week at the latest. If you turn the offer down or don't contact me, I shall tell Yasmine's father who you are. He'll get your name, date of birth and ID number, your address, copies of your passport and driving licence, your passport number, the registration number of your car, the names of everyone you know, your friends and acquaintances; he'll know everything you think, feel and do. Then it will only be a matter of time before he finds you and, given who he is, there isn't a place on this planet where you could hide from him. What he would do to you once he got hold of you is something I would prefer not to think about.'

'These are appalling allegations,' Staffan Nilsson said, getting to his feet. 'Accusations like this could drive an entirely innocent man like me to commit suicide.'

'I don't see how that applies to you,' Johansson said. 'To start with, you're guilty, even if I've chosen to disregard the fact that your crime has been prescribed. And you're far too self-important to kill yourself. If I turn out to be wrong on that point, I think I could live with the guilt. I'm strongly opposed to capital punishment, you know. That's why I'm giving you the chance to survive, to take your punishment. Joseph Simon, Yasmine's father, doesn't share my attitude. He takes a more Old Testament view of things. Eye for eye, tooth for tooth, if you're wondering what I mean. So call me. You've got my number on your answer-machine at home, in case you weren't sure. And you don't have to worry about any of the practical details. I can give you a lift to police headquarters myself. I can even help you get hold of a good lawyer.'

'You can forget that,' Staffan Nilsson said. There was hate in his eyes now, because fury had momentarily conquered his fear. 'If you breathe a word of these deranged allegations to anyone, I'll sue you for every krona you've got.'

'Rubbish,' Johansson said. 'Let's suppose you sued me for gross defamation, suppose you won and got a couple of hundred thousand in damages, because you wouldn't get more than that. You'd be dead before the court had time to publish its verdict. Anyway, that's small change for me and my brother.

'Do you know what?' Lars Martin Johansson went on, fixing him with the stare that he and his best friend used to save for the very worst cases. 'You're actually the worst person I've ever met in my entire life. But I'm still going to do you one last favour. I'm going to give you a chance to call me and tell me that you agree to take responsibility for what you've done. Call me, Nilsson. Seeing as you're already on your feet, I suggest you leave now before I change my mind and throw you out of the window instead.'

'If you like, I can do that for you, boss,' said Max, who was suddenly standing in the room, even though Johansson had told him to keep out of the way. His big fists were opening and closing, and his eyes were those of a wolf staring at its already wounded prey. His bony, expressionless face was as white as when he had talked about Nadjesta, his big sister in the life that had been forced upon him. Raped, drugged and asphyxiated when she inhaled her own vomit in the children's home they were both planning to run away from, to move to a house that no one else knew about, to have children of their own who they would spend all day kissing and cuddling.

'Let him go,' Johansson said. 'He'll be in touch.'

*

As soon as Staffan Nilsson reached the street, he hailed a taxi, got in and drove off. Well, then, Johansson thought. Regardless of his headache and the constant tightness in his chest, there was at least one man who felt worse than him. For good reason, he thought, and he called Lisa Mattei on her mobile.

'I've just spoken to Staffan Nilsson,' he said.

'I know,' Lisa Mattei said. 'He's sitting in a taxi and seems to be on his way home. In case you were wondering, Lars.'

'Good to hear,' Johansson said. This girl could go as far as she wants, he thought.

'My hunch is that he's not the sort to commit suicide,' Mattei said.

'I quite agree. But there's a chance he might hit upon the uniquely bad idea of trying to run.'

'I can't imagine where he might be able to hide. But, of course, right now he probably isn't thinking very rationally. So I've decided to keep an eye on him. If he were to get any ideas, I can always have a word with him. I can't hold him against his will, of course, as you no doubt appreciate, and there's not a great deal of enthusiasm here for giving him a protected identity, if I can put it like that.'

'There might be one way of solving that,' Johansson said. 'Lock him in a cell for a while to give him time to think.'

Then he told her about the report Nilsson had filed with the police in the Western District and the claim for damages he had probably already filed with his insurance company. Even if an attempt at aggravated insurance fraud was probably the last thing on his mind right now, despite his having just met Max.

'Worth trying, if he doesn't see sense,' Mattei said. 'I promise to bear it in mind. At best, we could probably lock him up for a month or so.'

'Sure,' Johansson said. 'And he'd be able to read about what he did to Yasmine in the papers while he's in prison. That would give him a bit of peace and quiet in which to contemplate what to do about that before we kick him out on to the street again.'

'Lars, Lars,' Lisa Mattei said. 'I didn't hear that last bit.'

'But that's what's going to happen, if the bastard doesn't take his punishment. I'll see to it myself if no one else wants to do the dirty work. I've given him a chance. If he doesn't take it, then he'll only have himself to blame. But I don't think he's quite as unbelievably stupid as that.'

'I hope you're right,' Mattei said. 'Good luck with the elk hunt, by the way.'

So you know about that, too, Johansson thought when he ended the call. Remarkable woman. Lies without any compunction and in the most believable way, even to a man who's twice her age and had been her boss and mentor for more than ten years.

96

Friday, 27 August to Sunday, 29 August

On Friday evening Johansson took a fond farewell of his wife. As fond as all his blood-pressure-lowering medication would allow, that is, as he hugged and kissed her, just to be on the safe side.

'Promise to take care of yourself,' Pia said.

'I promise,' Johansson said. I'll soon be back at the farm, and nothing bad can happen to me there, he thought.

Then he and Max headed out to Bromma Airport, where they drove straight out on to the apron and climbed on board the private plane his brother Evert shared with a couple of equally rich friends.

They landed in Kramfors an hour later and walked straight to the waiting helicopter. Three hours after leaving his home on Södermalm Johansson was standing in the farmyard of his parental home.

'Welcome home, Lars,' Evert said. He strode out on to the front porch dressed in green moleskin trousers and a chequered flannel shirt and gave Johansson a bear-hug which, oddly enough, seemed to ease the tightness in his chest.

'Thanks,' Lars Martin Johansson said. Home at last, he thought.

'Right, we're going to have a good time and just relax. Maybe shoot an elk or two as well, of course. I thought that you, me and Max could sleep here, in Mum and Dad's house, and the other lads can stay in the hunting lodge and make as much mess as they like.'

'When are they arriving?' Johansson asked.

'Sunday,' Evert said. 'We'll have the run-through and hunt dinner then. Until then, we'll have to manage on our own.'

'As long as you don't do the cooking.'

'Are you mad?' Evert said, putting his arm round his shoulders. 'I've got hold of a couple of women from the village. They're hard at work already. You'll get your herring and vodka and meat and potatoes, no need to worry.'

Evert kept his promise. As did Johansson. He refrained from a third vodka, because he could suddenly see Pia before him. He drank only two glasses of red wine with his pork stuffed with prunes and declined the apple pie to finish altogether. He contented himself with a cup of coffee and a tiny glass of cognac.

'I'm almost starting to worry about you, Lars,' Evert said, winking at him.

'How do you mean?'

'You're a reformed character. There's barely anything in that brandy glass.' He nodded towards the glass in Johansson's hand.

'Never too late to learn,' Johansson said. 'And now I'm thinking of getting an early night.'

*

523

Then he went and had a wash before getting into bed. He fell asleep without any help from his Greek ally and woke up the following morning as the first rays of sunlight were peeping between the edge of the roller-blind and the window frame.

He went out on to the meadow in front of the farm and stood there barefoot in the grass, watching as the pale sun rose in the east and dissolved the morning mist down in the valley.

This must be where Osslund stood, Johansson thought. Whether it was late winter or early autumn, as now, there was no more beautiful place on the planet.

Then he went back inside the house again, took his pills, had a shower, got dressed, breathing the way he used to, his head finally clear. Home at last, he thought. There was probably no more to it than that.

After a hearty breakfast they drove to Evert's very own shooting range so Johansson could practise with the elk rifle that the gunsmith had modified, which Max had already worn in for him.

It went far better than he could have anticipated. After just a couple of dozen shots he had no problem with his new trigger-finger. He could still twist his torso and hold the butt and barrel okay.

'I recognize you now, Lars,' Evert said with an approving smile.

Even Max had trouble hiding his surprise, even though he had never met anyone who could shoot better than him.

On Sunday evening he met up with the other hunters in Evert's hunting lodge, which, practically enough, lay in the middle of the forest, and right in the middle of the hunting ground. Everything was the same as usual: the same faces, the same stories, the same laughter, the same food and just as much vodka as always. Johansson even allowed himself a third glass and didn't spare his wife a thought as he raised his glass to drink a toast with the others.

'Damn, us rich chaps have a good life,' Evert snorted three hours later as he sat with his nightcap in front of the flaming fire.

'"Away, yearning and weakness from soot-blackened breasts, no more cares in our snow-covered home. We have fire, we have meat, we have liquor for guests . . ." Cheers, lads!' Evert said, standing up on slightly unsteady legs.

'Now I'm going home to put my brother to bed,' said Johansson, who was clearly the soberest member of the group, even though his wife was a thousand kilometres away. Apart from Max, of course, who hadn't drunk a drop all evening.

'You don't fancy a bit of arm-wrestling, then?' Evert said.

'Tomorrow,' Johansson said. Home, he thought. Properly home. Evidently, he needed a blood clot in his brain to make him appreciate what it was he had left behind fifty years ago.

97

Monday, 30 August

The first session that morning took place just a few hundred metres from the farm where he had grown up, at the edge of a large patch of felled woodland sloping towards the river a couple of kilometres further down. That was where they always began. As far back as Johansson could remember, the elk hunt started by sweeping the river valley and the banks below the farm.

'What the hell have you done to my tower?' Johansson said, nodding towards the wooden shooting tower where he had sat for the past twenty years.

The usual wooden ladder had been replaced by a flight of steps with handrails on either side. Like something from a professional sporting set-up, Johansson thought. He had taken over the stand from his father when he thought he was getting too old. Because Johansson's father thought he was a much better shot than his elder brother.

'Evert sent me up here,' Max said.

'When?'

'The day you got out of hospital, boss,' Max said.

'Very forward-thinking of him,' Johansson said. Must finally be feeling a bit guilty for everything he did to me when I was little, he thought.

No problem at all, Johansson thought as he climbed up and sat down on the broad bench.

'Where do you think you're going?' he said to Max, who was already halfway up the tower.

'I thought I'd sit next to you, boss.'

'You can forget that idea,' Johansson said. 'If you promise to keep your mouth shut and sit still, I might just let you sit underneath the tower. Otherwise, you can join the beaters.'

'I talked to Evert—'

'Forget it,' Johansson interrupted. 'Right, enough about Evert. We're here to have a good time. We're going to do some shooting.'

'Okay, boss,' Max said, then shrugged and did as he had been told.

Nothing on this planet of ours could be more beautiful than this, Lars Martin Johansson thought. He breathed in the clear morning air, the sharpness of autumn stroking his cheeks and chin. It doesn't get better than this, he thought, at the very moment someone squeezed his ribcage. Squeezed so hard he couldn't even gasp for air. Someone who was much stronger than Max, who was sitting just a couple of metres below his feet and had never met anyone stronger than him.

No bonus this time, Lars Martin Johansson thought, and that was the last thing he thought.

VI

Thine eye shall not pity . . .

Book of Deuteronomy, 19:21

On Monday, 20 September, three weeks after Lars Martin Johansson's death, the Director General and head of the Security Police decided to withdraw the surveillance on Staffan Nilsson. He was of the firm opinion that Johansson's death had intrinsically changed the situation. In the best-case scenario, Johansson was the only person outside the Security Police who knew that Staffan Nilsson had murdered Joseph Simon's daughter more than twenty-five years ago. Either way, Nilsson appeared largely to have reverted to his normal life and, if he were to apply to have his identity protected, he was free to do so in the usual way.

'What do you say, Lisa?' the Director General asked. 'Correct me if I'm wrong, but I have an idea that we have more pressing matters to spend our money on.'

'I'm in complete agreement with you, boss,' Lisa Mattei said. As she said this she put a protective arm round her stomach. Poor Lars, she thought.

On Friday, 1 October the bells of Maria Magdalena Church on Södermalm rang for a hunter and wanderer from Ådalen in northern Ångermanland whose earthly wanderings had come to an end just over a month before.

A month of nothing but grief for his wife, Pia, and when just a couple of days earlier she managed to fend it off for a short moment, it was only with the help of the anger she must have been storing up for much longer than that.

Bloody Lars, she thought. Why didn't you ever listen to me? Why didn't you do as I told you, just for once?

After the service the mourners gathered at Johansson's old neighbourhood restaurant to eat a belated but restorative lunch buffet. The whole of the extended Johansson family, his former colleagues from Stockholm Police, National Crime and the Security Police – all the old stalwarts turned out in force, with Jarnebring at their head.

It gradually turned into a fairly boisterous occasion. The dead man's name was on everyone's lips – Lars Martin Johansson wasn't the sort of man to be buried and quietly forgotten. There were far too many good stories that deserved to be told again.

Even Pia couldn't help laughing, even though she now lived alone in an apartment that was far too big for her and which she had already decided to sell, because it was now only a reminder of a different, better life. The night before she buried her husband she had lain awake while unanswered questions chased round her head. Should I laugh or cry? she wondered as she walked up the aisle of the church to the pew at the front, flanked by Anna Holt and Matilda.

First, she cried once more, for the umpteenth time. Then she laughed. For the first time. The funeral was over, her life was going on, a different life to before, but there was nothing she could do to change that.

'It's still a bloody shame,' big brother Evert declared as he stood at the bar, flanked by his brother's best friend and his own little lad. Red-eyed from crying for the first time in his life, almost eighty, and heedless of the fact that he, too, would die soon. Not today, not tomorrow, but sooner or later, just like everyone who had gone before him. Not that Evert had the slightest intention of doing any such thing. Especially now that his little lad had been restored to his father's house.

'It's still a bloody shame he wouldn't eat and drink like a normal person,' Evert said. 'That he wouldn't take any exercise. Except for when he was hunting, of course, because he could be quick enough then. He was only a young fellow, after all, just sixty-seven years old. That's no age, is it? Our father, Evert, lived to be ninety-three, and mother, Elna, was ninety-six. And I'm seventy-seven and I feel better than I have done in years.'

'I think he was just bloody unhappy,' Jarnebring said. 'When he stopped working, three years ago, it was like he'd made his mind up somehow. If he couldn't be a police officer any more, then he really wasn't that bothered.'

'The boss was a good man,' Max said. 'A good man who was unhappy. In the end he was very unhappy.' Because an evil man was eating him up from inside, he thought.

'I see,' Evert said with a nod. 'Lars was always a little unusual, of course. I hear what you're saying, but I had no idea that things were that bad. He always had the hunt and the forest. And the farm. We still own it together, of course, he and I. But now I suppose his lad will take over his share, Little Lars.'

533

'You can't think it was a coincidence that he gave up the ghost on the first day of the elk hunt,' Jarnebring said.

'Probably not,' Evert said, and his big shoulders shuddered. 'Take care of yourself, little brother,' he said, lifting his eyes towards the grey October sky above their heads. Raised his glass and downed it in one. 'Cheers, Lars,' he said.

'Cheers, Lars,' Jarnebring echoed. What the hell am I going to do now? he thought.

'*Nazdrovje!* Peace, boss,' Max said. I'm going to make sure you rest in peace, boss, he thought.

Just before midnight on the day of the funeral, a patrol car in the Western District found an abandoned car out on the islands in Lake Mälaren. It was parked by the side of the main road between Färingsö and Stockholm. A grey Renault, mid-range, clean and well looked after, definitely not a troublemaker's car, but they still decided to check it out. In the boot they found the badly beaten corpse of a man stuffed into a large blue sports bag. From then on, everything unfolded according to the usual routines.

The dead body was identified the following morning. A fifty-year-old man, the registered owner of the vehicle, and when Solna Police entered his home out in Frösunda they were immediately fairly certain that that was where he had been killed. There were large quantities of blood in the hall, kitchen, living room and bathroom. He had been beaten almost beyond what seemed humanly possible, but because he had evidently been alive for the majority of it, it was a mystery that none of his neighbours had heard a sound from the flat.

Superintendent Peter Niemi, head of Forensics at Solna Police, called his colleague Evert Bäckström. A Bäckström who sounded surprisingly perky when he eventually answered.

'I've got a body for you, Bäckström,' Niemi said. 'His name's Staffan Nilsson, born in 1960. Estate agent, single, no wife or children, lived out in Frösunda. Our officers found him in the boot of his car, which was parked at the side of the road out to Färingsö. I'm in his flat now, and it looks like a slaughterhouse, so I daresay this was where it happened.'

'Really?' Evert Bäckström said. Not a bad start to a new day, he thought. 'So how does he look, then?'

'To be honest, I don't think I've ever seen anything worse,' Niemi said. 'Eye for eye, tooth for tooth, if I can put it like that. But, according to our pathologist, our perpetrator did that in reverse order, to keep the poor bastard alive as long as possible.'

Single. Obvious, Bäckström thought. Sounds like a typical faggot murder, he thought. Those arse-bandits can be fucking lethal when they really let loose on each other.

'Typical fag murder,' Bäckström declared a few hours later when he had his first meeting with his investigative team. Not a particularly bright bunch but, seeing as he was the one in charge, it would doubtless turn out okay.

'How do we know that?' asked an officer who had been seconded from patrol. Judging by the length of his hair, he was of the same persuasion.

'I found an old case against him, for child porn. He admitted to being queer back then,' Bäckström said. 'And I also found an old boyfriend who looks pretty promising.' How the fuck can someone like that get into the force? he thought.

'Why does he look so promising? The boyfriend, I mean,' asked the long-haired constable, who clearly wasn't about to give up.

'He's an Arab,' Bäckström said, his voice resounding with the solemnity that naturally befitted one of the great legends of the force. 'His name's Ali Hussein.' Probably one of your mates, he thought.

Early in December, two months after Johansson's funeral, Evert's little lad, Max, handed in his notice so he could move to the USA. He had been offered a new job, his new employer had already sorted out a green card for him, and he would also have the opportunity to study as part of his job. Max was very secretive about what his new job entailed but, because he seemed happy and pleased, Evert saw no reason to investigate more closely. When Evert said goodbye to him out at the airport, he handed him a handsome bonus and gave him an old-fashioned bear-hug. Nothing could possibly have expressed more emotion between two real men.

'It's probably a good idea for you to see a bit more of the world, Max,' Evert Johansson said. 'Experience new things, not just hang around the farm with me and the wife. But if you ever change your mind, you know you're always welcome to come back home.'

On the Friday of the week in which Maxim Makarov flew from Sundsvall to Stockholm and then on to New York – his final destination remained something of a mystery – Anna Holt, police commissioner out in the

536

Western District, cut back the size of the investigative team looking into the murder of Staffan Nilsson.

Superintendent Evert Bäckström had, admittedly, found a number of Ali Husseins, but because he didn't appear to have found the right Ali Hussein, all the air soon went out of the investigation.

'You know what it's like, Anna,' Bäckström said when he explained the case to his boss. 'Sooner or later the bastard will show up, and then we'll have him.'

Investigation unsuccessful, Holt thought as she signed the documents that Bäckström had given her. But she had far more important things to think about because, that weekend, she was going to become a godmother for the first time. Godmother to Lisa Mattei's two-month-old daughter, who was going to be christened Anna Linda Elina. Anna Linda Elina Mattei. Anna after Anna Holt, Linda after Lisa's mother, and Elina in memory of someone the girl's mother didn't want to talk about.

Alongside his will, Johansson had left a private letter to his wife, Pia. Three short lines and, to judge by his signature, it had been written some time after 11 July that year. 'Stop snivelling, old thing. Find a new man. Take care of yourself.' Signed 'Lars'. Pia followed his advice and embarked on a new relationship shortly after New Year. Not anyone she was thinking of marrying, nor even of living with, but life went on, and she had to start somewhere.

A few weeks later, towards the end of January, Ulrika Stenholm moved to the USA. She got married in great secrecy to a man who was sixteen years older than her, and whose child she was already expecting. A girl, a love-child, whom she and her new husband had decided to call Yasmine. In the sixth month she suffered a miscarriage and their daughter died in the ambulance on the way to hospital.

The judges and their hangmen. Eye for eye, tooth for tooth.

By Leif G.W. Persson

THE BÄCKSTRÖM SERIES – AS SEEN ON TV

LINDA, AS IN THE LINDA MURDER

A young woman studying at the Swedish Police Academy is brutally murdered. Deeply unwillingly, Police Inspector Evert Bäckström is drafted in to head up the investigation. He thinks he is God's gift to modern policing, in reality he is egotistical, vain and utterly prejudiced against everything, a man with no discernible sense of duty, who thinks everyone with the exception of himself is an imbecile and really only has warm feelings towards his pet goldfish and the nearest bottle of liquor. If they are to solve the case, his long-suffering team must work around him, following the scant few leads which remain after Bäckström's intransigence has let the trail go cold.

HE WHO KILLS THE DRAGON

It should have been an open and shut case: two drunks fall into an argument and one of them ends their evening by savagely beating the other to death. It's a routine and yet strangely puzzling scenario to Detective Superintendent Evert Bäckström, whose legendary poor temper has not been improved by strict orders from his doctor to lead a healthier life. His gut feeling proves him right: within days, his team have another murder to contend with and have uncovered links to a high-profile van heist in which two people died.

THE SWORD OF JUSTICE

Finding a suspect for the murder of Thomas Eriksson – gangster lawyer and renowned defender of the guilty – is easy, but narrowing down the long list of people who wanted him dead is almost impossible. Fortunately, DS Evert Bäckström has spent his career cultivating a group of questionable acquaintances. His colleagues don't know that he only closes his cases with the help of these friends. Nor that Bäckström owes them a few favours. But this time they're all in for a surprise because even the dirtiest cop couldn't have predicted where this trail would lead.

By Leif G.W. Persson

BETWEEN SUMMER'S LONGING AND WINTER'S END
Stockholm. The dead of winter. A young American dies, falling from a tall building. It appears to be an open-and-shut case of suicide. But when Superintendent Lars Martin Johansson begins to delve beneath the layers of corruption, incompetence and violence that threaten to strangle the Stockholm police department, he reveals a complex web of treachery, politics and espionage that leads to the rotten heart of Sweden's government.

ANOTHER TIME, ANOTHER LIFE
Newly seconded to the Security Police, Lars Martin Johannson has reopened the files on one of the most renowned cases in Swedish history – the 1975 siege of the West German embassy. And in so doing, he discovers a trail which will take him from the murder of the Swedish Prime Minister in 1986 and the death of a civil servant three years later to a network of corruption and greed permeating the very highest level of Swedish society.

FALLING FREELY, AS IF IN A DREAM
Lars Martin Johansson, chief of the Swedish National Bureau of Criminal Investigation, has opened the dusty files on the 1986 murder of Prime Minister Olof Palme. He forms a new group comprised of a few trustworthy detectives to pursue fresh leads in a case that has all but gone cold – despite the scar the assassination has left on the country. Yet the more they uncover, the further away a resolution seems – sometimes the truth just needs to stay buried . . .